CATCHING KELLY

She caught her breath, startled by the unexpected sense of intimacy created by his touch. She hadn't been prepared to feel the warmth of his palm against hers, hadn't been prepared to feel the softness coursing through her.

First and foremost was an unexpected sense of comfort. How was it possible that his touch comforted her? She hardly even knew him.

But equally disturbing was an unwanted sense of sexual awareness and elemental recognition that he was man and she was woman, and that his touch was more than welcome. It was . . . exciting.

Her heart hammered and her breath seemed to thicken, and icy tendrils of panic began to fill her. She couldn't allow this, couldn't allow herself to feel attracted to this man when she didn't know him, didn't know what his motives and intentions might be.

But her body wasn't listening to her. Her body *liked* his touch, however innocent. And her body wanted more.

Other Avon Contemporary Romances by
Sue Civil-Brown

CARRIED AWAY
CHASING RAINBOW
LETTING LOOSE

SUE CIVIL-BROWN

Catching Kelly

AVON BOOKS  NEW YORK

AVON BOOKS, INC.
1350 Avenue of the Americas
New York, New York 10019

Copyright © 2000 by Susan Civil-Brown
Inside cover author photo by David Ewart Photography
Published by arrangement with the author
Library of Congress Catalog Card Number: 99-95338
ISBN: 0-380-80061-6
www.avonromance.com

First Avon Books Printing: January 2000

AVON TRADEMARK REG. U.S. PAT. OFF. AND IN OTHER COUNTRIES, MARCA REGIS-
TRADA, HECHO EN U.S.A.

Printed in the U.S.A.

WCD   10 9 8 7 6 5 4 3 2 1

Prologue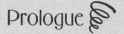

"Oh, no!" The words popped out of Kelly Burke's mouth the instant she finished reading the latest e-mail from her family.

She was sitting in her home office, surrounded by the clutter of her work life: stacks of papers, books, diskettes, compact disks, and several dust bunnies large enough to devour a big dog.

But all she could see were the words on her glowing computer screen.

"Dearest Kelly," the note began innocently enough, "we loved your new web page! Such beautiful design and color. Uncle Max is wondering why you don't pick up a paintbrush again."

Yeah, right, Kelly thought, remembering her painful attempts at oil painting under Uncle Max's tutelage when she was ten. He'd told her she had a wonderful future as an abstract artist. Kelly, who had simply wanted a duck to look like a duck— even a *toy* duck—had given up in frustration.

The note continued, "We're all doing splendidly here. Retirement seems to agree with us—at least the ones who are retired. Plenty of time for pursuing other interests or just smelling the daisies."

As if anyone in her family had ever done anything as mundane as smelling the daisies.

It was the next paragraph that set her pulse to racing, however, and had her alarm bells clanging in a deafening uproar.

"Granny Bea has turned over the guest cottage to a very nice young man named Seth Ralston. You've probably heard of him. He used to be a football star, but hurt his knee so badly he can't play anymore. Anyway, he and Granny are the best of friends, and she really enjoys his company. What's more, he's such a helpful young man. He's agreed to help us sort out our finances. Well, dear, you remember how badly tangled we got them when you were here. We're so relieved to have his help . . ."

That was the point where Kelly started choking. Help? From a stranger? A broken down ex-football player who probably couldn't add two and two? And what was he doing sniffing after her grandmother, anyway? What could a young man possibly want with a woman in her eighties?

Money. Lots and lots of money. Granny was wealthy, and the family finances had a habit of getting so messed up even an accountant couldn't tell if there was embezzlement.

What if this Ralston guy had blown every dime he had on wine, women, and song?

And Granny, who was the dearest, smartest, *craziest* octogenarian on the planet, had an ego big enough to believe that some young stud fifty years her junior could fall for her.

Instinctively she reached for the phone. Five minutes later she had a flight reservation. Twenty-four hours later she was driving into Paradise Beach, Florida.

By then, she was having serious second thoughts.

Chapter 1

Panic was a strange reaction to coming home after eight years, but that was exactly what Kelly Burke felt as she drove through Paradise Beach, Florida. As her panic deepened, she drove slower and slower, until she was being honked at repeatedly by drivers who sped past her shaking their fists. A glance at her speedometer told her she was doing ten miles an hour in a thirty-five zone.

She pressed harder on the accelerator, but speeding up only worsened her panic, so she slowed down again, surveying the familiar shops on each side of the road, pretending she was looking for something.

The minute she'd stepped out of the airport in Tampa, she had known this was a mistake. Traveling from winter-locked Denver into the brilliant sunshine and warmth of Florida had reminded her what she was doing. Coming home became real.

And it was getting more real with each passing moment. By the time she reached the narrow bridge that led to the Burke family's little island in the Gulf of Mexico, she could scarcely breathe.

On the other side of the bridge, she stopped her rental car and got out, willing herself to get past

3

her anxiety. Hyperventilating, leaning against the car for support while her knees turned to jelly, she gave serious thought to heading back to the airport and letting Granny get robbed blind. It wasn't *her* problem.

Man, oh, man, was she getting claustrophobic or something? The vegetation, so tropically thick, seemed almost to suffocate her. In Colorado she was used to seeing for miles from her little house in the foothills. Here nature seemed to slap her in the face. Everything was so disgustingly *green*.

And this *was* an island—with only one way off. The family loved the privacy it afforded them, but Kelly had always been aware of the lack of escape routes. Being raised in the middle of a three-ring circus could get a child thinking about such things. Taking on too many adult responsibilities at a tender age could make a child yearn for escape.

Claustrophobia, she decided. This reaction couldn't have anything to do with coming home to her loving family. Of course, it was never their *love* she had doubted. Just their sanity.

Worse, she had lived most of her childhood in a state of terrible anxiety, dealing with the family finances and the household, tasks that would have taxed an experienced adult. No one was more aware than she that she'd taken on those tasks of her own volition, so she didn't blame her family for dumping the responsibilities on her. No, she had taken them on because she had had a desperate need to make herself important and indispensable. Because she had needed to prove to them and herself that she wasn't a failure at everything.

But now the anxiety was returning, and it seemed to be all the worse for having been away so long. As if she were making up for eight years of freedom.

Pulling off her jogging shoes, she tossed them into the back seat and walked down to the narrow sandy beach that framed this side of the island. From there she could look out west across the sparkling water into the endless expanse of the Gulf of Mexico.

The open space was just beginning to soothe her when her privacy was disrupted by a limping, rather attractive dark-haired man who came from the other direction with a huge fawn-colored dog. Not only were both man and dog bigger representatives of their species than she had ever seen, but the dog snarled at her, and the man looked annoyed. Nonplussed by the unexpectedness of their appearance, Kelly stood gaping as if she hadn't a brain in her head.

He spoke. "This is a private island."

Kelly felt her dander rising, which was good because it banished her panic. Anger was a wonderful substitute for a great many feelings. It also made her heedless of the stranger's much greater size "I know. So who the hell are you?"

"None of your business," he said shortly.

"You're mistaken. It *is* my business."

The dog snarled again. The man made a brief gesture, though, and the beast—nearly as big as a Shetland pony—settled back on its haunches. "*You're* mistaken, lady," he said. "You'd better leave or I'll call the cops."

"*You'd* better keep a good eye on that dog. Aunt Zelda's tigers will make a snack out of him."

The man froze, his expression changing. Kelly was just beginning to savor her victory, feeling rather proud of herself for silencing this Arnold Schwarzenegger wanna-be, when he said, "Zelda? You know her?"

"She's my aunt. Why else would I call her Aunt Zelda?"

He started to smile, and for the second time Kelly realized that this behemoth was actually attractive. Even handsome. That did nothing to improve her mood.

"So," she said, "I'm family. Who are *you*?"

"I'm a guest of Bea's. Seth Ralston."

The light bulb went on, and Kelly felt incredibly stupid for not having guessed who he was at the outset. Which did nothing to improve her mood, either. "Ahh," she said. "The broken-down ex-football player."

He lifted a brow. "Was that her description of me?"

"No, it's mine."

His smile broadened, as if he thought she was funny. "You were reading between the lines, I gather. So you must be Kelly, the prodigal granddaughter. I suppose you're expecting them to slaughter the fatted calf now that you've deigned to come home for a visit."

"Deigned? Isn't that rather a big word for a linebacker?"

"Linebackers play on the defense. I was offensive."

The pun caught Kelly, suddenly pulling her in two directions. The urge to laugh nearly overcame her annoyance. Annoyance won. "You certainly are."

"I had a feeling you thought so." He looked down at the dog. "Bouncer, friend." Then he looked at Kelly. "Let him sniff your hand for a moment."

She took an instinctive step back as the dog approached. "Why?"

"So he'll accept you as a friend."

She scowled at him but obediently let the huge, drooling dog sniff her hand. "What's a big guy like you need a guard dog for?"

He shrugged. "Ask Zelda. She's training him."

"Oh, God." She caught another glimmer of amusement in his gaze.

"My sentiments precisely. See you around."

Then he turned and limped away with the dog at his side, leaving Kelly to wonder who had won the encounter and why it mattered. And where did he get off acting as if he owned the place?

But the encounter had a salutary effect. When she got back in her car, she no longer felt as if the foliage were crushing her, and as if coming home were the stupidest thing she had ever done.

It was probably only the second stupidest thing she had ever done.

The villa—the family always called it *the villa*—was a haven of landscaped sanity amid the insurrection of the surrounding tropical foliage. Kelly had long been convinced that the only reason the house nestled in neatly trimmed grass and formal gardens was because Granny Bea had decided years ago that she didn't want to be bothered with a yard. She'd hired a man from the mainland to oversee it, and he seemed determined to fight the chaos of nature with pruning shears, lawn mowers, and orderly flowers that were willing to obey his directives.

He had subdued the jungle and carved an English estate out of a couple of acres. Kelly suspected that if he'd tried to go any farther into the environs, he would have lost. Keeping just this little bit controlled was a full-time job.

The house itself, built of cypress and tropical hardwood, resembled an antebellum mansion with its wide verandas and blindingly white paint. It took another man most of his time to keep up that paint and the corrosion caused by the salt air.

So the villa, which wasn't a villa at all, appeared to be a neatly faceted jewel set amid the mayhem of the surrounding jungle. But as Kelly well knew, the appearance was deceptive. Inside was another riotous jungle: her family.

Out of habit she parked beneath the shade of an old oak tree, the biggest tree on the island. No one knew where that tree had come from on an island that was little more than a heap of sand held together by mangroves, but the tree and some of its smaller cousins thrived near the house.

Kelly stood beside her car for a few minutes, soaking up the serenity of the orderly gardens, then headed up the wide, sweeping staircase that led to the second story of the house. The ground floor was comprised of storage rooms and servants' quarters, because the storm surges of a severe hurricane could put it underwater. The second and third floors were where the family lived.

The steps creaked as she climbed them, as they always had, and she began to feel the anxiety once again. This was why she hadn't wanted to come back. This feeling of being ever on the precipice of a new major failure haunted her, along with trepidation about whatever zaniness she would meet inside.

It was very difficult for a child to realize that her entire family was crazy. At thirty, she told herself, she ought to find it easier.

Before she quite reached the door, it was opened by the family butler. Lawrence beamed at her, his balding head with its sparse feathers of white hair gleaming even in the shadows of the veranda. He was still wearing his usual uniform of khaki shorts and shirt with knee socks, looking as if he had stepped off the pages of a British army poster advertising the joys of serving in the tropics.

"Miss Kelly!" he said in the British accent she remembered so well, "What an unexpected pleasure."

Kelly was unprepared for the burst of warmth she felt at the sight of this man. For an instant she couldn't even speak, as her throat tightened. "Hi, Lawrence. How's it going?"

"Quite well, Miss. Thank you. Shall I get your bags?"

She hated to ask him to do it. He must be nearly seventy, and she was young and healthy. But she also knew how he'd feel if she didn't let him do his job. He'd made that clear a long time ago. "I didn't bring much. Just a suitcase and my laptop computer." She handed the car keys to him. "Where is everyone?"

"Miss Zelda is out feeding the tigers, Mr. Max is painting in the studio, Mr. Jules is practicing in the conservatory, and Miss Mavis is napping. And her ladyship"—he always referred to Granny as *her ladyship* because long ago she'd been married to a viscount—"is studying a script in her sitting room."

"I guess I shouldn't interrupt her, then."

"Actually, Miss, I think she'd be very annoyed if you *didn't* interrupt her."

Kelly considered the possibility, but decided she needed a few minutes to get used to being here again before she was ready to face anyone. "I've got a better idea, Lawrence. Leave my bags in the car, invite me to the pantry for a glass of something stronger than tea, and we'll chat first. Just you and me."

This clearly didn't agree with Lawrence's notion

of propriety, but he hadn't survived nearly forty years with the Burke family by being unadaptable.

"I should warn you, Miss, that Cook is on a tear."

"Cook is always on a tear. What's it about this time?"

"Miss Zelda fed the roast to the tigers."

An irrepressible bubble of mirth tried to rise from Kelly's stomach despite herself. "It couldn't have been big enough to satisfy the tigers."

"No, but with the addition of the turkey and the pork roast, it probably made a passable snack."

Kelly felt the corners of her mouth twitching.

"The meat delivery was late," Lawrence said by way of explanation. Every week a freezer-load of meat was delivered for the tigers. "Manuel has gone to see about it. And to replace the purloined food."

"So Cook will recover?"

"She always does," Lawrence agreed serenely.

The butler's pantry was just as she remembered it, lined with polished teakwood, dominated by a large mahogany table. She'd spent many hours here in her youth handling the family finances and the household, and had become closer to Lawrence than most of the rest of her family in the process— or so she had felt, sometimes. He'd been a surrogate father to her.

He poured two small snifters of brandy from his private stash and joined her at the table.

"To your health, Miss," he said in toast.

"My sanity," she replied, catching the faintest quirk of his mouth. "So what's this ballplayer doing here?"

"Ahh." He looked much enlightened. "Recuperating from his injuries. Her ladyship dotes on him." He tossed down his brandy and poured himself another. Lawrence had a taste for booze, which was probably the reason he put up with her family. No one else would put up with his occasional indiscretions.

"Dotes on him how?"

He shrugged. "She says he makes her feel young again."

"What do you think of that?"

He shook his head. "I couldn't say."

Which was the problem with picking Lawrence's brain. Unless you could get him drunk enough, he was a clam. Kelly was debating whether she was unscrupulous enough to refill Lawrence's glass yet again when he spoke.

"We've all missed you, Miss Kelly."

Kelly felt her throat tightening again. "I've missed you, too, Lawrence." And it was true: She *had* missed him—though she wanted to reserve judgment on how much she'd missed the rest of her wacky family.

"You really need to go up and speak with your grandmother, Miss."

But Kelly wanted to delay the moment as long as possible. "How is Granny doing?"

"Fit as a fiddle." Lawrence sipped his brandy. "Still working a little here and there, still ruling the roost, as it were."

"She not . . . um . . . getting senile or anything?"

Lawrence looked shocked. "I should say not! Sharp as a tack."

"But not too sharp to be taken in by some gigolo?"

Now Lawrence looked even more shocked. Appalled, even. "What in the world are you talking about?"

Kelly flinched inwardly at the disapproval in Lawrence's gaze. She was amazed to discover that a mere look from him could make her feel ten again. She had transgressed, and the steel in Lawrence's eyes let her know it. She backpeddaled immediately.

"I don't know what I'm talking about. I'm woozy from all the travel, I guess."

"Quite," he said, his expression softening.

Lawrence was apparently as taken in by this Seth Ralston as Granny, if he didn't know what she had meant. "So what's everyone been up to?"

"The usual. Miss Mavis makes appearances from time to time, usually for charity. Mr. Julius makes two or three concert appearances a year. Mr. Max is still painting. He had a gallery showing recently in London. Miss Zelda—well, she's Miss Zelda. When we had the oil spill last year in the bay, she dragooned us all into helping with the birds. Do you have any idea how difficult it is to hold a pelican while someone scrubs him?" He didn't wait for an answer but instead continued. "This place, frankly, looked like some kind of insane laundry and we all looked like a group of mad washerwomen. Then Miss Zelda didn't want to let the birds go until the oil spill had been sufficiently cleaned up, so we had seagulls and pelicans nesting everywhere. It took us a week to clean up afterward."

That was the family she knew. Almost in spite of herself, she was smiling at the image Lawrence evoked. "And what about you?" she asked him. "How have you been? And what have you been doing?"

"Oh, me," he said with a dismissive wave of his hand. "I'm right as rain, and looking after this household keeps me as busy as I could want to be. One needs to feel useful, you know."

She knew. The danger, though, was in becoming

so useful to others that nothing was left over for yourself. She remembered how Lawrence had always been there, a Rock of Gibraltar in her childhood. Why had he never been absent, pursuing his own life and interests? She felt a sympathetic squeeze of her heart. She knew how consuming the Burke family could be.

And as she watched him pour yet another brandy for himself, she wondered guiltily if she had made a mistake by asking him to share a drink with her. Lawrence had always had a drink or two in the late afternoon, but she couldn't remember him ever drinking more than that, except upon the rarest occasions. She wondered if his occasional bender had become something more constant. She'd have to keep an eye on that.

"What about the cousins?" Kelly asked. She had seldom seen them in childhood. Julius had been the only one of Granny's children to marry, apart from Kelly's father, and he had divorced when Kelly was seven. Her two cousins had been rare visitors because they had moved with their mother to Hong Kong.

"Well," he said, "Gerald is in a Trappist monastery."

Kelly started. "You're kidding!"

"He saw the light," Lawrence said, with just a small edge of portentiousness. "Never fear. He'll come to his senses."

"I can't imagine it."

"By this time, I would venture to say that neither can the other monks."

"He was always such a cutup." Actually, Kelly still thought of him as a nasty little boy who used to tease her mercilessly about being an orphan until Uncle Julius had caught him one day and threatened to box his ears. Not that Julius would ever have done such a thing, but the threat was so shocking it silenced Gerald.

"He hasn't changed much," Lawrence said. "He moves from one fanatacism to another like a freely flowing brook. I can, however, think of worse things for him to do with his life than be a monk."

So could Kelly. Easily.

"I realize that wearing studded black leather and makeup and prancing around on a stage while making the most grotesque sounds come out of that electric guitar of his made him quite wealthy and famous, but . . ." Lawrence caught himself, as if he suddenly realized he was about to commit an unseemly breach by commenting negatively on a family member.

Kelly took pity on him. "He is a character. And what about Verna?" Verna, two years her senior, had been a palid, thin little girl who had kept quietly to corners and sucked her thumb as if it were all that kept her alive. Kelly was convinced Verna had been permanently damaged by Gerald.

"Miss Verna," said Lawrence, "is with the Corps de Ballet in France. She wrote recently to say she thought she was getting a little old for dancing and she might be moving into choreography."

Count on Verna to have the family's talent. Kelly felt the sting of envy. "How nice."

"We're all quite proud of her, Miss. As we are of you."

But as always, the comment about her sounded tacked on, like a courteous afterthought.

Just then the pantry door flew open, and Kelly's Aunt Zelda burst into the room.

Zelda was a tall, thin woman in her fifties with a passion for bright, clashing colors. Her short hair was hennaed and tied back with a bright red bandanna. She wore lime-green slacks with a purple long-sleeved shirt and Kelly surmised she had been working with her tigers, since Zelda covered herself this way only when she was within the range of claws.

Zee had once been a circus performer, but after a few years had left the big top in disgust over the way animals were treated. Since then she had become a radical animal rights activist and had hatched more than one harebrained scheme to save mistreated animals. These days she was a licensed wildlife rehabilitator, considerably tamer by comparison.

"Lawrence," she said as she burst into the pantry, "you have to do something about Cook!"

Before Lawrence could answer, Zelda spied Kelly. "Kelly! My God, when did you get here?" She patted her niece's shoulder warmly, but returned her attention to Lawrence. "That woman won't let me into the freezer!"

Lawrence, who was well into his third brandy, was beginning to slouch in his chair. He merely raised an eyebrow at Zelda.

"*She* didn't pay for that food," Zelda went on. "*We* did! And my cats are hungry!"

"So feed Cook to them," Lawrence said, his words sounding slurry.

"Excellent idea." Zelda turned for the door, calling over her shoulder, "I'll be back in a few minutes, Kelly. I need to get the tigers first."

Lawrence hiccupped. "Pardon me, Miss," he said with exaggerated dignity.

But Kelly hardly heard him. She was out of her chair like a shot, hurrying after Zelda. "Aunt Zelda," she called after the woman, "you're not going to bring the cats in the house. You know how Granny feels about that."

"Mother will never know," Zelda said. She was

out the back door and heading toward the tiger enclosure, which accounted for nearly half the island.

"Zelda, no. I'll talk to Cook." She was starting to feel a little breathless as she struggled to keep up with Zelda, whose legs were a lot longer. "But you did feed our dinner to the cats."

"That freezer is full of food. No, dear, this is an insurrection, and that woman needs to be put in her place. She's a mere employee."

"But Zee, it's not her fault the meat didn't arrive. Manuel's gone to get it."

"And just where *is* Manuel?" Zelda drew up sharply at the gate to the enclosure and turned to look at her. "He went out first thing this morning! He should have been back with the meat long ago."

Kelly placed herself in front of the gate. "I can't let you do this, Zee."

Zelda reached out and patted her cheek gently. "You're a good child, Kelly. You always have been. But you're not going to stop me. In fact, you'd better move."

Kelly refused to budge.

"Look," Zee said, "you know I won't let anyone mistreat an animal, and Cook's refusal to let me get meat for my babies is tantamount to mistreatment. My God, the way some people treat animals is a crime. Not feeding tigers. Making elephants live solitary lives in their own filth. Elephants! A social species that needs the company of its own kind."

Kelly wondered how elephants came into it, but before she could ask, Zelda made a clucking sound. Moments later Kelly felt hot breath on her back. She didn't have to turn around to know the two Siberian tigers had emerged soundlessly from the jungle behind her in answer to Zelda's call. They were like ghosts, she had often thought as a child, invisible until suddenly, without even the merest whisper of sound, they were there.

The hair on the back of her neck rose, and she turned to see Nicholas and Alexandra, otherwise known as Nikki and Alex, right in front of her on the other side of the chain-link fence.

Lord, she had forgotten how big they were! Over six hundred pounds each, and nearly nine feet from the nose to rump. The two heads that were regarding her so calmly were as big as the steering wheel on a car.

But even after eight years, she could tell their faces apart. Each had its own identifiable stripe pattern. Nikki yawned lazily and regarded her unwinkingly. Alex sat back on her haunches and cocked her head.

"They remember you," Zelda said approvingly.

"Do they?" Kelly wished she could be so sure. Fifteen years ago she had helped raise the two cubs, which had been rescued from a breeder, bottle-feeding them when they were small. But now they were full-grown and powerful, and she wasn't at all convinced they saw her as anything but a potential meal. "It's been a long time, Zee."

"I can tell. But step aside so I can let them out."

"No, Zee. No. If something happens . . ."

But before Kelly could stop her, she reached out and opened the gate, clucking softly. "Time to go hunting, babies," she crooned. "I know it's not as satisfying as chasing down a deer, but that's civilization for you!" The tigers didn't look as if they relished this idea.

The football player—Seth Ralston, she remembered—chose that moment to come around the back of the house. He took in Zee, the open gate, and the tigers and came to a halt. "What are you doing, Zee?" he asked curiously.

Kelly answered. "She's planning to terrorize Cook into handing over the contents of the freezer."

"Ah," said Seth, looking amused. "It's war."

"No such thing," Zee sniffed. "It is *my* house. I'm merely handing down the law."

Seth looked around. "I don't see a burning bush."

Zee cracked a laugh, but stopped trying to coax the tigers out. Seth suddenly turned and looked around the house. "Bouncer, no! Stay!"

Oh, God, thought Kelly. The tigers would kill the dog.

Seth apparently had the same idea, and disappeared the way he had come.

"I suppose," remarked Zee, "that the dog would make a decent dinner for them, but I don't have the heart to allow it." Then she closed the gate and locked it. "You win, dear, much as I hate to capitulate."

Suddenly an upstairs window opened, and Granny Bea leaned her blue-tinted head out the window. "Zelda, for shame! You terrified the cook. Don't you ever let me hear of you doing that again."

"We need a new cook," Zelda called back. "Her tapioca stinks!"

"But her duck l'orange is fabulous," Granny called back. "Now you go apologize to her. Kelly, child, get up here right now before your aunt gets you into any more trouble!"

Kelly stifled a sigh and went to do her grandmother's bidding. But if one more person called her a child, she thought mutinously, she was going to sic Zelda's tigers on them.

Chapter 2 🐚

Beatrix Burke floated. Kelly had never understood how her grandmother did it, but the woman usually seemed to be drifting on some current of air, her favored lace and voile drifting gently around her. Not that she *always* wore old-fashioned gowns. Granny had been known to appear in men's suits and jodhpurs when the mood struck her, and somewhere in her huge closet she even owned jeans.

But most of the time, Granny floated, looking as if she ought to be reclining on a chaise with a mint julep in her hand. Instead of a mint julep, however, she usually held a pearl cigarette holder with an unlit cigarette tipping out of the end of it. Granny had quit smoking thirty years ago to avoid lines in her face, but she'd refused to give up her favorite prop, even when it went totally out of fashion.

This afternoon, Bea was wearing some gauzy creation suitable for a garden party with the queen. The ensemble lacked only a wide-brimmed straw hat trailing lavender ribbons. Just the mere sight of her grandmother made Kelly painfully aware of her own jeans and flannel shirt, and the icky, sticky feeling of travel soil in every pore.

19

Kelly's first impulse was to hurry over to her grandmother and give her a big hug, but the scent of gardenias assaulted her the moment she stepped through the door, and her sinuses began to shriek. Which was probably just as well, because Bea had never favored having her gowns crushed, even by hugs.

Bea was still looking out the window onto the back yard. "She's up to something. I know it."

"Who is?"

"Zee. I can smell it. She always starts doing crazy things when she's scheming something. It's like a barometer. She can't do just *one* crazy thing. No, she has to do a whole bunch of them."

Kelly wondered how anyone could discern when Zee was being crazier than usual. "I think she was just upset with Cook."

"Oh, certainly she was upset with Cook. But mark my words, she's up to something."

"Granny, can we talk somewhere else? You know I'm allergic to perfume."

"Is that any kind of greeting for your grandmother after eight years? And I'm wearing the damn stuff, so you'll just have to breathe it for a few minutes."

Kelly crossed the room, kissed her grandmother's cheek, then sat in the armchair, pinching the bridge of her nose. Bea floated to her own chair and settled as if buoyed by a cushion of air. That *had* to be practiced, Kelly thought. Nobody was born moving like goose down on a spring breeze.

"So," said Bea, "what brings you back so unexpectedly after all this time? I quite thought you'd disowned us."

Kelly shifted uncomfortably. "Don't exaggerate, Granny. I've called every week, and we exchange e-mails all the time. Anyway, I just had some free time and decided to come visit." Free time—right. That's why she'd brought her laptop with her, just so she could try to keep her head above water.

"How nice," Bea said rather astringently. "Well, if you're worried about me leaving the estate to Seth Ralston, you can forget it. I'm not crazy."

"Who said anything about Seth Ralston?"

"Aha! See, you recognized his name. I thought so! Who's been squealing?"

"Nobody's been squealing," Kelly said stoutly, hating the way her grandmother always honed in on exactly what was going on. As a child, she'd seldom been able to get away with anything.

"No? Then who told you about Seth? It must have been Mavis. She's quite convinced I've lost my mind."

Kelly decided to take the bull by the horns. "Have you?"

Bea sniffed. "Of course not! He's simply a pleasant young man who's experiencing some difficulties in his life right now. I can't see the least reason not to have him as a houseguest. Besides, he's the only gentleman who's bothered to show me a good time since I turned eighty."

If this speech was intended to be reassuring, it had quite the opposite effect. So this encroacher was wooing Granny, was he? She had been right to come. The only question was what she was going to do about it without sending Granny into a fit of stubborn pique that might well cause her to marry this young man just to annoy everyone.

"Besides," said Granny, "Liz had her young man."

Oh, God. "Are you trying to keep up with Liz?"

Granny waved an airy hand. "Hardly. We aren't even in the same league, you know. She was just a pretty face. I've always been an *actress*."

Granny had been competing with Liz ever since the younger woman had showed up on the Hollywood scene. "Well, you've married more times than she has."

"And to a viscount, too!"

Kelly hid a smile. "That's true."

"And I managed to have *five* children without losing my figure."

"Quite an accomplishment."

"So, as you see, I have no need to compete with her."

"None at all," Kelly agreed.

Granny beamed at her. "There. We're agreed."

"But how did you meet Mr. Ralston?"

Granny's blue eyes, once regarded as the most beautiful in Hollywood—until Liz came along—narrowed. "Back to that, are we?"

"I'm just curious. I met him on the beach and thought he was—well, he was nasty."

"Seth? Nasty?" She cocked her head, a graceful movement that in another woman would have been birdlike. "Well, I suppose he can be. After all, he's used to bashing people with his body."

"He was rude."

Bea laughed, a melodious sound that had once been considered as valuable an asset as Marlene's legs. "I suppose you were rude to him, too." She waved her cigarette holder gracefully. "Relax, dear. We've been having a terrible time with tourists this spring. He probably thought you were another invader."

"How did you meet him?"

"Oh, we did a commercial together a couple of years ago." She wrinkled her aristocratic nose. "I played a granny who was a football fan. I had to tackle him to get his autograph."

Kelly remembered that commercial. She hadn't

told anyone that that gray-haired woman in a flowered dress and jogging shoes who climbed the fence and ran across the football field in the middle of a play was her grandmother. Some things were better left unsaid. "That was Mr. Ralston?" She wouldn't have recognized him without all his gear.

"It certainly was. We hit it off wonderfully. After filming he took me out to dinner, and then we went to all these outrageous nightclubs together. I can't remember which one of us poured the other into a cab. Not that it matters, I suppose. We've kept in touch ever since."

"He took you *drinking*?"

"Well, of course. I drew the line at slam dancing, though."

Kelly had to cover her mouth with her hand to conceal her amusement.

"Crying into your beer is a good way to cement a friendship," Bea said. "Of course, I wasn't drinking beer. I stuck to champagne."

"Of course," Kelly agreed, keeping a straight face. "I suppose *he* was drinking the beer."

"Actually, no. He has a taste for fine scotch."

"Oh." This sounded worse and worse.

"Now, don't look so disapproving, child. You're not nearly old enough to criticize my conduct."

"I'm not a child, Granny. I'm thirty years old!"

"Which is still a child to me."

"Which makes Mr. Ralston a child, too, I suppose."

"Oh, my dear, no! He's a very mature man."

Kelly felt her heart sinking. This didn't sound good at all. "How long is he going to be here?"

"Until he finishes his recuperation. He blew out his knee, you know. Somebody—I can never remember the person's name—cut his knees and literally shredded all the ligaments."

Kelly instinctively winced. "That must have hurt."

"Not nearly as much as his divorce did, I'm sure. That woman cleaned him out."

For an instant, just an instant, Kelly thought she saw something amused and calculating in her grandmother's eyes, but before she could be sure, the expression vanished and Bea's face became a perfect moue of distress. Too perfect? The problem with dealing with an actress, Kelly remembered all too well, was that you could never be sure when you were getting the straight skinny or merely a role.

But if Granny was telling the truth, Seth was now broke—and all the more likely to be interested in her grandmother's fortune. Her stomach churned unhappily.

"So he's staying at the guest house indefinitely?"

"As long as he chooses."

Kelly felt her stomach plummet, but didn't know quite what to say.

"So how long are you planning to stay?" Bea asked. "More than a few days, I hope. We've all missed you."

The words unexpectedly tightened Kelly's throat again. Why hadn't she realized that coming home was going to unleash more emotions than exasperation and terror? She loved these people. She had always loved these people. She just couldn't stand to live with them.

"I'm not sure," she said, refusing to commit herself to something she might regret. If she could take care of this Seth matter quickly, she'd be out of here like a shot. "I've got work to do, and I'm not sure I can do it all from here."

"Well, of course. You're an important person."

Was that sarcasm? But a search of her grandmother's face revealed nothing. "I'm not important. I'm just a web designer."

"Your last page was quite impressive," Bea said serenely. Rising from her chair, she passed by Kelly, sending another wave of gardenia right up the younger woman's aching sinuses. "A little dark, I thought."

"That's the trend." And count on Bea to have a criticism of something she knew nothing about. But instead of getting annoyed, Kelly found herself remembering when she had thought Bea was the wisest woman in the world and that her grandmother had the answers for everything. Though that belief had worn off before she had left home, the memory still remained.

"Well, I'm sure you know best." Bea smiled fondly at her. "We've missed you, Kelly. Now why don't you go freshen up and rest a little from your trip? Everyone will talk you to death this evening at dinner."

Then Bea astonished her by giving her a tight, lingering hug. And suddenly the scent of gardenias seemed a whole lot more pleasant.

She found her bags in her old bedroom, and hoped Lawrence had managed not to drop the laptop on his way upstairs.

Her old room hadn't changed a bit. It was still ridiculously opulent with brocade wallpaper, damask seat covers, and a silk-embroidered bedspread, all in suffocating shades of rose. But at least it didn't reek of gardenias.

Kelly plopped down in one of the gold-leafed, damask-upholstered armchairs and looked around her, trying to fight the feeling that she was shrinking in size, reverting to the ugly-duckling child who had tried to take care of a family of swans. After eight years of standing on her own two feet, she was reasonably sure that her reaction was neurotic. With all the success she had achieved on her own, she shouldn't be feeling diminished just by coming home.

Her eyes suddenly alighted on the toy chest in the far corner. Because it had been purchased by her family, it was no ordinary toy chest. It didn't even look as if it had been made to house toys, and she would bet it was some hugely expensive antique, although no one had ever told her not to bang the lid down or not to sit on it and kick her feet. And the initials she had rebelliously carved on it at the age of ten had never brought her any punishment, though they certainly must have been noticed.

Curious, she went over to look more closely, and found the initials right where she had carved them. They were varnished over, so someone must have refinished the chest and left the initials intact. Her heart suddenly seemed to squeeze, though she couldn't have said why.

The top was still a comfortable seat, padded with more rosy damask. She decided to look inside, and was astonished to find her little china tea set still in its cardboard box. Her Legos were still in a plastic bucket, and two battered-looking Barbie dolls smiled up at her. Even her G.I. Joe, from the year she had decided she didn't want to be a girl *at all*, was still there, dressed in his camouflage, his helmet tipping precariously to one side.

Suddenly overwhelmed, Kelly sat on the carpet. Her ballet tutu, from when she was six, was folded neatly under the dolls, and the blue ribbons she had won in school science fairs were carefully tacked to the inside of the lid, along with the framed certificates.

Suddenly wondering what other pitfalls had

been saved for her to evoke emotions she really didn't want to feel, she jumped up and went to look in the closet. Oh, heavens, there was her white dress from her sixth-grade graduation, and the blue suit she had sewn for her eighth-grade sewing class, and the green organza she had worn to her first prom. And her first ballet slippers. Her first tap shoes. The sheet music from her early piano lessons. The oil painting of the duck that hadn't looked like a duck at all.

Anger filled her in a white burst, and she slammed the closet door. Damn them all to hell, she thought as furious tears spilled from her eyes. Damn them all to hell. How dare they make a shrine to her childhood as if it hadn't been painfully obvious to every one of them that she was a failure?

But even as the maelstrom of painful feelings whipped about her, she realized she was being ridiculous. This house was huge, and Granny was famous for being a packrat. She never threw anything away that might eventually prove useful again. And toys could always be useful when someone with children visited. As for the other things . . . well, maybe she thought they were things that Kelly didn't want to part with.

That made far more sense than the shrine. Far more. Soothed by the thought, Kelly gave up her anger. While she was here she'd get rid of the clothing, at least, and the old oil painting. But not right now. Right now she needed a shower, followed by a brisk walk in the warm spring air to clear her head before she had to face them all at dinner.

"So you met my granddaughter?" Bea greeted Seth. Since she was through rehearsing for the day, she had traded her tea gown for shorts, a wildly printed tropical blouse, and tennis shoes, and had headed over to the guest house.

She came and went from it as if she lived there, and Seth didn't seem to mind as long as she didn't trespass in the room he had turned into a study. But he wasn't in his study, he was out back in the seclusion of the fenced yard, chipping away at a huge block of cedar.

Bea didn't pretend to know what kind of shape he was trying to draw out of the wood, and she didn't especially care. What she did like was seeing Seth in nothing but a pair of white shorts and a headband, working up a good sweat. He'd lost some weight since his playing days, but he apparently hadn't lost any of those magnificent muscles.

And though she might be in her eighties, she was still appreciative of masculine beauty.

He grunted a noncommittal response and hammered his chisel into the wood again, taking a long shaving away.

"I take it the meeting wasn't auspicious."

He paused in his work and just looked at her.

"Funny," Bea said. "Her reaction was similar. I think she's taken you in great dislike."

He shrugged a shoulder and took another swipe at the huge block of wood.

"Where's Bouncer?" Bea asked.

"Zelda took him."

"Still trying to turn him into a vicious guard dog, hmm?"

"It amuses her."

Granny clucked. "Don't patronize her, my dear boy. You should never patronize a woman who has two Siberian tigers at her beck and call."

"I'm not patronizing her. I'm just letting her turn my sweet, lovable mastiff into a killing machine."

Which wasn't the case and he knew it, but the exaggeration suited his mood. "And I'm not quite sure why I'm allowing it."

"Perhaps because it amuses *you*."

He shrugged again, but there was a flicker of humor in his gaze that told her he wasn't indifferent to her teasing. She liked that about him—that he could appear so removed and yet still enjoy himself hugely. It was part of what had attracted her to him in the first place. When he *did* finally cut loose, Seth Ralston was something to behold. It gave her a great deal of appreciation for his self-control.

"So what happened between you two?" Bea asked. "Neither of you are the kind of people to take others in instant dislike."

"Maybe you don't know either of us as well as you think."

"Ahh . . ." Bea started to grin.

"Oh, cut it out, Bea," he said. "No great significance in it. I thought she was a tourist and told her to get off the island. She took exception." As he spoke, he limped around the block, studying the wood thoughtfully. Then he put his chisel to it and hammered away another shaving.

"Really?"

"Yes, really. So are you going to slaughter the fatted calf?"

She lifted elegantly penciled eyebrows. "The prodigal daughter returns? Is that how you see this?"

"Is there any other way?"

"Actually, yes, but I won't bother going into it. You've obviously made up your mind about Kelly."

"My opinion doesn't count."

She laughed. At eighty it wasn't exactly the light tinkle that had once been famous, but it was close.

"Everyone's opinion counts for something. That's what makes the world so marvelous."

He merely looked at her from beneath lowered brows.

"Well, regardless of what you think, I'm curious why Kelly seems to think you're . . . some kind of threat. At least that's the feeling I got. It's not as if I haven't had guests here before. So you'll join us for dinner this evening?" He sometimes did, and sometimes didn't, keeping his own hours with Bea's blessing.

"A gold-engraved invitation, Bea?"

"Fishing for time, Seth? Just come to dinner at seven. Nothing fancy. We aren't even dressing . . . although a shirt would certainly be appropriate."

With a gracious wave of her hand, she turned and walked back through the house, leaving Seth standing there staring after her, undoubtedly wondering what the hell was going on.

Which was exactly the way she wanted it.

Kelly went in to dinner with a great deal of trepidation. It was odd to realize that she felt nervous about seeing Max and Julius again, since she hadn't felt the least bit nervous with Granny Bea and Zelda. Of course, with Zelda there had been so much going on that she hadn't had time to feel nervous. And Granny had unsettled her as usual, leaving little room for any other feelings.

But it was different with her uncles. Since her parents had died when she was five, her uncles' opinions had always mattered more to her than anyone else's.

The walk had invigorated and given her back her inner balance, but entering the dining room took all that away.

Feelings from her childhood overwhelmed her as

she stepped into the huge room with its opulent furnishings and crystal chandeliers. So many evenings she had sat here with her family, listening to their wonderful stories about their wonderful lives, feeling her own school days pale by comparison. When they had asked about her activities, Kelly was sure it was only out of courtesy, since they all knew that she would never be one of the brilliant, beautiful people like them.

Max was slouched at his usual place, sketching on the small pad he always carried with him. She paused one moment on the threshold, feeling an overwhelming sense of love and resentment. Max had been born an artist, and from the age of three his sketches had amazed everyone. He'd had his first gallery showing at thirteen, where the critics had lauded his style and technique and had promised that maturity would bring depth to his work. It had, and these days a Max Burke sketch could bring tens of thousands of dollars, and a large oil could bring half a million. Max had even broken the rule that no artist was fully appreciated until he was dead.

Max's fame didn't interest him at all, though. He preferred this isolated island and the privacy it afforded so he could work to his heart's content. On those rare occasions when he'd had to venture into the larger world, he'd always taken Kelly with him to provide a buffer between him and the irritating aspects of being a businessman as well as an artist.

Remembering that now, Kelly felt her irritation easing. Max had needed her. And she remembered how good she had felt that Max deemed her essential, even when she was only ten. Max alone of this entire group had *needed* her.

"Kelly!"

Mavis's rich contralto tones came from behind

her. Kelly saw Max jump, glance her way, then start to smile as she turned in time to meet Mavis's assault. Her aunt was sailing toward her, wearing a plum-colored concoction that looked as if it were made entirely of scarves.

Mavis had always overwhelmed her. Everything, from her bosom to her voice, was larger than life. The stage presence that had been as important to her opera career as her voice filled a room and threatened to suffocate lesser beings.

Kelly found herself wrapped in a bear hug and pressed to her aunt's perfumed bosom. She had hated these hugs as a child, feeling that she was being swallowed, and was absolutely astonished to realize how good it felt *now*.

"Oh, we've missed you, child," Mavis trilled.

Kelly closed her eyes briefly, overwhelmed by the warmth of homecoming she was feeling. When Mavis let go of her, she regretted it in a most peculiar way.

"Kelly!" Her uncle Julius wore a white shirt and black slacks, his standard casual attire. His round face beneath a bald head was beaming wildly. "How wonderful!"

Max joined them in the doorway, his long graying hair slipping free of the rubber band that bound it in a ponytail, the piratical gold loop in his ear twinkling. He gave her a huge hug, lifting her off her feet and spinning her around as he had done when she was a child. Julius reached them, laughing and patting her back as she swung by him.

She felt like a child again but suddenly it didn't feel quite so bad. Kelly was given the place of honor at the foot of the table, where Julius, as Granny's oldest son, usually reigned.

"No, you sit there," he said when she protested.

"We all want to be able to look at you."

So she took Julius's seat, and the others clustered around her at her end of the table.

"Child," said Mavis, her voice ringing through the room, "we have missed you so *much*! Life just hasn't been the same without you to look after us. I have a terrible time keeping my appointments straight, I'm sure Max has been taken to the cleaners by those unscrupulous dealers, and Julius isn't booking as many concerts as he used to because he just can't manage his time the way you did."

"I haven't been taken to the cleaners," Max protested.

"How would you even know?" Mavis demanded. "You can't make heads or tails out of the accounting the galleries send you."

Max shrugged. "There's *enough* money, and then there's more money than anyone can possibly use. Since I have more than I will ever use, it's more than enough."

But Kelly felt a flicker of concern for her uncle. "Is it true, Uncle Max? You can't read the statements from the galleries?"

He shrugged a shoulder and grinned. "I never could, dear. I know it will appall you, but I have absolutely no idea how much money I have or should be making. But that's all right. As long as I can buy my supplies, I have quite enough, don't I?"

Kelly didn't know whether to envy his attitude or be horrified.

"Well, you don't need to worry about *me*," Julius said stoutly. "Slowing down is a good thing. Now I have time to collect books and enjoy other things. A concert or two a year is quite enough for someone my age. I'm semi-retired."

But something in the way he said it caused

Kelly's heart to squeeze. After a lifetime of being
in demand, her uncle Julius was probably beginning to feel that no one wanted him anymore. It
was possible, she supposed. There were younger
violinists out there who could probably play with
more passion and vitality, and who needed their
turns in the spotlight. Then again . . .

"Well, I'm quite all right, too," Mavis said. "I've
been retired for years. But it's just so embarrassing
to be invited to speak to a ladies' group or sing for
a charity, and then utterly forget that I've promised
to do it."

"You all need to get secretaries," Kelly announced. Looking after this lot was a full-time job
and a half, and she didn't have the time. Besides,
there was no way on earth she was going to rejoin
this insane household. Not after taking such strides
to escape it.

Her announcement silenced them for a merciful
minute. Then into the silence came Lawrence's announcement.

"Her ladyship and Mr. Ralston."

Chapter 3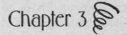

Bea wafted into the room on Seth Ralston's arm. He dwarfed her with his huge size, and Kelly realized her grandmother was enjoying the contrast the two made as a couple.

That set off the alarms again. Bea, after all, was the woman who had married a viscount simply because she had decided that a title would be nice to add to her collection. A startling contrast in size might be enough to make her do it again.

Besides, by marrying a handsome man nearly fifty years her junior, she could *really* outdo Liz.

Seth guided Bea to her chair, having just chuckled at something she said. Then she indicated the chair on her right hand for him. Kelly's worry soared.

Lawrence staggered across the room, grabbing a corner of the table to keep himself from falling. "Dinner is served," he said, slurring the words.

Bea looked down the table at Kelly. "You *didn't* have a drink with him when you arrived, did you?"

Kelly felt her cheeks heat. "Yes, I did."

Bea clucked. "You started him far too early in the day. Now he won't make it through dinner."

"I'm *fine*," Lawrence said firmly, drawing himself up. With exaggerated care, he staggered around the table, grabbing at chairs and shoulders for support. Then he zigzagged across the carpet toward the kitchen door, bumping into the doorframe with a thud. "How the hell did that get there?" he asked in a bemused voice just before he fell through the door into the kitchen and vanished.

Bea sighed and shook her head. "We may have to send Manuel out for burgers later." Then she brightened and looked at Seth. "Seth, let me properly introduce you to my granddaughter. Kelly is a very successful spider web designer."

"World Wide Web," Mavis corrected her.

Seth looked down the table at Kelly. "What's that?"

A Philistine, Kelly thought sourly. How could anyone not know about the World Wide Web?

"It's on the computer," Julius said helpfully.

"On computers all over the world," Mavis elaborated. "I'll have to show you, Seth. Kelly designs web pages for businesses, and anyone in the world can visit them and find out all about the business. Or even order things from them. But Kelly's work is special. Very artistic, don't you think, Max?"

Max nodded. "Very. So many web pages are bare-bones listings of information, but Kelly's always have a mood to them, a mood that seems to draw the viewer in. And her use of color is visually satisfying, beyond what most people seem to do." He looked at Kelly. "You have a great talent for design."

She flushed with pleasure; from Max this was very high praise indeed. Plus she hadn't realized how closely her family was apparently keeping up with her work.

Bea rapped the back of Seth's hand gently with

a fingertip. "Seth knows about the web. When he was still playing football, his team had a page just for him. Don't let him tease you." She batted her eyes at Seth, then wrapped her arm around his.

She turned back to Kelly, cooing, "Seth is a sculptor."

"Oh." She didn't know what else to say, and didn't particularly care whether she sounded friendly. A football player turned sculptor? Not very likely.

He grinned back at her, as if he knew exactly what she was thinking. He was proving to be the most unsettling man.

Manuel, the family's jack-of-all-trades, emerged from the kitchen pushing the large dinner cart. For the occasion he had slicked back his dark hair and added a linen handkerchief to the breast pocket of his green overalls.

Bea cocked a brow at him. "Lawrence is indisposed?"

"Falling-down drunk," Manuel confirmed. He began to serve the covered plates, setting one down before each diner with a thud. "Three sheets to the wind. In his cups. Chasing Cook around the kitchen."

Bea lifted a brow. "Chasing Cook? Again?"

Manuel sighed and shrugged. "She says she's going to sue for sexual harassment. After she finishes suing Miss Zelda for stealing food for the tigers."

Bea rolled her eyes.

Zelda, who was just entering the room, spoke. "Tell her to sue away, Manuel. I shouldn't have to liberate my own larder." She took her seat and Manuel dumped a covered dish in front of her.

"On the other hand," Bea remarked, "you really shouldn't threaten to bring the tigers in the house, Zee."

"I wouldn't have had to, if she'd just let me get the meat I wanted."

"And now," Manuel said, putting the last dish down, "I have to go to town again tomorrow because Miss Zelda fed all the chicken to her tigers." He shook his head. "I'll never get anything done if this keeps up." With a toss of his head, he disappeared back into the kitchen.

Kelly, thinking that nothing ever changed, lifted the cover from her plate and discovered some runny scrambled eggs. She looked up in time to see Bea frowning at her own plate.

"This is beyond enough," Bea said. "Scrambled eggs for dinner! Half-cooked scrambled eggs, besides."

"I think Cook is making a point, Mother," Julius said.

Max looked at him. "Duh."

"Don't you two start," Mavis said. "Mother, do you want me to speak with Cook?"

Bea sighed. "Don't bother. We'll send Manuel out for burgers and fries."

"That's what you think," Manuel said, returning with another cart, this one bearing a bowl of fruit. "I spent all day running around trying to find enough meat for two tigers and Cook. I cleaned out three supermarkets and got the nastiest looks from the other patrons."

"What happened to the meat I ordered?" Zelda asked.

"They don't know."

"Well, that is just too damn much!" Zelda threw her napkin down. "I need another supplier."

"They said they'll have it out here by tomorrow afternoon. Apple, anyone?"

"Me, please," Julius said.

Manuel tossed him the apple, lobbing it across

the table. "Orange?" He threw that one to Seth, who caught it handily.

Just then, Lawrence emerged from the kitchen, wearing the short white mess jacket with shoulder boards that he'd always adopted for serving dinner. It looked ridiculous over his khakis, but no one ever had the heart to tell him so. "I'll do that, Manuel," he said.

"Fine." Manuel threw a peach at him and disappeared into the kitchen.

Lawrence teetered uncertainly on his feet and picked up the bowl of fruit. With it in his arms, he staggered to the head of the table. "Milady?"

Just as Bea reached for a plum, Lawrence tipped forward onto the table, spilling the fruit. Apples and oranges rolled in every direction just before Lawrence's face landed in the green grapes, smashing them.

He was out cold.

"Well," said Bea, "at least he's not bothering Cook anymore."

At Bea's direction, Julius went to get the seven-passenger minivan out of the garage. "I was in the mood for a cheeseburger anyway," she announced. Lawrence was now lying on his back on the floor, snoring softly. She prodded him with her toe, but he didn't even twitch.

"I really need to convince him to go to AA," she said with a shake of her head. "Poor Lawrence. He's stuck here with us because no one else will have him."

"We're not *that* bad, Mother," Mavis said.

"You think not? Ask Kelly. She hasn't wanted to come back for eight years."

Kelly felt her cheeks growing hot again, but she refused to rise to the bait. All the way out here on the plane she had vowed she would remain cool, calm, collected, and mercifully distant from these people who had turned her childhood into a carnival of the unexpected. It wasn't that she didn't love them. She just couldn't stand the disorder of their thinking.

Kelly found herself sandwiched into the back seat of the van between her grandmother and Seth Ralston. Seth was such a large man that if her grandmother hadn't been so tiny, there was no way Kelly could have fit between them. Seth tried to give her more room by putting his arm across the back of the seat, but that simply made Kelly feel surrounded.

"I don't need to go," she said as she watched the others climb into the forward seats. "I'm not really hungry, Granny."

"Of course you're hungry. You've been traveling all day. Can you imagine, that woman serving runny eggs for dinner? I'm going to have to have a talk with her."

"There were chickens left, Mother," Zelda said from the seat directly in front of Bea. "Plenty of chickens. She could have cooked that for dinner."

Kelly reluctantly glanced at Seth, to see what his reaction to all this was. She had realized a long time ago that she tolerated her family a whole lot better when outsiders weren't present. They embarrassed her. And even though now, as an adult, she told herself that didn't matter, she still retained too many memories of how the other children had teased her about her eccentric relatives. Sometimes she didn't like herself very much. This was her *family*; she shouldn't be worrying about what anyone else thought of them.

But Seth seemed to be totally unaware of her. He

was smiling faintly, his gaze bouncing from person to person as they spoke.

"Still," said Bea, "you shouldn't have threatened to take the tigers into the kitchen. Cook has never responded well to threats."

"Cook never responds well to anything. I swear that woman is the most temperamental person I've ever met."

"Except for me," Bea said. She cherished her reputation for being artistically temperamental.

"Always excepting you, Mother," Mavis drawled. Considering she had a temper of her own, which had once stretched to throwing a vase full of long-stemmed roses at a stage manager, she might well vie with Bea for the title.

Julius hit the gas, throwing them all back in their seats. "Sorry," he said.

"Are you *ever* going to learn to drive?" Zelda demanded.

"If you don't like it, you come up here and do it."

Seth glanced down at Kelly, a smile in his eyes, but as soon as their gazes locked, his face froze. She looked quickly away, more convinced than ever that this man spelled trouble. Why else would he be so determined to dislike her?

Julius rocketed down the drive, through the gate, and onto the narrow bridge at a speed that was terrifying. Kelly wished there were something she could hang on to before she slid off the seat to the floor. Almost as if Seth sensed it, his arm closed around her shoulders, bracing her.

She sent a startled, annoyed look at him, and found him smiling. "Are you always so foward?" she demanded.

"Only when the opportunity arises."

"Well, this is not one of these moments. Let go of me please."

"Sure." He promptly obliged, and Kelly slid from the seat to the floor as Julius braked with a squeal of tires for a stop sign.

Seth leaned over her. "Are you more comfortable now?"

"What do you think?" She had the worst urge to pop him.

"Do you need help getting up?"

"I'd rather stay down here," she answered shortly.

"My, my," Bea said dryly. "You two get along so well!"

Kelly looked up at her grandmother. "We don't get along at all because we don't know each other, Granny. Which is exactly why he should never have put his arm around me."

"Hmm," said Bea, her blue eyes sparkling. She glanced at Seth. "Are you making passes at my granddaughter?"

He put a hand to his heart. "I'd as soon make a pass at a prickly pear."

Julius hit the gas again and wheeled sharply around a corner. Kelly found herself clinging to the arm of Zelda's seat. "All this for a hamburger!"

"Julius doesn't drive very often," Bea said calmly. "He'll get the hang of it again."

"Julius!" Mavis shrieked. "That was a stop sign!"

"I didn't see it," Julius said. Then, "Uh-oh."

"Uh-oh?" Zelda demanded.

"Cop," said Max. "You'd better pull over, Jules."

As Julius brought them to a bucking halt, Kelly reflected that her life at home was quiet, uncomplicated, and well within the confines of the law. Why had she ever come back here?

Seth leaned down. "You'd better get up on the

seat and put your seat belt on, Kelly. Or your uncle is going to get two tickets."

Reaching out, he caught her under her arms and lifted her onto the seat as if she weighed nothing at all. She didn't know if she liked that. But even less did she like it when he reached across her to grab the lap belt and pull it across her.

"I could have done that!"

"Not fast enough," he said, clicking it into place.

She glanced out the window and saw the policeman walking up alongside the van. When he reached the driver's window, he pulled off his sunglasses and looked in. "Hi, Julius."

"Blaise," Julius said. "How's it going?"

"It'll go a lot better when people stop running that stop sign."

Julius nodded, smiling pleasantly. "I'm sorry. I didn't see it until I was past it. In fact, I didn't see it at all. Mavis saw it after I ran it."

"You need to pay more attention."

"The sign needs to be bigger."

Kelly, listening to this, began to wince. Julius was going to talk himself into more trouble. It wouldn't be the first time.

"It's big enough, Julius. It's as big as every other stop sign in the world."

"Well, it's invisible." He unstrapped his seat belt and started to climb out. "I'll show you."

"Julius," said Bea, "just take the ticket from Chief Corrigan."

"No, Mother, I won't. That sign is invisible."

"Not so invisible *I* didn't see it," Mavis harrumphed.

"Well, *I* didn't see it, either," said Max. He, too, unstrapped and climbed out of the car. The chief stepped back to let Julius climb out, and the three men crossed the quiet intersection.

"I can't stand this," Kelly said. She pulled off her seat belt, struggled forward, and climbed out the side door. Everyone else piled out after her.

"Uncle Jules," Kelly called. "Let me drive for you."

"Absolutely not," Julius called back. "Just let me take care of this, dear."

"Let him," said Seth, coming up beside Kelly. "He's an adult."

She looked at him. "You don't understand. I've watched him make messes like this before."

Seth shrugged. "It's *his* mess."

"Are you always so callous?"

"I'm not being callous. He's a sixty-year-old man. If he wants to make a mess, that's his prerogative."

Ignoring him, Kelly caught up with Jules, Max, and the police chief, who had gone a little way up the street to view the stop sign.

"You see?" said Jules triumphantly. "It's too small!"

"It's as big as every other stop sign in the world, Jules," the chief said again.

"Well, it's too small for this corner," Julius said. "I never even saw it."

"Me neither," said Max again. A chorus of "Me neithers" arose from the entire group now gathered by the stop sign. Mavis, however, was looking rather satisfied by this turn of events.

Corrigan looked at the flock of eccentrics and started to smile faintly. "None of you should be driving, then," he said flatly. "That sign is as big as it needs to be, and bright red, to boot. Are you color-blind, Julius?"

The question was asked pleasantly and was not at all accusatory. At this point, Kelly thought, any sane person would take the ticket and drop the argument.

But not her uncle Julius. He looked offended. "You're not going to give me a ticket for this, Blaise," he said. "That sign is poorly placed and darn near invisible."

"Just give me your license and registration."

"How awful!" Bea said. "You're really going to do it."

"Of course he is, Mother," Mavis said tartly. "It's his job!"

"But surely he could overlook it just this once. Nothing bad happened."

"Look around you, ma'am," Corrigan said politely. "I might have been able to let it pass before you all got out of the car, but not now."

Kelly looked around and realized they had gathered a crowd of curious onlookers.

"This is an outrage!" Julius said. "I have a perfect record. And this sign is nearly invisible."

"That sign," Corrigan said patiently, "has been there for at least ten years, Julius. You drive this way every time you come off your island. Are you telling me you've been missing it for ten years?"

Silence fell, but only briefly. "I didn't see it *this* time," Julius said.

"And this time you're getting a ticket. Get your license and registration, please."

Julius folded his arms. "I will not."

"Jules," said Seth, speaking for the first time, "just take the damn ticket."

Jules hesitated, but only for a moment. "It might as well be the death penalty, for all I care. I didn't do it on purpose! I won't accept a ticket for a mistake."

"Take the ticket, you jerk," said a man in the crowd. "I'm sick of people running this stop sign. There are kids around here."

"There, you see?" Julius demanded triumphantly. "People run the sign all the time. It *is* invisible."

"It's as plain as the nose on your damn face," said another onlooker. "You old geezers shouldn't be allowed to drive. You're a danger to everyone else." Realizing that Seth was frowning at him, the man fell abruptly silent.

Julius started to step toward the loudmouth, but Corrigan held out his arm and stopped him. "License, registration, and insurance," he said again. "Or I'm going to have to take you in."

"You wouldn't!" said Bea in horror. "No one in our family has ever been in jail."

"Well, I'm going to be the first, Mother," Julius said firmly.

"Oh, for pity's sake," Bea said in disgust. "Just give him the information and take the ticket, Jules. I'm starving to death. Runny eggs for supper. I tell you . . . I'm going to faint if I don't get some food soon. Hand over your license."

"I can't," Jules said. "I don't have it. And even if I did, I wouldn't. You all just go on to dinner while Blaise carts me away. I'll be fine."

"No one is fine in jail," Kelly said tartly. "Quit being so noble. For heaven's sake, you'd think this was a matter of high moral principle."

"It is!"

"Do you *want* to go to jail?" Kelly asked.

"Absolutely! Then I'm going to hire the best attorney I can find and sue the police department."

"For what? For writing you a traffic ticket?" If Kelly hadn't grown up with these people, she wouldn't have been able to believe her ears. But she had, and she knew Jules meant exactly what he was saying.

"No, to make a point," Jules said. He thrust his

arms out suddenly, offering his wrists to Corrigan. "Take me away."

"Oh, for Pete's sake," said Corrigan. "Julius, don't be a jerk."

"I'm not being a jerk. I'm going to fight this."

"You could fight this after you accept the ticket."

"Well, I can't do that. I don't have my license. So you'll have to arrest me."

Corrigan sighed, tipping his head back and looking up at the evening sky. "I don't believe this," he muttered. "Okay, Julius, get in the back of my cruiser."

"Where are the handcuffs?"

"Forget the cuffs. You can force me to take you in, but you *can't* force me to put you in cuffs like a common felon. Quit being a fool and get in the car, dammit!"

With an air of smoldering martyrdom, Julius hunched his shoulders and went to do as he was told.

Corrigan turned to Kelly. "You're the sane one, right?"

"It's a possibility."

"Take them to dinner, then come down to the station. Julius will be ready to go home by then." He shook his head. "Assuming I can pry him out of his cell, that is."

The Burger Place was garish, dovetailing a beach theme with the streamlining of a fast-food place. When they arrived, the only patrons were a few groups of teenagers who stared as the Burkes and their guest walked in.

Seth and Max pushed three tables together, enthroning Bea at their head. Then Bea wrote everyone's orders down on her pocket pad, including an extra burger to take to Jules in jail, tore out the sheet, and handed it to Kelly along with some money. "You and Seth go place the orders, dear."

Kelly would have preferred to do it by herself, but there was no reasonable way she could disagree. Besides, she reminded herself, if she didn't start being pleasant to Seth, there was no way she was ever going to find out what was really going on with him. Having him constantly on his guard with her was only going to make things more difficult.

So, as they walked up to the cash register, she smiled at him. "I'm sorry," she said. "We got off on the wrong foot. I guess I was tired from all the traveling."

His brows drew together a little, as if he were doubtful of her sudden pleasantness. Then he nodded, albeit cautiously. "No problem," he said. "I wasn't exactly nice, either."

"So let's put it in the past?"

"Sure." He shrugged as if it were a matter of indifference to him.

"How long are you visiting Granny for?"

"We hadn't settled on anything definite."

"Oh." They had reached the gum-snapping girl at the cash register, and Kelly read the list to her as the girl punched the order in.

"It'll be a few minutes," the girl said. "You can wait over there."

"High-class service," Seth remarked, his tone amused as he and Kelly moved to one side to wait.

"At least the food will be fresh." She turned to face him, trying to keep a pleasant smile in place. "Don't you get bored on that island? I know I did."

"I couldn't possibly get bored with your family. They're all fascinating people. And I have plenty to keep me busy."

"Sculpting?"

"Among other things."

It was the other things that worried Kelly. "I just thought you must be used to a much more exciting life, being a star football player and all."

He tilted his head to one side, and one corner of his mouth lifted. "You don't know anything about what I'm used to."

She had the worst urge to punch him and rear-range those handsome features into something more suitable for a troglodytic ex-athlete. The impulse shocked her. "You're right," she said, smiling too brightly. "But you don't know anything about me, either."

"How could I?"

"Exactly." She stifled a sigh of annoyance. "But I'm trying to remedy that."

"Why?"

Now she was sure she wanted to punch him. Or hang him by his thumbs until he begged for mercy. The image of him begging for her mercy rather pleased her, and her annoyance vanished as she began to smile.

"What's so funny?" he asked.

She had to give him points for being perceptive. "Not a thing," she said airily. "How's retirement?"

"Pretty exciting, actually."

"Don't miss the game?"

"I didn't say that. But I'm keeping busy."

She nodded. "Keeping busy. The world's most popular euphemism for 'life sucks.'"

He almost cracked a smile at that. She caught the glimmer of it in the depths of his dark eyes . . . and she hated the feeling that she might find it possible to like this man.

He was certainly good-looking, if you went for the huge, muscle-bound type. She preferred nerds who spoke her own language. But that didn't keep her from wondering what he thought of her, with her short dark hair and a body just a little too plump from spending her whole life chained to a computer. He probably preferred the blond cheerleader type.

He spoke. "What brought you home after all this time?"

"You're the last person I need to explain that to."

"Maybe. But I feel very protective of your grandmother."

"Isn't she too old for you?"

"She'll never be old."

Her smile soured. "You've certainly got all the lines down pat."

"What the hell do you mean by that?"

She leaned toward him. "I know what you're up to, mister, and you're not going to get away with it."

His eyebrows lifted. "Are you taking your medication?"

"Medication? For what?"

"Paranoid schizophrenia."

"What the hell are you talking about?"

"I could ask you the same question."

She hated the way he was looking so amused, especially after he'd just insulted her. "I'm neither paranoid nor schizophrenic."

"You could fool me. So who told you I was up to something? Your voices? Or did the government beam the information into your mind?"

The urge to kick him in the shins nearly overwhelmed her. "Neither," she said between clenched teeth.

"Really?"

"Are you always so insulting?"

"Only when I'm accused of being up to something by someone who hasn't spent five minutes talking to me."

"I have my sources."

"Yeah? The Venusians?"

The worst part of it was that he was laughing at her. She could see it in his eyes, and it made her even madder to realize he was enjoying himself when she was so angry.

Now the laugh in his eyes turned into a grin on his mouth. "So," he said curiously, "is this your idea of getting off on a better foot?"

She was saved from having to answer by the arrival of their food: trays heaped with burgers, fries, and beverages. Seth picked up two of them, she picked up the third, and they went back to the table.

"Ahh," said Bea as the burgers were passed around. "A double cheeseburger! Ambrosia!"

Seth and Kelly sat in the last two chairs available, next to each other near Bea.

Kelly, whose appetite was already iffy, felt it sag even more as she watched Seth put three burgers in front of himself. Nobody ought to eat that much, not even if they weighed nearly as much as a diesel locomotive. Which, she found herself thinking, was probably a good analogy for what he had used to do as a player. She noticed, however, that he didn't take any fries.

"Well," said Bea brightly as she unwrapped her huge burger, "are you two getting acquainted?"

"Oh, yes," Kelly said, smiling falsely.

"No point in it, Bea," Seth said. "The Venusians have already warned her about me." He ignored Kelly's glare.

Bea puckered her lips. "Are you talking to the Venusians, dear?" she asked Kelly. "What country are they from?"

"There are no Venusians," she said shortly.

"Really?" Bea looked perplexed. "Then how can you be talking to them?"

"I'm not sure," Seth answered before Kelly could explode. "I asked if they were beaming messages into her mind, and she said no. So maybe they're sending her e-mail."

Which was so close to the truth that Kelly fell silent.

"Well," Bea said, "that's neither here nor there. You really should get to know each other. I think you'd become great friends."

"There's no point in it, Bea," Seth said yet again. "She'll be leaving in a few days."

Kelly looked at Seth. "What makes you think I'll be leaving?" Even though that was exactly what she hoped to do—assuming she could find a way to keep Seth from stealing her family blind.

"You," he said bluntly. "You've looked miserable ever since you arrived."

Bea suddenly reached out and covered Kelly's hand with her own. "Do we make you miserable, child?"

Kelly wanted to sink. This was not the time and place for this discussion. Certainly not with that hulk of a man sitting next to her, ready to stir up trouble.

"I know," Bea continued, "that we're not like other people. And I realize that must have been a trial for you as a child. Every child wants a regular mother and father who do regular mother and father things. But we've never been like other people, Kelly. And I'm very much afraid that if your father and mother had lived, they wouldn't have been normal parents, either."

"Probably not," she agreed through lips that were wooden.

"Kelly's parents," Bea said, turning to Seth,

"were Wanda Turner and Troy Burke. Troy was my oldest son."

"They made all those 'Love In' movies," Julius said. "*Love in Paris, Love in Athens* . . . Maybe you remember them."

Seth shook his head. "Sorry. Before my time, I guess."

"Troy and Wanda were quite popular with the younger set," Bea said proudly. "But not nearly stable enough to be good parents to a young child. Kelly cut her teeth jetting all over the world, staying in fancy hotels, being tended by nannies." She turned a sharp look on her granddaughter. "Do you remember much of that?"

"Not much," Kelly admitted.

"Well, it's a good thing your last nanny quit just before your parents flew to Rome, or we'd have lost you, too." She turned to Seth. "When the nanny quit, they had to leave Kelly with me—so she wasn't on that plane with them when it crashed. I'm so grateful to that beastly woman for quitting, I can't tell you."

"I can imagine," Seth said, and for an instant there was something dark and anguished in his gaze.

"I'm sure you can," Bea agreed. "Anyway, as proud as I was of Troy's accomplishments, I was never comfortable with him as a father to my grandchild. It wasn't just the rootlessness that troubled me, although I think every child needs a stable home, but the partying. They both drank entirely too much, and I suspect they were using recreational drugs. Well, that was very popular back then, especially in Hollywood. It got so I wouldn't go to parties anymore because everyone was smoking or snorting something illicit. Look what happened to Liz: She had to go to that clinic! Anyway,

I hate to say this about my own son, but I don't believe he was strong enough to resist the temptation. And I know for a fact that Wanda wasn't. Every time she left after a visit, her bedroom smelled like marijuana."

Kelly, who had never heard these things before, looked at her grandmother with mixed feelings. On the one hand, she was very curious about her parents. On the other, these revelations were disturbing. As a child, she had naturally beatified her dead parents, and as an adult, she didn't want to see them toppled from their pedestal.

Bea smiled at her and patted her hand. "So you see, child, coming to live with me wasn't the *worst* thing that could have happened."

"I never thought it was, Granny." And she hadn't, really. Trying, exhausting, and even exasperating, but never, ever the worst thing that could have happened to her.

"Oh, I'm sure there were times you thought exactly that. In retrospect, I believe we leaned on you entirely too much. But you were always so ... adept at management."

Also at parenting, Kelly thought. There had been many times when she had felt she was raising her relatives, and not the other way around. Yet however maddening her family could be, she loved them with her whole heart. At the same time, being complimented on her management skills felt like second prize. She had never been able to dance, or sing, or paint, or play an instrument, and as an actress she was an abysmal failure. Heck, even her cousin Verna was an accomplished dancer, and her cousin Gerald had been a famous rock musician. But Kelly had been completely passed over by the family talents, and had felt the lack her entire life.

"Well," said Bea, picking up a hamburger that

looked big enough to satisfy a stevedore, "Troy and Wanda were a lovely, sparkling couple, very much in love. They just burned the candle too quickly."

She bit into the burger and juice dripped down her chin, and she looked as happy as could be.

Kelly looked down at her own burger and realized her appetite had completely fled.

"Aren't you going to eat?" Bea asked.

"I'm really not hungry, Granny."

"Are you getting sick?"

"Maybe." It was a distinct possibility. "I'm a little nauseated."

"Then go get yourself a shake. Maybe that will settle it."

"That's the worst thing, Mother," Mavis said. "Milk will curdle on an upset stomach."

"An old wives' tale," Bea said with a dismissive wave. "It'll either settle her tummy or bring it all up. Either one will make her feel better."

"I'll just pass, Granny. I can always raid the pantry later for some crackers."

"True," said Zelda. "Kelly's the only one of us Cook pampers."

Bea spoke dryly. "That could be because Kelly doesn't invade the larder."

"Oh, Mother, just drop it. Those tigers are my responsibility. They're caged and can't hunt for themselves, so I have to make sure they're properly fed."

"I quite agree, dear. But you shouldn't have threatened Cook with them."

"Why not? She was threatening *them*."

Max shook his head. "Let's not run around in circles about this, okay? We've already been over it, Mother."

Bea was not so easily silenced. She turned to Seth and simpered. "I just want to know what Seth thinks about Zee threatening to bring tigers into the kitchen."

He looked faintly amused at the way Bea was gazing at him. "I figure the lady with the tigers makes the rules."

"Hah!" said Zelda, clapping her hands in delight. Bea frowned. "Chicken."

"Absolutely," he agreed. "I like tigers well enough, but I like them even better when they're well fed. And on the other side of a strong fence."

"So you don't want them in the kitchen?"

"Of course not."

"See?" said Bea, preening.

"And Zee wouldn't have had to make the threat at all if Cook had allowed Zee to get what she needed. Which Zee should have been able to do without a fight."

Kelly looked straight at Seth. "You're as crazy as the rest of them!"

He grinned suddenly, a gorgeous, entrancing expression. "You bet."

And that, she thought glumly, wasn't going to make her task any easier.

Chapter 4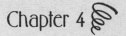

After dinner, Kelly drove them over to the police station to pick up Julius. As she feared, that wasn't as easy as Blaise Corrigan had made it sound.

"He's not exactly being cooperative," Corrigan said.

"Why should he be?" Bea demanded. "You arrested him! He's quite right to remain silent. Don't you watch TV?"

Seth smothered a snort of a laughter and Kelly looked at him, wishing she could find this all as amusing as he did. Instead she could only wonder if she should call the men with the butterfly nets for her uncle, for making such a big deal out of a ticket.

"I suppose," Bea continued sternly, "that you'll be using rubber hoses on him next."

Corrigan shook his head. "Why is it every time I arrest someone they start screaming about rubber hoses? We don't have any rubber hoses. We've been out of them for years. I keep looking for a new supply, and you know what? None of the police supply businesses carry them anymore."

Kelly began to feel an urge to laugh, too. A glance at Seth nearly cost her her self-control. His eyes were full of mirth.

Bea sniffed. "What have you done with him?"

"That's just it, Bea. I *haven't* done anything with him."

"Then where is he?"

"In his cell."

"You put him in a *cell*?"

"Actually, I couldn't keep him out of it."

"You can't possibly expect me to believe that."

He shrugged. "Believe what you want. As I recall, he was threatening to break every window in the place if we didn't lock him up immediately."

"Julius?" Bea appeared astonished.

"Yes, Julius."

"Well, you shouldn't have arrested him!"

"That's the point, Bea. I *haven't* arrested him."

"But you took him in your car!"

"Only to shut him up. I never said I was arresting him, and I never put cuffs on him. And he got into that car under his own steam. I was merely transporting him. And I'd really, *really* like to get rid of him, but I have a sneaking suspicion he won't go."

Bea threw up her hands. "You expect me to believe this?"

"Believe it, Granny," Kelly said. "That's Uncle Jules."

Corrigan looked at her as if he were relieved to find another sane person in the middle of an asylum. "Can you talk some sense into him?"

"Me? I doubt it. Nobody listens to me."

Bea frowned at her. "We *all* listen to you, child. You were always the sensible, practical one."

Practical. That ugly word again. "Practical or not, none of you ever listened to me when you took the bit between your teeth, and you know it. If Uncle Jules is determined to be arrested and spend the night in jail, then that's what he'll probably do!"

Bea was surprised. "You're not even going to try?"

"I spent my entire childhood trying, Granny. It never worked."

"Oh, dear." She suddenly looked sad. "How awful for you."

Kelly felt her throat suddenly tighten, and she had to swallow hard. This was not an appropriate time to discuss this.

Just then another officer appeared through a door. "Chief? That Burke guy is squawking, threatening to call the ACLU or something because the bunk is too hard. He also wants his dinner."

Corrigan perked up. "Really? Well, tell him he can have his dinner as soon as he gets his butt out of that cell."

Bea spoke. "He isn't locked in?"

"Hell, no," said Corrigan. "I told you, he's not under arrest. He can go anytime he wants."

"But what about the ticket?"

"I'm not going to write one. I checked on his license, and guess what? He doesn't have one. It expired eight months ago. If I give him a ticket now, he's going to have more trouble than running a stop sign. So . . . no ticket."

"Well, you could have just said that when you stopped us in the first place."

"I would have. Except that Jules wanted to fight about it. Now will somebody please convince him to go home?"

Bea turned and handed Kelly the bag containing the hamburger they'd gotten for Julius. "Use this, dear. If he's complaining about wanting his dinner, this ought to draw him out."

She looked at the bag Bea was holding out to her and gave in with a sigh. Why prolong the inevitable?

"I'll go with you," Seth said. "Or I'll go talk to him myself. Either way."

"Okay." She really didn't want Seth's help, but she didn't want to make an issue of it. She took the bag and looked at Blaise Corrigan. "Which way?"

He pointed toward a door. "The holding cells are right through there. Help yourself."

She walked through the door, aware of all the eyes on her and Seth, and found herself in a wide corridor with three cells on either side. Two rather decrepit-looking men sat in cells on the right side of the corridor, and she didn't like the way they looked at her.

Jules sat in magnificent isolation in the first cell on the left. He was perched on the edge of a metal cot, with his arms folded in a posture Kelly recognized all too well. Julius only folded his arms when he was feeling stubborn.

"Hi, Uncle Jules," she said.

"It's about time someone arrived to visit me. Where are the others?"

"Out front."

"I was beginning to wonder if you'd all gone home and forgotten to come bail me out." He looked rather pouty.

"We'd never do that, Uncle Jules."

"Why aren't the others coming in? Are they ashamed of having a jailbird in the family?"

"You aren't a jailbird."

"No?" He waved an arm, indicating the cell. "Then just what is this?"

Kelly smothered a sigh and tried not to give in to the feeling that this was hopeless. Jules was evidently enjoying the role of wronged motorist and was prepared to play it to the hilt.

Seth spoke. "Jules, you're not under arrest. Chief Corrigan isn't even going to give you a ticket."

Julius looked almost disappointed. "No?"

"No. The cell isn't even locked." To prove it, he reached out and swung the door wide open. "See?"

Jules appeared dumbfounded. "Now, why in the world would they do that?"

One of the men across the aisle went to his own door and rattled it to see if it, too, was unlocked. "Hey," he said, "that's not fair!"

"Of course it's fair," Kelly said tartly. "*You're* under arrest. My uncle isn't."

"Then what's he doing in that cell?"

"Ask him. I haven't the foggiest idea."

The man looked at Julius. "Are you crazy?"

"I've always been crazy," Julius said, hunching his shoulder. "Artists are always crazy."

"Really? What do you paint?"

"I don't paint. I'm a violinist."

"Now, that *is* crazy. Why don't you play something real, like a guitar?"

Julius sniffed. Kelly interrupted. "Look, Uncle Jules, crazy or not, you've got to come out of there. Everyone's waiting to take you home."

"I'm not coming out of here! I've been arrested."

"No, you haven't."

"What do you call it when a cop puts you in his car and brings you to the station?"

Seth pointed at him, speaking with quiet thunder. "Transportation for an idiot who's refusing to just take his ticket and go!"

Jules gaped at him, his round face sagging. "Are you angry with me, Seth?"

"No, but I'm getting there."

"But why? I didn't do anything wrong! That stop sign was invisible. It's not my fault I missed it."

"You were driving, which makes it your fault. But it doesn't matter, because you're not going to get a ticket for it, so just come out of there."

Jules looked mulish.

Kelly waved the food bag at him. "Look, I have your dinner right here."

"If he doesn't want that burger," said the inmate across the aisle, "*I* do."

"I'll keep that in mind," Kelly replied dryly. "Now, Jules, are you coming home or not?"

"Not until I've talked to a lawyer."

"A lawyer? About what?"

"About the way I've been treated. I'm going to sue!"

"For what?" Kelly felt her temper rising, and was almost at the point of beaning him with a double cheeseburger. How had she ever managed to deal with these people when she was a kid?

"For false arrest!"

"You haven't been arrested! You were simply removed from a public street where you were making a scene. I'm surprised Chief Corrigan didn't arrest you for trying to incite a riot. Did you see how angry you had those people who live there? I don't blame them for being sick of people who whiz through that stop sign."

"Well, if I did something wrong, he ought to give me a ticket."

"That's right," said the other inmate. "He ought to get a ticket."

Jules frowned at him. "Will you stay out of this, please?"

"Hell, no. You're sitting there in an unlocked cell and you won't go home. If I've got to live next door to you for the next week, then I'm going to say what I think. It's a free country."

"The First Amendment doesn't apply to private conversation," Jules said stiffly.

"Really?" The other inmate looked astonished. "Are you sure about that?"

Seth folded his arms and looked sternly at Jules. "You can't hire a lawyer. If you tried, he'd just laugh you out of the office. You haven't got a case."

"I certainly have!"

"Not when he hears that Chief Corrigan didn't even cite you for running a stop sign and driving with an expired license."

"Man," said the other inmate, "you ought to be in deep doo-doo."

"I am in deep doo-doo."

"Not with your cell standing wide open."

"Jules," Kelly said, her tone sharp, "get out of there this instant and come home!"

Jules looked stunned. "You have never talked to me that way before!"

"That's because before I was a child. Now I'm a grown-up. And you'll have to excuse me for saying this, but it's time you grew up, too!"

"Well, I never!"

"Jules . . ."

"Excuse me," Seth said politely enough to Kelly. Then he turned to Jules, the thunder in his voice rumbling louder, and jabbed a finger at him. "Jules, get your butt out of there, or you'll miss tomorrow's game."

Jules, who was still gasping like a beached fish over Kelly's unexpected outburst, suddenly clamped his mouth shut and looked at Seth.

"Come on, Jules," Seth said again. "You owe it to the team."

Jules unfolded his arms and rose to his feet. "You're right," he said calmly. "I mustn't be selfish about this."

Then he strode out of the cell and headed toward the door.

"Hey," yelled the first inmate. "What about that burger?"

Jules paused to look over his shoulder. "Give it to him, Kelly. I'm not hungry anymore."

Astonished, Kelly hardly felt it when the inmate snatched the bag out of her hand. She stared at Jules's departing back, sure she had stepped through some kind of reality warp.

"Game?" she said. "Team?"

But nobody answered her. Nobody ever did. She suddenly had the worst urge to jump into her bed and pull the blankets over her head.

Seth called to Bouncer, and together they stepped out into the muggy night air. Life was getting too complicated, he thought. He'd accepted Bea's invitation to stay in the guest house because he'd needed a place away from the world to lick his wounds. The world, in the form of Kelly Burke, seemed to have found him anyway, and he was feeling annoyed and irritated.

He didn't know what to make of the woman. He'd imagined her as a dried-up, mousy prune, and had been predisposed to dislike her because of the way she had been avoiding her family all these years. Instead she had turned out to be as lovely as her mother—which he knew because Bea had once showed him photos of the notorious Wanda and Troy.

Once he had learned who she was, he had decided he was going to like her even less because she was beautiful. He distrusted beautiful women, largely because he'd been married to one and she'd proved to be as shallow as a rain puddle on pavement.

But tonight, watching Kelly with her family, he'd realized that she had no idea she was beautiful. She wore not even a dab of makeup, her hair looked as if she might have cut it herself, and she dressed in loose clothing that concealed whatever other charms she might have.

But more, he had noticed how she seemed to shrink in the company of her relatives. Especially when they praised her in some way.

He couldn't begin to figure that one out. This entire wacky family doted on Kelly. He hadn't been here two days before he'd discovered that, and he'd wondered more than once why they were so fond of her when she couldn't even be bothered to come home to visit. Now he had to wonder what was really going on here.

The Burke clan were all crazy, but he liked that. Hell, he was crazy himself. Only a lunatic would go out onto a football field week after week, year after year, even when his body had been so banged up he wanted to scream when he crawled out of bed in the morning. So he was nuts, and he tended to respect that kind of nuttiness in others. It was the thing that made you reach for the absolute best in yourself, the thing that made you continue to strive after others had long since given up.

The Burkes had it in spades in their respective endeavors, and maybe that had been difficult for a child to grow up with. But that didn't explain why now, as an adult, she still seemed to shrink around them, and seemed to look at them with a mixture of doubt and love that was almost painful to behold.

They had reached the narrow strip of beach, where the calm waves of the Gulf were lapping gently, and Seth looked down at Bouncer. "It's stupid to wonder about this, isn't it?" The dog returned a soulful look.

"I thought so. The woman's not my problem. In fact, I'm going to stay as far away from her as I can. I've got too many problems of my own these days."

Bouncer wagged his tail.

As if to remind him of his problems, Seth's knee twinged sharply and he smothered a groan. He ached all over most of the time. He could, if he thought about it, remember nearly every body slam and tackle he'd experienced in his years of playing ball. Elbows hurt, shoulders hurt, ankles hurt, and muscles reminded him of pulls and tears at the most awkward times. But this damn knee was really getting him down, more than anything ever had.

Because it had ended his career. Ended his marriage. And, apparently, ended his fatherhood. Velvet was bound and determined to keep the kids from him no matter what it cost, and since he was paying all the bills, including her legal fees, that added insult to injury.

He missed the game, all right. But he missed his two young children more. He swore softly and yanked his thoughts back from that cliff edge. He had to believe his attorney's promises that he was going to get court-ordered visitation, because he couldn't bear to believe anything else.

All of a sudden Bouncer, who would have crawled through fire at Zelda's command but who listened to Seth only when he felt like it, took off down the beach. Seth tried calling him to heel, but the dog disappeared into the shadows farther down the beach.

"Damn dog," Seth muttered, hurrying after him as fast as his gimpy leg would permit. The problem was, Bouncer knew his master was a pushover who'd love him no matter how bad he was. Velvet had hated the huge mastiff, once he'd grown out of his puppy stage, and Seth figured he might have overcompensated a bit too much. The dog walked all over him.

Seth rounded a sand spit, swearing inventively with every painful step, and found Bouncer standing over a supine figure who was pleading desperately, "Down, Bouncer. Off me, you big beast!"

Bouncer was licking Kelly's face as if she were chocolate ice cream—which the dog wasn't supposed to have at all, but still managed by dint of mournful eyes to get from time to time.

Seth halted, taking in the picture, and started to grin.

She spied him. "Damn it, Seth, get this monster off me!"

"Why? He's just kissing you. He likes you."

"I don't care if he *loves* me. I'm drowning!"

"There's just one small problem, Kelly."

"What's that?" She shoved vainly at the dog's face, and for her trouble received another huge lick from her chin to her forehead.

"He only listens to me when he feels like it."

"Just try it, damn it!"

"Okay." But he couldn't quite keep the tremor of amusement out of his voice. The dog outweighed Kelly by a hundred pounds. Neither of them was going to get Bouncer to do anything he didn't want to. "Bouncer, heel."

The dog licked Kelly again.

"Bouncer, no! Bad dog!"

He hated to say that to the animal, and rarely did. Perhaps it was the rareness of it that brought Bouncer's huge head up and drew his eyes to Seth. Kelly seized the opportunity to wiggle out from between the dog's legs and jump to her feet.

"My God!" she said, pulling up the tail of her T-shirt and wiping her face. "That dog *drools*!"

"Mastiffs tend to do that. But he's not as bad as most."

"Aren't I lucky." The reply dripped sarcasm.

Bouncer, deprived of his game, sat down with a forlorn *humph* and looked from man to woman.

"You ought to feel flattered," he pointed out.

"Flattered? That two hundred pounds of drooling dog knocked me flat and tried to drown me? Are you out of your mind?"

"Maybe." He couldn't erase his grin, even though he was sure it was infuriating her more. But the more irritated she grew, the funnier the whole thing seemed to him.

"You need to teach him not to jump up on people," she groused as she tried to brush all the sand off her clothes. "You have no idea how terrifying it is to see this huge shape hurtle out of the darkness and jump on you! I thought for sure I was dead."

"He's just a puppy dog at heart."

"That might be more believable if he weighed twenty pounds. He's *dangerous*."

Deciding that it hurt entirely too much to stand, especially if they were going to argue about the dog's behavior, Seth sat on the sand. Bouncer immediately belly-crawled in his direction and put his ears back, begging for forgiveness.

And as always, Seth forgave him, giving him a good scratch behind the ears. "Look," he said to Kelly, "I'm sorry you were startled and got knocked over. But frankly, this dog does what he wants to. The most I can expect is occasional cooperation. And he hasn't got a mean bone in his body; you're the first person he's ever knocked over that way. I guess he really, really likes you."

Kelly, eyeing the dog suspiciously, dropped down on the sand, too, sitting cross-legged a few safe feet away. "He's got a funny way of showing it. I thought Zelda was training him."

"She is, when she feels like it. And he listens about the same way: when he feels like it."

She surprised him with a reluctant laugh. "He *is* kind of big to argue with."

"Well, it's my fault, I suppose. I didn't realize it at the time, but you have to get the upper hand with a mastiff while it's still a puppy. I indulged him too much, so he's got the idea he only needs to listen when he wants to. Most of the time it's not a problem. We coexist peacefully." He looked at her. "Don't you like dogs?"

"I love dogs. But that's not a dog; that's a Shetland pony. Why did you want such a big dog anyway?"

"I didn't. My ex-wife did. At least, she did while he was still a puppy. Around about the time he reached a hundred and thirty pounds, she changed her mind, but there was no way I was going to give him up." He reached out again to pat the dog. "She always did like puppies, and kittens. Babies. Funny how her attitude changes when they start to grow up."

She scooped up sand and watched it run through her fingers. The moon was rising higher, and the beach was awash in silvery light. She spoke hesitantly. "Did you . . . do you have kids?"

"Two. Johnny and Jenny. Aged four and six."

"Do you see them often?"

"I don't see them at all. Yet."

She looked right at him. "Why not?"

"My ex is claiming I'm an unfit father." It hurt to say it, but he'd been making himself practice the words for months now, because they were the dimension of the real problem that was tearing his life apart. Beside that, a bum knee didn't matter.

Her gaze never wavered, and he gave her points for that. "Are you?" she asked bluntly.

"Nope." He didn't want to say any more about it, didn't want to discuss it with this strange woman who hadn't visited her family in eight years. He had a feeling she would be on Velvet's side in this. So he went on the attack. "What brought you home after all this time?"

She stiffened, then lifted another handful of sand and watched it spill through her fingers. "It's none of your damn business."

"Neither are my custody problems yours, but you asked."

"You brought it up."

"No, you did. I mentioned that my ex didn't like the dog once it started to grow up. You asked about kids."

"Are you always right?" she asked acidly.

"No. Just occasionally. And I hate to be wrong." He felt that ridiculous grin growing on his face again. If he didn't watch it, this woman was going to think he was a full-blown lunatic. But what did it matter, anyway? Her prickliness kept making him want to laugh, though he was damned if he knew why.

"That was rude; what you said earlier about me being a paranoid schizophrenic."

"Well, you have to admit that it looks kind of odd when someone you've just met for the first time says, 'I know what you're up to, and I'm not going to let you get away with it.' Or words to that effect."

She didn't answer.

"So what am I up to?" he asked.

"Never mind."

"No, I'm not giving up that easily. I'd like to know what you're accusing me of."

"It doesn't matter."

He decided to let it lie, because he found himself thinking that Kelly was one thornbush that looked beautiful in the moonlight. It silvered her skin and softened her edges in a way that made his hands itch to sculpt her.

He had the worst urge to say something sappy, like, "Moonlight becomes you." Except he could imagine how a remark like that would be perceived. She'd be accusing him of being a pervert before the words were out of his mouth.

Perplexed, he sat stroking Bouncer's fur and looking at the puzzle who sat before him, pouring sand through her hands. She didn't seem in any particular rush to get away from him, yet she gave him the distinct feeling that his company was unwelcome.

Maybe she felt she'd been here first, and that he ought to be the one to move on. The devil in him was tickled by the idea: It showed spunk.

"So," he said, deciding to enjoy her thorns since there was no other alternative except walking away, which he was oddly reluctant to do, "do you always hang out in the moonlight looking like a nymph?"

"Do you always make asinine comments?"

"Sometimes." The urge to laugh threatened to get the better of him. "Are you always so predictable?"

"What do you mean?"

"I knew you'd bark at me for complimenting you."

She jumped to her feet, brushing the sand off her shorts. "I'm going in now. I wish I could say I'd enjoyed your company."

He couldn't resist a parting shot. "Seems like I'm not the only one who hates to be wrong."

But this time she didn't retort, and a minute later he was all alone with the lapping waves, the silvery moonlight, and a lot of sorrowful, angry memories.

Kelly awoke in the morning to hear shouts of "Go, go, *go!*" from the back yard. She groaned and rolled over to look at her clock. Seven A.M. That was obscene!

She tried pulling the pillow over her head to drown out the racket, but it didn't help much. She was awake now, and once she woke up, she could never go back to sleep.

Groaning, she sat up and swung her legs over the edge of the bed. She winced as she discovered that her bottom was feeling a little bruised from her tussle with Bouncer last night. She hadn't sat down that hard since she'd been a toddler learning to walk.

But her fatigue was a worse problem than a little bruise. Back home in Colorado it was only five A.M., and her internal clock hadn't had time to adjust to the change. Even worse, she was a night owl, often preferring to work into the wee hours and sleep until noon. But then, at home she didn't have people shouting under her window at dawn.

Yawning hugely, she pushed herself up from the bed and padded barefoot to the window, absently rubbing her sore bottom. She could still hear the shouts, but couldn't see what was going on outside. If she wanted to know what all the shouting was, she'd have to go downstairs and look.

She groaned again and decided to take a hot shower. Maybe that would wake her up and ease her stiffness. The shouts followed her into the bathroom, then were drowned in the sound of running water when she turned on the shower.

She forgot about them and stood under the hot

spray so long that her fingers wrinkled. But finally she could stay there no longer and she got out and dressed in a T-shirt and shorts.

She felt like lead this morning, and not just because of her tumble in the sand. The dog hadn't really hurt her, and if she were to be honest about it, she hadn't even been all that scared, once he'd started licking her face. She just didn't like being bowled over by a dog twice her size.

A perfectly reasonable objection. And last night she had been so crabby anyway, after an exhausting day and Jules's and Zee's hijinks, that she'd had every right to feel irritated.

So why was she feeling guilty about it, as if she'd committed some kind of social solecism?

Sitting down to put her shoes on, she paused and thought about that. She hadn't been *that* waspish with Seth, and he deserved it anyway, considering he couldn't control his dog. Considering what else he might be up to here.

She wanted to stiffen her resolve, but instead all she found herself remembering was how Seth had looked in the moonlight last night. Living out West, she'd pretty much convinced herself that she liked men in jeans, western shirts, and boots.

But there was nothing quite like a man in khaki shorts, a polo shirt, and deck shoes. Particularly a man with strong legs like Seth's.

It created a powerful image in her mind: an image of moonlit beaches, palm trees, and a blanket in the sand. Even the cigarette poster cowboy hadn't attracted her that much when, at thirteen, she'd been on a western kick.

What was happening to her? She'd fled Florida and all its crowded tackiness, and now she was discovering that there was a magnetic pull to these same beaches and to men who dressed like tropical beach bums?

Sheesh, she'd even sworn off Jimmy Buffett when she moved away. She'd dumped the sand out of her shoes, thrown out all her seashells, and persuaded herself that the aspens in autumn were more beautiful than a Washingtonia palm against a tropical sunset. She'd traded the sea for the mountains, and swore there was nothing more gorgeous than the Rockies.

But just one evening at home had her longing for this place, longing for a man on the sand in the moonlight?

A man she intended to cordially dislike? A man who was probably scamming her family? A man who was considered an unfit father by his ex-wife?

It had to be the air, she decided. There was something in the Florida air that made everyone crazy. It made ninety-year-old women wear skin-tight capri pants and tank tops in garish colors, and now it was sending her over the edge.

Maybe she ought to send away for a bottle full of clean, bracing Rocky Mountain air. Something to clear her head, which seemed to be fogging over with the soft sea air—or growing mold, the way things were wont to around here.

Kelly bent over to tie her shoes, and tried not to remember the powerful response she'd felt to Seth last night when they were sitting in the sand and actually talking like two normal people. Tried not to think about how much she wished she could just lean over and rest her head on his powerful shoulder.

That last thought snapped her bolt upright and filled her with indignation. My God! She was a modern woman, thoroughly capable of taking care of her own affairs. The thought of leaning on a man for anything made her want to toss her cookies.

Better to be alone than leaning, she told herself sternly, and started downstairs. But somewhere deep inside, a little voice whispered that being lonely was the worst thing of all.

She ignored that traitorous little voice. It didn't know what the hell it was talking about.

Chapter 5

Cook tried to shanghai Kelly as she was heading for the back door. "Your breakfast is ready, Miss Kelly."

"In a minute, Cook. Thanks."

"No, Miss, it'll get cold. I heard you showering, so I scrambled the eggs."

More eggs? Kelly felt her stomach turn over as she remembered the runny mess that had been put in front of her last night. "I'll heat it up if necessary. But I'll only be a minute."

Cook stiffened. "You can't treat me this way!"

Oh, cripes, Kelly thought. Not another uproar. Not this early in the morning. She turned to look at the rotund woman, swaddled in her massive white apron, and saw the light of battle in the cook's eyes. In any other household in the world the cook wouldn't be this uppity, but in the Burke household, everything was turned on its ear. The cook was temperamental, the butler was a lush, and Manuel . . . well, she wasn't sure about Manuel, but if he was hanging around with these birds, he was probably as weird as the rest of them.

"Okay," she said finally, deciding that peace was preferable to World War III. "I'll take my plate outside with me."

"You want to eat with the mosquitoes?"

"Sure, why not?" she replied with a fixed smile. At least outside she could dump the runny eggs behind an oleander.

Muttering under her breath, Cook disappeared into the kitchen and returned a minute later with a tray, which she handed over with the air of someone who was mortally offended.

"Thank you," Kelly said, and marched out the back door.

Standing on the wide veranda one floor above the ground, she nearly dropped the tray as she saw what was going on in the back yard.

Granny, her aunts and uncles, and Lawrence were all running around shouting, tossing what was unmistakably a football. Well, they weren't exactly running. None of them were spring chickens anymore, but they were doing an admirable jog on the trampled grass.

On the sidelines, leaning on a cane, his knee wrapped in an Ace knee brace, Seth stood calling out directions. If he'd been gorgeous last night, he was even more so in the morning light with his hair toussled. He wore a 49ers jersey over tight white athletic shorts that left little to the imagination. Knee brace and cane notwithstanding, he still looked like a man who could barrel into three hundred pounds of defensive lineman and move the lineman as if he weighed next to nothing.

Kelly had never in her life seen such power this close, and her reaction astonished her. For the first time in her life, she felt a totally unprovoked sexual urge—a desire to run her palms over all that tight muscle, an urge to touch and explore and discover. And worse, an urge to feel the strength of those arms wrapped tightly around her.

Stunned, she stood frozen with the tray in her hands.

Zee hefted the football and tossed it. Julius caught it, his face breaking into a huge, triumphant grin, and he headed for the makeshift goal line, marked by two folding chairs. Moments later he crossed it, then spiked the ball with all the verve and panache of an older Deion Sanders.

Seth blew a whistle and began to applaud.

"I did it, I did it," Julius crowed like a little boy, hopping from one foot to another. "I did it!"

Granny, wearing black spandex shorts and a grass-stained white T-shirt, scowled at him. "Don't rub it in. Our team is at a disadvantage."

Julius stopped dancing. "But Mother, you have Lawrence *and* Max."

"And I'm eighty-something. No help at all."

"Cut it out," Seth said from the sidelines. "You may be eighty, but you're as fast on your feet as Mavis. Don't be a poor sport, Bea."

Bea brushed grass from her shorts. "Being beaten by one's children is very lowering."

"And you won the last game, so suck it up, lady."

Bea lifted an elegantly penciled brow. "Is that how coaches talk to players?"

Seth laughed. "Coaches talk a lot worse to players. I'm censoring myself."

Bea's expression became wry. "Really." Then she turned to Julius. "Just don't crow all day, Jules. It irritates me."

"You crowed all day yesterday when you won. Well, most of the morning, at any rate," Julius said.

"Fine," said Bea. "You may crow until noon. In another room. Far away from me."

Zee spoke. "You're a sore loser, Mother."

"Yes, I am. Which is why I usually win." Bea

clapped her hands. "Into the showers, everyone."

Kelly, still holding the tray, stepped aside as her relatives mounted the steps and passed her on their way inside. Her aunts and uncles were dirty, sweaty, and effervescently talking as they trailed after the equally dirty Bea like chicks in the wake of their mother. They did, however, pause long enough to say good morning.

"Did you see?" Julius asked her, his eyes alight. "Did you see my catch and my touchdown?"

"I sure did," Kelly said warmly. "It was wonderful, Uncle Jules."

"I never played football before. Ever. And I always wanted to."

But Kelly was of a different mind. Setting her tray on the wrought-iron table, she walked over to the wooden railing and looked down at Seth.

"I suppose," she said, "this game was your bright idea."

"Good morning to you, too," he answered.

"You realize these people are all older."

He cocked his head, looking up at her. "What's your beef, Kelly? Feeling left out? I can probably use you as a replacement player when one of them gets winded."

Her hands tightened around the railing, and anger burned in her throat.

"Are you out of your mind?" she asked him. "You could give one of them a heart attack! And if Granny falls, she'll probably break every bone in her body! What are you trying to do? Kill her off?"

"Take a chill pill, lady. They wanted to do this. They're enjoying it. And none of them has to play any harder than they want to. It's just *fun*. Do you have a problem with *fun*?"

She didn't like the way he said that. Come to think of it, except for his gorgeous legs, she didn't like a single thing about Seth Ralston. She didn't like the way his dark hair curled in the humidity, she didn't like the way his broad shoulders were way too wide, and she certainly didn't like the way he limped. An actor could have done a more convincing limp.

"Listen, you lamebrain, these people are too old to be involved in strenuous activity."

"Really?" He stepped closer to the porch, his eyes narrowing. "I suppose you never bothered to find out just how much time they put into keeping in shape. Every one of them jogs on a treadmill every day. They lift free weights. You probably aren't in as good shape as they are."

"I'm a hell of a lot younger!"

"So? Look at you. I'll bet the only time you ever move your butt is to go from your computer to the fridge."

"That's not true. I jog!"

"Yeah? Once a year?"

Her cheeks were flaming, and she wanted to strangle him. She might have even tried to, except that she doubted her hands could close around that massive neck of his. "You don't know anything about my habits."

"Yes, I do. You're pasty, pale, and you have circles under your eyes. Do yourself a favor and get some sun while you're here. And try excercising something other than your mouth for a change."

"Why you . . . you . . . troglodyte!"

"Check your dictionary, Ms. Burke. A troglodyte is a cave creature. I spend most of my life in the sunshine."

He turned and limped away, leaning heavily on his cane.

She hated him. She absolutely, positively loathed him, so it was a crime against nature that she couldn't help noticing his tight rump as he walked away. Couldn't help wishing her own bottom were half as toned.

A soft throat-clearing drew her attention to her left. That was when she realized Lawrence was still down there on the grass and had heard every word of the exchange. Her cheeks grew even hotter, and embarrassment made her even more angry.

"What is it, Lawrence?"

"I believe your breakfast is growing cold, Miss."

"Screw my breakfast."

"Well, if you don't want to eat it, I'd recommend dumping it over the fence for the tigers. Cook is easily offended."

"Too easily offended."

"Be that as it may." He coughed gently and clasped his hands behind his back. He made an odd sight, standing so formally while wearing grass-stained clothing. Even his knees were stained with dirt. "Miss, your family is quite enjoying this game. You really needn't worry."

Her anger eased a little. "I'm scared to death one of them will get hurt."

"I understand." Lawrence ventured closer, coming to the foot of the stairs. "I think, Miss, that you've been away so long it looks to you as if they've aged a great deal. But let me assure you, they haven't. They do all work out every day, quite seriously. After you left, they began to feel old, you see."

Kelly hesitated, finally relaxing her death grip on the railing. After a moment she came to sit on the top step and look down at Lawrence. "Why?"

"Because all the youth was gone from the house. You kept them young for many years, Miss. Then you were gone."

Kelly felt a twinge of guilt. "I had to leave, Lawrence."

"Yes, of course you did. It was inevitable. Children have to leave home and make their own way before they can come back as true adults. No one blames you for leaving, Miss."

"But?"

"But they felt older. Much older. And they grew depressed. So their doctor recommended an exercise regimen, and they've been sticking to it quite faithfully. If I may say so, Miss, physically they're younger now than they were when you left."

Kelly nodded slowly, feeling suffocating waves of guilt over the way she had avoided her family. Maybe she'd been too determined to prove her worth. Maybe she'd been too selfish. "But Granny is in her eighties, Lawrence. Her bones must be brittle."

"Actually, her bones are quite fine. She has them checked regularly. You'll be glad to know that osteoporosis doesn't seem to run in the family."

"That's good." She sat there with her elbows resting on her knees and thought about what Lawrence had said. Maybe she *was* overreacting. Then she remembered the way her uncle Julius had looked when he made that touchdown. Maybe some things were more important than caution. "You know, Lawrence, when you're not in your cups, you're a pretty remarkable guy."

Lawrence almost smiled. "Actually, Miss, even when I'm in my cups I'm pretty remarkable." Then he turned and entered the house on the ground level, where his room was.

Kelly sat for a while listening to the breeze clatter the palms, and to the cries of birds. One of the tigers emerged briefly from the woods to stare at her, then disappeared silently back into the thick growth, too quickly for her to identify which one it had been.

She guessed she owed Seth an apology. She'd been awfully rude to him. But before she abased herself, she was going to see what she could find out about *exactly* what he was doing here. Maybe he was trying to kill off her relatives with his football game, she thought darkly.

She dumped her breakfast over the fence for the tigers, who promptly came out of the shadows to enjoy the runny eggs and burnt bacon. Then they sat purring and looking at her as if they wanted her to come inside the fence and play with them. There was a time she would have, but not after eight years away from them. Purring or not, they might view her as dessert.

She found Mavis a short while later. Her aunt had just showered and was sitting at her dressing table in a burgundy terrycloth robe, her hair wrapped in a shocking pink towel.

"Come in, come in," Mavis said warmly in her trilling contralto. "Kelly, you have no idea how we have missed you! It does my heart good to see you again."

"I've missed you, too, Aunt Mavis." The problem was, she was beginning to realize that she needed to take her family in small doses. Or even just one at a time. They were overwhelming when all together.

"Did you see much of our little football game? We've been having so much fun with it. When I was a girl we weren't supposed to do such things, and I always resented it. It's so refreshing not only to be able to play such games, but to actually find a man encouraging us to do it. But then, Seth is a refreshing man. I'm glad your grandmother invited him to come stay with us."

Kelly felt a sting over the way her family obviously doted on Seth, but she told herself it wasn't really jealousy. No, it had to be annoyance that they were so charmed that they didn't realize he might be planning to hurt them.

"Everyone seems very fond of Seth," she remarked in what she hoped was a casual tone.

"Oh, yes! Very." Mavis pulled the towel from her head and began to fluff the tightly permed iron-gray curls. "He's actually a lot of fun, and no trouble at all. We've had a lot of guests in the past who were far more discommoding, I'll tell you. But Seth? He's never, ever a bother."

"How nice."

Mavis smiled at her. "We think so. Zee has certainly taken to him. Although, if you ask me, Zee is hatching some kind of plot again and wants Seth's help." She sighed and shook her head. "It scares me when she plots, Kelly. Last time we wound up with two Siberian tigers."

"I know." Zee had rescued the cubs from an unscrupulous breeder who was keeping them in hellacious conditions. And she'd done so without regard to the law, which had caused further uproar. "Do you know what she's planning?"

"I haven't a clue. I never do until it happens. Oh, well." She sighed and looked at herself in the mirror. "But to get back to Seth. He livens things up without putting us out, if you know what I mean."

"I think I do. So Granny is sweet on him?"

"Absolutely. He's brought the sparkle back to her eyes." Mavis stopped fluffing her hair and looked at Kelly. "In a nice way, of course. Mother needs to know she can still be attractive to attractive men. What woman doesn't? But I'm sure they're not . . . you know."

"Planning to get married?" Kelly supplied, being deliberately obtuse.

Mavis looked surprised. "Married? Oh, I don't know. But that would make it all right, wouldn't it?"

Kelly was afraid to ask what "it" would be made all right with marriage. If that man was having an affair with her grandmother, she was going to pull his toenails out. Young men just simply *did not* become genuinely attracted to women in their eighties. No way.

"Would Granny really consider marrying again? She always said six was enough."

Mavis sniffed. "You know Mother. She marries and divorces the way other people change socks. A viscount for a title, a tycoon for a large fortune . . . It escapes me how she managed to remain married to John Burke long enough to have five children."

"The amazing thing to me is that having five children didn't destroy her career."

"Oh, she was careful about that." Mavis waved a hand. "Nine months off every two years hardly caused her a flutter. The studio worked around it. But she really became a big star when she finished having her family and went back full-time. In the forties, you know. But it escapes me how she managed to remain so youthful-looking after five pregnancies. When she was thirty-five, I swear she didn't look a day over twenty."

"And now she's eighty-something and doesn't look a day over fifty."

"Amazing, isn't it?" Mavis frowned, touching her own crow's-feet as she looked in the mirror. "I wish I looked half so good."

"You look wonderful, Aunt Mavis." And it was

true. At fifty-eight, Mavis didn't look a day over forty.

"Well, I'll look better once I get my face on." She turned back to the vanity mirror and reached for her jar of foundation. "Are you worrying about Seth, dear?"

"What makes you say that?"

"Well, you seem concerned about his relationship with Mother. So either you're worried about him or you're interested in him yourself."

"Me?" Kelly was appalled. "No way!"

"It's high time you started thinking about marriage, Kelly. The biological clock is ticking. I waited too long. I was *so* career-oriented. And now I have no career and no children. Well, other than you. I'll always think of you as a daughter."

"Thank you."

"So, consider me a mother when I say you're thirty years old and it's high time you thought of settling down."

"I *am* settled, Aunt Mavis. I'm very happy with my life. Why would I want to mess it up with a man?"

Mavis looked at her, dismay flickering over her features. "My dear, I realize that it's quite all right for—I certainly wouldn't object to anyone else's choices—but . . . my dear . . . you aren't . . . ?"

Kelly was tempted to let the question go unanswered, but she couldn't bear to leave her aunt looking so unhappy. "No, really, I'm not interested in women. I'm just not very fond of men."

"Oh, thank goodness! Not that I object to *that*, but we were really hoping for grandchildren."

"Well, I'm in no hurry to do that. Men are basically selfish, you know."

"Oh, yes, I *do* know," Mavis said. "They expect one to cater to their egos and their every wish, waiting on them as if they were pashas. But surely you can find someone who's a cut above average."

"Not so far."

"Then perhaps you're looking in all the wrong places."

Kelly really didn't want to discuss her love life— or lack thereof—so she moved quickly back to Seth. "You said in your note that Seth is handling the family finances."

"He's helping out, yes. And we're so grateful. None of us has ever been a wizard with a checkbook. I'm sure you remember. Everything's in such a tangle that we'll never figure it out now. Seth is much better with figures than we are."

Kelly seriously doubted that. A man who'd had as many concussions as most football players probably had Jell-O between his ears. Besides, nobody with a brain would ever play a sport like that. "Well, maybe I could take a look at it for you."

"Why should you? You're on vacation. No, dear, just leave it to Seth. I'm sure he'll fix it all up." Reaching over, Mavis offered her a bottle of sunscreen. "Watch those wrinkles, dear."

Just how Seth might fix it all up was what was worrying Kelly, but she didn't know how to express her concern to her aunt, who would think Kelly was being ridiculous. Mavis clearly thought Seth could do no wrong.

Next, Kelly went looking for Zelda. Zelda had always been the most down-to-earth of the bunch. Zee wasn't in the house, though, so Kelly went outside to look for her. Her aunt usually worked with her tigers in the morning while it was still cool, because in the afternoons they preferred to sleep in the shadows beneath the trees.

She spotted Zee immediately. Wearing a khaki safari shirt and yellow stretch pants, she was standing just inside the fence, feeding a bottle of milk to one of the tigers. Rather disconcertingly—or it would have been if Kelly hadn't seen this before—Nikki was standing on his hind legs with his forepaws on Zelda's shoulders. Zee was holding the bottle as high as she could over her head, and he was drinking enthusiastically. Zee always said that bottle-feeding the tigers kept them sweet, and kept them thinking of her as their mother. So far it had always seemed to work.

"Zee?" Kelly called.

"Just give me a few minutes here, dear. Unless you want to come in and feed Alex? She's waiting for her bottle."

"Maybe I'd better wait."

"I'm sure they remember you. You helped raise them, after all."

"If you don't mind, I'd rather not test that right now." Even though she had once known these tigers very well, her hair was rising on the back of her neck. It would only take one swipe of Nikki's paw to finish Zelda off, and Kelly found that eight years away from this backyard zoo had given her a lot more respect for that fact.

"Well, have it your way, dear. It would be nice if you'd go into the house and get us something cool to drink, though. Feeding my babies always makes me thirsty, for some reason."

Fear? wondered Kelly. Maybe Zelda wasn't quite as comfortable as she pretended with six hundred pounds of Siberian tiger looming over her. "Sure," she called back, and returned to the house.

Inside, she found a woman in a white maid's uniform industriously mopping the hallway outside the kitchen. She had almost passed by when she drew up short and took a second look.

"Manuel?" she said tentatively.

He straightened, smoothing his skirt. "Yeah?"

"Oh! I almost didn't recognize you."

He shrugged and smiled, turning a pirouette. "It's better than overalls, don't you think?"

"Umm . . . yes, I guess." His hair was pinned up, too, she realized, held in place with a large, shiny clip, and his face was tastefully made up with lipstick and eye shadow.

"I dress to suit my mood," he explained, flashing white teeth. "Today I'm in touch with my feminine side."

She wasn't quite sure what to say. "Umm . . . you look very pretty." And he did. It was also apparently the right thing to say. He gave her a huge smile, then returned to his scrubbing.

Feeling dazed, Kelly passed through into the kitchen, where she found Lawrence sitting at the island with Cook, both of them looking mournful.

"Um, hi," she said uneasily. "Manuel's wearing a dress." She hadn't meant to say that, but somehow the words came tumbling out.

"He does that all the time," Lawrence said. "He has quite a wardrobe, in fact. Wouldn't you agree, Cook?"

Cook nodded, giving Kelly a baleful glare. "You threw my breakfast to the tigers."

Oh, God, thought Kelly. Not this, not now. "I'm sorry. I just wasn't hungry."

"You don't like my cooking? You got a problem with my cooking?"

"I didn't say that!"

"No, you just threw the food to the tigers."

Something inside Kelly snapped. She felt as if she'd been tiptoeing for ages, even if it was only half a day, and she was screamingly sick of all the egos in this house. "Your scrambled eggs suck and the bacon was burned!"

"No!" said Lawrence, leaping to his feet. "Don't say that—"

But it was already too late. Giving a look that could kill, Cook stomped out of the kitchen.

"Oh, Lord," Lawrence said, sinking back down onto his stool. "Now who's going to cook lunch and dinner?"

"Cook will make lunch and dinner or she's going to be fired. I'll see to it."

"You don't understand," Lawrence said mournfully. "Nobody else will put up with us. Now I'm going to have to find some way to appease her." He gave Kelly a resentful look. "You have absolutely no idea how difficult it is to keep this house in order."

"I think I do, Lawrence. I used to oversee everything. And nothing was this bad when I was here."

"Everything *was* better when you were here. But we're all getting older, Miss. And more eccentric. Trust me, last time Cook left in a dudgeon, we ate frozen pizza and canned soup for a month. Everyone we hired quit after only a day. I can't face a month of frozen pizzas. None of us can."

Kelly slumped onto another stool. "Okay," she said finally. "Okay. I'll make it up to her. Lawrence, what do you know about Seth Ralston?"

"Ralston?" He sighed and left the island, disappearing into the butler's pantry. When he returned, he had a bottle of scotch and two glasses. He poured one for himself and looked at Kelly.

"None for me," she said. "The sun isn't past the yardarm. And you shouldn't be drinking either, Lawrence."

"I know, but I need to regroup to deal with Cook. Now, about Ralston . . ." He trailed off and downed his whiskey. "Not my affair, you know."

"It may not be your affair, but you've certainly noticed what's going on."

"Certainly I have," he said darkly, and poured himself another drink. He downed it immediately.

Kelly reached for the bottle. "That's quite enough regrouping, Lawrence."

He snatched the bottle back and cradled it to his breast. "I'll take my comfort where I can find it."

"You won't be any good to anyone if you collapse in the scrambled eggs again."

"I won't." He poured yet another drink, but this time he sipped it. "Too much blood in my alcohol system makes me dizzy."

It was an old joke, but coming from Lawrence, it was strangely poignant to Kelly. Giving up, she said, "What about Seth?"

"I suspect Miss Zelda has some use for him, but other than that it's not my place to speak, Miss."

"Oh, cut it out! You've always gossiped with me about everything that goes on here."

"Ah . . . but this is different. Mr. Ralston is not a member of the family. And you've been gone so long." He looked at her. "One doesn't quite trust your judgment any longer, Miss."

That hurt about as much as anything anyone could have said to her. "Why?" she asked, feeling the corners of her mouth tremble. "Why wouldn't you trust my judgment? I'm worried about my family!"

"If you were truly worried, Miss, you wouldn't have stayed away so long. As for Mr. Ralston, you'll have to question him yourself."

The shaft went straight home, leaving Kelly aching and speechless.

"And now," said Lawrence, rising with exaggerated dignity, "I have to go deal with Cook before she persuades Manuel to drive her to town." He looked down at her. "And *that* is why I don't trust your judgment, Miss. You used to deal with these things a whole lot better."

Kelly watched him leave, and wondered if he might not be right. And wondering that made her hurt worse than ever.

Chapter 6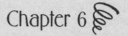

Time to beard the lion in his den, Kelly decided. Avoiding Seth Ralston wasn't going to help the situation at all. She needed to confront him and find out just what he was made of.

She gathered some frosty glasses of lemonade and took them onto the veranda as Zee had requested, but both Zee and the tigers had disappeared. Either the tigers had eaten her or she had decided to play Mowgli and take her usual morning stroll with them.

Seizing the opportunity, Kelly hurried across the gardens to the guest house, where she knocked on the front door. No answer. She knocked again more loudly, wondering if Seth had gone for a walk. That didn't seem likely, considering he'd been using a cane this morning.

Why was he using the cane, anyway? A ploy for sympathy? Ugly suspicions about that man kept filling her head. He seemed to elicit them the way chum in the water drew sharks.

She knocked again, then decided to go around back into the private garden. Maybe he was holed up there, pretending to be a sculptor. She wanted to see some of his work, sure it would prove he was a sham.

But even as all these negative thoughts were roiling inside her, some part of her felt they were forced, as if she were trying to reassure herself that there must be something bad about Seth. As if she were trying to defend herself against him. As if she were trying to quash the attraction she was feeling more strongly with each passing hour.

Kelly found a huge block of wood out back, some kind of dark, twisted wood that showed evidence of chiseling and planing. It reminded her of a fantasy wraith emerging from the wood, but she was sure that had more to do with the original shape of the wood than anything Seth had done to it.

But no sign of Seth. Feeling stymied, she stood there and tried to think where next to look for him.

Then she heard groaning coming from within the house, drifting out to her through an open window. The hair on the back of her neck stood up, and she wondered if he was hurt.

"Seth? Are you hurt?"

There was no answer immediately, but then she heard another groan, followed by a loud thud.

"Seth?"

He was suddenly at the window, peering out through the screen. "Spying?" he demanded.

Irritation surged in her, the more so because she was doing precisely what he accused her of. "I heard you groan," she said sharply. "I was worried you might be hurt. And why would you worry that I'm spying unless you have something to hide?"

"Ah," he said, and disappeared. A few moments later, the back door flew open and he limped onto the porch. "So," he said, grinning down at her, "guilt by innuendo. I'd sure hate to have you on my jury."

"What are you talking about?"

"You're in my backyard. Did I invite you here? If you're not spying, what are you doing?"

"You're evading my question."

"You're evading mine. Standoff."

She frowned at him. "I simply wanted to talk to you. When you didn't answer the front door, I thought you might be out here *sculpting*."

"Why is it you say that word with such sarcasm? Could it be that you don't think I'm a sculptor?"

"Let's say I find it hard to believe."

"Why? Because some banged-up jock couldn't possibly aspire to the arts?"

That was exactly what she thought, but she'd go to the stake before she would admit it. "Pardon me?" she asked stiffly.

He stepped forward, until he came to the edge of the porch. "Is it just me you object to, or do you object to jocks in general?"

"Both," she said, before she could consider the wisdom of her words.

"Well, I can understand your attitude toward jocks. It seems to be a common one, however inaccurate. But objecting to me even before you get to know me is sheer idiocy."

"Idiocy? I am *not* an idiot!"

"Then don't act like one."

"I'm not. I'm concerned about my family."

"Why? The last time I checked, I wasn't a serial killer. In fact, most of the people I know actually seem to think I'm an okay guy. So what is *your* problem?"

Stung, she blurted out her question. "Why are you handling the family checkbook?"

He stiffened. "I'm not *handling* the checkbook."

"Mavis says you are."

"Then Mavis misspoke. I have, against my better judgment, agreed to take a stack of check registers, bank statements, and deposit slips and try to figure out exactly where the family stands. That is hardly *handling* the account. In fact, if you're so worried about it, I'll be more than happy to hand the damn thing over to you and let you try to work it out. If you think I *want* to sort out two years of checks written by five people on the same account, you're out of your ever-loving mind."

In spite of herself, she felt a twinge of sympathy for him. She knew what a headache it was. But she wasn't going to let him know she was softening. "I am not out of my mind."

"That's a matter of perception, don't you think? This family needs a business manager. And they also need to maintain separate accounts."

"I know. I've told them that over and over." The words were out before she realized she was going to say them, and she regretted them the instant she saw his expression soften.

"You used to deal with this for them, didn't you?" he said almost kindly.

She didn't want his kindness, and she hunched a shoulder, wishing she didn't suddenly feel like crying. A little bit of sympathy shouldn't bring tears to her eyes. God, was her life so arid that a few kind words could make her feel like weeping?

Disturbed, she turned away and reached for her anger again. "I suppose that wood is a sculpture."

He didn't answer for a moment, and when he spoke, his tone was almost brittle. "Actually, I just started it. I wouldn't call it a sculpture yet."

"Neither would I."

"At last, a point of agreement."

She turned to him, prepared to bite his head off, but found her anger dissolving when she saw the humor in his gaze.

Then, simply by saying gently, "What made you

so angry and defensive, Kelly?" he totally de-stroyed her defenses. She turned swiftly away, wrapping her arms around herself, battling the tears that blurred her vision.

She heard him swear softly, then heard his cane bang as he limped back into the house. She listened as the screen door slapped closed, then creaked open again. There was a thud, and curiosity drove her to turn around and look.

He had dumped a large box full of papers on the porch. "All yours," he said with a grand wave of his hand. Then he went back in the house.

She stood there wondering if she should take the box and leave, or if she should apologize to him. After all, she admitted, agreeing to balance the checkbook *was* a far cry from handling it. Handling it implied that he had access to it. Apparently he didn't.

The morning was warming up, and she could feel the prickle of the hot sun on her skin. The breeze was soft with the smells of the sea and the humidity. Palm fronds clattered aimlessly, almost like the ticking of a clock, as she wondered if she was wrong about this man.

She hated to be wrong. She knew it was a juve-nile attitude, but that didn't change her reaction. Being perfect seemed to be her major goal in life, and every time she fell short of it, she hated herself.

Seth appeared again, this time carrying two tall, frosty tumblers. "Iced tea," he said. He limped down the steps and handed her a glass. "I took a flier and didn't sweeten it."

"I don't like it sweetened," she admitted as she accepted the glass. "Sugar makes me feel hotter. Thank you."

He lifted a brow and smiled at her. "Don't choke on the words. You don't have to say them."

"Yes, I do."

He shrugged. "Have it your way. Would you mind if I sit on the porch? My knee is killing me."

It amazed her that he was being so nice to her after what she had just accused him of. But he appeared unfazed as he climbed the steps again and settled into one of the wicker chairs.

After a moment, she followed him and sat next to him. Finally, to be polite, she asked, "Will your knee get better?"

"I hope. But it's possible I'll need to have it replaced eventually."

"I hear that's rough surgery."

"It can be. But I'm used to pain, so I'm not worried about it."

"That's sad."

"What?"

"That you're used to pain."

He looked at her from dark eyes. "My choice. I knew before I started that playing football was going to leave me banged up. Just one of life's trade-offs. There's a price on everything, don't you think?"

She wanted to disagree with him, but she couldn't. He was right. Everying had a trade-off. Being a computer geek had virtually narrowed her life to one room and a computer screen. Discomfort made her change the subject. "Where's Bouncer?"

"Zee took him. I suppose she's teaching him to go for the throat."

"I hope not."

He laughed. "With your aunt, you never know. By the time I leave, she'll probably having him doing the Mexican hat dance and whistling 'Dixie.' "

He really could be quite charming, Kelly thought as she laughed reluctantly. "If anyone could do it, Zee could," she agreed. "She's amazingly talented with animals. She claims it's because she treats them like people."

"She might be right. Most people underestimate animal intelligence. Bouncer taught me not to. Scam artists could take lessons on manipulation from that dog."

Scam artists? Why had he mentioned them? An ugly suspicion began to crawl through her mind again, but she tried to hold it at bay. Getting angry and accusatory clearly wasn't going to get her anywhere with this man. As her grandmother had often said, you caught more flies with honey than vinegar.

"Well," he said magnanimously after a moment, "I forgive you."

She twisted to look at him, wondering if he was naturally irritating or if he worked at it. He certainly seemed to have an unerring instinct for provoking her. "For what? I don't recall asking for your forgiveness."

"You don't have to ask. I'm offering." He flashed a smile. "I forgive you for having suspicions about me. Considering that Mavis told you I was 'handling' the checkbook, I can see why you thought I must be up to something. I'd have thought the same thing."

"Really?"

"Really." He gave her an almost boyish grin. "So I forgive you. And I'm more than happy to give you all that stuff in the box. It's been a headache just trying to figure out which numbers on the deposit slips are the dates. And as far as I can tell, every bit of their money is going into checking. They need a savings account. IRAs. Planning."

She didn't tell him that thanks to her they had all those things, and at the time she'd left, they'd had enough socked away to take care of them all for the rest of their lives and beyond. If he thought that all they had was in checking, so much the better. There was no reason a stranger ought to know the net worth of the Burke family, or that she had arranged for twenty percent of everything they received through their agents to go directly into a trust for them. She'd figured out by the age of sixteen that that was the most painless way to ensure they saved. They just never saw the money. They'd agreed to it readily enough, signed all the papers, and left Kelly in charge of the trust. Which to this day she still managed, though she had no part in their other affairs.

"I tried to hire a financial manager for them," she said after a moment. "It was hopeless. They drove him crazy in a matter of weeks."

"Why?"

"Well, he couldn't do anything without consulting them, you see."

He laughed quietly. "That would do it. I can't imagine getting the five of them to agree to anything."

"Or trying to explain bonds versus stocks. It's as if they all go into a panic the minute anyone starts talking numbers."

"But they're wonderful people," he said seriously. "Eccentric, but wonderful."

"Yes." They were. Just impossible to live with. She sipped her tea and tried to figure out how to bring the conversation around to him again. Finally she asked, "Have you always wanted to be a sculptor?"

He shifted. "Well, it's really just a hobby. I don't have any delusions of greatness, but your grandmother seems to like my work. Anyway, to answer your question . . . I suppose so. I used to whittle a lot when I was a kid. I started with balsa wood and worked my way up to harder woods. Then I started to go for bigger pieces. I guess I've been doing it all my life, in one form or another. Something about it is soothing."

"That's a pretty big block you have there. Where'd you get it?"

"I don't remember. I'm always on the lookout for pieces that I think would make interesting sculptures and anytime I find one, I snatch it up. Most of them aren't quite that big, though."

"I'd think not."

He chuckled. "My ex complained that there was no room in the garage because of my 'forest,' as she called it. I had blocks stacked to the ceiling. They're all in storage now, and have been ever since she decided she wanted to live in Manhattan."

"Do you ever sell anything?"

"Sometimes. Mostly I give them as gifts."

That didn't fit in with the idea of a con artist. She couldn't imagine that a man willing to do just about anything for money would give away sculptures he could conceivably sell. Even if they were lousy sculptures, they probably had commercial value because of who Seth Raltson was. She could imagine any number of beer-swilling, body-painting NFL fans willing to put down money for something signed by this man.

Feeling inexplicably disgruntled—well, not inexplicably, because she was beginning to realize that she *wanted* this man to be conning her family—she looked away from him. Why did she want that? she wondered. Granny would be terribly hurt, and so would the rest of them. They liked and respected this man.

She ought to be hoping Seth Ralston turned out to be exactly what he appeared. So why was she hoping otherwise?

She glanced at him and had a sudden gut feeling of attraction, a feeling so deep that it was like an earthquake, changing her inner landscape forever. Despite all the biting words they had exchanged, she was drawn to him. She wanted to get to know him better. She wanted to see him smile and hear him laugh, and know what it was like to have his arms around her.

The feeling nearly panicked her. Her experiences with men had all been disappointing. Invariably they turned out to be selfish bastards or users who wanted to have a fling with her and then move on to the next green pasture. Even her friends who had married had wound up divorcing after love turned to disappointment and bitterness. Basically, she was totally disenchanted with men.

And that was why she had to do everything in her power to keep Seth Ralston at a distance. He threatened the equilibrium she had managed to find. He threatened her self-image as an independent woman. And she was sure, in her heart of hearts, that whenever he looked at her he saw someone who was lacking.

She had no brilliance, no standout characteristics or talents. She would never be like her luminous family, and to Seth, who had also had a talent large enough to win national fame, she must seem rather dull.

But regardless of her own feelings, she needed to be fair. Maybe viewing some of his sculpture would give her a better measure of his honesty. "Can I see some of your work?"

He didn't even hesitate. "No."

"No? Why not?"

"Because my ego couldn't handle hearing your opinion."

Somehow she very much doubted that. He

seemed to have an ego big enough for ten. "Don't be ridiculous. You said my grandmother likes your work."

"She does. But she also likes *me*. You loathe me. Ipso facto, there would be a huge gulf between what your grandmother thinks about my work and what you think of it."

"I don't loathe you."

"You've been shooting sparks out of your ears and eye sockets since the instant we met. You think I'm a stupid jock who's trying to worm my way into your family's affections so I can rob them blind."

If the ground had suddenly opened up and swal lowed her, Kelly would have been thrilled. How- ever, the ground remained solid, and her own nasty suspicions hung in the air between them, seeming to point fingers at her and laugh merci- lessly at her discomfiture. "I never said that!" she protested weakly.

"No, but I can add." His grin was not comfort- ing. "Two plus two makes four, and you've been talking all around four since I met you."

"I have not!" But she had a sudden, painfully embarrassing memory of having just last night said to him, *I know what you're up to.*

"Ahh," he said with evident pleasure. "Gotcha."

She hated the ease with which she blushed, and right now her cheeks felt hot enough to fry a steak on. Miserably, she looked out at the garden and wished the ground would open up and swallow *him*.

"You haven't got me," she said sharply. "You're leaping to conclusions."

"So are you. I guess that makes us both grass- hoppers." He grinned.

Except that she had been the one doing the leaping, she realized with annoyance, while he had been drawing logical conclusions from what she had said. And since she prided herself on logic, it was very humbling to realize she was being illogical. Which only made her more illogical.

"I don't see what's so funny," she snapped.

"Apparently not. Have you had your eyes checked lately?"

It did nothing to improve her temper to realize that he was enjoying himself hugely. She could see it in the crinkles at the corners of his dark eyes. He was *laughing* at her. Frantically she sought a retort, but came up blank. "You're not being very nice," she said quietly.

"Why should I be? I wouldn't want to disappoint you. After all, I'm an unsavory con man and you can't stand the sight of me."

"Quit putting words in my mouth."

He sighed, but the humor still lurked in his gaze. "What are you trying to tell me, then? That you're really wildly attracted to me and the only way you can keep from jumping my bones is to tell yourself that I'm some kind of crook?"

Then she really did want to die, because what he'd said in jest came entirely too close to the truth. "You are despicable."

"Good. That's what you want, isn't it? Should I keep at it?"

Seething, she stared out at the garden and tried to pretend he'd just fallen into a huge sinkhole.

"Look," he said after a moment, his tone kinder, "wouldn't it just be easier to declare a truce and promise each other that we'll stop leaping to conclusions?"

Since she was doing most of the leaping, it would be a bigger concession for her and she was sure he knew it.

"Good," he said. "If you promise to stop assessing my character until you know more about me, I'll promise to stop wondering what kind of a woman ignores her family for eight years."

That stung and she turned on him. "I haven't been ignoring them. I call every week. I e-mail nearly every day. I've just been really busy building my business."

"Well, I can understand that. Being self-employed tends to be a twenty-four-hour-a-day job."

"Yes, it does."

"So," he said slowly, "what's your real problem with them?"

She opened her mouth to tell him it was none of his damn business, but the words that came out were something else entirely, and they sounded so raw that they even shocked her. "You'd never understand."

"Try me," he said quietly.

But she couldn't. She was afraid to trust him. Besides, how could such a successful man ever understand that she hadn't been able to come home until she'd gained enough confidence in herself to face this houseful of extraordinary people? How could a man like him, so big and powerful, ever understand how inadequate she felt when she came through those doors? There couldn't possibly be any point of comparison in his life.

When she stayed silent, he said, "Maybe another time." Then he said the most extraordinary thing. "You're going to be all right, Kelly."

Her throat tightened and her eyes prickled, betraying her. She was all right right now, she told herself. She was just fine.

But she knew she wasn't. Not when she was on

the verge of tears every time she turned around, and over nothing at all except a little kindness.

Just then Bea came into the yard through the back door of the guest house. "Ah, there you are!" she said with satisfaction, her blue eyes hopping from one to the other. "Did I interrupt?"

"We're just discussing sculpture," Seth said. "Join us."

"No, no, I haven't time." She smoothed her diaphanous silver crepe dress and patted her hair. "I just need someone to drive me to town in a little while. I was hoping one of you could do it. I certainly don't trust Julius after last night."

"Sure," Seth said. "I'd be happy to."

"I'll ride along," Kelly said swiftly. She might be revising her opinion of Seth, but she wasn't prepared to leave him alone with her grandmother, especially when Bea was dressed to kill. "Doesn't Manuel usually drive you?"

"Not when he's in a femme mood. Not that I mind it, but he gets treated rather poorly sometimes. And of course, being Manuel, he doesn't take it lying down. I'd really rather not have to try to break up a brawl. Although I must say I could kill him myself for looking better in a tennis skirt than I do. Of course," she finished, almost preening, "he has me to thank. I taught him how to do his makeup correctly, and how to choose clothes that enhanced his assets. He used to be so ... dowdy."

Kelly didn't know quite what to say to that, so she elected to change the direction of the conversation. "Where do you need to go?"

"To the studio in Paradise Beach. I have to film a TV commercial this afternoon. I'm playing the bride's grandmother." She pivoted, swirling her skirts. "Perfect, don't you think?"

Kelly was surprised. "There's a studio in Paradise Beach?"

"Well, of course. I built it myself, dear. I just can't see why I should drive into Tampa when I could do most of it on my doorstep. And it's so easy to drag the crews out here to do the filming when I charge them only cost for using the studio."

"It would be," Kelly agreed. "But is it financially wise?"

"Of course it is. I can agree to do a lot more commercials now that I don't have to travel all over to do them. It all comes out in the wash."

Kelly doubted it, but didn't say another word. Given Bea's age and financial situation, she suspected it was more important to her grandmother to keep working and feel useful than it was to make money.

"Half an hour, then?" Bea asked.

"Half an hour," Seth agreed.

"I'll meet you at the car out front." She turned and left, walking back through the house.

"Does she always walk through your house?" Kelly asked.

"Always," Seth said. "Sometimes it feels like a shuttle terminal."

Kelly laughed then. For the first time that day she really, truly laughed. It felt so good to know that her family was driving someone else crazy, too.

Kelly carried the box of bank statements back to the house and changed into something a tiny bit dressier for going into town. Not that T-shirts and shorts weren't perfectly okay for the beach community, but for some reason she felt she needed to do a little more.

Of course, she told herself, it had nothing to do

with the fact that she was going with Seth. She changed into a newer pair of white shorts and a royal blue tank top. The dab of makeup was purely for her own benefit. Period.

She found the van parked out front with the engine running, but no sign of Bea or Seth. The two emerged from the house a minute later, laughing over something, and Kelly felt a twinge of jealousy.

Bea stopped on the top step. "Why is the car running? Where's Manuel?"

"I don't know," Kelly said. "I just got here."

Bea sighed. "He's offended."

"Offended? About what?"

"That I don't want him to drive."

"How do you know that? Maybe he left the car running because it was difficult to start."

Bea shook her head. "You don't know Manuel." She turned and went back into the house. Seth and Kelly exchanged looks, then followed.

Bea found Manuel cleaning the ceramic tile floor in the conservatory. He was still wearing his white maid's dress and was on his knees, scrubbing industriously.

"Manuel?"

He didn't look up. "Yes?"

"Manuel, why did you leave the car running?"

He let out an exaggerated sigh and put his brush down, but still didn't look at them. "Did you want me to wait for you to come out? There are important things that need doing, like this floor. Besides, I didn't want to be a spectacle."

Bea rolled her eyes and looked at Kelly before she spoke again to Manuel. "Spectacle? Who said you were a spectacle?"

"No one has to say it," he said bravely, his voice trembling. "You don't want me to drive you to town. You're ashamed to be seen with me."

"That's not it at all."

"No." He sniffed and reached for the brush again, saying in die-away accents, "It doesn't matter. I understand. I'm a freak. It's all right. I'll just stay here and mop the floors."

"Manuel . . ."

"No, no," he said, his voice breaking, keeping his back to them. "It's perfectly all right. I understand. My own mother doesn't want to be seen with me. Why should you?"

"I'm not ashamed to be seen with you," Bea insisted.

"No, of course you'd never say such a thing. Don't worry about me. This floor really needs a good scrubbing. I'm going to take a toothbrush to the grout, you know. It's needed it for a long time."

Kelly looked at the expanse of flooring and thought Manuel was crazy even to consider such a thing. He was also playing the martyr exceptionally well.

"Manuel," Bea said, "you know I hire that job out. It's simply too much for one person to do."

"Oh, I have the time now," Manuel said with forced cheer. "You just run along and have a good afternoon. I'll be just fine here, doing what I'm *fit* to do."

There was a sudden, slow clapping from the other doorway, and they turned to see Lawrence leaning against the doorjamb.

"*Bravissima*, Manuel," he said, still clapping. "You remind me of my ex-wife! Did you study under her?"

Manuel rose to his feet and put his hands on his hips. "What are you talking about, you silly old lush?"

"Martyrdom," Lawrence said, and hiccupped. "Come to think of it, you remind me of my mother, too." He looked at Bea. "You run along and let Manuel have her dudgeon. Don't ruin it for her. And while you're out, see about getting a load of frozen pizzas. I can't find Cook anywhere. I hope Miss Zelda fed her to the tigers." Then he turned and staggered away.

"This is beyond enough," Bea said, throwing up her hands. "My cook is a temperamental dragon, my butler is drunk at noon, and my handyman—"

"Maid," Manuel intervened. "Today I'm the maid."

"And my *maid*," said Bea, glowering at him, "is having a temper tantrum because I wanted someone else to drive me today! Has everyone forgotten who pays the bills around here?"

Manuel waved a hand, pretending courageous indifference. "You're right, of course. You pay the bills. And I'm the *maid*, and I'd appreciate if you'd just let me do my job. Run along and have fun. Maybe you'll come home in a kinder mood. And don't worry about *me*."

"Fine, I won't," Bea said. She swept from the room, Seth and Kelly hurrying after her.

It was only once they were in the van, driving toward the bridge, that Bea broke into laughter.

"What's so funny?" Seth asked her.

"The inmates are running the asylum," she said, and laughed again. "Manuel! When he gets in these femme moods of his, no one does it better. I swear, he really *is* a woman at heart."

"Well," said Seth, "I have to admit my ex-wife also used to do essentially the same thing. Especially that line, 'Don't worry about me. I'll be fine.' Every time I heard that, I knew I was in deep doo-doo."

"Exactly," said Bea, chuckling again. "I've used

that line more than once in my life. It always works like a charm."

Kelly laughed, too, but found herself thinking how difficult it must be for Manuel to be a man if he really felt like a woman. How sad.

"And I wonder what happened with Cook," Bea went on. "She seemed fine this morning."

"That's my fault," Kelly admitted. "I told her her eggs were runny and her bacon was burnt."

Bea looked back at her. "Oh, my dear child, you didn't! We'll be eating frozen pizza for a month."

"No, we won't," Kelly said. "I'll cook until we find a replacement. Granny, you can't keep letting the employees run your life."

"Whyever not? As long as they do what I need, I'm perfectly willing to accommodate their personalities. They accommodate *ours*."

"But you're paying them."

"So? We've all been together so long, we're family." She sighed. "But I will admit that placating Cook is a major headache." She shook her head. "Runny eggs and burnt bacon. Oh, my dear, you hit her right where it hurts."

"Then maybe she should remember how to cook. She used to be a marvel. And while I'm thinking about it, Lawrence really needs to go to AA."

"I know he does. I've tried everything I can think of to persuade him."

"Well, we need to do *something*. His drinking is going to kill him." With a sense of shock, she realized that she had said *we*. But these problems weren't hers anymore. In a few days she would be flying back to Colorado, putting this whole mess behind her. Surely she couldn't be proposing to get involved. But apparently she had.

"If you think of something, let me know," said

Bea. "Losing Lawrence would be more painful than six divorces. He's been with me forever."

After they dropped Bea at the studio, Seth suggested Kelly and he take a stroll along the beach and possibly get lunch. "We've got three hours at least, probably four. I gather Bea is usually overly optimistic about how long it's going to take."

Kelly was surprised to realize that she wanted to walk on the beach with him, and the desire made her want to flee. A typical guy would take a girl out, promise to call, and she'd never hear from him again. Or he'd stand her up. Or he'd act like having sex with her was reasonable payment for a twelve-dollar dinner at a burger joint. So she'd begun to avoid the whole problem.

But Seth was a larger-than-ordinary problem, and not just because he was so big. She still hadn't figured out exactly what his relationship with her grandmother was, and there were a lot of possibilities that could wind up causing her a great deal of heartache if she became involved at all with him.

On the other hand, she couldn't toss her heart over the moon just by walking down the beach.

"Sure," she said.

"Whew!" He flashed a smile. "You were taking so long to answer, I was beginning to wonder if asking a woman to walk on the beach had become a transgression of feminist rules."

She felt herself smiling back at him. "No," she said. "Not that I've heard. I just don't care to spend time alone with men." There, she thought, that ought to keep him in line.

"Oh?" The way he lifted his brow told her exactly what he was surmising.

"Not *that*," she said for the second time that day. "I just think most men are juvenile jerks."

"Well," he said agreeably, "they are."

"But you're an exception, right?"

He wiggled his eyebrows. "I didn't say that. But you never know. I might surprise you."

"In your dreams," she said tartly. But he only laughed.

They crossed the dunes and reached an expanse of white beach. There weren't a whole lot of bathers out today. Florida was in the "between" season, right after most of the tourists had gone home, but before the natives started taking vacations. The sand was smooth, freshly groomed, and trashless. They made their way down to the water's edge and walked along the damp, harder sand, where it was easier.

The gulf was light lime green today and the breakers were small, no more than a foot. Terns and seagulls wandered around and a half dozen pelicans patrolled over the water.

As Seth wielded his cane with the ease of long familiarity, Kelly finally asked about it. "Why do you need a cane today?"

"I slept wrong on my knee last night. It feels like it keeps wanting to buckle."

"Was that why you were moaning earlier?"

He looked down at her. "Curious kitten."

"Sorry. It's none of my business."

"No, it's not."

The urge to feed him to alligators was growing again, but at least that eased her apprehension about spending time with him. As long as she wanted to turn him into a snack for the local wildlife, she was safe. Surely. "You didn't have to agree with me," she said tartly.

"No, but I was raised to believe that a gentleman never disagrees with a lady."

"Cheap, Ralston. Cheap."

He laughed. "Are you saying I'm being disagreeable by being agreeable?"

"Exactly." While he might have Jell-O between his ears, Seth Ralston had more than a few functioning brain cells left.

"Tell you what," he said. "If you'll tell me the truth about why you haven't been home in eight years, I'll tell you why I was groaning this morning."

"How can you even ask after today? Granny is right, the inmates run the asylum."

"Ah, but they're such charming inmates."

"In small doses. Unfortunately, I O.D.'d by the time I was sixteen."

He was certain that there was a great deal more to it than that, but he let it slide. There were some questions you couldn't ask until you were better acquainted, and he really didn't want to get better acquainted with any woman right now—especially one as prickly as Kelly.

"Your turn," she reminded him.

"I was exercising my leg," he said promptly. "I have to do all kinds of strength training to keep it from stiffening up. Sometimes I yell for the sheer joy of it."

"I doubt that." She glanced down at his leg, seeing the scars in the daylight. "You've had it operated on before."

"Oh, sure. Cartilage repair and removal. Ligament reconstruction. Routine stuff. This time they couldn't do a full reconstruction. I shredded too many ligaments too badly. I've only been out of the immobilizer for about six weeks."

"I'm sorry."

He sensed she really meant it, and he felt himself softening toward her. Maybe somewhere inside the virago, there was a nice person hiding.

She was looking out toward the water, so he took the opportunity to study her. She was still too pale, and too tired-looking, but she *was* an attractive woman. Right now the sun was setting her dark hair on fire, bringing out all the deep red highlights. A bit of tan and a proper haircut, he thought, and she would be eye-catching.

His gaze wandered lower of its own volition, and he found himself noticing the fullness of her breasts, and the attractive curve of her hips. Womanly. Nothing like the model-thin woman he'd married. He'd bet Kelly didn't exist on rabbit food.

"You know," he heard himself saying, "I got so sick of sitting down to dinner with my wife every evening and finding her eating a plate of salad while I ate a steak or chops."

She looked up at him, lifting her brows as if surprised at the direction he had taken. "Why?"

"How can you enjoy your food when you're sitting next to someone who's deliberately starving herself?"

"Anorexia?"

He shook his head. "Nope. If she'd carried it that far, she probably couldn't have had two healthy children."

"That's a good point." She shook her head. "Well, as you can see by my hips, I'm not overly fond of starvation."

He looked down at her, then startled her by reaching out to take her hand. "Your hips are just fine."

She caught her breath, surprised by the unexpected sense of intimacy in his touch. She hadn't been prepared to feel the embrace of his palm against hers, hadn't been prepared to feel the warmth coursing through her.

Instinct made her want to jerk her hand away, but it was as if her palm had become welded to his. They continued to walk, Seth leaning heavily on his cane, Kelly staring fixedly ahead as she tried to deal with the emotions that were flooding her.

First and foremost was an unexpected sense of comfort. How was it possible that his touch comforted her? She hardly even knew him.

But equally disturbing was an unwanted sense of sexual awareness, an elemental recognition that he was man and she was woman, and that his touch was more than welcome. It was . . . exciting.

Her heart hammered and her breath seemed to thicken, and icy tendrils of panic began to fill her. She couldn't allow this, couldn't allow herself to feel attracted to this man when she didn't know him, didn't know what his motives and intentions might be.

But her body wasn't listening to her. Her body *liked* his touch, however innocent. And her body wanted more.

For the first time in her life, she felt as if she were of two minds, one speaking her body's needs, and the other shouting warnings. The division almost paralyzed her.

But the sense of comfort grew, and finally it was to the sense of comfort that she clung.

He spoke. "So you're a web designer?"

Her thoughts had strayed so far that she had to take a moment to digest what he was asking. "Partly. Actually, I'm what's called a 'new media designer.' I design interactive media, web pages, graphics. Just about anything you might want to do on a computer or online."

"So you're a computer geek."

"Exactly." She didn't take it amiss. She'd striven

hard to become exactly that. "An *artistic* computer geek." It felt good to say it, although a bit brash.

"Sounds like it could be fun. Or a great big headache."

"It's both, I guess. I do a lot of programming as well as graphic design."

"And you have your own business?"

"Yes."

He glanced down at her. "That's probably where most of the headaches come in."

"It seems like it. Compared to people, computers are easy."

He laughed. "I wouldn't know. My computer skills extend to turning it on, sending e-mail, and word processing. I guess the computer has one advantage, though: When it's not working right, I can turn it off."

She smiled at him, and found herself noticing the way the sun glinted off his hair, revealing blond highlights, and how his dark eyes seemed to sparkle. But mostly she noticed his smile. It was warm, crinkling the corners of his eyes, transfiguring him.

How, she found herself wondering, could any woman divorce this man?

The thought hit her like a cold shower. She didn't know anything about him, she reminded herself. The smile didn't make the man. He might be an absolute beast. His ex-wife might have very good reasons for trying to deny him custody of their children.

The turn of her thoughts darkened her mood and she tugged her hand from his grasp.

"What's wrong?" he asked.

"I'm getting off balance."

"Oh?" He grinned suddenly. "I know. You don't want to be caught holding hands with a dumb jock in broad daylight."

"You're right," she replied tartly. "It'll ruin my reputation."

He laughed, shook his head, and let her remark go.

But then her curiosity got the better of her. "Don't you mind being called that?"

"What? A dumb jock? Why should I? It doesn't reflect on me; it reflects on the person saying it."

Stung, she sent him a dark look.

"Gotcha," he said for the second time that day, looking quite satisfied with himself.

"You're being juvenile."

He wiggled his eyebrows. "I'm glad you noticed."

Forget the alligator, she thought sourly. An alligator would probably choke on his tough hide.

But what he had done, quite effectively, was to kill the sexual tension that had been growing within her. Had he somehow sensed what she was feeling? The thought mortified her.

Forget the alligator, she thought again. What she needed was a *Tyrannosaurus rex*.

Chapter 7

They decided to have lunch at the Paradise Beach Bar. They had just been seated at a small table on the deck with a view of the water when Kelly knew she had made a serious mistake.

The hair on the back of her head stood up when she heard a familiar voice say, "Kelly Burke! What a nice surprise."

Seth immediately rose to his feet.

Turning with a sense of impending doom, she tried to summon a smile for Miss Mary Todd. Mary was an octogenarian, the doyenne of Paradise Beach society, and a great friend of her grandmother's. With a halo of white hair and sharp, dark, birdlike eyes, Mary was a beautiful woman, but also a pain in the neck. She spoke her mind, and had made a career out of saying things that others would never dare say, and of poking her nose where it wasn't wanted.

Mary tottered over to them, leaning heavily on an ebony cane, and looked down at Kelly. "Who cuts your hair, gal? It's awful!"

Kelly felt her cheeks heat and her smile faltered. She cut it herself because she never had time for the hairdresser. "I don't believe I asked for your opinion, Miss Todd."

"Nobody ever does, but they get it anyway." Mary turned to Seth. "You must be the football player Bea's been talking about."

"Kindly, I hope," Seth said. "And you're Mary Todd. I've heard a lot about you."

"None of it good, I expect. I'm an outspoken old busybody, and everybody knows it. So are you two an item?"

Kelly began to have visions of crawling under the table, or running out and burying herself in the sand. Or maybe she could simply walk out into the gulf and never be seen again. "No," she said sharply.

"No," Seth agreed, more mildly. "We're just waiting for Bea to finish a commercial. Would you care to join us?"

Kelly wanted to strangle him then. There was no time to wait for a tyrannosaur to show up.

"Sit down, sit down," Mary said to Seth. "I'll pull up my own chair."

"Allow me," said Seth, reaching out to snag an empty chair and hold it for her.

"A gentleman, eh? I thought they'd gone the way of the dodo bird. Well, except for a handful." She sat and beamed at them.

Kelly decided that if the tyrannosaur showed up, she'd feed Miss Todd to it, too.

"My beau is late," Mary said. "Ted and I were supposed to meet here for lunch. It *is* lunchtime, isn't it? Well, he probably got something mixed up. I swear he's getting senile. We seem to get our wires crossed more and more often." But she didn't look disturbed by the fact. Instead, she turned her sharp eyes on Kelly. "Finally decided to come home, did you?"

"Yes." Despite her best efforts, Kelly found herself nearly speaking through her teeth.

"Oh, don't get your on high horse with me, miss! I've known you since you were in kindergarten. When a young woman doesn't come home for eight years, people are bound to remark on it."

"Most people wouldn't actually *say* anything directly to her, though," Kelly said evenly.

"Probably not, but I'm not most people."

Maybe, Kelly thought, an alligator could deal with Miss Todd. Her hide couldn't be as tough as Seth's.

Mary's eyes brightened. "You'll do, gal," she said approvingly. "Backbone's a good thing."

"Is that what it is?" Seth asked innocently.

Mary turned her sharp gaze on him. "Don't be a pain, lad."

"I'm not being a pain," he said innocently. "Basically I've never understood the difference between stubbornness and backbone."

Mary laughed. "You're trying to distract me, aren't you? Well, pardon me, but I don't believe any professional football player would fail to understand the difference."

Then she leveled her gaze on Kelly again, and Kelly had the feeling she was looking down the twin barrels of a shotgun.

"So," Mary said, "you don't want to discuss it. Well, that's all I'll say."

Kelly doubted it, but she was willing to cling to the hope.

Mary patted her forearm gently. "I heard about Julius's little scene at the jail yesterday. Relatives like that would probably suit me to a tee, but others would probably find them a sore trial."

Kelly kept mum, although she felt a strong inclination to defend Julius.

"On the other hand, relatives like mine would be a trial for anyone. My nephew is trying to have me committed again."

"Really?" said Seth dryly. "I can't imagine whatever for."

Kelly felt an unexpected bubble of laughter trying to emerge. Seth, it seemed, had no qualms about dealing with Mary Todd on her own terms.

Mary cracked a laugh. "He wants my land. He's bound and determined to become a big developer, and my property in Paradise Beach would get him well on his way. Of course, I haven't told him that I have every intention of outliving him just to spite him." She laughed gleefully.

"But he can't do it, can he?" Kelly asked. "Have you committed, I mean?"

"No, of course not. They've changed the law so it's gotten even harder than it used to be. And if he couldn't do it before, he certainly won't be able to do it now—especially when I have the chief of police on my side. This past week, when Aldo claimed I was being violent and needed to be picked up by the police, Blaise Corrigan told him to stuff it. Aldo was furious." Mary appeared to savor that fact.

"I remember Aldo," Kelly said, ransacking her memory. "I think I met him once or twice. He was obnoxious."

"That's Aldo, all right." Mary shook her head. "Hard to believe we both crawled out of the same gene pool."

The waiter appeared and they placed their orders for sandwiches and soft drinks. When the waiter left, Mary resumed her discussion of her nephew.

"Aldo is primordial ooze." She formed her mouth around the words as if she savored them. "He's still at the single-cell stage of development. And what can you do with one cell? Civilizing it is hopeless."

Seth laughed. "What a description."

"I've had years to develop it. Lesser epithets don't satisfy me as much." Her dark eyes were twinkling, and Kelly had the distinct impression that Mary actually enjoyed crossing swords with her nephew. "But then, men tend to be on the lower rungs of the evolutionary scale. Present company excluded, of course."

"Why exempt me?" Seth asked. "I have it on good authority that I'm a dumb jock. And I certainly spent a good portion of my life doing nothing but battering other jocks."

Mary laughed, but Kelly felt herself blushing again. "Look," Kelly said, "I'm sorry I ever said that!"

"Why? Because I keep throwing it in your face? Don't be such a coward."

"I am *not* a coward!"

"Then stick by your opinions."

She wanted to bean him, especially since his expressive eyes were laughing at her. "All right, then, I'll stick to it. I suppose the only thing you read is X's, O's, and arrows."

"Well, at least that makes me literate. Can you read them?"

"Of course I can."

"So if I scribble my X's, O's and arrows on a napkin, you'll know exactly what play they represent?"

Now she really wanted to use him for fish bait. He'd taunted her into rashness, then backed her into this corner. Worse, he was laughing at her.

"All right," she said stiffly. "You have football knowledge."

"Sure. Which means I have at least *three* brain cells. One for X's, one for O's, and one for arrows."

Kelly didn't want to laugh. She absolutely, positively didn't want to . . . but she did anyway. Stubbornly, however, she refused to back down. "Well, three cells is hardly an overload."

"True," Seth agreed. "But there might be a few more in there. Sometimes I hear them rattling around."

Again Kelly laughed, and gave up trying to stay annoyed with Seth—at least for the moment.

Mary, who had been watching the two of them, now shattered the moment of shared laughter. "So," she said to Seth, drawing out the word, "why exactly did you get divorced?"

His faced clouded. "That's none of your business."

"Certainly it is—not that that would matter, anyway. You're staying with my best friend, and having lunch with her granddaughter. I quite naturally want to know if you crawled out of the ooze recently."

He turned his head so that he looked directly at Mary, and his face became set. "You want the dirt?"

"No, just the significant details. Did you cheat? Beat her? Psychologically abuse her? I'm not interested in anything else."

Seth simply stared at her, then shook his head. "That's a hell of a laundry list, Mary. Are you sure you can believe my answers?"

"Actually, yes. I'm a human lie detector. And since I'm concerned about Kelly and Bea, I'm sure you'll answer me."

"Cripes. You know how to push the buttons, don't you?"

"How else have I been so successful at minding other people's business for eighty-odd years?"

He laughed reluctantly. "Okay, okay. I didn't abuse her—physically, psychologically, or otherwise. I didn't cheat on her, either."

"So what happened?"

"I refused to take a network sportscasting job."

"That's all?"

"It was enough. She liked the limelight and the fast lane, and when my career ended she assumed I'd just move on to broadcasting. Of course, she never bothered to tell me what her expectations were, so I found myself in a lot of trouble when I turned down the network."

"And she couldn't get over it?"

"Not enough to stop making my life hell. After six months I moved out and she filed. End of story."

"Well, she couldn't have been very happy all along or she wouldn't have done such a thing."

"It *has* occurred to me that the only reason she married me in the first place was because I was reasonably famous and making a pretty good income."

"Well, you wouldn't be the first man who's been seen as a bootstrap to wealth and fame."

"I suppose not."

Kelly decided to forgive Mary for her bluntness. She never would have dared to ask Seth these questions herself. "That's awful," she said, feeling true sympathy for him.

He shrugged. "Live and learn. I'll never make that mistake again."

"Not *all* women are like your ex-wife," Mary observed.

"That may be, but I'm far from ready to yield to logic."

"I can understand that," Kelly remarked.

Mary looked from one to the other. "My, my," she drawled. "Agreement! Will wonders never cease?"

After lunch, Seth and Kelly decided to walk

down the boulevard on their way back to the studio.

"Mary Todd's quite a character," he remarked.

"She always has been, as far back as I can remember."

"I can certainly see why she and Bea would get along. They're very much alike in some ways."

"Well, Bea is a lot more dramatic. Mary's very down-to-earth and practical."

"But neither is afraid to speak her mind."

Kelly laughed. "I'm not sure that's always a good thing."

"No, I can see where it might be a problem. But I get the definite feeling that Bea and Mary only speak their minds when it serves their purposes. And Mary strikes me as being much more calculating, though I'm not sure why. She didn't really say anything that would justify that feeling."

"Bea's always referred to her as 'that crazy schemer, Mary Todd.' "

He grinned. "Really? Well, count on Bea to know. She's one of the canniest women I've ever met, behind that dramatic veneer."

Kelly supposed that was true. While she might occasionally criticize her grandmother for her nuttiness, she had never, ever thought Bea was stupid.

"I wonder," she said aloud, following a train of thought from Bea to Manuel to Cook, "if Cook has reappeared or if we really need to get those frozen pizzas."

"I thought you said you were going to cook."

"A moment of sheer insanity on my part. I hate to cook."

"I find it relaxing."

"Compared to playing football, I suppose it is. But when you have to do it every day, it gets to be a drag."

"I am doing it every day."

And to think she'd started to feel charitable toward him. She was beginning to think he just liked to disagree with her. "Do you always have to disagree with me?"

"No."

"Then why do you?"

"Because I enjoy the fireworks?"

She gave an exasperated sigh. "You're being juvenile again."

"God, I hope so. You're never too old to be a kid again."

It was a strange philosophy, one that felt deliberately directed at her. But of course, he couldn't know that she'd missed half her childhood by assuming so many adult responsibilities on behalf of her family. He couldn't know that being an adult was the only thing she felt reasonably sure she knew how to do. "Just don't revert to diapers," she said tartly.

"Nah, but I could do with a pacifier."

They paused to enter a few of the more interesting shops along the boulevard, but when they came to the bookstore, Kelly was lost. It had been ages since she'd had the opportunity to read any fiction, and she was soon buried in the shelves, scanning titles and cover blurbs eagerly. Seth disappeared in the nonfiction section.

Some time later, she emerged from her preoccupation to discover she was holding nearly a dozen paperbacks, everything from romances to thrillers. A glance at her watch told her they needed to meet Bea in ten minutes.

She headed for the checkout and found Seth was just ahead of her, buying tomes with titles like *Dealing with the Disruptive Child, Behavior Modifica-*

tion for Educators, and *Studies in Adolescent Psycho-pathology.*

Kelly leaned over, peered at the titles, then look at him. "You're into self-help?"

"Actually, I thought the pages would make wonderful wallpaper." But he didn't tell her more, leaving her to wonder why an ex-football player would want books like these.

"Oh, you're Kelly Burke," said the lovely strawberry blond behind the counter when Kelly handed over her credit card.

"Yes?" Kelly said uncertainly.

"Don't mind me. I'm Jillie Corrigan. My husband is Blaise Corrigan, the chief of police. He mentioned that you were in town visiting your family. Which almost makes me feel like I know you, because I'm crazy about your whole family."

Kelly felt herself smiling. "*Crazy* is probably the best word."

Jillie laughed. "That's part of their charm, don't you think?"

Kelly wasn't so sure about that, but she didn't want to say so to a stranger.

"Sometime when you can, stop in again," Jillie suggested. "We can have tea or coffee together and get acquainted."

"I'd like that," Kelly agreed, although to be quite honest she didn't plan to be in Paradise Beach long enough to get to know anyone.

"Your fame precedes you," Seth remarked as they stepped out onto the sun-drenched street.

The air outside had grown still and sultry. Kelly, who was a long way from being acclimated to the sun and heat here, found it almost insufferable after the air-conditioned interior of the store.

"I just remembered why I left this place," she

announced, ignoring Seth's comment. "God, it's hot!"

"Humid," Seth said.

"Humid, whatever. There you go disagreeing again."

"Well . . . it's really not that hot. Maybe eighty-five."

"Hot enough."

"The 'feels-like' temperature is probably closer to a hundred."

Kelly kept waiting for a wisp of the usual breeze that old-timers had once called God's air-conditioning, the only thing that made the barrier islands tolerable in the summertime. But the air had become as still and heavy as a sauna. Instinctively, Kelly looked toward the sky and saw the lowering green clouds of a storm approaching over the gulf.

"We're gonna get it," she remarked, indicating the sky. "I hope Bea is done."

Seth nodded. "Me, too. That looks really nasty."

Florida, she thought with disgust. If you weren't boiling, you were drowning or blowing away.

Bea wasn't quite ready, though, and from the sound of it, she wouldn't be ready in a few minutes, either. She wanted to retake one segment because the camera angle was unflattering, but the director disagreed with her.

"This is a *commercial*!" the man said in exasperation. "Not a screen test for ingenue number two!"

"That is precisely the point," Bea told him firmly. "It's not a screen *test*. It's a commercial that will be on national television. Look, Reuben, if you had once been one of the most beautiful women in the world, and now you were over eighty, and every day you had to look in the mirror and see just an ordinary old woman, how do *you* think you'd feel about an unflattering camera angle?"

The director sighed. "It's *not* unflattering, Bea!"

"Yes, it is. I look old enough now without having to look *haggard*."

The director threw up a hand. "Have it your way. We'll do another take. But I want it perfect the first time. I have another appointment to get to, and I'm already running behind."

"And a storm is coming in, Bea," Kelly interposed gently, feeling an urge to wrap her grandmother in a tight, comforting hug. She had never guessed how aging might have affected Bea's feelings about herself. Bea had always seemed so strong and content with her lot. "You know how hard it is to get over the bridge when the waves are rough."

"One take is all I need," Bea said firmly. "And softer lighting. And make *sure* that camera doesn't get me from the left side this time!" She patted her cheek. "It doesn't show much when I'm animated, but that little stroke I had last year has made the left side of my face look . . . older."

Stroke? Kelly almost had one herself when her grandmother said that. No one had told her! Why hadn't they called?

Bea caught her expression and paused on her way back to the set. She patted Kelly's arm. "I wouldn't let them tell you, child. It was just a little spot of bother, and it's all just fine now. Why, I was out of the hospital in three days! I wouldn't have mentioned it at all except that Reuben can be so dense sometimes."

Kelly managed a weak smile, but she felt as if a dark cloud had settled over her mind. Bea, indestructible Bea, had had a stroke. It seemed stupid to be shocked, but somewhere in her mind she had always believed that Bea would never really grow old.

When everyone else had left the room and moved into the studio, Seth looked at Kelly. "I gather she didn't tell you about the stroke."

Kelly compressed her lips, holding back ineffable grief and fear, and shook her head.

"It wasn't that bad," Seth said. "Really, it wasn't. She apparently got a little dizzy and felt weak on one side, so she went to the hospital. The doctor said it was a transient ischemic attack, a mild kind of stroke, and that it was caused by an irregular heartbeat. Almost all the symptoms were gone in twenty-four hours, and he treated her heart problem. Since then she's been just fine."

"You were there?" she asked.

"Mavis called me. I flew right down."

It was too much. Kelly turned and fled, going out to the parking lot. The storm was closer now and the breeze had freshened, taking on a restless feeling. She hardly noticed it, hardly saw that the gulf had turned steel-gray.

All she could think of was that her grandmother had had a stroke. That her grandmother hadn't wanted anyone to tell her. That the family had called for Seth, rather than her.

And it was all her own fault. They should have been able to turn to her in a time of trouble, but she had put so much distance between them they hadn't felt they could.

But she'd been a disappointment to them all along. Why should anything change simply because she'd grown up? What had they thought she would do, pitch a fit of hysterics? But they had always considered her to be the practical one. It didn't make sense.

But while she tried to tell herself that it was just

an extension of the disappointment they had felt in her as a child, in her heart of hearts she knew it was more. She had virtually cut them off. Why should they feel they could turn to her?

A hand touched her shoulder and she jumped. It was Seth, and he was looking at her with a gentleness that made her throat ache.

"I'm sorry," he said. "It never occurred to me they hadn't told you. I would have gotten your number and called you if I had known."

She shrugged a shoulder defensively. "It doesn't matter now, does it?" But she could certainly understand why he was so down on her about not coming home for so long, especially when her grandmother had had a stroke. She was certain she deserved every ill thought he'd had of her—and was probably still having. It seemed she was no good at anything—not even at being a granddaughter, something that seemed to come naturally to everyone else in the world.

"Yes, it does. I love your grandmother, Kelly."

Something inside her started to freeze. He loved her grandmother. Well, maybe she should just pack her bags right now and get the hell back to Colorado, where at least she had people who wanted her around.

"She's a great friend," Seth continued. "A real doughty old lady. A pistol. Did I leave anything out?"

He was trying to make her smile, but he was only succeeding in making her feel worse. She managed to say tightly, "I don't know."

"Whatever," he continued, his voice soothing, almost gentle. "She's a pisser. And I like that in people. I can't explain it, but we hit it off in a way most people never do, and our age difference never seemed to matter. In fact, your family is full of pissers. And sometimes they get so wrapped up in themselves they don't realize the annoying impact they're having on other people."

It was true, she thought. In all the times they'd made her feel inadequate or stupid, she had never once thought they were doing it on purpose. "So?" Her throat was so tight she could barely squeeze the word out, and her eyes felt swollen and hot. *Please, God, don't let me cry in front of this man.*

"So, they're difficult to deal with. Much as I love your grandmother, I can only feel for someone who was raised by her. She has at least as many cock-amamie ideas as she has good ones, and she tends to be a steamroller. She's trying to steamroll me right now, you know."

"Mm?"

"Yeah, she's trying to get a gallery showing for my sculpture. And no matter how many times I tell her that it's just a hobby, that I don't want to do it professionally, that I prefer to *give* my sculptures to friends, she plain won't listen."

"Mm."

"Maybe," he said quietly, "you had a damn good reason for staying away so long. And if you want to cry, it's okay."

But she wasn't going to give him that satisfaction. "I'll be okay," she said stubbornly.

"Sure you will." But he put his arm around her shoulders and hugged her briefly anyway.

When he took his arm away, she felt more bereft than she had ever felt in her life.

"Bea better hurry up," he remarked casually, as if they hadn't just walked through an emotional minefield. "Look at that sky."

For the first time, she became truly aware of the shift in the weather. The gulf looked choppy, the waves high and foamy, and the wind carried the scent of ozone and rain. The clouds had turned a deep gray-green and had blotted the sky all the way to the east.

"That happened fast," she said, feeling as if she were shaking off a dark dream. Later, she thought. Later she could think all of this over. Right now was a bad time because she wasn't alone, especially since she was torn between both wanting and *not* wanting Seth's kindness.

"Let's go see how it's coming," he said. "The take couldn't be more than three seconds long."

"Until Bea gets involved with directing," Kelly replied, remembering countless episodes like this from her childhood. How many times had she sat silently in the corner of a studio while her grandmother had performed the same scene a dozen times until she and her director were both satisfied?

But Bea was coming out the front door just as they reached it.

"At last," she said. "We're done." Then she noticed the weather. "Why didn't you tell me it was this bad?"

"We tried," Seth said. "You're rather single-minded, Bea."

"Well, single-mindedness is essential to success. You can't tell me you weren't single-minded when you were playing."

But she was hurrying toward the van, her silvery sandals tapping quickly on the pavement, and they hurried after her. Seth climbed behind the wheel, and Bea insisted Kelly sit up front with him while she sat in the back.

By the time they reached the bridge, spray was splashing up over the sides, dousing the pavement. Seth turned on the wipers and slowed down. Gusts of wind kept catching them and Kelly had the uneasy feeling that they might be blown right off the bridge into the roiling waters.

But then they were over and into the shelter of the trees, and the world seemed once again calm. It still hadn't started raining, and the woods were dark, mysterious-looking.

"We made that just in time," Bea remarked. "No thanks to Reuben. That man is getting more difficult with each passing year."

Seth spoke. "I'm not sure he's the only one, Bea."

She laughed. "I've *always* been difficult. I haven't changed a bit."

Seth dropped them off at the front door, announcing he had some business to attend to, and Kelly and Bea went inside together. The house was dark and quiet, and it felt as if no one else were there.

"I wonder where everyone is," Bea said. "Usually you can hear Mavis warbling somewhere, and Jules playing his violin. Oh, well, I'm going up to change, dear. Afterwards, let's talk."

Kelly nodded, but regarded the idea with trepidation. Her "talks" with Bea in the past had always involved Bea going on endlessly about some point until Kelly agreed with her out of sheer desperation.

She supposed she could go upstairs and do some work of her own, but instead found herself wandering into Max's studio. He had turned on all the lights in the room, driving the stormy darkness away, and was cleaning his paintbrushes. The familiar smell of turpentine tickled Kelly's nose and made her feel nostalgic.

This room had once been one of her favorite haunts. As a child she'd spent many hours here playing while her uncle worked, or watching him paint. From the time she'd been six, he'd often given her a small canvas of her own at a tiny easel, where she spent hours splashing colors around. And never had he complained about the expense of the oils she was wasting, or the mess she always managed to make of herself and everything within five feet.

She found a stool and sat, watching him fondly.

"Too dark to paint," he said to her as he shook turpentine out of a brush. "I hate to waste a day."

She nodded. "I feel that way, too, when I can't work."

"Well, in all fairness, I managed to start at around eight this morning, so I've really gotten enough done. It's just that I hate to stop when it's going well. It *does* feel like I'm wasting time. Oh, well."

He reached for another brush and began to work the turpentine through the bristles. "Do you still paint?"

"Not if I can avoid it."

He looked over at her and smiled. "Your standards were always too high."

"Too high? I could never make anything look the way I wanted it to."

"So? Do you think my paintings are exactly the way I want them? The hand and the brush often fail the mind's image. Sometimes I think Beethoven was lucky that he became deaf before he could hear the Ninth Symphony performed. At least he never heard the purity of his mind's composition deformed by an errant piccolo player, or a faulty tenor, or some conductor's mistaken interpretation."

"I never thought of it that way."

Max shrugged. "I think of it all the time. I'd be a lot happier with my work if I could never see it on canvas. But that's neither here nor there. The point is, I wanted you to have *fun* painting. I wanted it to be child's play for you. But you always wanted it to be something more."

Feeling suddenly uncomfortable, because that wasn't the way she remembered it at all, Kelly changed the subject. "What are you working on now?"

"I've switched to seascapes again." He waved to the easel. "Take a look."

Kelly slid off the stool and walked around to look at the large canvas. She caught her breath as she saw the painting of storm-whipped waters beneath a lowering sky and noticed the little boat that was being tossed about on the huge waves. As so many of his paintings did, it seemed to reach right out and touch her.

"It's wonderful, Uncle Max. Wonderful."

"Thanks. I'm doing a whole series of moods. The others are over there in the corner."

But she kept staring at that little boat. "That's the difference between you and me, Uncle Max."

"What is?"

"I feel like that little boat. You make me *feel* it, when I look at your paintings. I could never do that."

"You did it in other ways, Kelly. Some of us *have* gifts. Others of us *are* gifts. You were always a gift."

Her throat tightened again, and she forced herself to look away from the painting. Her uncle was looking at her with smiling love.

Then he tossed his brush and cloth aside and opened his arms. "Come give your uncle Max a hug, child. I've missed you like hell."

The strength of his arms around her and the smell of the turpentine combined to make her feel small and safe again.

And for the first time since she arrived, she truly felt that she was home.

Chapter 8

Seth was working at his computer, taking care to save his file often because of the hammering storm outside, when he heard a different kind of hammering. Someone was pounding on his door.

Reluctantly, he saved his file again and went to find out which of the Burkes had ventured out into the gale to disturb him.

It was Mavis, looking like a drowned rat. "Seth," she said in her ringing voice as she pushed sodden strands of iron-gray hair away from her face. "You've got to help."

"Sure, if I can."

"It's Kelly," Mavis said. "Cook hasn't come back, and Kelly's trying to cook our dinner, only . . . I don't think she knows how. She's stomping around the kitchen complaining there are no cookbooks. And certainly none of the rest of us can cook. If you could give her a little guidance before we all starve to death?"

Guidance, Seth thought with an inward surge of amusement. Kelly would probably find that about as welcome as an appendectomy. Which was reason enough to agree. "I'll be there in a minute, Mavis."

"Oh, thank you so much," she trilled. "Kelly was muttering something about how we ought to have hot dogs in the refrigerator like everyone else. Hot dogs!" She shuddered.

Seth, who was rather fond of the occasional ball-park frank himself, manfully refused to disagree with her. "Just give me a minute, Mavis. I need to unplug my computer."

"Unplug it? Whatever for?"

"Just in case of lightning. No point running the risk when I'm not working. Can you get back all right by yourself?"

"Certainly I can."

"Then you go on ahead and dry off."

He watched her disappear into the downpour and wondered why she hadn't even bothered to pull on a raincoat. Probably to evoke sympathy, he thought with amusement. None of the Burkes, with the possible exception of Kelly, could pass up an opportunity to do that.

He also found it a little bit difficult to believe that none of them could so much as heat a can of soup for themselves. Which led him to the inevitable conclusion that they were up to something. But what?

Shaking his head, he went to get his poncho.

When he entered the Burke house five minutes later, he found Kelly standing at the kitchen island staring at a leg of lamb big enough to feed a football team.

She looked up when she saw him. "They want leg of lamb for dinner," she said almost pathetically. "Leg of lamb! This thing is frozen so hard a Neanderthal could use it to bring down a woolly mammoth!"

So, he thought, there *was* more to it. This wasn't a case of Kelly being able to cook nothing at all.

His antennae began to vibrate madly. The family was up to something, and he'd put almost nothing past them.

"Well, then, they can't have leg of lamb tonight," he said. "Unless they want you to serve it just like that."

She looked at him. "You know, it looks entirely too much like part of an animal. I don't think I could eat it even if I could figure out how to thaw it. It's too big to go in the microwave."

"It's too big to cook before tomorrow, regardless."

She frowned. "You're right. I can't believe none of them have any idea how long it takes to prepare something like this."

Neither could he, but he resisted saying so. He had a feeling they had known *exactly* what they were asking Kelly to do. "Do you by any chance remember that old Alfred Hitchcock piece about a leg of lamb?"

"You mean the woman who beat her husband to death with a frozen leg of lamb, then cooked it and served it to the investigating detective?"

"That's the one."

They both looked at the meat.

"Nah," they said at almost the same time, then laughed.

"Unfortunately," Seth said after a moment, "forensics are a lot better these days. They'd find pieces of lamb in the wounds."

"Yup."

"You could always serve it just the way it is."

"With a sprig of mint on the side." She sighed. "I'd better put it back and figure out something else."

She started to lift the lamb, which must have weighed fifteen pounds or more, but Seth reached for it and carried it toward the walk-in freezer. "You pick out something else while I put this back."

She followed him in and stood looking at the shelves, which were stacked with butcher-wrapped meats, all neatly labeled.

"Wonderful," she said. "Hamburger and more hamburger. T-bones. Sirloins. Tenderloins. Chickens whole, and chicken parts. Duck. Goose. Lobster. Shrimp. Cod . . ." She shook her head. "What I'd really like to do is find a cookbook!"

"What about lamb chops?" he suggested. "If they're in the mood for lamb."

She gave him a sour look. "At this point I don't care what mood they're in."

"Ah. I forgot you hate to cook."

"Not only do I hate to cook, but I'm lost without a cookbook. And there doesn't seem to be one anywhere!"

"I can help," he offered.

She looked as if she would rather swallow nails. "I'll manage," she said stiffly. "You just go back to banging on wood, or whatever it is you were doing."

"Could we carry on this conversation somewhere besides the freezer?" He was beginning to feel chilled, and he could see goose bumps all over Kelly's arms. "I prefer to argue when I'm warm."

"Just go, then. I still have to decide what to make."

"Can you cook *at all*?"

The glare she gave him could have bored holes in steel. "If I have to. Look, I'll manage, all right? I always manage."

"I'm sure you do. No need to get defensive. I was just trying to help."

"You can help by just staying out of my way."

"Okay." He walked out of the freezer and took a seat on one of the stools at the island.

She emerged from the freezer a few moments later with a package. "Hamburgers," she said.

"A culinary triumph in the making."

"Don't be nasty."

"I'm not being nasty," he said virtuously. "There's a lot you can do with hamburger, actually. Meatloaf. Burgers. Stew. Chili. Spaghetti."

"Not without a cookbook, I can't."

"I can. So let me kibitz."

"Speaking of kibitzing," she said as she put the meat in the microwave and punched the buttons, "why are you here?"

He considered the possibility of lying to spare her feelings, but he'd never been one to lie. "Mavis showed up at my door looking like a drowned rat and asked me to come over and help you because you're lost without a cookbook."

"She did, did she?" Kelly turned on the microwave, then leaned back against the counter, folding her arms. "Now, why do you suppose she would do that? And how come there are no cookbooks anywhere in this kitchen?"

"I don't know about the cookbooks. But as for why she would come get me . . ." He hesitated. "I sometimes get the feeling I'm being manipulated."

"Aha!"

"Aha?"

"Aha."

He waited, but finally prodded her. "Aha what?"

"They're great manipulators."

"I'm beginning to think so."

"They're up to something."

"It's crossed my mind."

She nodded, satisfied. "Well, that would explain a great deal."

"What would it explain?"

"Why I got this rather strange e-mail from Mavis a few days ago mentioning how Bea dotes on you, and how you were handling the family finances."

"I'm not handling the finances."

"So I gather. And this afternoon, when I took a few minutes to look things over, I realized they're not really in a mess. I don't know why Bea told you you needed to sort all that stuff, but as near as I can tell, the checkbook couldn't be more than a few dollars out of balance compared to the statements."

"So why the hell did they give me that song and dance about not being able to figure out how much money they have in the bank?"

"Beats me. Except that it worked as a great excuse to get me to come home."

"Ahh." Suddenly things were getting clearer. "So you came charging back to rescue them from a scam artist, namely me."

"I sure did."

He nodded. "I hate to tell you this, Kelly, but I've got more money than I could probably ever spend. I don't need anyone else's."

She nodded. "It's possible."

"Not only possible, it *is*. I'm a reasonably good financial planner. Even after my wife took half of everything, I still have enough to live the rest of my life in comfort. I sure don't need your family's money."

"She took half of everything?"

"Well, half of everything I'd made during our marriage."

"You must be pissed."

He shook his head. "That doesn't bother me; I've got other things to be bothered about. But we're getting away from the question here. I can see why they might try subterfuge to get you home; they've all missed you. But why the hell have I been hornswoggled into coming over here to help cook dinner?"

"I was just wondering that."

He thought it over for a moment, then said tentatively, "Matchmaking?"

"Matchmaking!" She repeated the word with distaste.

"Well, sheesh," he said with a lopsided grin, "you don't have to be so repulsed by the idea."

"Yes, I do! Matchmaking with a man who keeps reminding me he can cook better than I can? Don't make me laugh."

"I have the same sort of visceral response to the word," he admitted. "I'm never going to marry again. One Velvet in a man's life is enough. And you'd never want anything to do with a dumb jock."

"Will you quit throwing that word up at me?"

"Why? You put it into play." He couldn't quite help himself, and a grin escaped. "Let's stick to the problem, okay? How should we deal with this?"

"Oh, I don't know. How about a really rotten dinner?"

"I've got a better idea," he said. "Chili. A really *good* chili. A really *hot* chili."

He was tickled when Kelly began to smile.

"No beans?" she asked an hour later.

"No beans. Real chili doesn't have beans."

"A matter of perspective, I assume."

"Or regional preference," he agreed amiably enough.

"Is that really going to be enough for everyone?"

"Everyone?"

"Well, you helped cook it, so you have to eat it."

"There's plenty," he assured her. "As spicy as this is, a little goes a long way. Add a few tortilla chips and it's a meal."

Just then they heard a crash and a series of thumps from the direction of the butler's pantry. They exchanged looks.

"I'd better go see what's wrong," Kelly said. "Lawrence might have hurt himself."

"Go ahead. I'll watch the pot simmer."

She knocked gently on the door to the pantry, then heard another thud. Worried, she opened the door.

Lawrence was standing there, his arms full of liquor bottles.

"Are you all right?" Kelly asked.

"I'm fine," he said, weaving a little. "I've decided to go on the wagon." With that he dumped his armload of bottles into a large green plastic trash can. Then he turned and pulled several more bottles out of the liquor cabinet on the wall.

"Um . . . Lawrence?"

"Yes, Miss?"

"That's the household stock."

"I know, Miss. But one cannot go on the wagon when one shares a room with a liquor cabinet that's stocked as well as most bars."

"True," she admitted, then winced as another bottle fell into the trash can. This time it shattered, and the smell of bourbon filled the room.

"I cannot have it in this house," he announced almost grandly, dumping yet another bottle. "I cannot serve it. I cannot smell it. I cannot know it's there."

"Understandable." But she had a feeling the rest of the family might not agree that they should all become teetotalers. Granny occasionally liked a martini before dinner, and Max was fond of his shot of whiskey in the late afternoon. And Zee . . . well, Zee could knock back scotch with the best of them when she got in the mood. "Lawrence? Are you drunk?"

"Yes!" He stood up straighter and looked at her. "I am drunk. I am drunk most of the time. I am drunk right now. And if I don't clean out this cupboard, I may be drunk forever."

"Um . . . maybe you should get some medical help with this."

"There is no medical help. Just let me finish cleaning out the cupboard and the wine cellar—"

"Wait a minute, Lawrence. *Not* the wine cellar."

He regarded her with dignity. "I don't wish to become a wino. That goes, too."

"But there's the Château Lafitte and the Moet . . ." She trailed off, having sudden visions of disaster. Granny had been collecting fine old wines for many years, and while she might not use them very often, since she didn't entertain as much anymore, there was a sizable investment in that wine cellar—which wasn't really a cellar at all, but a room set aside for the purpose. "Lawrence, don't touch the wines until I get Granny."

"Fine. I'll deal with the cooking sherry next."

Kelly went back to the kitchen. "Lawrence is throwing out all the booze. I've got to get Granny before he hits the wine cellar."

Seth frowned. "Do you need me to stop him?"

"Just don't let him get to the wine cellar. Man, she must have thirty thousand dollars in wines in there . . ." Her voice trailed off as she hotfooted it toward her grandmother's rooms.

She found Bea primping for dinner at her vanity. A loud roll of thunder shook the house unexpectedly and drowned the first words out of Kelly's mouth.

"The thunder is just terrible," Bea said when it trailed away enough to speak. "Don't tell me lightning has set the house on fire. My dear child, whatever is wrong? Has Zelda finally hatched her scheme? Oh, Lord, don't tell me she's going to rescue a rhinoceros this time! We'll never keep it behind a fence!"

"Lawrence is throwing out all the liquor."

Bea's hand, holding a mascara wand, froze halfway to her eye. "Why?"

"He says he needs to go on the wagon."

"Well, it's about time. We could all do with less booze in the house."

"But Granny, he's planning to empty the wine cellar."

Bea frowned. "Really? That could be quite expensive."

"Seth's going to keep him away from the cellar, but I think maybe you'd better come down and talk to Lawrence."

"If he'll listen to me. He rarely does, you know. I take it Cook hasn't turned up?"

Kelly shook her head. "Seth and I are making dinner."

"You know, I'm beginning to feel that my staff are getting way above themselves."

"They've *always* been above themselves."

"Well, everyone in this house is above themselves. But when the servants start running you around in circles, there's serious trouble." She sniffed and patted some powder on her cheeks. "I'll be down in a moment. Tell Seth to sit on Lawrence, if he must."

But Seth didn't have to sit on Lawrence. The butler was passed out, sitting on the kitchen floor and leaning against the cabinets, a bottle of cooking sherry in one hand and a bottle of rice wine in the other. Seth was sitting on a stool, his lips puckered as if he were trying to decide what to do about this.

"What happened?" Kelly asked.

"He was taking down the cooking wine when he suddenly announced he was tired. Then he sat down and passed out."

"Poor Lawrence," she said sadly.

"Has he always been like this?"

She shook her head. "When I was a child, he used to tipple a little. You know, a drink before dinner, a brandy after. No one thought much of it. But it gradually grew worse over the years. By the time I left he was drinking rather steadily, but nothing like this. He was always so genteel about it that it seemed like a foible, you know?"

"The man needs help."

"He certainly does," Bea said as she swept into the room in her dinner dress of rose brocade. "Dear, dear, dear, passed out again! He never used to do this."

"We need to help him go on the wagon," Kelly said.

"Yes, of course we do. The problem is, he won't remember this in the morning. He won't remember that he was throwing out all the liquor. And he'll very probably be angry at me."

Kelly looked at her grandmother. "So?"

Bea nodded. "Exactly. So? He'll just have to be angry, and he can quit if he wants, but I'm not going to turn a blind eye to this any longer. It not only sets the household on end, but the poor man is going to kill himself. I can't allow that. Kelly, get the others, will you? And Seth, if you would be so kind, would you see if you can find Manuel? We're going to take care of this right now."

Kelly got the rest of the family, wondering why Bea needed the entire household to cart Lawrence off to a hospital. But Bea surprised her.

When the entire clan, save Cook, was gathered, Bea announced, "We've got to help Lawrence before he kills himself. Therefore, I want every bit of booze out of this household before Lawrence wakes. And that includes the wine cellar."

Jules winced. "Mother, the cellar is worth a fortune! And where are we to put it?"

"You can't throw it in the water," Manuel announced. He was wearing a black maid's uniform tonight, with a frilly white apron. "That's polluting. You could get a big fine."

"I wasn't suggesting any such thing. Zee, what if we dump all the bottles in the tiger enclosure? Lawrence would *never* set foot in there, and when we want a few bottles, Zee can retrieve them."

"Well, I suppose," said Zelda. "As long as the bottles aren't open or cracked. I don't want my tigers getting drunk."

"Wait one minute," Mavis said. "I'm perfectly willing to share this island with tigers as long as they're on the other side of a strong fence, but I have no desire to trespass in their domain."

"I'll put them in the kennel," Zee said impatiently. "Just the way I do when the vet comes. Don't be a wimp, Mavis."

"It's hardly wimpish to have a reasonable respect for the claws and teeth of six hundred pounds of predator."

Max was pondering a rather different matter. "I suppose this means I have to give up my afternoon bourbon."

"We're *all* giving up liquor," Bea said firmly. "It won't hurt any of us to go on the wagon with Lawrence, and it might actually do *some* of us some good." She shot a significant look at Max.

"That's all well and good, Mother," he replied,

"but I seem to remember that you like your martini before supper."

"All I know," said Jules, "is that if you all give up drinking, life is going to be hell around here."

Mavis stiffened. "Are you implying we're addicts?"

He shrugged. "How would you know? You've never had to do without your afternoon drink before."

She glared at him.

"This is getting us nowhere," Bea said impatiently. "What we need to do is decide the quickest and easiest way to remove all the wine and liquor before Lawrence wakes up."

"Well," said Kelly, "he's done pretty well in the pantry. I think all the liquor is in the garbage can in there."

"That's assuming he doesn't have a secret stash," Manuel said. "I know these drinkers. Pretty cagey."

"We can only do our best," Bea replied firmly.

"Mother," Mavis said, "there must be a thousand bottles of wine in the cellar. How are we to move them all."

"No, no, there are only a few hundred."

"Why don't we just lock the cellar?" Max said.

Kelly spoke. "In my opinion, short of turning the wine cellar into a vault with a combination lock before Lawrence wakes up, you couldn't keep him out."

"You're right," said Manuel. "He'd just pick the lock. I saw him do that once."

Bea was aghast. "My *butler* was picking a lock? When?"

Zee reddened. "I lost the key to the lion enclosure. Lawrence picked the lock for me."

"Well, just a padlock . . ."

"He also locked him and me out of the house one night," Manuel said.

"All right, all right," Max said. "I get the picture. The wine goes. Just tell me we don't have to carry it all bottle by bottle."

"Oh, no," said Manuel. "There are two wheelbarrows in the garden shed, and Miss Kelly's little red wagon."

They still had her little red wagon? Kelly was amazed. Then she recalled her room. Why in the world had they kept all these things? The answer that was beginning to push past all her resistance made her throat tighten.

"I've got a cart," Seth volunteered. "I got it to move my sculptures around. It doesn't have sides, but I can probably rig something."

"There, you see," said Bea, well pleased. "It won't be that difficult at all."

Lawrence punctuated the proceedings with a loud snore. Bea looked down at him. "And we'll start with him. Mavis, take those bottles from his hands. Max, Seth, will you please move him to his bed? Kelly, you and Manuel go to the garden shed and get the wheelbarrows."

"Not so fast," Manuel said. "If I'm going to be running around in the jungle, I need to change into something more suitable. I don't want to run my pantyhose."

Bea clucked. "Really, Manuel, we don't have to go into the woods. Just getting the wine on the other side of the fence should be enough."

"You don't know Lawrence," he said darkly. "You'd better put it where he can't see it, or he *will* forget the tigers and climb the fence."

"Manuel is probably right," Max said. "If the cats aren't in sight, he'd probably try it. Then, *poof!*"

"Yup," agreed Seth. "Lawrence tartare."

"Ewww," said Mavis. "Don't be disgusting!"

"I'm not being disgusting, I'm being practical. If Lawrence climbs that fence, he'll be dead meat."

"All right, all right," said Bea. "Enough. We'll take the bottles back far enough that he can't see them from the fence. Zee, go lock up the tigers. And the rest of you, get hopping. Since Manuel's going to change, I guess you and I should as well, Mavis."

A few moments later, Kelly, Max, and Seth were alone in the kitchen with the loudly snoring Lawrence.

"Well, this ought to be something," Max remarked, a small grin on his face. "There's more wine in the cellar than Mother thinks. We're going to be all night carting and hiding those damn bottles like a bunch of idiots getting ready for an Easter egg hunt. And in the dark, no less."

"Do you have a better idea?" Seth asked.

"Unfortunately, no. The tiger enclosure is the *only* place Lawrence won't go."

"Neither do I. So let's just move Lawrence to his bed. It's going to be a long night."

"The tigers are penned," Zee said, emerging from the enclosure. The others stood in a long line, two wheelbarrows, the wagon, and Seth's cart already loaded with wine bottles. At Bea's direction, the women had been designated loaders and unloaders, while the men had been turned into transport mules.

"Which best suits their temperament," Bea had added, bringing scowls from the men. She seemed neither to notice nor to care. She was all decked out for this expedition in safari khakis and a pith helmet. The rest had settled on more prosaic slacks and jeans, except for Zee, who was wearing orange capris and a purple silk blouse.

Bea now walked along the line spraying everyone with a choking fog of mosquito repellant. "Malaria's becoming a concern again, you know," she said when Mavis protested that she couldn't breathe.

Bea returned to the head of the cavalcade, lifted her riding crop—why she had a riding crop, Kelly couldn't imagine—and pointed forward. "Onward, gentlemen."

Manuel, now garbed in tight black leather pants and a flowing poet's blouse, led the way, pulling the little red wagon. Max and Jules followed with their wheelbarrows, and Seth pulled his cart, by far the heaviest load. He was limping noticeably, and Kelly fell into step beside him.

"Are you all right?" she asked him. "Should you even be doing this?"

He shrugged. "What's a little pain? It won't do any damage. It just hurts."

"I tend to stop doing things that hurt."

He flashed a smile, his teeth white in the darkness. "That's why you never played pro sports."

She harrumphed, then added, "This is a cockamamie idea."

"All the best ideas are cockamamie."

"We could have just hired some movers to come and take it all away in the morning."

He slapped his forehead. "Why didn't you suggest that sooner?"

"Don't be sarcastic."

"Sorry." He sighed, then staggered a little as he came down wrong on his bum leg. "I think the point is to remove temptation before Lawrence wakes up. And I think the other point is that your grandmother doesn't really want to give up her wines."

"Probably not. It took years to collect all these vintages."

"I imagine so. But I think you seriously under-estimated the value of her cellar."

"I guess I did. There must be a thousand bottles in that room. Which means, that the value is prob-ably closer to eighty or ninety thousand."

"It's an interesting retirement plan. Sell it for money if you need to, or drink yourself into obliv-ion. Better than a bank account."

She had to laugh.

"Oh, gawd," Julius suddenly said up ahead. "Oh, gawd, I've stepped in cat poop!"

Zelda, who was nearby, shone her flashlight on his feet. "It's not shit, Jules," she said. "It's rotten meat."

"Oh, gawd," he said again. "Even worse! I'll have to throw these shoes away!"

"Probably," Zee said indifferently.

One of the tigers roared from the pen, and every-one froze.

"Don't mind them," Zee said. "They're annoyed. They don't like it when I leave them alone in the pen. Besides, they know we're trespassing out here. Just hurry up, will you?"

"Why?" asked Jules. "Won't the pen hold them?"

"It should," Zee said. "But I've never really seen them very angry before."

"Just lovely," remarked Max.

They crossed the open, grassy area behind the fence, then stepped into the darker, thicker woods. Palmettos whipped at their legs, and Spanish moss caught at their hair. And also . . .

"Spiderwebs!" Mavis shrieked. "I hate spiders! Get it off me!"

"Don't be such a wimp," Zee said sharply. "What can a little bitty spider do to you?"

"I hate crawly things!" Mavis shrieked, dancing wildly and batting at herself.

As if in answer to her shrieks, the tigers roared from the pen a hundred feet away. Mavis froze.

"You're exciting their hunting instincts," Zee said. "If I were you, I'd shut up."

Mavis did exactly that, but kept wiping at her arms and face, trying to remove whatever was on her.

"Zee, that was cruel," Kelly told her aunt.

"Compare the threat of a spider and a tiger." Zee was clearly unrepentant.

Kelly found herself glancing uneasily back toward the pen. She'd grown up thinking of tigers as extremely large cats that had to be handled with care, but she'd never had to think of her aunt's tigers as a threat. Was Zee kidding or was she being truthful? The nape of her neck began to prickle.

By the time they had dumped the first five loads in the palmettoes around a huge old oak tree, they were all sweating, irritable, and exhausted, and the tigers were getting more and more excited.

"Mother," Mavis complained, "we can't do all this in one night."

Bea, leaning against a tree and panting, agreed. "I guess not. I had no idea I had so much wine. But if we don't finish tonight, Lawrence might get into the wine tomorrow."

"Why don't we take a break?" Max suggested. "Some cool drinks and a half hour of rest ought to get us up to snuff again."

"Maybe that's all *you* need," Mavis sniffed. "It's well past my bedtime and I'm beginning to see things."

"What things?" Jules asked curiously.

"I thought I just saw a tiger behind that tree."

Jules started to laugh, but bit the sound off suddenly. "A tiger?" he asked, his voice hushed.

That's when they all realized that the tigers were no longer roaring or growling from the pen.

"Oh, no," said Zee.

Chapter 9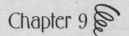

The group clustered together in a tight knot, wheelbarrows, wagon, and cart surrounding them. The woods were dark, except for the beams of the flashlights that Bea and Zee held.

"Are you sure you saw a tiger, Mavis?" Max asked in a whisper.

"No, I'm not sure," she said irritably. "I hallucinate when I stay up too late. Besides, it's dark. But I thought I saw a tiger in the shadows over there."

They all followed her pointing finger with their eyes.

"I don't see anything," Max whispered.

"Me, neither," agreed Jules.

"They're being too quiet," Zee said flatly. "They're stalking."

"Oh, God," whimpered Mavis.

"Don't get hysterical, now," Zee said sharply. "Save it for after we get out of here."

"We'll *never* get out of here," Mavis groaned.

"We certainly won't if you freak out."

"The point," Seth intervened firmly, "is what do we do now, Zee? You know your tigers. Do we split up?"

"If we split up they can only catch two of us," Zee said.

Mavis whimpered again.

"On the other hand, if we stay together, they'll probably leave us alone. Their teeth are still good."

"Their *teeth* are still good?" Bea repeated in tones of horror. "Is that supposed to be good news?"

"Actually, Mother, it is. Tigers prefer not to eat humans. Apparently we don't taste all that good. They only start preying on us when their teeth get bad and they can't catch their usual prey."

"Oh." The word carried a wealth of meaning, none of it positive.

"Well," said Seth, "it's nice to know I'm not the top item on a five-star menu."

"Besides," Zee said, "they're well fed. They're not hungry."

"So they won't bother us at all?" Mavis asked hopefully.

"I didn't say that. Unfortunately, they're also territorial, and we're in their territory."

"Eeps."

Kelly, whose heart was pounding uncomfortably, was scanning the woods frantically, looking for any sign of the tigers. "So, we just stick together and walk out of here, Zee?"

"It's the best plan. They may watch us, but as long as we don't threaten them, we should be okay."

Julius spoke. "Can't you just tell them to sit or roll over or something, Zee? I thought you had them trained."

"I do. But right now it's night and they're stalking. It's not a training situation at all. I don't think they'd kill me—I feed them milk every day, after all—but I'm not sure about the rest of you."

Mavis made a small, despairing sound.

"This just gets better and better," Seth remarked. "It's nearly midnight, darker than pitch thanks to the storm, and two annoyed tigers are stalking us. Does that about cover it?"

"Did you have to remind us?" Kelly asked.

"Well, I've only got three brain cells. I wanted to be sure I fully understood the situation."

"I'm surprised you could fit all that into three brain cells."

"Must be the others I occasionally feel rattling around."

"I can't believe," Mavis said, "that you two find this funny."

Seth looked toward her. "Did you hear us laughing? I didn't."

"Me neither," Kelly agreed. But Seth's patter was keeping her distracted just enough to prevent her from giving in to terror.

Seth reached out, and in the darkness squeezed Kelly's hand comfortingly. She felt her own fingers wrap around his and cling. "Zee," he asked, "should we leave the wagons?"

"Yes. Let's just walk out of here. Together."

"Where," Max sighed, "is a whip when you need one?"

"I'd rather have an elephant gun," Jules retorted.

"Stop it, you two," Zee said sharply. "Don't you threaten my tigers."

"I rather think it's the other way around right now." Max bent and picked up a bottle of wine. "Damn, I wish I had a corkscrew." He grabbed it by the neck. "Anything that comes near me gets a concussion."

"No." Zee was horrified. "Don't hurt my tigers!"

"I won't, as long as they don't try to eat me."

The group, keeping to a tight knot, began to edge toward the gate. The distance, which hadn't seemed very long mere minutes ago, suddenly looked like miles.

"Keep looking backward," Max advised. "They might come up behind us."

"Dammit," Jules swore, "don't step on my toes, Manuel."

"Sorry."

Kelly, who was right beside Seth, was glad when he reached out to tug her behind him, deeper into the moving knot of her family. His broad back before her seemed like a bulwark.

Just then, visible in the pale light of the two flashlights, a tiger came running out of the trees, straight toward Seth. The group shrieked and fell backward, except for Seth—who did the most amazing thing.

He crouched into a three-point stance just as if he were on the scrimmage line of a football game. The tiger loped toward him while everyone held their breath.

"Seth . . ." Kelly took a step forward, thinking to yank him out of the way of the charging tiger.

But within five feet of Seth, apparently confused by this strange human response to his approach, Nikki screeched to a stop, sliding forward on the damp grass until he was only three feet away.

The tiger shook his head, almost as if he were surprised by his skid, then crouched, staring at Seth. Seth stared right back.

"What now, Zee?" Seth asked.

"Damned if I know."

"Thanks. That's reassuring. Cripes, my knees are killing me," he muttered.

The tiger growled low in its throat.

Seth growled back.

The tiger's ears pricked, and his head cocked to one side, as if he were trying to decide what to make of Seth.

Seth's eyes never wavered. Look for look, he met

the tiger's stare. Nikki growled again. Seth growled back.

Kelly thought her heart was going to hammer its way out of her chest. "Maybe you should back off, Seth," she suggested quietly. "You're challenging him with that stare."

He ignored her, growling back at the tiger.

"You really don't want to wrestle with a tiger," Zee insisted, for the first time sounding genuinely concerned about this mess.

"No, I don't. Which is why I'm not going to look away."

Everyone stood frozen as the tiger and Seth faced off, growling, neither giving ground. Nikki, apparently more sanguine about this standoff than Seth, paused once to lick his front leg, then resumed the contest.

Seth growled again. The tiger looked away.

"That's good," Zee said quietly. "That's good. Maybe he's losing interest."

"God, I hope so." Seth growled the words deep in his throat for the tiger's benefit. "My damn knees are shrieking."

Nikki lifted his head, sniffing the night breeze. Seth didn't move a muscle.

Nikki cocked his head inquisitively.

Seth didn't move a muscle.

Nikki crouched.

"Look out," Zee said. "He's getting ready to spring."

"Then he's in for a shock," Seth replied.

Kelly was holding her breath, her nails digging into her hands. That tiger could kill him with one blow.

Then Nikki sprang. And while the tiger was in midair, Seth lunged upward in a classic rip move, his right hand catching the beast beneath its armpit. Seth's entire body seemed to explode upward through his right side with a massive *huummph* of expelled breath.

Nikki went sailing five feet through the air, twisting madly, but landing on his feet. Once again on the ground, he shook his head, as if a little confused. Then he gave an enormous stretch and licked his shoulder as if the whole thing were of total unconcern to him.

Seth was standing now, but bent, as if his knees wanted to buckle. He and the cat exchanged looks, then Nikki rolled over onto his back. A moment later the cat had vanished once again into the shadows.

"Now," said Zee. "Now! Let's go."

This time they moved a lot more quickly. Two minutes later they were all safely out of the gate.

"Jesus Christ!" Max wiped his forehead with a shaky arm. "Don't anybody ever again suggest I go into that enclosure!"

"Look," said Kelly, pointing. Nikki was coming out of the woods again at a lope.

"What now?" wailed Mavis.

The tiger stopped at the fence, right in front of Seth, and began purring, a deep, loud rumble of contentment.

"Wow," said Zee. "He likes you."

"I think he was playing all along," Seth said. "I don't think he'd have come head-on like that if he was really intent on hurting any of us."

Just then there came a plaintive roar from the direction of the kennel.

"Oh, hell," said Zee. "I guess Alex is still caged. She sounds pissed."

"Really?" said Mavis. Then, ending the evening on a perfect note, she fainted on the grass.

*　　*　　*

Seth was in his element, Kelly thought. He was looking quite pleased with himself as the entire family and Manuel gathered around the dining room table and talked about their adventure. She supposed he had every reason to feel pleased, considering the outcome, but he'd taken a foolish risk by facing off with the tiger. What if Nikki had perceived that as a threat?

Max had broken open the bottle of wine he'd carried out of the enclosure and poured everyone a glass. Then they'd heisted a couple more from the remaining bottles in the cellar. Granny didn't even complain that they were drinking her best vintages.

"It was a standard football move," Seth said in answer to Max's question. "I used to do it all the time."

Max shook his head. "Against three-hundred-pound players, maybe. That tiger is over six hundred pounds."

"Well, I bench-press five hundred," Seth said modestly. "And squat eight hundred. I suppose adrenaline helped a little, too. Besides, the cat had no idea what was coming." He shrugged. "I was fairly certain that if the tiger sprang, I'd be able to toss him."

"As long as he didn't swipe you with a paw in the process," Kelly said tartly. Everyone stared at her disapprovingly. Apparently they didn't want to hear any common sense while they were bestowing laurels on Seth. Diplomatically, she decided to change the subject.

"I suppose *that* was the groaning I heard this morning. You lifting weights."

He didn't answer, his dark eyes almost twinkling.

"You really shouldn't do that without a spotter—you could kill yourself."

Now there was a definite, devilish sparkle in his eyes. "I didn't know you cared."

The rest of the family helped considerably by making a knowing "Oooooo" sound. Kelly glared at them.

Manuel spoke. "I spot for him," he said.

"You couldn't have been spotting for him this morning," she argued. "You were in here scrubbing the hallway."

"I wasn't working out then," Seth said. "I was doing physical therapy."

"Oh." For some reason she couldn't fathom, she suddenly felt small and mean for picking on a man who had to do physical therapy.

"Well, that was sure some move." Julius chortled as he poured himself another glass of wine. "Nikki looked astonished."

Bea stirred in her chair. "I don't imagine tigers are used to being thrown through the air."

"It was awful," Mavis said. "Utterly awful. I don't know what you're going to do with the rest of the wine, Mother, but you can count me out of any more attempts to move it into the tiger enclosure."

Zee, who had been staring into her wine, looked up. "We couldn't anyway. Nikki's kennel is knocked down."

Bea looked at her daughter. "However are you going to handle that?"

"I suppose I'll have to have the vet tranquilize them so Manuel and I can get in there to do repairs."

"Me?" Manuel shook his head vehemently. "I'm never going in there again."

"They'll be asleep, Manuel."

"But for how long?"

Zee tossed down the last of her wine. "Well, maybe I'll put them in their travel cages. I hate to do it because the cages are so small, and the cats really don't like them. But I can do it, I suppose. Good night, all. I've had enough."

"*She*'s had enough," Mavis remarked after her sister vanished. "Whose insane idea was it to put the wine in the enclosure anyway?"

Everyone professed to have forgotten.

Mavis poured herself another wine. "Well, I'm going to bed, too. All of this uproar is *terrible* for my voice."

"It's not good for anyone," Bea remarked. "And we still have to get rid of the wine before Lawrence wakes."

Seth spoke. "Just put a guard on the cellar until we can figure out what to do with the rest of the bottles."

Bea frowned at him. "Lawrence tends to wake *very* early. And in a terrible mood, especially after he's had too much to drink. Are *you* volunteering?"

Seth shrugged. "I guess I just did."

"You don't know what you're asking for."

"After a tiger, I hardly think Lawrence offers any threat."

"You don't know Lawrence," Bea said darkly. Then she, Jules, and Max all headed for their beds, leaving Kelly and Seth alone.

Kelly had a sudden thought. "I forgot all about the chili!"

"We all did. I imagine it simmered itself into a burnt block by now."

"I need to go turn it off."

She headed for the kitchen, aware that Seth was right on her heels. He would be a whole lot easier to deal with if he weren't so attractive, she thought.

It thoroughly annoyed her that his stupidity with the tiger tonight made her feel an admiration for his strength and prowess that was entirely at odds with her intention to dislike him.

The chili had cooked down to almost nothing. Kelly switched off the burner and looked at it. "I suppose I can't clean it till morning," she observed, for the sake of saying something—anything—that would alleviate the sudden thickness of the air. "Do you have to stand right behind me?"

"Not really," Seth answered amiably. "But I kind of like the way your hair feathers the back of your neck. Does it tickle?"

She turned and found herself trapped between him and the stove. She tried to lean backward, but the heat from the pot warned her that wouldn't be wise. So she stepped to the side. Seth immediately followed her.

"You're crowding me," she complained.

"Really?" He smiled, but didn't move.

"Are you drunk?"

"No. Just . . . relaxed."

She wished *she* could feel relaxed, but right now she felt coiled as tight as a compressed spring. Every muscle was tense, ready to explode—or ready for something else. It was getting harder to breathe, and she began to think that Seth was just like Nikki earlier, ready to pounce. "Back off, meat-head," she said. But the words didn't come out as sharply as she had intended. They came out throatily. Huskily. She had never imagined she could sound like that.

His smile broadened. "Do I scare you?"

"No!" The response was instinctive. It was also a lie, because suddenly he terrified her. Not because she feared *him*, but because she feared herself.

"Good. Because I'm scaring myself."

His words arrested everything inside her, holding her suspended. Her claustrophobia vanished, and with it her fear. "Scaring yourself?" she repeated stupidly.

"Terrifying myself," he amended.

"Why?

"Because I want to kiss you. And I can't think of a more dangerous thing to do."

Her mind snagged on the word *kiss*, like a stuck record. *Kiss . . . kiss . . . kiss . . .* There was a reason she shouldn't want that, she realized in some dim recess of her mind. There were excellent reasons why she ought to run away right now. But she couldn't remember them. Her mind, what was left of it, was sinking into a sea of quicksand, leaving her unaware of anything except a growing heaviness at her center and a yearning in her heart.

"Seth . . ." Her lips must have spoken in reaction to a signal sent long ago, because now the words had no relation to what was going on in the wreckage of her brain. "No . . ."

Somehow his face moved even closer, until she could feel the whisper of his wine-scented breath on her cheek. "No," he agreed. "It would be stupid."

"Dumb." Single words seemed to be all her lips were capable of speaking now.

"Foolhardy."

"Foolish."

"Good. I've always been a foolhardy fool."

She stared at him almost blankly, sensing that he'd said something that didn't quite fit with the rest of their conversation, but too swamped by yearning to want to think it through.

His face came even closer, then she felt the lightest touch of his lips against her, a mere brush.

"Wine," he said.

That must explain it, she thought hazily. Wine.

"You taste like wine."

So did he. A remarkably brilliant observation.

His mouth touched hers again. "Soft."

"Mmm . . ."

He moved closer, and she could feel the slight pressure of his hard chest against the peaks of her breasts. The sensation poured champagne into her legs, making them feel warm and weak.

Another light kiss, this time with the tickle of his tongue against her lips. Her legs nearly buckled, and her hands flew out to grip the edge of the counter for support.

"Hang on to me," he said huskily. Reaching out, he lifted her arms and put them around his neck.

It was a thick neck, heavily corded, descending into shoulders that were as hard as rock, and clinging to him felt as safe as clinging to an ancient oak tree in a hurricane. Solid. Strong.

He moved closer still, and she was pressed between the counter and his hard bulk, trapped and uncaring. This time when his mouth touched hers, it was no light caress. He came back to her like a pirate, taking what he wanted as his arms closed around her back and held her securely.

He plundered her mouth, foraging with his tongue against hers, finding every sensitive little spot and teasing her with promises of greater delights. Her fingers dug into him, holding on tight as she began to feel like a little boat being driven before an undeniable wind. There was a small whimper . . . her own, no doubt.

Then his hands slipped down to her bottom and lifted her until she was perched on the edge of the counter with her legs wrapped around his hips.

When he lifted his mouth from hers, she was

dazed and lost, and wanting only to have him closer still. Long past caring that she was in a shocking pose with a man she hardly knew.

"You go right to my head," he whispered roughly, and began sprinkling kisses over her cheeks and throat.

The words filled her with elation. Never in her life had she gone to anyone's head. Never.

When his mouth found the hollow of her throat, she dropped her head back . . . and cracked it on the handle of the cupboard.

"Ouch!" She jerked her head forward and cracked it on his chin. He jumped back.

"Damn!" he swore. "Are you okay?"

"I'm fine." Rubbing her head, though, she knew she wasn't fine at all, at least not emotionally. "I just cracked my head."

He started to grin. "You could have just said no."

"I did," she said, annoyed that he could find this funny. "Why didn't you just listen to me, dammit?"

He rubbed his chin, still grinning. "You didn't want me to."

"Oh, you . . . !" Frustrated, feeling horribly empty that he'd pulled away and angry at her own behavior, she grabbed something from the counter and threw it at him. Unfortunately, it was a jar full of rice. The jar shattered on the tile, and rice went everywhere.

He backed away cautiously. "Do you always attack men who kiss you?"

"I haven't ever been kissed when I didn't want to be before!" She rubbed the back of her head again and felt the growing bump. "Do you always concuss the women you kiss?"

"Did you see stars?"

"Stars?" She couldn't believe his gall. "Nothing you could do could make me see stars!"

"Then you don't have a concussion."

She pushed herself off the counter, ready to give him what-for, but as soon as her shoes hit the spilled rice, her feet went right out from under her.

With amazing speed, Seth reached out and grabbed her before she hit the floor. They were bent over, he above her, and she was suddenly at his mercy again.

He looked down at her, an odd smile playing around his mouth. "Next time you enjoy a man's kiss, at least be adult enough to admit you liked it."

"Why, you . . ." Words failed her as indignation filled her.

Straightening, he set her on her feet, and let go of her only when he was sure she was safely balanced.

"But don't worry," he said as he headed for the door. "I won't touch you again. I've got enough problems in my life without fooling around with a self-deluded geek."

Then he was gone, leaving her to sputter and wonder why she felt like she'd just been through a train wreck.

Kelly cleaned up the rice, which proved to be quite a job. The jar had exploded nicely, almost like a bomb, sending rice grains and glass all over the kitchen. By the time she finished, her back was aching, her head was throbbing, and her mood was not improved.

It was all too humiliating, she thought. First the kiss, from a man she wanted to believe was up to something unsavory. Then her humiliating behavior. She should have been stronger, should have stuck by her guns instead of giving in to desire like some kind of ditz.

And throwing the rice at him . . . that was a brilliant move. In her entire life she'd never thrown anything at anyone. It was horrifying to discover she was capable of such childish, even criminal, behavior. Whatever the provocation, she owed him an apology for that.

Done with the kitchen, including the chili pot, she switched off the lights and headed up to her room. She was feeling glum and disinclined to try to pull herself out of the mood. Everything was going to hell, and she didn't see any reason to be a Pollyanna about it.

Just as she reached her bedroom door in the dimly lit hallway, she heard sounds from the room across the way. No one slept in that room.

Her heart was suddenly in her throat and her mouth was dry. Had someone broken in?

Moving quietly, keeping to the wall so the floorboards wouldn't creak beneath her, she edged down the hall and picked up a huge porcelain vase from one of the hall tables. Grabbing it by its base, she held it over her shoulder like a weapon and approached the door of the room.

The creak of a floorboard sounded thunderous in the silence of the house. She froze, but whoever was in the room was apparently unconcerned. The sounds of stirring continued. A drawer slid open, then closed. Floorboards creaked from within, and someone sighed.

Reaching the doorknob, Kelly twisted it, and wondered if she was out of her mind. If someone had broken in, she ought to call the police. What if he had a gun? What good would a porcelain vase be against a bullet?

But her whole family was sleeping and vulnerable. By the time she called the cops and the police got out here, whoever was in that room might already have done their dirty work. She couldn't risk it.

So she decided to crash through the door and charge ahead like a crazed demon, hoping that she would scare the intruder. If nothing else, the noise would alert the rest of the family. She even had a satisfying image of the intruder leaping out the window in fright at the unexpected attack.

She reviewed the self-defense classes she'd taken a couple of years ago, imagining the moves she might need.

Then, twisting the knob, she hurled herself through the door with a scream that would have done Bruce Lee proud.

And nearly gave Cook a heart attack. The rotund woman took one look at the avenging fury that leaped through her door, screaming and wielding a vase, and keeled over on the bed.

Adrenaline still pumping wildly in her veins, Kelly drew up short and looked at the woman on the bed. "Cook?"

Cook didn't answer.

But Kelly's scream had done its job. Seconds later, Max burst through the door, wearing boxer shorts and carrying the nineteenth century Wilkinson ceremonial sword that was one of a pair hanging on the wall of his bedroom.

"What the hell?" he said as he saw Kelly standing over Cook with the vase in her raised hand. "Look, I know her cooking stinks, but don't you think that's a bit extreme?"

"I thought she was an intruder."

Before Kelly could lower the vase, pajama-clad Uncle Julius charged in, waving a baseball bat. "My God, Cook! Who hit her? Where's the intruder?"

"Kelly hit Cook," Max said. "She thought there was an intruder."

"Good God," Julius said, looking at Kelly. "There's no call to beat the poor woman up."

"I didn't hit her!"

"Then what's she doing unconscious? And why are you holding that vase?"

"I thought I might need a weapon. But I never laid a finger on her!"

Julius and Max looked at the Cook. "Right," they said.

"I suppose we can come up with a story," Max observed. "Cook isn't likely to remember who hit her."

Julius nodded. "I hear people always forget what happened right before a blow to the head."

"I didn't hit her," she said in a burst of frustration. "I never laid a finger on her! She fainted."

"That's a good story," Julius agreed. "She fainted and knocked her head when she fell. That'll explain the goose egg."

Kelly was ready to scream. "Look," she said between her teeth, "she won't have a bump because no one hit her. She *fainted*."

"It works for me," Julius said.

"Me, too," Max agreed.

Kelly gave up.

"Is there any water in that vase?" Max asked. "Maybe we can rouse her."

They were saved the necessity by Cook, who chose that moment to moan and sit up.

"Take it easy, Cook," said Max, taking charge. "You might have got a concussion from that bump on the head."

"I don't have a bump," said Cook grumpily. "I fainted when Miss Kelly came screaming through the door."

"See?" said Julius to Max. "It'll work. Cook already believes it."

Cook looked at the men like they were mad. Then she glared at Kelly. "What did you think you were doing?"

"I didn't know you were in here. I thought someone had broken in."

Cook harrumphed.

"I'm sorry I scared you. But what *are* you doing in here?"

"Hiding."

"Whatever for?"

"Miss Mavis told me to hide so that you'd cook dinner. I don't know why."

Kelly stared at her as her mind suddenly made some blinding connections. Then she looked down at the tempting vase in her hands.

But no, she decided. She was going to find a much better way to get even with Mavis.

Chapter 10

Morning came with a steady rain and Kelly was relieved. It prevented the touch football game, and she was in no mood to try to pry Seth away from her besotted relatives.

Cook had returned to her normal role as if yesterday hadn't happened, and breakfast was on the sideboard. The eggs were a little better this morning and Kelly was starving, so she helped herself to a large portion.

Afterward, she set out for the guest house. Rain drummed steadily on her umbrella and dripped sorrowfully from the leaves. The paving stones where slippery beneath her feet and she moved cautiously.

When she reached Seth's house, though, she was suddenly reluctant to talk to him. How could she explain that she had proof her crazy family was actually up to a matchmaking scheme? He'd probably laugh himself sick at the mere idea, and she didn't know if her ego could handle another bruising.

She didn't want to watch Seth get his jollies because it was so ridiculous that he might be attracted to her—even if it *was* ridiculous.

175

And after the way she'd behaved last night, she couldn't blame him if he seized every opportunity to needle her.

Besides, she remembered, they'd realized last night that there was something afoot, and Seth had even suggested a matchmaking plot. So she didn't need to tell him she'd all but confirmed it, did she?

In short, she was feeling like a coward. And the more she considered knocking on his door, the more reasons she thought of to turn around and walk away. *Chicken*.

Just then, his door opened and he filled the frame, wearing nothing but gym shorts, shoes, and a towel around his neck. He looked bigger than ever this morning, she noted unhappily. That might have had something to do with the fact that he wasn't wearing a shirt, so the full expanse of his broad chest was visible to her. Never had she seen a better chest.

Or legs, for that matter. His were powerful, and while she'd always believed she preferred lean runner's legs, there was something about those powerful columns that reached her at a visceral level.

"Why are you skulking out here?" he asked.

She felt her cheeks burn. "I was debating whether to bother you."

"Well, you've already bothered me, so close the bumbershoot and come on in." He disappeared into the house, leaving the door open on the apparent presumption that she would follow.

It would have been an excellent time to run, but instead she went inside. Now that she'd been discovered, running would have been too cowardly to bear. She stepped up onto the porch, shook the umbrella off, and left it loosely folded by the door.

Inside, the house was cool and dark. She had no idea where to go after she took two steps into the entry hall, because she had no idea where Seth had gone.

He reappeared a few minutes later wearing a navy-blue sweatsuit. "Sorry," he said, "but I was getting chilled. Come on into the kitchen and I'll make us a warm drink."

She couldn't imagine how he could stand being in that sweatsuit. To her Colorado-acclimated blood, the day was entirely too humid and warm for comfort. She was grateful for the air-conditioning that had apparently been chilling him.

He wasn't using a cane today, she noticed. Pretty impressive, after all the stumbling they'd done over rough ground last night.

"Is anyone guarding the wine cellar?" he asked.

"I think we all forgot. I haven't seen Lawrence this morning, though."

"Well, I didn't exactly forget. He doesn't usually start looking for his first drink until just before noon, so I left a message on the wine room door."

"Saying what?" Kelly asked.

"That I'd counted all the bottles, and if I found any missing I'd turn him into a pretzel."

"He won't believe that."

Seth smiled faintly as he pulled cocoa powder off a shelf. "No, but it'll give him pause. Long enough for me to get over there, anyway." He glanced at his watch. "Twenty minutes before he starts jonesing for booze. That's time enough for a quick cup of cocoa."

He spooned powder into two mugs, filled them with milk, and stuck them into the microwave. "So everyone forgot about poor Lawrence this morning, huh?"

"Well, I did," she admitted. "I had something else on my mind."

"That something else being what has you lurking in front of my house?"

She nodded.

"Hmm. Is this a game of twenty questions?"

She flushed again, and hated the ease with which he made her blush. "No, it's not. First, I wanted to . . . well, apologize. For last night."

He leaned back against the counter and folded his arms, giving her an almost evil grin. "Never apologize for getting a man's motor running."

Her flush heightened, and she decided he was every bit as crazy as the rest of her family. "I wasn't apologizing for *that*," she said tartly.

"Oh. Good." He waited.

She didn't know quite how to continue, especially when he was looking so Sphinx-like. He wasn't exactly encouraging her.

"Okay," he said finally. "Twenty Questions it is. What are you apologizing for?"

Her cheeks grew even hotter. "For throwing the rice at you."

"Oh."

"Is that an acceptance of my apology?"

"Sure. If you need it."

"Look," she said in exasperation, "throwing the rice at you was a terrible thing to do."

"Really? They throw rice at weddings."

"Not anymore. The birds eat it and it swells in their stomachs and kills them."

"I didn't know that."

She sighed. "Let's not digress, okay? The problem with throwing the rice was that it was still in the *jar*. I might have hurt you."

"Sweetie, if that jar had come anywhere near me, I'd have caught it. I'm a football player, remember?" He was grinning again. "And if you meant it to hit me, your aim needs a hell of a lot of work."

"I'm not your sweetie. Are you always such an impossible jerk?"

"Probably. And hey, that's a great way to apologize, asking me if I'm always a jerk."

She flushed with annoyance. "This is already humiliating enough! And no, I didn't mean it to hit you."

"Then no apology is necessary. Except maybe to Cook, who'll discover the rice is gone and decide she can't possibly make dinner when she comes back, because even though she had originally planned a turkey and stuffing, now that the rice is gone she'll be absolutely convinced she was making paella."

Kelly couldn't help laughing, because he'd described Cook so perfectly.

Seth's smile grew friendlier. "You know, I've been wondering since I got here. Does Cook have a name?"

"Of course she does. But it's some completely unpronounceable Eastern European thing. I used to be able to write it on her checks, but none of us could ever say it."

"Makes sense. Does she mind not having a name?"

"I think she likes being called Cook better than the hopeless attempts we used to make. I mean, how in the world do you pronounce a six-syllable word that doesn't have any vowels?"

"You sputter?"

"That's about what we did."

Laughter danced in his eyes, and she felt herself warming to him—until she remembered what else she had come here to discuss.

He pulled the two cups of cocoa from the microwave and set one in front of her at the dinette.

"Grab a seat," he suggested, and she did so. "So that's it? You wanted to apologize?"

"Well, unfortunately there's more."

He sat across from her, and now the twinkle in his eye grew devilish. "I know I didn't make you pregnant."

Her cheeks heated again. "Stop! You're awful!"

"I'm sorry." But he didn't look it.

"It's about Mavis. Maybe just Mavis or maybe all of them, who knows? But remember we were saying they were up to something?"

"They are. There's not a shadow of a doubt in my mind."

She nodded and used the excuse of sipping cocoa to delay revealing what she'd discovered. "Mm. This is good, Seth."

"Thanks." The smile around his eyes deepened. "Come on, quit stalling. It can't be *that* bad."

"I suppose that depends on how you look at it." She took another sip of cocoa and plunged in. "I found Cook last night."

"Where was she?"

"Hiding in one of the bedrooms."

"Better than taking a dive off the bridge, I suppose."

"Actually, she was hiding because Mavis told her to. So that I'd have to cook dinner."

"Ahh. And Mavis came to get me to help you last night."

"Exactly. And I've got a sneaking suspicion that there was a reason I couldn't find a cookbook anywhere."

"Probably." A chuckle escaped him. "My God, what a conniver. Well, we suspected it, didn't we? This just confirms it."

At least he wasn't laughing at the idea that he could be attracted to her, Kelly thought with relief, and felt more kindly toward him. "We need to do something about it."

"Why?"

"Because they'll drive us both crazy with their little schemes if we don't call a halt."

"No, they'll just find a different way to throw us together." He rubbed his chin and winced. "You have a hard head, you know."

She colored again. "I'm sorry. I was just so shocked when I banged my head on the cupboard."

"It's no big deal."

"I wouldn't think so, for a football player."

"Actually, I'm used to having a face mask. Maybe I should get one to wear when I'm around you."

"Oh, cut it out."

He laughed, holding up a hand. "Okay, okay. Well, my solution to the matchmaking problem is to act as if it's working."

"What? And encourage them?" The thought horrified her, because nothing her family had attempted so far had come close to what she knew they *could* do.

"Not exactly. But if they think the matchmaking is going well, they'll leave us alone."

"You don't know my family. They'll be encouraged and decide to speed things up."

"If they do, we'll be prepared. In the meantime, it's the only thing I can think of trying that won't encourage them to get more devious."

Kelly realized something. "You're enjoying this."

He shrugged. "Sure. Why not? We're both immune, and it might be funny to watch them scheme."

Somehow the idea of him being immune didn't make her feel as good as he apparently thought it should.

He glanced at his watch again. "Oops. I gotta get up there to keep Lawrence out of the wine cellar. Bring your cocoa if you want."

He pulled on a slicker and she picked up her umbrella. Together they walked back to the villa.

"They're probably watching us from the windows," he remarked as they stepped out from under the trees into the formal gardens. Rain was still falling steadily, and from the enclosure one of the tigers made a disgusted sound.

"I hope not," Kelly said. "I don't like feeling like a bug under a microscope."

"Pro sports kind of inures you to that."

Big words again, she thought. Much as she hated to admit it, she was beginning to think Seth was a well-educated jock. "Why?"

"Because you're in a fishbowl. Everything you do is second-guessed by every reporter and armchair quarterback in the country. Not to mention your coaches and teammates. And the other teams. And every move you make is caught on videotape."

"I'd hate that."

"Eventually you learn to compartmentalize. You stop listening to anyone but your coaches and teammates. After all, it's really easy to kibitz from the safety of a press box. Then you figure out there's the public you and the private you, and you try not to let the things said about the public you affect the private you too much. You realize that the ballplayer is only part of you, and that part is just a piece of meat that is owned by everyone from the team to the fan who watches you on TV."

"How awful!"

He shrugged. "It's not that bad. It has its compensations, and I don't just mean money. But you realize that you're no big deal, that your value in the sport is only as good as your last game. Only as good as your knees, your back, your shoulder. And you figure out that your identity is a whole lot more than that, and that it doesn't depend on the game."

"So what do you get out of playing, except money and a lot of injuries?"

"The joy of the game."

It was a simple answer, but to Kelly it seemed to encompass so very much.

They entered the house through the service door into the kitchen and found Cook pitching a fit while Lawrence stood in the doorway of the butler's pantry looking ready to spit nails.

"The woman is insane," Lawrence said tautly to Kelly and Seth.

"Why?" asked Kelly, edging nervously around Cook, who was wielding a hug steel ladle as if it were Max's sword.

"She threw out all the liquor, and now she's accusing me of stealing her cookbooks."

Kelly and Seth exchanged looks. "You were right," Seth said.

"And my rice jar!" yelled Cook. "You stole my rice jar!"

"Madam," said Lawrence stiffly, "I did no such thing."

"Yes, you did! And you're going to tell Lady Bea I threw all these things away so she'll fire me. I know what you're up to."

Seth let out a piercing whistle that momentarily silenced Cook. "In the first place," he said, "Lawrence, you threw out the liquor last night. In the second place, Cook, if you want your cookbooks, go talk to Mavis."

"And the rice?" Cook demanded, waving her ladle. "Where's the rice? I'm making paella tonight."

Seth coughed, clearly trying not to look at Kelly. "Umm . . . Kelly had an accident last night when she was cooking dinner."

Cook turned on Kelly, jabbing the ladle at her. "Then *you* go to town and get more. I need it. How is a woman supposed to cook when the tigers are eating her meat and the household is stealing her cookbooks and her rice? Huh? Tell me!"

But Kelly was spared the necessity of trying to answer at ladle point, because Cook turned and hurried away to find Mavis.

"I wouldn't want to be in Miss Mavis's shoes," Lawrence remarked. He leaned against the doorjamb and folded his arms. "So, I threw out the liquor last night?"

"Yes, you did," Kelly told him. "You said you were going on the wagon and you couldn't do it with any liquor in the house."

Lawrence winced. "That was foolish of me. There must have been several hundred dollars worth of liquor in the cabinet."

"At least. But you were determined."

He sighed. "Please tell me I didn't throw out everything in the wine cellar. Her ladyship would never forgive me."

"No. We took care of most of that."

"Took care of it?"

"We hid it. And we're going to get rid of the rest of it, too."

He shook his head. "I don't know if that's necessary."

"Why not? You want to stop drinking."

"Be that as it may, Miss Kelly, it remains that I simply have to drive to town to get another bottle. There was no need to hide the wine. If I do indeed go on the wagon, I'll need to be able to do it in a world with a liquor store on nearly every corner and next to every grocery."

He had a point. Kelly reached out and pulled a stool away from the island so she could sit on it. "What are you going to do, Lawrence?"

"I don't know." He came to the island and sat across from her. Seth joined them, sitting next to Kelly. "It's very lowering, you know, to have a weakness of this kind."

Kelly nodded sympathetically.

"It's not simply a matter of saying I'll never drink again. I've tried that. And I've tried AA, too. Somehow it doesn't help my willpower at all to get up in front of a bunch of other drunks and say I'm an alcoholic. It just makes me want a drink even more so I can forget how weak I am." He shook his head.

"I have a friend who had to go to AA," Seth said. "He said that at first it made him feel even worse, just like you're saying. But he stuck it out, and he started to feel better about himself. Counting up those sober weeks apparently helps."

Lawrence grimaced. "It's not my style at all. One simply does *not* launder one's dirty linen in public."

Seth looked at Kelly. "There's something to be said for that."

She nodded, looking at Lawrence and feeling a deep wellspring of affection, and aching for him. "Do you remember how I used to sit on your lap when I was little, Lawrence?"

"Yes, Miss." His face softened.

"When Granny was entertaining, and I had to stay out of the way because I was too small, I used to come to the pantry and stay with you. We had fun, didn't we?"

"Yes, we did," he agreed, suddenly looking

misty. "You taught me how to play Monopoly."

"And you taught me how to play cards. And you told me the most wonderful stories about all the places you visited when you were in the army. India, Singapore, Cyprus."

"And Africa." He nodded reminiscently. "You used to like my stories about Africa best of all."

"Lawrence . . . are you feeling useless?"

He appeared taken aback. "Of course not! Certainly there's less to do these days, now that the family doesn't entertain as often. But we're all getting older and need an easier schedule, you know."

"What I'm trying to say is, maybe looking after this house isn't enough for you anymore. Maybe you need to get a hobby, join a club—find something for yourself, Lawrence. A lady friend?"

He shook his head. "No one could replace my Gwyneth."

"That doesn't mean you couldn't find a companion to go out with and do things with. There must be something in this world you want to do besides look after the house and family."

"I've always been a servant, Miss. Even in the army. This is the life I was bred to. My father and grandfather were butlers before me."

"Which is wonderful—we'd have been lost without you. But when the hours hang heavy in the afternoons or the evenings, you might consider getting out of here and doing something else. You might go fishing. Or dancing. There must be something. After all, at one time you had enough of a taste for adventure that you went into the army before you started being a butler."

"That's true." He sighed. "Well, I'll certainly think about it. The busier I am, the less likely I am to start thinking about liquor."

But his gaze grew distant and for a moment he

looked ineffably sad. "I can't leave her ladyship, you know. She needs me to look after her. I left my previous post to stay with her, and nothing will pry me away."

"I'm not suggesting you quit, just that you find some things to enjoy during your free time."

"Well, I shall apply myself to the problem and think of something. Thank you for your concern, Miss. I'll be all right."

Kelly nodded, watching as he rose stiffly and disappeared into the pantry, closing the door behind him.

Seth spoke. "Poor old guy. This is one hell of a monkey to have on your back."

"It's terrible. I wish there was something I could do to help."

"Considering how heavily he's been drinking lately, I'm not sure it's wise for him to go into a complete, sudden withdrawal."

She hadn't thought of that. "You think he might get the DTs?"

"I think we'd better keep an eye on him, yes."

"Maybe I ought to call the family doctor and see if he has any suggestions."

Seth nodded. "That's a great idea."

Kelly rose, planning to go find a private phone, but what Seth said next caused her to sit right back down.

"Lawrence is in love with your grandmother."

"How do you know that?"

"The way he looked when he said he would never leave her. The old guy's carrying a torch."

"Then he ought to say something."

Seth shook his head. "There's this class thing involved, Kelly. In Lawrence's world, mere butlers don't aspire to the lady of the manor."

"How medieval!"

He nodded. "But telling Lawrence that isn't going to change his perception of his proper place in the scheme of things."

"Then maybe I should speak to Granny about it."

"What? And make her so uncomfortable that he'll know? Best to stay out of it. This is one thing the two of them need to figure out. So why don't I take you fishing this afternoon?"

"In the rain?"

"That's when they bite best. We might come up with a little grouper for dinner."

The idea of fishing had never really appealed to Kelly, but the idea of being out of this house for a few hours with nothing to trouble her but the rain was *very* appealing. "I've never gone fishing." She felt obliged to give him the warning.

"No problem. I'll bait your hook for you."

Cook reappeared with an armload of cookbooks, which she dumped with a thud on the counter. "You were right," she announced. "Miss Mavis had them. Now, why would she do a thing like that? This whole family is crazy, I tell you. *Crazy.*"

"You've got that right," Kelly agreed. Rising, she went to look for a private phone. So Lawrence was in love with Bea? That might explain a great deal.

She phoned the family's doctor, who said he'd call in a prescription for sedatives for Lawrence. "But the bottom line, Miss Burke, is that if Mr. Lawrence begins to get at all incoherent, confused, or delusional, you need to bring him to the hospital. In the meantime, give him Vitamin B, and have him take a sedative when he starts to get anxious."

"When will the prescription be ready?"

"I'll have my nurse phone it in as soon as I get off the phone."

"Thank you."

After she hung up, she went looking for Seth. He

was still in the kitchen, listening to Cook bemoan her lot and the general state of insanity in the household.

"I need to go to town and get a prescription for Lawrence," Kelly told him. "I will also get the rice for Cook. And maybe we shouldn't go fishing at all, not when Lawrence needs to be watched."

"We can ask the others to watch him."

"I'd never do that to the poor man. They'd be all over him every second, watching him as if he were a criminal about to commit a robbery."

"You're probably right." He pursed his lips thoughtfully. "What about asking Manuel to keep an eye on him? Besides, you *really* need to get away."

Manuel agreed, but first he had to change into something more appropriate than his gardening clothes. He appeared twenty minutes later in a white dress and white shoes, which he apparently felt were more suitable to the role of nursemaid.

"A wrestling outfit might have been more appropriate," Seth remarked.

Manuel waved a hand. "Lawrence would never hit a lady."

Some part of Kelly recognized the absurdity of that statement, but it was a sign of how accustomed she was getting to the lunacy that it also seemed perfectly reasonable. "I'd better let Lawrence know what I'm doing. I don't want him to be offended."

But Lawrence was in no mood to be offended. He was in the library, rather morosely supervising the day maids who came in to clean twice a week. "Bertha, you must—really you *must*—dust the lintels. Don't spare the feather duster. We can always get another."

"I just dusted them last week, Mr. Lawrence."

"Unfortunately, Bertha, dust just keeps settling.

And plan on doing the books again next week."

Bertha sighed, but did as he bid.

"Hired help," Lawrence muttered as he followed Kelly back out into the foyer. "And now I need to go see how Lydia is doing. She has a tendency not to vacuum behind the furniture."

"In just a minute," Kelly said. "Lawrence, I called Dr. Haycroft about your decision to give up alcohol."

Lawrence's expression grew even gloomier. "I suppose he wants me in hospital."

"Not yet. Maybe not at all. But he's calling in a prescription for sedatives. He says you need to take them if you start to get anxious. I'm going to pick them up now."

He nodded. "I suppose I can manage that much."

"Good. And don't worry about your duties. If you need to take one of the pills, the rest of us can manage. It will be only for a few days, after all."

He sighed and looked to heaven. "You would *not* believe what a mess this household can get into in three days."

Kelly felt the corners of her mouth twitching. "Actually, I can imagine it very well. I used to live here, remember? I think I can fill in for a few days, don't you?"

"Yes, Miss." He sighed again. "I'm not indispensable."

"I didn't say that." She felt awful suddenly, realizing how Lawrence had interpreted what she said. "Lawrence, I may be able to fill in for a few days, but no one, absolutely no one but *you* could run this household indefinitely. Heck, no one else would *want* to."

She was relieved to see a glimmer of amusement in his gaze. "You're right, of course." Squaring his shoulders, he marched off toward the drawing room, intent on checking up on Lydia.

Five minutes later, Kelly and Seth were in his pickup truck, headed toward town.

"I thought you'd have a Corvette or a Porsche," she remarked.

He flashed her a wry grin. "I'm a rather large guy; I need room. Besides, the truck is handy for carrying big blocks of wood."

He certainly *was* large, she thought, watching him out of the corner of her eye. And for some reason she found herself remembering the way he had kissed her last night, found herself wishing that she could repeat those exhilarating moments when nothing else in the universe had mattered.

Instead, she was running to town to take care of Lawrence and Cook, and preparing to take over the management of the household, something she had sworn she would never be dragged into again.

Feeling blue and resentful, she looked out the side window, watching the sheets of rain wash over the glass. Why should this surprise her? The Burke family was like a huge whirlpool, drawing everyone who came within reach into the maelstrom at the center, making escape nearly impossible. Look at Lawrence. Nearly forty years with the Burkes had turned him into an alcoholic, yet he couldn't leave, not even for his own sake.

"What are you thinking?" Seth asked.

She stirred and looked at him. "Gloomy thoughts on a rainy day. No big deal."

"What's wrong?"

"Nothing, really. I was likening my family to a whirlpool. If you get too close, they'll swallow you."

"Wow. That's some image."

"Look what they've done to Lawrence. He used to be a sane, healthy man."

Seth didn't answer for a minute. When he did, his voice was gentle. "Did you feel that way before you left?"

"I'm feeling that way now. The longer I stay, the deeper I get drawn in. Now I've told Lawrence I'll manage the household for the next few days while he gets through withdrawal."

"What did you think you were going to do? Fly in and fly out unscathed a few days later?"

She had been hoping exactly that, but hearing him say it made it hit home.

He shook his head and braked for the stop sign that Jules had missed the other night. "Look, I don't know what your real problem is with your family, but you're damn lucky to have them. They're not a whirlpool, they're just a family. Admittedly zanier than some, but just a family. And there isn't a mean bone in the bunch."

"That doesn't mean they don't swallow you whole if you let them. What's your family like?"

"My parents, you mean? My dad was an abusive alcoholic. My mom finally ditched him when I was ten. She had her own problems, but she was supportive of me."

"What kind of problems?"

"After years of living with my dad, she was a pretty frightened, pretty timid woman. Neurotic. Hypochondriac. But she never let that get in the way of anything *I* needed. And she never told me I couldn't do something. I half expected her to laugh at me when I was eleven and announced I was going to play pro football."

"But she didn't?"

"Not once. Instead she found a way to make sure I got to practices and had everything I needed.

When I realized I was never going to be a quarter-back—I didn't have the arm for it—I got all depressed. And you know what she said to me? She said, 'There are thirty other players on the team, Seth. Where would the quarterback be without them?'"

"Very wise."

"I thought so, even then. And for all her fears, she always said something to me that I've never forgotten. She said, 'Don't ever let me hear you say you *can't* do something. Not until you've tried your best.' Sometimes I'd get so angry at her for that, because there were things I was sure I couldn't do. Or because I was sure she didn't understand the problems involved. But she wouldn't lay off of me until I *proved* I couldn't do them. Which is why you see before you a former Pro-Bowler who also sculpts."

"She sounds like a remarkable woman."

"She was. At times. At other times she was very human and weak. Throughout most of my high school years she had one illness or another, and I had to take care of her. That's how I learned to cook and clean. Now, I could have felt she was weighing me down, trapping me. But I didn't."

Kelly's cheeks flushed. "I didn't mean to sound as if I feel my family is trapping me. Not exactly."

He pulled the truck into the pharmacy parking lot and switched off the ignition. "They're trying to snare you right now."

"I know that. That whole e-mail that Mavis sent me was calculated to get me hotfooting it back here. But that's not what I meant. There's . . . an emotional pull. And it can swamp you. It nearly swamped me."

He released his seatbelt and turned to look at her. "How so?"

"Because they're so overpowering. Because they really *do* need someone to look after them. Because they're so damn talented and eccentric. A kid can get lost in an environment like that, even when they try to make her feel like a queen."

His dark eyes were gentle. "I think I can understand that."

"Anyway, it doesn't matter now. I have my own life, and I'm going to go back to it. Once Lawrence gets better, anyway."

"So you no longer think I'm a threat?"

She shook her head. "No, I don't think you're going to rob them blind anymore."

"Well, that's a step in the right direction."

He came around to open her door for her, a courtesy she wasn't accustomed to and that made her feel special. She walked a few steps toward the door, then paused and looked up at him. "Seth? What about your children?"

His face set in a hard line. "I'll get them. Because the bottom line is, they're going to cramp her style, and sooner or later Velvet will be looking for someplace to leave them."

"But why is she making such an awful claim about you?"

"Because she's furious at me. I didn't take that broadcasting job, so she's using the kids to get even. She hasn't got a lick of evidence for her claim, so sooner or later the court is going to award me reasonable visitation. It's just rough in the meantime."

"I wish I could meet your kids." She was surprised to realize she meant it. She'd been too busy the last eight years even to think about children, but she found the idea appealing, somehow.

"I wish you could, too. I think you'd like them."

Maybe he wasn't so bad after all, Kelly thought when they went into the store. But somehow, feeling kindly toward Seth didn't make her feel any better at all.

Chapter 11

The rain had lightened considerably by the time they pulled up in front of the house. "Perfect for fishing," Seth commented. "I just hope Manuel isn't having a problem with Lawrence."

But Manuel was indeed having a problem. When Seth and Kelly entered the house, they found Lawrence lying facedown on the floor and Manuel sitting astride his back, with his skirt hiked up until the top of his pantyhose were showing.

"Get off of me, you numbskull," Lawrence was shouting.

"Uh-uh," Manuel replied. "You quit drinking."

"That was last night! This is today. If I want to have a glass of wine, I'll have a glass of wine, you nincompoop."

"Sticks and stones may break my bones," Manuel chanted, "but names will never harm me."

"I'm going to pull your hair out by the roots."

"It doesn't have any roots. It's a wig."

"Oh, dear heavens!" Bea wailed. She was standing on the gallery above, literally wringing her hands. Kelly had never seen anyone actually do that before, but trust Bea to have it in her repertoire.

"Manuel," Bea cried, "get off of my butler!"

For an instant, Manuel froze, looking non-plussed. Lawrence seized his advantage and nearly bucked him off. Manuel grabbed frantically for the back of Lawrence's coat and hung on as if he were riding a wild bull.

"This is too much," Bea said, still wringing her hands.

Kelly noted with a cynical eye that Bea was putting on a good act. Her grandmother had never, ever been helpless in any situation. The fact that Bea was remaining upstairs and moaning over the railing was a pretty good indicator that she didn't want Manuel to stop restraining Lawrence.

"What's going on?" Seth asked mildly.

Manuel waved his free hand as Lawrence bucked again. "I've had to chase him away from the wine cellar three times since you left. This last time, he said he was going to rip my eyebrows off my face."

"Lawrence?" said Bea in failing accents. "Lawrence said that?"

"I said no such thing," Lawrence protested. "I merely told this cretin that he had no business blocking my access to the cellar."

"And that you were going to rip my eyebrows off if I didn't stay out of your way."

"I think that's enough," Seth said, his tone still mild. He crossed to the pair on the floor, and with an amazing strength lifted them both by their collars until they stood on either side of him. "What do you want me to do with them, Bea? Knock some sense into their heads?"

"Oh, my dear, no!"

Seth shrugged and released both men.

Lawrence glared at him. "I don't appreciate being manhandled."

"No one does. Don't give me an excuse to do it again."

Bea hurried along the gallery and came floating down the stairs. "I can't have this in my house," she said firmly. "The maids left a half hour ago because Lawrence was driving them crazy. I wonder if they'll be back come Monday." She looked balefully at Lawrence, who managed to look ashamed.

"And Manuel," she said, turning to her handyman, "if you're going to wear skirts, you really need to learn not to straddle things."

"But I had to stop him."

"No, you didn't," Bea said firmly. "If Lawrence wants to be a lush for the rest of his days and pass out in my mashed potatoes, that's his business. Although really," she said turning to the butler, "it's so unappetizing. And you might suffocate."

Lawrence looked even more shamefaced.

Bea continued, looking every inch the queen she had once played. "No one can prevent Lawrence from drinking, however much we might love him and worry about him. He must do that himself."

"That's right," Lawrence said stubbornly.

"Yes, it is," Bea agreed. "Although I must say that after all the trouble we went to trying to hide the wine last night—nearly getting devoured by the tigers in the process—you could be more grateful for our efforts. But it's your choice."

Lawrence nodded, his chin set stubbornly. Then he looked from one face to the next, and something in him seemed to soften. He turned to Kelly. "Did you bring the sedatives, Miss?"

She handed him the bag.

"Then I shall take one and retire to my room." He faced Bea again. "My apologies, my lady."

When he had disappeared, Bea frowned at Manuel. "Put on something more suitable," she said to him. "You'll be serving dinner tonight."

Manuel threw up his hands and walked toward the back of the house, muttering, "I was just doing what Miss Kelly told me."

Bea looked at her granddaughter. "What *did* you tell him to do?"

"To keep an eye on Lawrence. The doctor was worried about withdrawal problems."

"This is too terrible. I'm worried about this, child. *Very* worried. I wish someone could persuade Lawrence to go to a hospital."

"*You* probably could convince him," Kelly said. "He listens to you."

"Hah! That man has never listened to me." She sniffed. "He's always been enamored of the Pygmalion concept. From the minute I married the viscount, Lawrence began to try to make me over into a proper lady."

Seth spoke. "You *are* a lady, Bea."

"Of course I am. But not elevated enough for Lawrence. He's always given me the feeling that he thinks he lowers himself by associating with me."

"Yeah. Uh-huh. Sure." Kelly shook her head. "That's why he left his job with the viscount to come to Florida with you. That's why he's stayed here nearly forty years."

"I never could understand that, really." She sighed again and began to move in the direction of the butler's pantry. "I'm going to check and make sure he took that pill."

Seth and Kelly watched her float away.

"Imagine that," Kelly said after a minute. "Lawrence makes Granny feel inadequate. I never would have imagined it."

"Me neither. Bea is always so sure of herself."

She turned to look at him. "Does it bother you that Lawrence is in love with her?"

"No. Why should it?"

Kelly's last remaining doubt about Seth crumbled. She had realized already that he wasn't a con man, but now she no longer had to wonder if he was sweet on her grandmother. And if he wasn't sweet on Bea . . .

"How about that fishing trip?" she asked, deciding that she needed to get out of this house before she started having crazy thoughts of her own—such as that Seth was a remarkably attractive and completely unattached man.

"Sounds good to me. I'll get the gear."

Half an hour later, they were standing in the drizzle on the side of the bridge with their lines dangling in the water. Seth was using frozen shrimp for bait, from a package he'd happened to have in his freezer at the guest house.

"Rather expensive bait," she remarked.

"It was either that or run to town again to get some. This'll do."

"Well, it's better than big old nasty bugs."

He laughed, his eyes dancing. "You don't want me to get crickets, then."

She shuddered. "The whole idea of eating a fish that's just devoured a cricket makes my stomach heave."

"But you cut the guts out of the fish before you cook it. The cricket would be gone."

Kelly looked at her line dangling in the water and decided she didn't like this fishing thing at all. She began to reel it in.

"What are you doing?"

"I think I prefer my food in plastic packages from the supermarket."

"Why?"

"Well . . . it's this whole killing and gutting thing. Some poor grouper who's minding his own business, looking for food on a rainy day, is going to bite my hook and get yanked out of the water. Then he's going to be beheaded and drawn and quartered."

"That's what happens to the fish you buy in the market."

"True. But when I buy it, it's already dead." Finished reeling in her line, she set her pole down and tried not to look at the swollen, nibbled shrimp that was left on her hook. "I won't buy live lobster, you know. I won't even buy it in a restaurant."

He began to reel in his own line. "You're definitely not a fisherman."

"Don't stop on my account."

He gave her a smile that crinkled the corners of his eyes. "Somehow, I just don't want you to think of me as a murderer of poor little fishies."

"I wouldn't. Intellectually, I don't have a problem with fishing. I just don't want to do it myself."

"I can understand that. Somehow I don't see myself working in a slaughterhouse, either. When it comes to beef and pork, I'd rather buy it in plastic packages, too. So I understand where you're coming from."

Seth picked up her pole and the bait bucket, and they started walking back toward the house with Bouncer at their side. The road was muddy and getting slippery, so they had to walk carefully. As it led them into the heavily wooded area, the drizzle seemed to grow louder as it tapped on the leaves and palm fronds and the sound echoed.

"I love the sound of rain," he remarked.

"So do I."

"There don't seem to be too many days like this

around here. Mostly it's severe storms and tornado warnings."

"When I was about nine, Granny and I stood in an upstairs window and watched a waterspout. It pulled out a whole bunch of trees on the south side of the island."

"You must have been frightened."

Kelly thought about it. "No, not really. I always felt safe with Granny." And she had, she realized. Even though she had spent most of her life feeling as if she were a disappointment to the Burkes, she had always felt secure. But the dichotomy had created a tension in her, one that still troubled her, she realized. Even with all her success as a media designer, she still felt inadequate.

"Penny for your thoughts," he said.

"Oh . . . when I left home I was still a child. Coming back as an adult is . . . strange."

"Things don't look quite the same, do they?"

"No."

"They look more human?"

She shook her head. "Not exactly. They've always been *very* human. I used to go nuts trying to deal with their foibles."

"A bit much for a child, maybe."

She glanced at him. "Are you always this good at listening?"

"Of course not—I'm just pretending." But his smile was warm. Friendly. It belied his teasing.

"Anyway . . . I used to wish I had a normal family. You can't imagine what it was like to have the five of them show up for my school conferences. Bea would arrive dressed as if she were going to a premiere, and everybody would whisper and point at her. Every time Mavis opened her mouth, she could be heard all over the school."

"She *does* project well."

Kelly had to chuckle. "That she does. And Max and Jules would argue with the teachers about everything. They felt school was stifling my creativity. And Zee . . . well, Zee was Zee. Wearing some outlandish circus-type garb and cussing, and telling one teacher that she'd better watch her step because the tigers were very protective of me."

"She didn't."

"She did. I wanted to sink. They never went to a conference that they didn't wind up in a quarrel among themselves about whether the teacher was right, whether the teaching methods were adequate . . . oh, just about anything at all. Max was ready to get my art teacher fired because she gave me a C on some assignment I did. He gave her quite a lecture on how she wasn't a qualified art critic."

"Ouch."

"Exactly. When I didn't make the cut for choir because I couldn't carry a tune, Mavis descended on the school and went on a tear about how *anyone* with proper training could carry a tune."

"What happened?"

"The school wouldn't back down, so Mavis gave me voice lessons." Kelly grimaced. "I'm still not a very good singer. And the next year I *really* didn't want to go out for choir, because I'd been so embarrassed. But Mavis made me go to tryouts."

"What happened?"

"I was able to carry a tune and they put me in choir."

"So she was right?"

"Apparently so. But I quit after a week because all the other kids said I'd only gotten in because Mavis made such a stink."

He reached out and took her hand. "That's rough."

"It was." She shook her head. "But looking back

at it now, I see it all happened because they were so protective of me. Their intentions were the best."

"The road to hell and all that." Stopping, he tugged her hand until she faced him. "It doesn't hurt as much now, does it?"

Her face must have answered him, because he dropped the fishing poles and the bait bucket and reached for her, drawing her into a tight hug. "Some things are a whole lot easier for adults to handle. I think your family is fascinating and a lot of fun. But I can understand why you needed to get away."

He didn't understand the half of it, she thought, but she didn't feel like talking about it anymore. Not when he was holding her so close and she could feel the beat of his heart beneath her ear. Somehow when he held her, the whole world seemed to recede into the distance, and a strange kind of peace settled over her.

She knew this was dangerous, knew it with every fiber of her being. There was his divorce and his references to never wanting to get involved again, and his stated disinterest in her. Besides, she had her own life to get back to. But despite the danger she couldn't make herself back away.

He spoke, his voice a deep rumble, almost like a purr. "It's all a game, you know. Life's a game just like football. Sometimes you win, sometimes you lose, sometimes you make a perfect play, and sometimes you get hurt. But what matters, all that matters, is that you play it with everything you have. Your family does that—wholeheartedly. That's why they seem so different. Most people don't commit so fully."

"How can you do anything but commit?"

"You can always hold yourself back. Color inside the lines. Avoid the risks. Dream small. There are lots of ways to half-play the game. Or you can jump right in and play it with all you've got, and enjoy the flood, the mud, the tears, and the sweat."

"That's how you felt about football, isn't it?"

"Exactly. I loved everything about it. One of my favorite memories is of a game we played against San Francisco. It was raining and it just kept getting muddier and muddier until finally we all went into a pile and it was so muddy we couldn't get up. Hell, we couldn't even hang on to the ball. Everything was squirting out of our grip and we were sliding like we were on ice. It wound up getting so silly that we were all laughing, and by the time the game was over the only part of us that wasn't hidden in mud was our eyes."

"And that was fun?"

"You better believe it. How many adults have an excuse to play in the mud?"

She felt herself smiling. "I've never played in the mud."

"Never? You're missing one of life's great pleasures. Of course, it's a whole lot more fun when you're grown up and nobody's going to yell at you for it."

She laughed then and looked up at him. In that instant, the world stood still. He had such a beautiful smile, such a warm smile, and it seemed to reach out and hold her the way his arms were doing. She felt everything inside her growing warm and weak, heavy with yearning.

As if he felt the change in her, his smile faded and his eyes grew sultry, heavy-lidded. His lips parted, and she knew, just knew, he was going to kiss her. And she knew, just knew, that she wanted it more than she had ever wanted anything in her life.

Instinctively, she started to go up on tiptoe. It

was a mistake. Her feet slipped in the mud and went out from under her. Apparently he thought she was trying to get away, because he slackened his grip on her and she felt herself falling.

Then, realizing his mistake, he reached out for her, but his knee buckled. An instant later they were both lying on their backs in the muddy road, with the steady rain drumming on them.

"Damn knee," he said philosophically, looking up at the sky through the lace of leaves.

"Gave out, huh?" she said, equally calmly.

"Sure did."

She could have been annoyed, or disappointed, but instead she felt like laughing.

"Did you get hurt?" he asked.

"No. The mud's soft. You?"

"I'm fine."

"Good." She pushed herself up on one elbow and looked down at him. "Well, since we're already in the mud . . ." She scooped up a handful and dropped it on his chest.

He looked startled, then broke into laughter. "Wanna play?"

Before she could answer, he caught her around the waist and rolled her right over until he was on his elbows above her. She felt the mud soaking her back, felt the mud she'd dumped on his chest soaking into her front.

"Mud pies?" he asked. "Or mud balls?"

She reached out, closing her fingers around a handful of mud. "Mud balls," she decided. Moving swiftly, she brought the mud up and shoved it down his collar.

"Why, you . . ." He levered himself to his feet, slipping a little, and scooped up a huge handful of mud. Kelly jumped up, too, skating a little until her shoes found some gravel. She grabbed a handful of mud, but before she could throw it, Seth hit her square in the shoulder. The mud was cold and soft as it ran down her arm.

He was already grabbing another handful, so she hurled hers and danced away. The grass verge was nearly as slippery as the mud, though, and she had to skitter to keep her balance. Another mud ball hit her in the hip.

Deciding she needed to take extreme measures, she grabbed mud in both hands and hurled both, striking Seth on his chin and stomach.

"Hey," he said. "Double-barreled, huh?"

That was a blunder, she thought as she watched him grab two handfuls. Turning, she started to run.

That proved to be a mistake. Her feet slipped and she fell facedown in the mud, sliding a few inches before she stopped.

Seth was there instantly. "Are you okay?" He knelt beside her. Bouncer, who'd been watching them as if they'd lost their minds, loped over to sniff at her ear.

"Sure." Rolling over, she gave Seth a mud pie on the side of the head. Bouncer began to bark excit edly.

"No fair." But Seth was grinning.

"Fair's a matter of perspective," she said virtuously.

"True. And all's fair in love and war."

Before she could wonder what he meant, he was leaning over her and kissing her. She was covered with mud, he was covered with mud, but neither of them seemed to notice as mouths and bodies met full-length on the road. When Kelly ran her hands over his back, it wasn't the slick mud she noticed, but the power in his shoulders, the way the muscles rippled as he held her. And when his hands cupped her bottom and drew her closer to him, she was sure he wasn't noticing how wet and dirty she was.

Sparkles of sheer delight zinged along her nerve endings, warming her in places that had been cold for far too long. With each teasing stroke of his tongue against hers, she felt herself being lifted upward into a strange new world where a simple caress could paint fire and a touch could explode into fireworks.

When his hand closed over her breast and squeezed, she arched upward, seeking more of him, feeling as if she were more alive than she had ever been in her life. When he traced her nipple through the wet fabric with his fingertip, she thought the ache that raced to her groin would make her cry out. Never, ever, had she imagined desire could overpower her like this.

It was the approaching growl of an engine that brought them to their senses. Like startled deer, they jerked apart and looked at one another.

"Oh, God," said Kelly.

Seth pushed himself to his feet, wincing as his knee protested, then tugged her up beside him. Just in time. The van came skidding around the corner and slid to a stop in front of them.

Manuel leaned out. "Doing it in the road, huh?"

Kelly felt her cheeks burn. "Manuel . . ."

"Hey, it doesn't bother me. I'm going to get fresh seafood for the paella. Anything you want from town?"

Kelly shook her head. Seth said, "No, thanks."

Manuel nodded, rolled up the window, and drove off.

Kelly looked at Seth. "How did he know?"

He looked at her, then started laughing.

"What?"

But he was laughing so hard he couldn't answer.

Kelly began to feel very annoyed. "What the hell is so funny?"

He straightened, still laughing, and pointed.

She looked down and gasped when she saw the unmistakable muddy print of a hand on her left breast. "Oh, my God . . ." She was mortified. She wanted to die. She wanted to sink into the mud and vanish forever.

"Here," he said, his laughter fading. "Let me fix it."

"Fix it?" Before she could ask how, he reached out and smeared the handprint beyond recognition, rubbing her breast as he did so, and reminding her all too clearly of how he could weaken her knees.

"Seth . . . !"

But he looked unrepentant as he stepped back and admired his handiwork. "Much better." Then he leered, wiggling his eyebrows. "Want me to smear the other side, too?"

"Oh!" Feeling at once frustrated and indignant, she turned her back on him and began to march toward the house. The gesture would probably have been a lot more dignified if she hadn't been covered in mud and slipping on every other step.

Seth caught up with her. "I'm sorry," he said. "I didn't mean to embarrass you."

"Get lost."

"Kinda hard to do on an island this size."

"Did anyone ever tell you that you're uncouth?"

"No, not that I recall. But then, I associate with dumb jocks. They wouldn't know what the word means."

"Oh, cut it out!"

"Why?"

"Because you're not a dumb jock, and you know it!"

"Hmm. A change of heart?"

"Leave my heart out of this."

He walked another few steps beside her in silence. Finally he asked with what sounded like genuine curiosity, "Are you always this difficult to deal with? Or is it just me?"

The question seriously irritated her, especially since he was justified in asking it. Since she had arrived here she'd been far more prickly and irritable than was her wont, but she didn't want to admit it, and certainly not to him. "Just you," she snapped.

"Oh, okay. I'm glad to know that."

That brought her up short, and she stopped to glare at him. "Why?"

"Because if you were like this with everyone, I'd never have a hope of seeing you without that chip on your shoulder."

Point, set, match, Kelly thought as she watched him limp up the road, leaving her behind. And the worst of it was, she deserved it.

Chapter 12 🕊

Seth stood at the window, watching the rain fall on the tarp he'd put over his sculpture, thinking about Kelly. He'd been invited up to the house for dinner, but had excused himself. The last couple of days, he'd found himself getting more entangled with that family than he really wanted. Especially with Kelly.

It had all seemed so simple when Bea had suggested he hole up here after his divorce became final. He liked Bea a whole lot, and enjoyed the rest of the clan, and they provided distraction at a time when he desperately needed it. He hadn't imagined that the quiet existence he'd been promised, with solitude in which to work on his sculpture and his psychology dissertation, would wind up exploding this way.

The fact that Mavis might be matchmaking didn't trouble him nearly as much as the creeping suspicion that Bea had planned this from the start. Behind those delicate airs and the old-fashioned femininity she projected, he was certain, lay solid brass and a calculating brain. It was entirely possible that she'd been planning for months to get him together with Kelly. Hell, she wouldn't even allow him a respectable time to recover from his divorce. Bea didn't believe in letting moss grow under anyone's feet.

He should have been amused. He would have been a lot more amused if Kelly weren't getting under his skin.

And she definitely was. He wanted not to like her—she had more thorns than a rosebush—but he found himself liking her anyway. Which would have been okay, except that he kept having fugitive thoughts of making love to her.

At errant moments, when he was sure he was thinking of nothing but his dissertation, or his sculpture, or whatever Burke catastrophe was currently brewing, he would find himself having vivid images of things like running his palm over Kelly's smooth thigh. Or kissing the hollow of her throat. Or laying her beneath him and feeling her soft curves yield to his weight.

He was waking up aching in the dead of night with her image floating before his mind's eye. When he worked on his sculpture, he found the curves becoming Kelly's curves. And the little witch had managed to do all this to him in just a handful of days.

He couldn't believe it.

He wasn't happy about it.

He ought to pack up and leave before he got in any deeper. He didn't have room for this in his life right now, nor the heart to commit to a woman who needed commitment. Nor did he really feel he had the emotional energy to deal with her problems.

He suspected she still had hangups due to the death of her parents, and she certainly had difficulties from her childhood in this house of lunacy. What she'd said today about school conferences had given him just an inkling of the dimensions of that particular problem.

But what could he do about it? People had to resolve their own conflicts. Nobody else could do that for them. In the meantime, anyone who got too close to that woman was going to find himself bleeding from her thorns.

And he'd already bled enough for one lifetime.

Besides, he reminded himself, she wasn't trustworthy. Any woman who could walk away from her family for eight long years wasn't a woman he felt he could trust.

He wandered into the kitchen, planning to make himself a salad and maybe a steak, when the phone rang. He picked up the receiver, expecting to hear Bea on the other end with some new catastrophe. Instead he heard a silky voice that made his blood go cold.

"Seth, it's Velvet."

"What's wrong?" His heart slammed as he started to imagine every kind of catastrophe that could befall two small children.

"Nothing," she said impatiently. "Nanny's going on vacation and I want you to come home for two weeks to take care of the children. I need to go to Paris."

Reading between the lines, he understood that she'd found another lover. "I don't know if I can," he said, though he wanted nothing more. "You're suing me for custody, remember? Claiming I'm unfit?"

Velvet had never let such details get between her and something she wanted. "Don't worry about it; I'm asking you. Just come home and take care of the children for a couple of weeks. Isn't that what you want? To see the kids?"

He did. Oh, God, he did. For just one minute of

holding their warm little bodies in a bear hug, he'd have given both his legs and his arms. But Velvet had taught him caution. "I'll need to call my lawyer first."

"Fine!" She was both sharp and impatient now. "But get back to me right away, okay? I need to make my flight reservations soon."

"I'm not sure I'll be able to get ahold of Will tonight. If not, then first thing in the morning, okay?"

"No later than that. I don't want to take them with me."

Of course she didn't. They would interfere with her romantic interludes. "I'll call as soon as I know," he said, and hung up.

His palms were wet and his mouth was dry. It angered him that that woman could still have such an effect on him after all that had happened in the last year. Or maybe it was the thought of having his kids again that was doing it.

Instinctively, he went to the room he was using as a study and picked up the framed photo he kept beside the computer, where he could look at it often. Two towheaded children, Johnnie and Jenny, Jenny eighteen months older. Two children he loved more than life. He felt his eyes begin to sting and he put the photo down quickly, then reached for the phone to page his lawyer.

Will Collins called him back twenty minutes later. "So," he said first thing, "what new scheme has the Velvet devised to make your life hell?"

"She wants me to come home and take care of the kids for two weeks while she goes to Paris."

"Wonderful!"

"Wonderful?"

"Sure, it undermines her claim that she considers you unfit. If you're so unfit, why is she leaving the kids with you for so long? That's good. On the other hand . . ." He trailed off thoughtfully.

"Yes?"

"To be on the safe side, it would be best if you took the kids someplace where you'll be among your friends rather than hers. Just in case. You never know, but she might come back from Paris and claim all kinds of psychological damage to the kids. I wouldn't put anything past her."

"Neither would I." He thought about it. "Well, I'll see if I can bring the children here."

"That might be good. You've got, what—five people there who can testify you're not a bad parent?"

"More than that. But I'll have to clear it first."

"Let me know what you decide. Maybe I can get this before a judge in the next couple of days and get her custody case dismissed. The fact that she's dumping the kids on you so she can go away for a couple of weeks ought to be sufficient."

Seth hardly dared to let himself hope this could be settled so easily. He'd been living with the nightmare of losing his kids for months now, and it had begun to seem as if daylight would never come.

After he finished talking to Will, he called the villa and spoke to Bea. She professed herself to be thrilled at the idea of having his children on the island for a couple of weeks, so, before he could have qualms about the wisdom of his decision, he called Velvet back.

"I'll take the kids," he told her, "but I'll come up there tomorrow to get them. I want them down here with me."

She hesitated, and he wondered what new scheme of hers he'd interfered with. "I'm not sure they should be uprooted that way, Seth."

"I'm not uprooting them, I'm taking them on a Florida vacation. Any kid on earth can handle that."

"Why can't you just stay up here with them?"

"Because I'm working, Velvet. I need to work."

"On that stupid sculpture of yours, I suppose. Well, fine, then, but just make sure the kids don't get near your tools. They might get hurt."

As he hung up, he had the really horrible thought that she might actually hope something of the kind would happen. No, not even Velvet was capable of that.

Yet she had taught him that when it came to her, nothing was ever simple. So even as he began to look forward to having his children again, he was thinking of ways to protect himself from her.

"Wanna fly to New York and back tomorrow?" Seth asked Kelly.

She was sitting on the back veranda, working on her laptop, trying to whip a client's web page into shape. Behind her, a hundred-foot phone cord ran into the house to the phone jack near the butler's pantry. Her mind had shifted into symbolic logic and programming, and it took a minute for his words to penetrate.

She looked up at him, and found him silhouetted against the bright spring day. "Why would I want to do that?"

"I need to go get my kids. My ex is going to Paris for two weeks."

"I thought she claimed you were an unfit parent."

"Going to Paris is apparently more important. Anyway, given what she's been saying about me, my lawyer thinks it would be best if I have witnesses to the fact that I don't abuse them."

She nodded, able to understand that. "But it won't prove anything, if you're being watched."

"That's not what we're worried about. We're worried that she'll go off on her fling, then come back and make new charges. So we want to head it off at the pass."

"Sounds like a good idea." But flying to New York and back in one day . . . "That's a marathon you're proposing."

He pulled one of the wicker chairs over and sat facing her. "I can't wait," he said.

The simplicity of his answer revealed how much he loved his children. She felt herself softening. "Well . . ."

"I know it's a really big favor to ask, Kelly. But I'd feel better not having to face her alone, without a witness. If it's too much, just say no."

But she didn't want to leave him in a lurch, or leave him open to more trouble from his ex-wife. She'd never been the kind of person who could do that. "I'll do it," she said, just as Lawrence staggered out the back door.

He stumbled over toward them and sank onto one of the chairs, holding his head in his hands. He groaned.

Kelly leaned toward him, concerned. "What's wrong, Lawrence?"

"Those sleeping pills the doctor gave you. Lord, the hangover . . ." He lifted his head, looking hang-dog. "I've had smaller headaches after cracking my head on concrete."

"I'm sorry."

He groaned again and put his head in his hands. "At least with a real hangover, a Blood Mary would fix it. Nothing is helping with this."

"Still," Seth said encouragingly, "this is your second day sober."

"It's not worth being sober if this is how I have to feel."

Bea emerged from the house, looking less like the queen than usual, and more like a very tired woman of her years. She plopped down in the chair next to Lawrence. "*Neither* of us may survive this. We were up all night."

Lawrence looked at her. "I *told* you that you didn't have to sit up and hold my hand."

"As if I was going to leave you to face this all alone!" Bea looked indignant. "I realize you think I'm a flighty, useless old woman, but I *do* have a sense of common decency."

"I don't think you're flighty, useless, or old." Lawrence sounded truculent.

"Well, I'm almost old enough to be your mother."

Lawrence rolled his eyes, then groaned as if the movement hurt him. He put his head in his hands. "At my age, I don't need a mother."

"No, you need a keeper."

Something about the way Lawrence's shoulders shook suggested to Kelly that the butler was stifling laughter. At least she hoped that was what it was.

Zee came out of the house carrying two large stainless steel feeding bowls filled with raw chicken necks. "Mavis and Jules are at it again, Mother," she said as she headed for the tiger enclosure, where the cats were already waiting.

"At what again?" Bea called after her.

"Mavis says she needs the music room all day because she's promised to sing the national anthem at a school soccer game on Friday. Jules says he can't go an entire day without practicing because his fingers will get stiff."

Bea looked at Kelly. "No household should have

two musically gifted people. It's impossible. Thank God Max paints."

Zee opened the gate to the tiger's lair cautiously and threw the bowls in as if they were Frisbees. Feeding time was the most dangerous time with the animals, and Zee rarely stuck more than a hand in the enclosure until they'd finished their meal. The tigers, who had been lurking at the edge of the woods, sprang forward and began to eat voraciously. Even at this distance, the crunching of chicken bones was audible.

"Gross," said Bea.

Zee heard her. "No more gross than us eating eggs, Mother."

Bea sighed. "When they're little, children are so easy to handle. What in the world happens when they grow up?"

Seth smiled. "They get minds of their own."

"Well, yours are still young. Your turn will come, Seth."

"I'm sure it will. I hope it will." For an instant his gaze grew distant and his expression became haunted.

"So," said Bea briskly, "when are your children coming?"

"Kelly and I are going to fly up to New York tomorrow and bring them back.."

"Wonderful." The way Bea's eyes settled on Kelly, she found herself wondering just what Bea thought was wonderful: the children coming or Seth and Kelly going away together.

Zee, coming back to the porch, paused and looked up at them. "You're going away? But I *need* you."

"We're coming back tomorrow, too," Kelly hastened to say.

Bea said, "That's a rather long trip to make in

one day. Why don't the two of you stay overnight?"

"No, Mother!" Pulling off her leather gloves, Zee mounted the porch steps. "I was counting on Seth and Kelly to be here."

Bea waved a hand. "A few days won't make any difference."

"Yes, it will."

Seth spoke. "What is it you need us for, Zee?"

Bea held up a hand. "Don't ask. I don't want to know. I've been saying for days that she's scheming something. I knew it the minute she threatened to bring the tigers into the house. Every time she does something insane like that, she's in the middle of plotting something even more insane. It's like a weather vane."

Zee tossed her gloves on the wrought-iron table. "Don't be ridiculous, Mother. I'm not plotting a thing. I just need some help picking up an abused animal."

"Hmph," said Bea. "No more tigers, I hope. Or lions."

"Nothing at all like that."

Seth intervened before Bea could say any more. "I'll be glad to help when I get back, Zee." He looked at Kelly. "I'm sure Kelly will be glad to help, too."

"I'm not so sure about that," Kelly said. "I've been clawed by ferrets, butted by goats, pecked by pelicans—all in the name of helping Zee rescue some poor critter."

Zee shook her head. "And here I thought you agreed that abused animals should be rescued."

"I *do* agree with you. There's nothing as awful as penning an animal so it can't take care of itself and then abusing it."

"So what is your problem?"

"I just said I wouldn't be *glad* to help. I didn't say I wouldn't help at all."

Zee looked relieved. "Good. These other coots are all too useless or old to help me."

Bea sighed and waved her cigarette holder. "Now I'm a coot. I get no respect from my children."

Seth looked at Kelly. "Did I make a mistake by agreeing to help?"

"Probably. What are we rescuing this time, Zee?"

"I'll tell you later. Don't worry about it." Then she picked up her gloves and disappeared into the house. She couldn't have said anything more calculated to make Kelly wonder what kind of catastrophe she was getting into now.

Bea looked at Kelly and Seth, suddenly smiling sweetly. "Are you *sure* you don't want to spend a week in New York?"

Seth shook his head. "No," was all he said, leaving no room for discussion.

She had to learn that word, Kelly thought. She had to learn to say it just that way, without any polite explanation tagged on. It would make life so much easier.

Kelly and Seth landed at LaGuardia the next morning around eleven o'clock. A driver was waiting for them, holding a placard with Seth's name on it. Ten minutes later they were ushered into a stretch limousine.

"I could get used to this," Kelly said as she sank back into padded leather cushions and looked around.

"I thought it would be easier with the kids. I don't usually bother."

"I'm not complaining."

He laughed. "It's comfortable, isn't it? I'll bet you

two-to-one the kids want to ride backwards."

"Probably. I'm considering it myself." Curious, she opened little panels and discovered temperature controls, radio controls, a TV, a phone, and a small, equipped bar. "Wow. Can I have some water?"

"Help yourself."

She pulled out a bottle of Evian, then on impulse poured it into two champagne glasses and offered one to Seth.

"To your kids," she said, toasting him.

"My kids," he agreed, and drained his glass.

"Are you nervous about seeing them?"

"A little," he admitted. He put his glass in the holder beside them. "It's been a while, and I'm not sure how comfortable they'll be with me. Velvet has probably been making me out to be the bogeyman."

"I really can't understand parents who do that to kids."

"Neither can I. But I never thought Velvet would lie about me to a court, either."

"Hell hath no fury, et cetera."

"Oh, I wouldn't limit that to women. Besides, she's the one who scorned me."

"I'm sure she has herself convinced it was the other way around." Kelly put her own glass aside and leaned back against the cushions. "I don't think I'd like your ex very much."

He almost grinned at that. "Right now, neither do I."

"Do you ever find yourself wondering why you married her?"

"No." He shook his head, his smile fading. "I *know* why I married her. I loved her. She wasn't perfect, but who is?"

Kelly wondered if he was still carrying a torch

for Velvet, then shied away from that line of thinking, sensing that it would only depress her though she didn't know why. "So, no regrets?"

"Only that it fell apart. How could I have any regrets? I was in love, I married the woman I loved, and I got two beautiful children out of it. You don't regret something like that if you have an ounce of sense."

Either he was lying or he was a remarkable man. Since she had the feeling that he was painfully honest, she had to give him the accolade of remarkable. It made her uncomfortable to do so, considering what she'd thought about Seth when she first met him. However, she prided herself on being able to change her mind when she was wrong.

Velvet Ralston lived in an elegant brownstone fronted by trees surrounded by cast-iron fences. The leaves were just budding, giving them a feathery look. The street was quiet, and the cars parked along it were expensive. A nice neighborhood.

The limousine waited while she and Seth climbed the steps. He was limping badly and had been ever since they got off the plane. Sitting in one position for so long had stiffened his knee up, apparently.

He rang the bell. Faintly she could hear it from inside the house.

The door opened and a dark woman with white hair, wearing a black dress and white apron, opened it to regard them suspiciously. "Yes?"

"Mr. Ralston to see Mrs. Ralston. She's expecting me."

The maid stepped back, giving them entry, then ushered them into a small sitting room off the hallway.

"My," Kelly said quietly, taking in the decor that looked as if it had originated in the mind of some

half-crazed but expensive designer. Nothing like
the Burke home, where the hodgepodge of gener-
ations melded into comfort and familiar discomfort. This was color-coordinated down to the last
pale little rosette in the crown molding. Sterile, especially the thoroughly modern, colorless chrome
and white furnishings.

"Ugly, isn't it?" Seth said. "There isn't a room in
this house where you can feel comfortable putting
your feet up."

"*Children* live here?" she asked.

"Actually, they have a nursery."

"Oh."

The corners of his eyes crinkled, apparently
amused by her evident disapproval. "I agree," he
said quietly. "And if I hadn't been tossed out, that
wouldn't have continued."

The sound of footsteps drew their attention toward the door, and a few seconds later a tall, beautiful woman appeared. So this was Velvet Ralston,
Kelly thought with a sinking heart. Blond, picture-
perfect, looking ready to step onto the cover of
Vogue. She wore a green silk suit and pumps, and
her hair and makeup looked as if she'd just left the
chair of a cosmetologist. Flawless skin, too, Kelly
noted. Absolutely flawless. The woman didn't look
as if she owned a single pore.

"Seth," the woman said, then looked disapprovingly at Kelly, who was now feeling utterly grungy
in her cotton khakis and running shoes. "Did you
really need to introduce your children to your paramour?"

Kelly considered scratching Velvet's eyes out,
then calculated the possible prison time and decided it wasn't worth it. Yet.

"This is Kelly Burke, Bea Burke's granddaughter.

She is *not* my paramour, or my girlfriend. Or anything at all except a friend."

An elegant brow arched disbelievingly. "Really? Then why is she here?"

Seth smiled unpleasantly. "To prevent you from having an opportunity to accuse me of anything else unsavory."

"Ahh." Velvet smiled as if she liked the idea that she had her ex-husband over a barrel.

"What exactly are you going to Paris for?"

"That's none of your business anymore, Seth."

"Really? Considering that you've opened every detail of my life to scrutiny with your charges, it seems only fair that you should face the same scrutiny."

She wrinkled her nose. "Let's forget that little unpleasantness, shall we? I've decided to drop it."

"I'd like that in writing."

She shrugged. "I'll tell my attorney."

"Good. I won't ask why you're having this change of heart, especially since we have a return flight to catch. So, if you could get the children, I'd appreciate it."

"Lou is getting them right now. They'll be here in just a minute."

"Thank you."

"You'll bring them home in two weeks."

"Sure."

"I've made arrangements for them to be out of school that long but no longer. You'll find one of their cases contains all the schoolwork they need to do. See that it gets done."

"Of course."

She nodded. "Well, you don't need me for anything more."

She turned to leave, but Seth stopped her. "You'll phone the children, won't you?"

She shrugged. "Perhaps."

His face suddenly became hard. "There is no perhaps about it, Velvet. They're young and they're going to miss you. So call. Pick a time each day and call to talk to them for a couple of minutes."

She sighed, as if it were a huge imposition. "Say four o'clock in the afternoon your time."

"That'll be fine."

Then, without so much as a good-bye, she left the room.

"Bitch," Seth muttered under his breath.

Kelly agreed with him, but didn't want to say so for fear of being overheard. Five minutes later, two young children looking as alike as peas in a pod appeared in the doorway, followed by the maid who had opened the door. She was carrying their suitcases.

"Daddy!" shrieked the girl, and threw herself into the air, landing in her father's welcoming arms. The boy was a little shyer, approaching more cautiously but coming to rest finally against his father's powerful leg, clinging tightly while Seth's hand caressed his head and shoulder.

For a long time Seth just stood there with his eyes closed, holding his children close. Kelly felt her throat aching, and finally she had to look away and blink rapidly.

Then he broke the silence, smiling broadly and speaking cheerfully. "So, are you two ready to go to Florida and see tigers?"

"They don't have tigers in Florida," the girl said, giggling.

"Actually, they do, sweetheart. We're going to stay with a lady who has two big tigers and you'll get to see them."

Talk of tigers animated the boy and carried the conversation all the way out to the limousine, where the children settled, as expected in the back-facing seats. Then their excited conversation revolved around the limousine. They were only a few minutes from the airport when the children settled down enough to become interested in Kelly.

Seth introduced her to them, and them to her, and explained to Johnny and Jenny that they were going to be staying with Kelly's grandmother.

"You're too old to have a grandmother," Johnny said.

She had to laugh. "No, I'm not. And you're going to meet her."

Jenny had a more pressing question. "Mommy said Daddy was staying with a movie star. Are you a movie star?"

"No, but my grandmother is."

"Really? With real diamonds and everything?"

"With everything," Seth assured her, his dark eyes twinkling.

"All of it," Kelly agreed. Then she sat back and watched the children talk eagerly with their father, chatter that didn't end until nearly two hours later when the two happy children fell asleep on the plane.

"The children," Bea said later that evening to her own children, "are a definite hindrance."

"Yes, they are," sighed Mavis. "I don't see how Kelly could possibly get romantic with Seth when the children are always around."

"We have to come up with a new plan. The financial thing didn't work. I gather Kelly figured that out almost as soon as she got here."

"Then she's probably figured out what we're up to," Max said. "She's always been extraordinarily bright."

"Ah, but not about people," Bea said. "Regard-

less, we got her home and that's what we most
wanted to do. Now we have to figure out how to
keep her."

"I don't know about you all," Zee said, "but she
doesn't seem to me to be in any hurry to leave now
that's she's here. Why not just leave well enough
alone?"

"Because," said Bea, "I want great-grandchildren
and my time is running out. Jules's children show
no sign of *ever* marrying."

Jules snorted. "You know, Mother, I can't think
of a worse reason for Kelly to marry and have children."

"I didn't say she should do it to please me. But
I'd be delighted if it happened."

"Just leave well enough alone."

"My dear Jules, I have never in my life left well
enough alone. If I had, I wouldn't be where I am
now."

"I'm not so sure that would be a bad thing."

Bea clucked at him. "You're getting far too big
for your britches, boy."

"Really? The scale says I haven't gained an ounce
in twenty years."

"No," Mavis said acidly. "It's just rearranged itself."

Bea sighed, wondering why God had taxed her
with four squabbling children. She couldn't recall
ever having done anything *that* bad. "Enough," she
said in her sternest mother voice. "We need to
come up with a new plan."

The others knew better than to argue with her,
but all of their faces reflected reluctance.

"Sure, why not?" said Max finally. "What's the
worst that could happen? We could alienate her
permanently and not see her again for the next
twenty years."

Bea frowned at him. "Why have you always been such a pessimist?"

"I'm an artist, Mother. We're given to drink and despair."

"Well, you need to practice some optimism, and I suggest you start right this minute."

"Yes, Mother."

Satisfied she'd had the last word, Bea began to spin her plan.

Chapter 13

Seth looked at Kelly. His two children slept on the other side of him, curled up in their seats. They were getting close to some of the late afternoon thunderstorms that were a regular occurrence in Florida, and the plane ride was becoming bumpier. He noticed that she was gripping the arms of her seat until her knuckles were white. He half expected that the turbulence would wake the children, but they slept on undisturbed.

"Not much longer now," he said.

"No." The pilot had just announced that they had passed Jacksonville. Or maybe it was Gainesville. She didn't know; she hadn't been paying attention to anything except the dark clouds outside the window.

"I'm sure we're flying around the storm," he assured her.

She nodded. Looking past him out the window, she could see the late sun highlighting the cumulus clouds in shades of gold. An otherworldly landscape, it would have been breathtakingly beautiful if the plane hadn't been bouncing and dropping in sickening lurches.

"Don't you like to fly?"

She fixed her eyes on him. "I like it just fine. What I don't like is turbulence."

"Need an airsick bag?"

"I'm not going to lose my lunch. However, I might scream."

He lifted his hand from his lap and covered hers with it. Her fingers maintained their grip on the armrest.

"I hate it, too," he admitted.

"Don't patronize me."

"I'm not. Even with all the flying I did when I was in the NFL, I still hate it. I hate the turbulence. I hate knowing the ground is thirty thousand feet below. Did I ever tell you I'm terrified of heights?"

She turned her head so she could see him better. "Really?"

"Honest to God." He shrugged. "Great hero material, huh? That's why I never take the window seat, and why I almost never look out the window."

"I didn't think you were afraid of anything."

"Why? Because I was willing to bash heads and bodies with a bunch of guys who were as big or bigger than I am?"

"But you weren't afraid of the tiger the night before last, either."

"Wanna bet?" He gave her a crooked smile. "I just did what I felt I had to. That's a long way from not being afraid."

Which gave her something to think about.

"So anyway," he continued, "I'm as much of a coward as the next guy."

Just then, the plane lurched and took a drop long enough that Kelly's stomach had time to climb into her throat, and someone on the plane let out a small shriek. The aircraft steadied, but by then her hand had turned over and now clung to Seth's as if it were a lifeline.

"Planes fly through this weather all the time," he told her.

"I know. That's what I keep telling myself."

"Me, too." They exchanged a look, and for the first time Kelly felt that they had a genuine meeting of minds. In that look, so much was exchanged, from wry humor to sympathy and understanding.

Seth looked away first, glancing at his kids. "I don't understand how they can sleep through this."

"I'm glad they're not awake."

"Yeah."

The plane lurched again.

"It's getting worse," Kelly remarked.

"Uh-huh. So let's think about something else. What do you suppose Zee wants us to help her rescue?"

"I have no idea. When we rescued the tigers, I was fourteen, and she wouldn't tell me what we were doing, except that she was going to buy a pet. So we arrived at this breeder's place near Sebring and she handed me a camera and told me to take pictures of everything like some kind of ditzy tourist. Then we went in, talked to the breeder, and went out to look at the cubs. God, it was awful. He had the cats penned in these tiny cages, living in their own excrement—but we weren't supposed to see those animals, just the two cubs he wanted us to look at. They were in a clean pen up front, but Zee kept motioning me to wander off, so I did, and took a whole bunch of pictures. By then I kinda figured out what she was up to."

"Were you scared?"

"A little. I figured the guy was going to get really mad at us, and I remember thinking that Zee ought to do her own dirty work. Except that I felt so bad for all those tigers. Then I found the liger pen."

"Liger?"

"Crossbred tigers and lions."

"Why in the world would anybody do that?"

Kelly shook her head. "I don't get it, either. Apparently there's a huge market for exotic pets. People with too much money who want something different to impress their friends with, I guess. And Zee says a lot of these animals are raised for private game reserves, where people can hunt them. Most of them are so inbred they're not healthy, and even a zoo wouldn't take them. So, most of the animals we found that day had to be put down."

His jaw tightened and his mouth compressed into a hard line. "Go, Zee," he said quietly.

"I thought so, too. Anyway, the guy found me taking pictures of the ligers, and he pitched a fit and grabbed my camera away. So I started babbling about how I really wanted one of the ligers because they were so cute and Zee told me we weren't going to do business with any man who would steal my camera and treat me that way. He calmed down and we bought Nikki and Alex, and left with them. And Zee turned over all her pictures to the authorities. They had the guy shut down in less than a week."

"Good!"

"It was awful." Kelly shuddered. "I had nightmares about it afterwards. Those poor animals. Nikki and Alex were only about ten weeks old at the time, and they were so sick. Full of parasites, and their paws were a mess from standing in their own filth. They were malnourished, too thin . . . Anyway, Zee and I nursed them back to health, but it took a few months. If Zee hadn't wanted to keep them, they'd probably have been put down, too."

"Well, I'm glad she did. They're beautiful animals."

"They are." The plane lurched again, reminding her they still weren't out of the storm. She gripped his hand harder.

"What other animals have you guys rescued?"

Kelly took a deep breath and willed her stomach to settle down. "They've mostly been common breeds. Zee busted a puppy mill one time in pretty much the same way. She's rescued pelicans that were tangled in fishing line—which was how I got pecked. Man, those birds are big and strong. She rescued an alligator once from a pond in a subdivision. The folks who lived there got permission to have the gator killed because it was eating their dogs, so Zee went out there with a couple of her friends and caught the darn thing. Only Granny wouldn't hear of having it on the island, so Zee took it up into Pasco County and let it go in an isolated lake. I suppose it's still living there."

"She didn't take you on that rescue?"

"Heck, no." Kelly shook her head. "I wouldn't have been any help at all. You need someone who's experienced in dealing with an alligator to do that."

"Well, I hope she isn't wanting to rescue any gators when we get back."

"No. It's probably another puppy mill, or something like that."

"That I can handle." The plane jolted again and he sighed. "But I don't know about this turbulence. What got Zelda off on this animal rescue thing?"

"She worked in a circus for a while as a lion tamer."

"Really?" He raised an eyebrow. "I thought only men did that."

"Don't be an MCP."

"I take it that means male chauvinist pig?"

"Brilliant deduction, Watson."

"I'm not an MCP."

"Yeah? What about playing pro football? No women allowed."

"There used to be a female in pro football."

"Yeah, right."

"I kid you not. Her husband was a placekicker. You know, the guy who kicks the ball for field goals and extra points, and usually the kickoffs? They'd always worked as a team. She held the ball for him in practice. Anyway, these placekickers are squirrely. Everything has to be just so, from what kind of shoe they wear—or don't wear—to how the ball is held. I'm not sure exactly how it came about, but the team picked her up as a holder, and put her in uniform and on payroll. And every time this guy went onto the field to kick the ball, his wife was there to hold it for him."

Kelly was fascinated by the story, but not yet ready to give up. "So, she got to hold the ball. Big deal. What if she wanted to play a regular position?"

"Sure. If she's fast enough, big enough, and strong enough. Be realistic, Kelly. Would any woman weighing one-twenty *really* want to tackle or be tackled by some guy who weighs three-forty and is as fast as a competition sprinter? Would she stand a chance? But I've got no problem with it if *she* weighs three-forty, stands six feet, and can squat eight hundred pounds, just like all the rest of the team."

He had a point. "I'm sure there must be women like that."

"Me, too. But as far as I know, they haven't tried out for a team. That might just be because they aren't being encouraged to go out for JV football.

Or it might be because they don't want to do it. Look, when they have that punt, pass, and kick competition for kids every year, they have a girl's section as well as a boy's section. It's not that the NFL is dead set against women; it's that the women qualified to play pro just haven't turned up."

"They sure aren't being encouraged to. Admit it."

"But it could happen," Seth said. "Why not? Look at Warrick Dunn. He's, what . . . five-eight, one-eighty? That's not out of reach for a woman. If she could move like him, I'd want her on my team any day."

"Okay," she said. "You're not an MCP."

"I'm relieved to hear it. The way that standard keeps moving, you never know."

"It does not keep moving. What a *male* thing to say!"

He shrugged. "I've found that the position of the bar depends on the woman who's setting it. And every woman seems to have a different idea of when a man has crossed it."

"Poor baby."

He grinned. "Yup. Life is tough for us meat-heads."

"Oh, will you please just stop it?"

Another lurch and drop kept him from answering. After a moment, he reached into the seat pocket in front of him and pulled out two airsick bags. He passed one to Kelly. "Have a barf bag on me."

"Be still my beating heart."

"I knew that would grab you. I'm a generous kind of guy."

"Who sets the bar on that one?"

"Me, of course."

"Naturally." Kelly closed her eyes, hoping the lurching would bother her less, and found herself thinking about Seth. She realized, turbulence aside, that she was really enjoying this trip with him. She *liked* sitting next to him, liked being so close to him. Even liked their little rounds of verbal sparring.

The attraction that she'd felt from the very start was growing, and it scared her. She might have gone a long way in building her self-confidence these last eight years, but she wasn't sure it was strong enough to handle coming in second best yet again. And compared to a woman who looked like Velvet Ralston, she could never be anything but second best.

She knew that, and accepted it. So why did her heart insist on aching?

When they got back to the villa with the children, the sun was setting in a blaze of red tropical glory. Seth introduced the children to the family before taking them to the guest house with him, and instead found that his kids were being abducted.

"They'll stay here tonight," Bea announced firmly.

"But Bea . . . look, I haven't seen my kids in nearly six months."

"I understand that. But you promised to help Zee, and she needs your help *tonight*."

"It can wait."

"No, it can't," said Zee. "It really *can't*. An animal could die."

Seth raked his hand through his hair and looked down at his children. "I can't leave them."

"It's only for a couple of hours," Bea said. "Look. We'll all have dinner together, then you can play with the children until their bedtime. Once they fall asleep, you can help Zee. You'll be back in a couple of hours, and you can stay here with them or you can take them back to the guest house—although I really don't think you should wake them once they're asleep."

Seth squatted in front of Johnny and Jenny. "What do you think about that?"

Jenny spoke. "You promised to help with the animals, Daddy. You have to keep your promise." Johnny seconded her.

"You won't mind?"

They shook their heads.

They went in to dinner. Cook had outdone herself for some reason known only to herself, and had provided a child-winning meal of homemade pizza and soft drinks. Lawrence, looking better than he had yesterday, served the meal flawlessly.

By the time they were done with a dessert of chocolate pudding, the kids were no longer shy, but were talking like little magpies to all the adults.

After dinner, a junior version of Clue was brought out. Seth and Kelly played with the children, with much cheering and joking from the rest of the family.

When Seth took the children upstairs to put them to bed in one of the guest rooms, Kelly remained with her family, sitting in the lamplight, listening to the perpetual breeze whisper outside the open windows.

How many evenings of her childhood had been spent just like this, with one or more of her relatives playing games with her, or reading her a story? Nearly every one, except when Bea was entertaining, and then Lawrence had filled in.

As a solitary child in a house full of adults, she could have expected to spend a great deal of time alone, occupying herself. Instead she had had a family full of playmates. Her family had been unstinting with their time. Uncle Jules had crawled around in the dirt with her playing with cars and trucks. Uncle Max had always been ready to have a tea party with her. Aunt Mavis had never refused to play with Barbie dolls, and Granny Bea had spent countless hours with her using the Easy Bake Oven to make little cookies and cakes. They'd played Chutes 'n Ladders and Candyland with her until they must have wanted to scream. They'd taught her old maid, and eventually hearts and rummy. They'd played checkers and dominoes and Parcheesi for hours. At one point, much to Granny's horror, Max and Jules had even taught her several variants of poker.

They might have turned her over to a television set or a nanny, but they never had. They had loved their little ugly duckling.

So what, she wondered now, was her problem? The fact that she'd never been talented enough? Had one of them ever said a word about that? No, never. But she had believed they must have felt it. She had been anomalous in the family. How could they not have felt it?

But maybe the pressure she had felt, the pressure to perform above average in some way, hadn't been applied by them. Maybe she had applied it to herself.

The thought disturbed her, unsettled her view of her life, and left her feeling dismayed. Could she really have been so far off base?

Seth returned more than an hour later, looking sad and thoughtful.

"Are they okay?" Kelly asked.

"Sure." He shrugged. "Bathed, read to, and sound asleep. It's going to kill me to give them back."

She didn't know what to say to that, except, "I'm sorry."

"Me, too." He shoved his hands into his pockets, looking as if this were a subject he couldn't bear to contemplate any longer. "Okay, Zee, what do you need?"

"I need you to get some boots on. These animals are living in their own shit. You, too, Kelly. I have a pair you can use if you need them."

"What exactly are we rescuing?" Seth asked.

"You'll see soon enough."

Kelly knew they were in trouble as soon as she saw the big trailer truck. Seth had driven them into Tampa in the van, to the house of a friend of Zee's. There, the friend turned over the keys.

"I need it back by ten in the morning," he said.

"You'll have it. This shouldn't take too long."

Kelly stood looking at the trailer and truck, taking in the garish logo of a small family circus. "What do we need this for, Zee? What are we rescuing? A whole herd of cows?"

"You'll see soon enough," Zee said again.

"Why is this guy lending you this truck? I thought you said circuses mistreat animals."

"Some do, some don't. This one doesn't. This one doesn't even have any animal acts except for dogs. Hank decided a long time ago that circus life was unnatural for most animals."

Seth lifted his brows. "Interesting. You wouldn't have had anything to do with that, would you, Zee?"

"I wouldn't know."

"Well, I've never driven a trailer truck."

"Me neither," Kelly said.

"*I* have," Zee announced. "Climb aboard. Time's a-wasting."

Zee walked around to the driver's side of the truck, leaving Seth and Kelly to look at one another.

"I don't know about this," Kelly said.

"She's *your* aunt. You know more about what we're getting into than *I* do."

"Which is to say exactly nothing." She sighed.

"Well, I could tackle her and refuse to let her go until she gives us some answers."

"Men. You always think in terms of violence."

"Women. You get so fussy about little things."

"That could well be. Maybe we don't see any fun in hurting other people."

"Really? Tell that to Velvet. And while I'm on the subject, this had better not be anything illegal we're doing. Getting my butt thrown in jail is hardly going to help my custody case."

"Zee's never done anything illegal that I know of."

"Why does that feel like such small consolation?" He reached up and opened the truck door. "Climb up."

The cab was roomy enough for the three of them, with Kelly in the middle. Zee switched the engine on, and the loud rumble filled the night. A few minutes later, they were barreling down I-4 toward Orlando.

"I've got a bad feeling about this," Seth murmured in Kelly's ear.

"It's a little late for that." But now that they were driving this truck down the highway, it began to worry her, too, that there might be more to this than Zee's usual animal rescue. It was night and they were driving a huge truck. This was a far cry from going out to take some pictures and buying a couple of tigers.

Forty minutes later they were off the interstate

and heading up a county road. It was nearly midnight now, and traffic was almost nonexistent.

Kelly spoke. "Zee?"

"Yeah?"

"Isn't it kind of late at night to be doing business?"

"It's exactly the right time of night."

Kelly looked at Seth. In the dim light from the dashboard, his eyes were unreadable.

He spoke. "We're not doing anything illegal, are we?"

"Hell, no," Zee said. "I'm paying for the animals."

Kelly suddenly realized that she could breathe easier. It was only then that she knew some corner of her mind had been wondering if Zee was planning to steal some animals.

Seth must have had the same thought, or must have read her mind, because he reached out unexpectedly and took Kelly's hand in his. Then he spoke. "We won't do anything illegal, Zee. You might as well know that right now."

"I told you, I'm paying for them."

Kelly, amazingly awash in comfort from Seth's touch, squeezed his hand back. Too bad he was probably no more reliable than the rest of his species, she thought. But she didn't want to think that way right now. Right now she wanted to pretend that he was going to hold her hand forever.

He adjusted his hold on her hand, and sent tingles of pleasure running up her arm by the simple expedient of gently caressing her palm with his thumb. All of a sudden, she couldn't think of anything except how good it felt to have him touch her, and how much she'd like his thumb to make caressing circles like that on her breasts. Between her legs. Meltdown.

Zee hit the brakes, slowing the truck down, then turned onto a rutted side road. "Almost there," she announced, oblivious of the fact that the atmosphere beside her was thickening with something dark and hot.

Jolted, Kelly pulled her hand out of Seth's. She thought she heard him sigh.

A half mile later, they pulled up in front of a frame house set amid live oaks. Zee stopped the truck and set the brake. "Just a minute," she said, and grabbed an envelope from the visor. She got out, and climbed the front porch steps to stick the envelope in the crack between the door and frame.

Then Zee climbed back in again and they jolted farther down the rough road.

"This feels almost like the plane ride earlier," Seth remarked.

"Are you getting sick?" Kelly asked.

Before he could answer, Zee said, "Hey, don't puke in here. Frank'll never forgive me."

"I'm fine," Seth said. "Just fine. Where the hell are we going?"

"Right up here a bit, just past those trees."

When they passed the trees, Kelly saw a small corral. In it were two dark shapes, one huge, the other considerably smaller. There was no moon, though, and until the headlights caught the shapes, she wasn't sure what they were.

"Elephants?" she asked as she recognized them. "*Elephants*?"

"Yup. A mom and her two-month-old baby."

"Zee, what in the world are you going to do with them?"

"Find a home for them. A home where they won't be living in their own shit. This jerk *never* cleans up after them, and the corral is way too small. And the baby's looking thinner all the time. I think the mother's so depressed she isn't feeding him anymore."

"We're not stealing them, are we?"

"I told you, I bought them."

"Why does this guy have them?"

"He had some stupid idea about opening a wild-life park. He never got any further than the elephants. Couldn't get zoning or something, I don't know. Anyway, these two are slated to be sent to one of those safari hunting things."

Kelly felt her heart turn over. She loved elephants, and couldn't imagine anyone wanting to kill one. She also couldn't imagine anyone treating them the way Zee said these two were being treated. Her resolve stiffened. "Let's go."

Seth nodded and threw open the door. An instant later he swore, and Kelly felt her stomach heave.

"What is that stink?" Seth asked.

"I forgot how bad elephant poop smells," Kelly remarked, covering her nose and mouth with her hand. "God."

"You practically need a gas mask," Seth said.

"Didn't have time to get any," Zee said. "We have to get these babies out of here tonight or they'll be shipped to the hunting preserve tomorrow."

Kelly should have realized right then that something was wrong with the picture Zee was painting, but the foul odor of elephant excrement was fogging her brain, and all she could think of was those poor elephants having to live with this all the time. Apparently Seth felt the same, because he said not another word, simply climbed out of the truck and helped Kelly down.

Zee joined them and took a minute to pull on

waders over her shoes. Kelly began to wish she had something better than the rain boots Zee had lent her. As for Seth, he apparently hadn't any boots with him at all and was wearing regular street shoes.

"What now, Zee?" Seth asked. "Just how do you persuade an elephant to climb on a truck?"

"Shouldn't be hard."

Kelly hoped Zee was right.

They could see the elephants clearly now, and neither one of them seemed particularly happy to see human beings. They moved to the far side of the corral, watching suspiciously, the little baby sticking close to his mother's side.

"What we do," Zee said, "is try to get the mother to come out. Christ, will you look at that? They haven't even got anything to eat!"

"Well," said Seth, "I guess this means we walk through elephant dung."

"Maybe not. Let's see what happens when I open the gate."

The gate, unfortunately, was chained closed and locked.

"Damn," Zee said, "I should have brought a hacksaw."

This began to penetrate Kelly's odor-fogged brain. "Zee, if you're buying the elephants, how come you need to hack off the chain?"

Seth spoke. "I was afraid you were going to ask that. There are some things I don't want to know."

Kelly looked at him. "Chicken."

"Absolutely. There are times when ignorance is bliss, and right now I'm staying resolutely ignorant."

"I paid for them," Zee said. "Fair market value. The guy's out of town tonight."

"Hmm," said Seth, looking at Kelly.

"Hmm," she said back.

"Well, what's it going to be?" Zee demanded. "Are you going to help or turn tail?"

Seth and Kelly looked at the animals in their tiny corral, and at the foot-deep carpet of hardened elephant excrement.

"Oh, hell," said Kelly, "I can't leave them like this."

"Me neither," said Seth. "And I know a good attorney." Then he reached out, examined the chain, and with one mighty jerk of his hands, broke it. He tossed it away and brushed his palms on his pants. "Let's go."

Zee opened the gate and motioned them to stand back. The mother elephant watched, her head swaying from side to side a little as if she were measuring the situation. Then, lifting her trunk, she seemed to taste the air.

A moment later she began a hesitant lumber toward the open gate. The baby followed.

Zee began to croon. "That's a good girl. Come to mama, sweetie. We'll get you out of this hellhole."

But at the gate, the mother elephant balked. She wasn't very trusting, and Kelly could certainly understand why. Zee went back to the truck and returned with a six-foot-long wooden pole, which she handed to Seth.

"Just go behind her and pat her gently with this on the rear."

"You're kidding, right? You want me to stand at the business end of that animal?"

"Stand to the side. You just need to tap her gently."

He rolled his eyes, but did as she bade. Then Zee told Kelly to move to the other side of the gate. "You stand over here so she won't walk that way.

We want her to move toward the back of the truck."

"Sure. Uh, Zee? You haven't opened up the truck yet."

"Agh! Seth, wait. Don't do anything until I get the truck open."

"Do you need help with that? I'm willing to do anything that will get me out of this elephant doo-doo. By the way, Zee, some of this stuff is *fresh*."

"Naturally." She ran around to the back of the truck. Moments later there was a clang and a thud as the doors opened, followed by something that sounded like rattling chains. A minute later she was back.

"Okay, let's do it."

Seth tapped the big elephant gently. She didn't move, simply turned her head to get a look at him. "I don't think she likes this, Zee."

"They never do. But give her another nudge anyway."

So he tapped her again, just a little harder this time. This time the elephant moved, walking out of the corral with the baby on its heels. One look at Kelly was enough to make the elephant head the other direction—very flattering, she thought.

Zee was waiting at the end of the truck. Kelly had no idea how she was going to persuade the animal to walk into that dark, confining space. She tagged along to watch the miracle, and realized Seth was right beside her.

Zee walked up to the big elephant, which was watching her warily, and began to pet the animal's trunk. Mamma elephant seemed to like her touch, and after a few minutes wrapped her trunk gently around Zee.

"Good girl," Zee said approvingly. Then she tugged gently on the trunk and guided the animal

up the ramp and into the truck. The baby followed
instinctively.

Seth looked at Kelly. "You *do* realize she could
have done that from the outset. *She* could have
walked into the corral and made friends with them,
instead of asking *me* to go in there with that stick."

"Well, of course," Kelly said. "Zee's not stupid.
She didn't want to step in the dung."

"Obviously. However, *she* had the waders."

"You'll recover." Kelly chuckled.

"Hey, don't overwhelm me with sympathy."

"There," said Zee, reemerging from the maw of
the trailer. "That was easy. Now let's get out of
here."

Five minutes later they were on their way with
two elephants. They had to keep the windows of
the truck open, though. Whatever Seth had stepped
in when he went into the corral hadn't come off
when he wiped his shoes on the grass.

Finally he told Zee to pull over at the next rest
stop. When she did so, he climbed out and threw
his shoes in the nearest trash can.

"Much better," he said when he climbed back
into the cab.

"So, Zee," Kelly asked when they were once
again on the highway, "how many years can we
get for stealing two elephants?"

"I bought them," she said again. "And you won't
get any years if you just remember that fact."

Kelly looked at Seth, and he looked at her. "I was
afraid of that," he said.

Kelly nodded. "My family. Aren't they wonderful?"

"They do take the cake. I wonder if the judge
will believe that I didn't know what was going on."

"Sure he will. You only have three brain cells,
remember? Too many concussions."

"Ahh, good point. And you'll testify to that fact for me, right?"

"Any day of the week."

"I knew I could count on you."

Chapter 14

When they got back to the villa it was shortly after two in the morning. Zelda simply unloaded the elephants into the yard.

"Um, Zee, they're going to make a mess of the gardens," Kelly pointed out.

"So? We can always have it fixed later. I sure can't put them in with the tigers. Not the baby, at any rate."

The elephants, apparently deciding in an instant that they liked their new environment, began grazing on the shrubbery.

"God, Bea is going to be mad."

Zelda apparently didn't much care.

"What if they wander off the island?" Seth asked. "They swim, don't they? Or they could cross the bridge."

"They won't cross it if I close the gate. Come on, let's shovel the shit off the truck and hose it down so I can take it back to Frank."

Elephants apparently had very busy bowels, Kelly thought as they climbed into the truck and began to shovel the mounds out of the back end. Bea was not only not going to dislike having her garden dined on; she was also definitely not going to like these steaming, stinking piles of dung.

An hour later, the truck was clean and Zelda drove off, leaving Seth and Kelly standing in the yard with two munching elephants.

"Well," Kelly said, "I guess there's nothing to do now except go to bed."

"Yeah," he said, but didn't move.

She was feeling enervated, she realized. The soft, moist air of the Florida night seemed to caress her skin, and her limbs felt heavy and warm.

"Well," he said presently, "that was an adrenaline rush. I kept waiting for some guy with a shotgun to show up. Or some cop to stop us."

"You, too?" She'd tried not to think of it, but all the way home part of her had been expecting to see flashing lights in the mirrors. "But Zee *did* pay for them. I'm sure that's what was in the envelope she left on the door."

"I wonder if that mitigates the situation any. Oh, hell, I'm not going to worry about it tonight. I need a shower. I stink. If I stay here much longer, that elephant is going to think I'm one of her babies."

They went inside and climbed the stairs together. At Kelly's door, they paused.

Seth looked down at her, his eyes unreadable even in the warm golden glow of the hallway lights. "You know," he said slowly, "this was fun. I haven't done anything so outrageous since I was a kid."

"I'm not sure I *ever* did anything this outrageous."

A smile curved his mouth, then he bent and kissed her lightly on the lips. Her response was electric, but before she could do any more than register it, he had straightened and was moving away.

"Maybe," he said, "you ought to be be outrageous more often." Then he disappeared into the children's bedroom.

For a minute or so, Kelly couldn't even move. She remained rooted to the spot, hoping against hope that Seth would come back out. But he didn't, and finally she went into her own room, trying to ignore the disappointment that was making her ache.

She took a shower, well aware that it would probably wake her up even more, but there was no way she could avoid it. The smell of the elephants clung to her, and she wasn't going to climb into bed stinking like that.

The shower did leave her wide awake, and what was more, she realized she was hungry. She argued with herself for a few seconds, then decided to just go downstairs and get a glass of milk and a few crackers.

The house was quiet except for the sound of the breeze through the open windows. Padding downstairs wearing nothing but a terrycloth bathrobe, Kelly found herself remembering how she had done this as a child, particularly during her teen years. And how Cook had never once said a thing about the missing ice cream, cake, or cookies.

Odd, she thought, how her childhood was gradually taking on a different color since she'd come home. Maybe all her confusion and poor self-esteem had been a bad lens through which she had received a fractured view of life with her family. And maybe now that she was feeling better about herself and her abilities, she was able to see more clearly.

Or maybe time had simply made her nostalgic.

She found a quart of chocolate Häagen-Dazs in the freezer and sat at the island with it, eating it right out of the carton. Since leaving home she had refused to do this, except for a couple of times when she had broken up with a boyfriend—usually after only a few dates—and had over-dramatized the whole thing. Then she had eaten the ice cream defiantly. Tonight she was eating it sadly, reaching for memories that seemed to slip right out of her grasp.

And Seth. She didn't want to think about him, didn't want to think about the fact that she was craving him even more than the ice cream. Her sexual attraction to him was strong, but more than that, she was coming to like him, coming to feel that he could be a trusted friend if she just let him. And all of this mess, and all of her doubts, seemed to be combining in her mind into a devil may care, what-the-hell mood that made her want to have an affair with him.

She'd never done anything that harebrained in her life, and she wasn't about to start being stupid now. But that didn't keep her from fantasizing a fling with him as she sat there eating. Just a fling, a safe little night or two that she could remember fondly when she escaped back to Colorado. No emotional upheaval. No broken heart. Just a fun fling.

Not that she was genuinely capable of such a thing—her hormones and her heart seemed to run pretty close together—but it didn't hurt to fantasize herself as one of those people who could have sex for the sheer joy of it and emerged unscathed. It was just fantasy, after all.

A fantasy fueled by memories of how his hard body had felt against hers when he had kissed her in this very kitchen the other night. Mmm, he had certainly felt good against her, and her palms still remembered the strength of his muscles as she had caressed them. As for the strength of her attraction—well, if she could have forgotten she was rolling in mud that other time they had kissed, it was some strong attraction.

And the ice cream wasn't cooling her ardor one bit. Instead, she was growing increasingly aware of the way her robe brushed her skin each time she moved. And with that awareness, a heaviness was growing between her thighs that made her clamp them tightly together.

She would never get to sleep tonight.

She was almost done with the ice cream, and was wondering what other comfort food she might be able to find, when a whisper of sound drew her attention to the doorway. Only the stove light was on, and Seth stood in shadow.

"I can't sleep, either," he said, his voice hushed.

She was suddenly aware that her hand was freezing from holding the carton. She put it down quickly. "I think there's more ice cream, if you want."

He didn't answer as he walked into the room. He didn't say a word as he came to stand beside her, looking down at her.

"You know why I can't sleep?" he asked.

"You're worrying about the elephants?"

He shook his head. "I keep thinking about *you*."

Her heart skipped a beat, and the air suddenly seemed thick. "Me?" Her voice cracked on the word.

"You. And you want to know why I'm thinking about you?"

She managed a nod, never taking her gaze from his face.

"So do I."

That wasn't what she had wanted to hear, and for an instant the fog of desire that was clouding her brain lightened just a little.

Then he said, "Tell me I'm crazy."

Speaking was difficult, but she managed, "You're crazy."

"Good." He backed up, working his way around the island until it was between them. But adding three feet to the distance between them didn't seem to lessen the thickening of the air. "I know I'm crazy."

"Why?"

"Because I'm coming off a bad marriage, and the last thing on earth I want to do is get involved with a woman. Especially a woman who hasn't come home in eight years."

The words should have hurt, but somehow she was past feeling any hurt. Maybe because he was saving them both with his reservations. She nodded. "Very wise."

"I think so." He reached for the carton and her spoon, and ate a mouthful of melting chocolate ice cream. "I always try to do the right thing. Sometimes that's cold comfort, but I try anyway."

"Yeah. Do you ever get sick of it?"

"Of trying to do the right thing? Sure. Who doesn't?"

Kelly nodded, feeling wistful and irritated all at once. "I sure do. I feel as if I've spent my entire life trying to be perfect. The really irritating thing is that the harder I try, the less perfect I seem to become."

He nodded and ate another spoonful of ice cream. "So . . . what's the real story with your family, Kelly? I've watched you with them, and I can see you don't hate them. But you seem to . . . shrink when you're around them."

She sighed and looked down at her hands, realizing that she didn't feel quite so reluctant to discuss her problem with him anymore. "It's not their fault," she said finally. "It's mine."

"How so?"

"I could never measure up."

He put the spoon down and pushed the carton to one side. "Funny, but from where I sit, it's obvious that they dote on you. They wouldn't change a hair on your head."

"Maybe not. But *I* would. Maybe you can't understand, because you're a famous football player and you managed to do something really spectacular with your life. But I was never spectacular, not in any way. They tried to teach me to paint, to dance, to sing, to play an instrument... and I couldn't do it. I was born without a lick of talent."

"Well, we'll leave the issue of talent for later. For now I'll accept your assumption."

She rolled her eyes at him. "Trust me, I *know* better than anyone that I haven't got any talent. Not even a little bit."

"So they were disappointed?"

She shook her head. "No, *I* was disappointed. They encouraged me, and I kept letting them down. I felt like an utter failure."

"They sure don't describe you that way."

"Maybe not." She shrugged a shoulder. "It didn't matter what *they* thought, only what I felt."

"I can see that." His hand moved on the countertop, as if he wanted to reach out to her, but then it stilled.

"Anyway, to fall back on a fairy-tale analogy, I felt like the ugly duckling in a family of swans. I guess I still do to some extent."

"That had to have been hard on you."

"Funny, isn't it, how we make our own problems? I sure made mine. I kept hoping that somehow, some way, I'd suddenly blossom with a talent. That I'd be a prodigy like the rest of them. But I never did. And I started to feel more and more like a failure. So I overcompensated."

"How?"

"I started running the house. Silly, but I felt I had to make myself feel indispensable in *some* way. In retrospect, I'm surprised they let me do it. I was so young, and they'd have been justified in saying so. But they let me take over. Before long, I was running the house, controlling the budget, handling all their appointments. They let me take over wherever I chose to."

"Maybe they understood why you needed to."

She thought about that for a minute, then nodded slowly. "Maybe so. They seem to have been getting along all right without me since then. And they managed to get along before I stepped in. Anyway, I managed to make myself feel indispensable."

"Did it help?"

She shook her head. "I started to resent it. Not so much because it was a lot of work, but because it was a lot of stress trying not to mess up. I worried all the time."

His tone was infinitely gentle. "That had to be tough."

"Oh, it was. It was too much for a child to be responsible for, but I dug my own grave, as they say. And I wouldn't back down or back off, because that would have been another failure. Finally, I kind of blew a gasket. I figured out that I couldn't keep on that way, that I needed to find another way to validate myself. So I took off, spent a couple of years working for a new media company, then started my own business. And I've been successful."

"That's a good thing."

"That depends." She looked at him, meeting his gaze sadly. "I'm beginning to realize that cutting off half of yourself is a high price to pay for anything. And that's what I did. I cut my family off. Oh, not entirely. I kept in touch, calling every week and so on, but I distanced them. I thought they threatened me."

He nodded slowly. "How do you feel about that now?"

"That I was crazy. And very, very wrong. The only person who's ever threatened me has been me. And now I'm a failure again."

"Aren't you being a little harsh?"

"I doubt it. Like you said, why should you trust a woman who abandoned her family for eight years? It's pretty ugly, when you think about it. My biggest failure."

He didn't say anything for a while, just drummed his fingers absently while he thought. She watched him, half expecting him to condemn her foolishness, half wishing he would because it would confirm her own sense of iniquity.

But he surprised her. "Maybe you just needed to be away long enough to develop your own strength. You've got to be strong to deal with this family. They'll run over anybody who gets in their way. Not intentionally, but they're awfully single-minded. I can see how they would be overwhelming for a child."

"But it was more than that."

"No, I don't think it was. I think you needed a base of confidence from which to deal with them. You tried running their affairs for them, but it was too much. So you found another way. The question is, have you succeeded?"

It was Kelly's turn to think about it. "No," she

said eventually, "I guess not. Because all I feel right now is guilt."

"For what? They're adults. They can take care of themselves. Maybe you should have come home a few times to visit, but you're doing that now, aren't you?"

"I still feel guilty. They didn't do anything wrong, Seth. If anything, they bent over backwards for me. It's not their fault that they're such strong, successful personalities that I couldn't handle it."

He got up and filled a couple of glasses with ice water, then gave one to Kelly. "I don't know about you, but ice cream always makes me thirsty."

"Thanks."

He remained near her, leaning his hip against the edge of the counter. "I read somewhere that children of famous parents often have psychological problems. Growing up under a parent's shadow is evidently debilitating."

"God. I hate the idea that I fit a psychological profile."

He laughed softly and reached out to touch her cheek with a fingertip. "It ought to be reassuring. There isn't anything wrong with *you*; the situation is just too much for a child to handle."

"How come you know so much about it?"

"I don't, really. But I'll let you in on my deep, dark secret: I'm actually in the process of finishing my doctoral dissertation. In psychology."

That set her back on her heels. "So . . . um . . . your brain isn't Jell-O?"

"Not yet." Laughter sparked in his eyes.

"What are you going to do with the degree?"

"I want to work as a counselor with troubled children."

"I guess you're starting with me." That stung.

"I'm not counseling you. In fact, I'm making a

concerted effort to do nothing of the kind. I'm just trying to be a friend."

He couldn't have said anything more calculated to get behind her defenses—because she'd never had a friend who'd known the truth about her past. With her friends in Colorado, she'd always acted as if she had no real family to speak of. It had been easier—and safer—than trying to explain. But having someone who knew about her ugliness and didn't turn away was more affirming than she would have believed possible.

"Anyway, even though I'm just acting as a friend, I can't totally forget what I've studied and read. Kids with famous or extremely successful parents often turn out mixed up. You're actually probably less mixed up than most, which is remarkable because you didn't have to deal with just one highly talented parent, but an entire family of successful talent. Basically, I'm telling you that you're not weird, and you're not an ugly duckling, either."

She felt her throat tighten painfully, and she had to look away. "I feel ugly."

"But you're not. You're an ordinary mortal who had the misfortune to be born to a family of demigods. It's hardly surprising you feel dull by comparison. But in fact, you're quite bright and talented yourself in comparison to other normal people. Look at what you've managed to do: Not every woman of thirty can say she owns her own successful business."

"Maybe." But she wasn't quite ready to consider herself in that light. Truth be told, she still felt lacking because her name wasn't on a marquee somewhere.

"You're not ugly at all, Kelly," he said again, his

tone gentle. "Maybe a little prickly, but definitely not ugly."

She gave a choked laugh. "Here I was hoping I'd turn into a swan one of these days, and you're telling me I'm a cactus."

"Have you ever seen a cactus flower? When a cactus blooms, there's nothing prettier in the world."

She looked at him then, which proved to be a big mistake. Something inside her leaped, as if it wanted to jump right out of her chest and into his arms.

"I'm crazy," he said.

"So am I."

"I don't want to hurt you."

"Me neither."

"So we're agreed on that?"

She nodded, her heart hammering.

"Good." But he didn't back away. "I'm, um, in the mood for a fling. With you."

She nodded again, finding speech impossible. A fling couldn't hurt, she told herself. Not if she understood the rules from the outset. She was an old hand at protecting her heart.

What she didn't realize, or refused to realize, was that her defenses were already down.

"So . . . like . . . tell me to get lost?" he suggested.

But she couldn't make herself do that. Her body was heavy with yearning, and her breath was locked in her throat, and for the first time in her life she felt a hope and anticipation almost too painful to bear. And she felt so fragile that she was sure the merest breath would shatter her into a thousand pieces.

The feeling had come over her so quickly that it swamped her before she could fight it or run. She was past considering consequences, driven by a

fear that she would never know what she most
needed to know: what it was like to be loved by
Seth Ralston.

"I guess," he said thickly, "you're not going to
be my conscience. And mine seems to have
died . . ."

His voice trailed off and he reached for her, lifting her off the stool and into his powerful arms,
making her feel as light as feather down.

"Last chance," he said.

She didn't want the last chance. She threw her
arms around his neck and gave in to the absolutely
indescribably wonderful feeling of being held by
him. Deep inside, she felt that if he ever let go of
her she was going to die.

He carried her out of the kitchen, down the hall,
and through the foyer. She felt as if she were floating on air, and was vaguely surprised how safe a
man's strength could make her feel.

Then they reached the stairs.

"Um, Kelly?"

"Hmm?"

"I'd really like to carry you up the stairs, but I
can't trust my knee. If I fell . . ."

Reluctantly, she nodded against his shoulder,
and wanted to cry out with disappointment as he
lowered her feet to the floor. The touch of hard
wood beneath her was too real, and for a moment
she felt her resolve flutter.

But then he was behind her, holding her hips in
his large hands, urging her up the stairs. She could
feel his chest against her back with every step, and
somehow reality drifted away again, consigned to
that painful place she was determined not to visit
again this night.

At the top of the stairs, he lifted her into his arms
again, as if he were afraid she might vanish. The

movement surprised a little laugh out of her.

"Shh," he said in a stage whisper. "Someone might hear."

"I don't care."

"I do. I don't want Bea to decide I'm a bad influence on you."

She smothered another laugh in her hand. "Bea's been a far worse influence than you could ever be."

He grinned. "Wanna bet?"

"How much?"

"Mmm . . . if I win you get to undress me, and vice versa."

Something deep inside her clenched deliciously. She'd never imagined a guy talking so openly about what they were about to do. Her experience had been limited to, "Hey, babe, want some action?"

"Well?" he asked, pushing the door of her bedroom open.

"Okay," she agreed.

He put her gently on the bed and kissed her long and hard before straightening. "Wait, I've got a better idea. I'll be right back."

He was only gone for three minutes, but three minutes were long enough to give her a brief bout of sanity. Maybe he had intended to give her an opportunity to rethink this, away from his intoxicating presence. But even as her mind tried to rustle up all the reasons she shouldn't do this, her heart was saying something else.

She needed this, and some part of her knew it was more than the sex that she needed. She was feeling so bruised that she needed to be wanted. Really wanted. By someone who wasn't part of her family. She needed some proof that someone found her attractive.

Then, before she could really sort her thoughts

or completely lose the glow he'd awakened in her, he was back. With a can of whipped cream.

He sat beside her and wiggled his eyebrows. "This is even better. I win, you lick whipped cream off me. You win, I lick whipped cream off you."

Her cheeks flamed until they felt hot, and a helpless giggle escaped her. "You're shameless!"

"That's the only way to be. So what were we betting about?"

"Whether you're a worse influence on me than Bea."

"That's right."

Reaching out, he pulled the neck of her robe open a little and sprayed a small dot of whipped cream just above the curve of her breast. Bending, he licked it off, sending shimmering shivers of delight through her. "There," he said, his dark eyes bright with laughter. "That's worse."

She shook her head slowly, feeling that she was going to love this game. "No way. Bea gave me my first sip of bourbon at seven."

"Seven?" He arched an eyebrow. "Really? You're kidding."

"Nope, I'm serious."

"How come?"

"I wanted to know what it tasted like."

"What did you think?"

"It was awful. I still don't like the stuff."

"So that wasn't bad; she cured you of a taste for bourbon. You've got to do better than that."

Tugging her collar down a little farther, he put another dollop of whipped cream on her, this one just an inch above her nipple.

"Come on," he said. "Worse than I'm about to do."

"What *are* you about to do?"

"This." He followed the word with the action,

licking the sweet stuff off her skin, and unleashing another cascade of sheer delight in her. "See," he said, lifting his head just enough to look into her eyes. "I'm seducing you."

She was breathless and found it difficult to speak. "You're damn good at it."

"I think so." He spritzed her again from the can, this time right on her hardening nipple. "Now, for this one, you've really got to convince me that Bea was *bad*."

"Well, she let me use swear words at home when I was little. She thought it was funny."

"A mere peccadillo. All kids know those words and say them, even if their parents have a fit." Bending, he took the whipped cream into his mouth and her nipple along with it.

Kelly drew a quick, ragged breath as quivers of delight shot through her. Some part of her wanted to resist, fearing the moments of utter vulnerability that lay just ahead, but that part was a small voice, silenced by the rising drumbeat of passion.

None of her other lovers—not that she'd had many—had been so playful, and Seth's playfulness was unlocking her inhibitions in ways she'd never dreamed possible. Instead of being uptight and nervous, she was sinking fully into the experience he was giving her.

She was gasping when he at last lifted his head and surveyed his handiwork. "Mm, strawberries and cream. So . . . you've got to have something worse to report about Bea than her laughing when you swore."

Kelly's mind was so fogged over that she could scarcely think, but she tried, because she didn't want this game to end. "Umm . . . she let me stay home from school just because I didn't want to go."

"You win," he said, standing up abruptly. He

tossed the whipped cream aside, then threw his clothes and shoes after it. "Major transgression. She let you break the law."

A laugh tried to bubble up from somewhere within Kelly, but it didn't quite make it, because she could scarcely breathe. Nor did she ever want to breathe again. Seth Ralston was a gorgeous man, and he looked even better with his clothes off. He no longer looked disproportionately large or heavy because of his huge shoulders and thick neck. He just looked powerful—powerful enough to take the weight of the whole world on his shoulders.

Then he was beside her, tugging her robe open and slipping his arms around her inside it, so they met skin to skin, head to toe.

Nothing had ever felt so good.

"I wanted you to win," he confessed, a sparkle in his dark eyes. "And the sooner, the better."

But she'd already forgotten their game. In her mind there was one thought, and one thought only: to loop her arms around his neck and bring him even closer.

He seemed to agree with her. He hugged her tighter and rolled her gently over until he was lying atop her, between her legs. She could feel his weight, and more, she could feel the hardness of him, a flattering promise of things to come.

He gently caught her face between his hands and looked straight into her eyes. "You're not ugly," he said. "You're beautiful in every way. Beautiful enough to make me lose my head."

That was the last coherent word to pass their lips. Seth seemed to swallow her in his touches and kisses, covering every inch of her with flaming sensation. She came alive for him in a way she had never come alive for anyone, discovering places in herself that were uncharted territory.

She writhed and moaned, and reached for him with a hunger that was almost painful.

When he lifted himself at last and plunged into her, she felt utterly complete for the first time in her life.

A long time later, in the sweaty, glowing aftermath, she lay in his arms and whispered, "You win."

"Hmm?" He sounded sleepy and content.

"You win. You're a worse influence than Bea."

"Then you owe me."

"Yup."

And together they fell into deep slumber.

Chapter 15 🌀

Seth was gone when Kelly awoke in the morning. Disappointment surged through her, then she saw the note on the bedside table: *Didn't want the kids to wake in a strange place alone. XXXOOO*

It was a perfectly good reason, but it struck her as an excuse anyway, and she buried her face in the pillow and tried not to cry. She should have known better. Men only wanted one thing, then they headed for the hills.

But then she remembered their conversation last night. She had agreed to a fling. He had offered nothing more than that, and had given her plenty of opportunity to say no. There was no one to blame for feeling bruised this morning except herself.

Feeling that she'd been drowning in self-pity for entirely too many years, she rose, washed, and dressed for the day. Denial was a useful thing, and she planned to take full advantage of it today. She was going to pretend the entire thing had never happened. It had been an aberration, a moment of madness, and she was going to bury it six feet deep before it caused her any more trouble.

There was no breakfast waiting in the dining

room, so she wandered into the kitchen. Cook was there, sitting at the island, reading the morning paper.

The woman looked up with a suspiciously self-satisfied expression. "Breakfast is on the back veranda this morning, Miss."

"Oh, thanks." Kelly turned and headed that way, wondering why the break with tradition. Then she remembered. The elephants. Cook had done this to get Zee in trouble before the day got too old. It was revenge, pure and simple.

Kelly made it to the back porch just in time to hear Bea cry, "My garden! Oh, my poor garden!"

Seth, Johnny, and Jenny were sitting at the wrought-iron table, eating their breakfasts. Johnny and Jenny were giggling, and trying to stifle it by putting their hands over their mouths. They were evidently enjoying the sight of two elephants trampling the roses and eating the leaves off the magnolias. Kelly was careful to avoid looking at Seth because she was sure she'd either blush or have a palpitation if she did.

Bea collapsed into a chair with thump. "Oh, my poor garden," she said.

Kelly sat beside her and took her hand. "The elephants were slated to be sent to a hunting preserve this morning, Granny."

"I'd shoot them myself, but I don't have a gun."

Both children's eyes grew huge, and Kelly hastened to assure them, "She wouldn't do that."

Bea looked at her. "I wouldn't?"

"No, of course you wouldn't, and you know it. The garden can be repaired."

Bea covered her eyes with her hand. "And *someone* is going to get them out of my garden before this day is over."

"Besides," said Seth, "elephant manure is a great

fertilizer. It won't be long before your garden is more beautiful than ever."

Bea parted her fingers just enough to glare at Seth. "Don't you dare be amused by this."

"Just trying to give it a positive spin, Bea."

Bea dropped her hands and stared at the elephants. "I don't believe this."

"It is rather strange," Seth agreed. "Not what one usually expects in one's garden."

"Unless one lives with Zee," Bea said tartly. "I always suspected I was making a mistake by not spanking my children."

Jenny's eyes grew huge. "Are you going to spank Aunt Zee, Granny?"

"No, dear. But I may yell at her a little bit."

"That's okay."

"I'm glad you think so. My word, not one but *two* elephants. A *baby* elephant."

Kelly spoke. "We couldn't let them be sent to a hunting preserve, Granny."

She sighed. "No, of course you couldn't. I quite understand that. What I *don't* understand is why she couldn't find some more appropriate place to take them. Now not only is my garden trashed, but the children have nowhere to play. They certainly can't be out there where they might get stepped on. Or where they might step *in* something." She sniffed. "Oh, the odor is terrible! How can they live with themselves?"

"The elephants don't seem to mind it at all," Seth remarked. "Frankly, I'd like to have a gas mask."

"Look," said Bea, "the tigers have even disappeared. They're usually hovering at the edge of the woods waiting for food at this time of day."

Max emerged from the house at that moment, and looked from the group at the table to the elephants grazing in the garden. "Uh-oh," he said.

Bea merely sighed again.

"Well," Max continued, "I guess there *is* a reason that Blaise Corrigan is at the front door looking for Zee."

Bea pressed her hand to her brow. "This is too much."

"Where *is* Zee, anyway?" Max asked.

Seth answered. "She went to get the vet. She wants him to verify that the elephants were mistreated."

"Oh." Max took another look at the elephants. "Maybe it's my imagination, but they look as happy right now as pigs in—well, you know." He shrugged. "Okay, I'll tell Blaise to come back later."

"Maybe I should go talk to him," Seth offered.

Kelly felt her heart climb into her throat. No way, not when he was in the midst of a custody battle for his two adorable children. "Are you crazy?" she demanded. "You don't know anything about this. *I'll* talk to Blaise."

"Wait a minute," Bea interrupted. "Maybe it's time Zee dealt with her own messes. Max, ask Blaise if he wants to come in for some coffee while he waits. And you two," she added with a glare at both Seth and Kelly, "just shut your mouths. This is Zee's problem."

A minute later, Max returned with Blaise, who greeted them all politely. When Bea asked him to sit and join them for breakfast, he took a chair readily enough, but waved away the offer of anything except coffee. "Thanks, but I already had breakfast."

Then he looked at the two elephants. "Those animals wouldn't happen to have appeared in your garden overnight, would they?"

"How did you guess?" Bea asked him. "I've been

staring at them, wondering what in the world I'm going to do with them."

Kelly looked at Seth, who laid his finger across his lips warningly. She got the message. Bea would probably deal with this better than either of them, simply because she hadn't been involved in the heist.

Heist. Oh, God, what had she gotten into last night?

"Well, that's real interesting," Blaise said as he sipped his coffee. "I got word two elephants were stolen last night over in east Hillsborough."

"Really? Now, why do you suppose somebody would steal elephants and leave them here?"

Blaise arched a disbelieving eyebrow, but said only, "So Zee's gone to get the vet?"

"Yes. When she found these poor dears here this morning, she immediately recognized that they'd been mistreated."

"Personally," said Seth, "I think Bea's being very magnanimous about this. Those animals have torn up her garden, but she's still concerned about their welfare."

Bea glared at Seth, and Kelly choked down a laugh.

"Very magnanimous," Blaise agreed. "So how do you know they were mistreated?"

Kelly opened her mouth to tell him about the pen they'd been kept in, but Seth gave her an almost imperceptible warning shake of his head and she bit her lip.

"Well," said Bea, "you'll really have to ask my daughter. She's the one who knows all about animals. But that baby looks awfully thin to me. What do you think?"

Blaise looked out at the animals. "I don't know,"

he said. "Maybe a baby elephant is supposed to have all that saggy skin."

Kelly spoke. "I've never see one that thin in a zoo."

Mama elephant chose this moment to uproot a shrub, bringing a soft moan from Bea. Then the baby decided to nurse, and Bea grew thoughtful.

Max, who'd been silent as he drank his coffee and ate his breakfast, now spoke. "It's too thin," he said flatly. "No baby in the world has skin that hangs in folds like that. Unless you want to count a shar-pei."

"That's true," Kelly agreed.

"Well, I'll wait to hear what the vet has to say," Blaise decided. "But that might do more good for Zee in front of a jury than it's going to do her right now."

"Jury!" Bea sounded horrified, but something about her expression was ever so slightly false. Kelly had a feeling her grandmother was seriously annoyed with Zee over this.

Come to think of it, Kelly was annoyed, too. Not because Zee had rescued the animals, and not because Zee had asked for her help, but because Zee had dragged Seth into it, and Seth couldn't afford trouble of any kind right now. Not with his children in the balance.

They didn't have long to wait. Before Blaise had finished his coffee, Zee plowed through the back door with the vet in her wake. When she saw Blaise, she drew up short.

"What are you doing here?" she demanded.

"You left your calling card at a house in west Hillsborough last night. At the moment you're a wanted woman."

"Hell," Zee said in disgust. "I *paid* for the animals."

The vet, an attractive man named Mike Halloran, looked uneasy. "These animals are stolen?"

"They are *not*," Zee said firmly. "I *paid* for them. With a cashier's check."

Blaise spoke. "You'd have done better to pay with cash. It couldn't have been traced."

"Precisely," Zee said with disgust. "And Junior Roscoe would have taken the cash, hidden it, and claimed the elephants were stolen. So I provided proof that I paid for them."

"Unfortunately," said Blaise, "you didn't have Roscoe's agreement to the sale. You're still on the hook."

"I won't be, after a jury hears my story."

"Maybe not."

"She won't be," Kelly said hotly. "You wouldn't believe how that man was keeping those animals."

Blaise's thoughtful gaze settled on her. "What do you know about it? Come to think of it, they believe there had to be more than one person involved to get those animals on a truck."

"Nobody was involved but me," Zee said hotly. "Don't be getting any crazy ideas, Blaise. I can move a couple of elephants without any trouble."

"Maybe." But he was looking thoughtfully at Kelly.

Seth then put his foot in it. "Kelly didn't do anything, Chief. *I* helped Zee."

"Actually," said Max, "*I* was the one who helped her. Seth's just trying to protect me."

"Nobody helped me," Zee said. "I took some witnesses along so they could testify to the conditions, that was all. And it doesn't matter anyway, because I paid Junior Roscoe exactly the amount of money he was going to get from that hunting preserve."

Blaise stiffened. "Hunting preserve?"

"Yes, hunting preserve," Zee spat. "He was sending those poor animals off to be hunted down by rich yuppies looking for an artificial thrill."

Blaise nodded thoughtfully. "Do you have any proof of that?"

"I've got letters from Roscoe. I wrote a ton of letters trying to stop this, and he wrote back."

"I'd like to take a look at them. After the vet looks at the elephants."

Mike Halloran, who'd been waiting patiently, said, "So it's okay for me to touch them? It won't make me part of this band of desperadoes?"

The corners of Blaise's mouth quirked upward. "No. Somebody needs to check them out."

"Okay." Mike was down and off the porch in a shot, walking up to the elephants with the confidence of someone who wasn't at all intimidated by several tons of nervous animal or the mounds of manure that were growing among the shrubbery.

"My poor garden," Bea said. "Oh, well, it's for a good cause. And you may as well know, Blaise, that I was the one who helped Zee. Nobody else was involved."

Kelly had a feeling that her grandmother was seeing herself as Sharon Stone on death row.

"Great," said Blaise. "Nobody else was involved. That's fine by me. Having Zee involved is quite enough."

Bea grimaced at Zee. "It certainly is," she told Blaise.

Kelly rose and went to join Mike as he looked over the animals. "That baby's too thin, isn't it?"

"Way too thin," he agreed. "From the looks of it, I'd guess he'd have been dead in another week or so. But look at the backs of mom's legs." He pointed out an assortment of scars, some barely healed. "Somebody's been jabbing her hard. And look at her flank here. More scars. This animal is not only underweight, it's been seriously mistreated."

Back on the porch, he gave Blaise his report. "Serious abuse," he said flatly. "The mother is about fifteen hundred pounds underweight. It's a wonder she's making any milk for the baby—and she probably isn't making enough, which is why he's so thin. There's also evidence of beating and prodding with a sharp instrument, some of it recent—maybe within the last week."

Blaise nodded slowly, then set his cup down and rose. "Okay. I'm not taking you in, Zee, but don't go anywhere. Doctor, you give me that report in writing. Time to do a little horse trading."

Mike gave instructions to Zee for caring for the elephants. Then he said he'd be back in two days, as planned, to look at the tigers. He and Blaise departed together.

"What did Blaise mean, horse trading?" Zee asked.

"Oh," said Seth, "I think he's going to suggest to Junior Roscoe that if he doesn't drop the charges against you, he might find himself charged with criminal animal abuse."

Zee sat down, looking smug, and reached for a cruller. "That's what I figured would happen all along."

Bea frowned at her. "Don't get too full of yourself, dear. You're not off the hook yet. And you're going to pay for having my garden fixed."

"Yes, Mother."

Not that it mattered, Kelly thought. They all used the same bank account. She supposed it was the principle of the thing—or just Bea making her point in the most dramatic way possible.

Right then, Manuel came around the corner of

the house, stood looking, then said flatly, "I'm *not* cleaning that up. I may do windows, but I don't do elephant poop." Having announced his position, he returned the way he had come.

"I have to feed the tigers," Zee announced. "And then I have to go get some hay for the elephants."

Bea turned to look straight at her. "You're not *keeping* them."

"No, of course not. Only until I can make suitable arrangements for them."

The back door opened and Lawrence stepped out onto the porch carrying a fresh pot of coffee. "Oh, God," he said, staring at the elephants. "It's the DTs."

He turned quickly and hurried back into the house, with Bea hot on his trail saying, "Lawrence . . . Lawrence, you're not seeing things. There really *are* elephants in the garden."

Shaking his head, Max rose to follow. Seth and Kelly were left alone on the veranda, with no one to overhear them except the animals and the children. Kelly turned to Seth. "You shouldn't have said you were involved."

"Hell, I wasn't going to let *you* take the rap for it."

"But . . ." She looked significantly at the children, who had run to the far end of the veranda and were standing at the railing talking to the elephants. "You have more important things to consider, Seth."

He nodded. "They're important, all right, but I've never refused to accept the consequences of my actions. It would be a terrible example to set."

Then he flashed an unexpected grin. "Besides, they think I'm a hero for saving the elephants. And what's the worst that could happen? A fine and a slap on the wrist. That's a small price to pay for being a hero."

"We're talking grand larceny here."

"No, we're not. Zee told us she'd paid for them. And she did. Nope, the worst we're in for is a laughing attack from a judge."

"I hope you're right."

He astonished her by reaching over and taking her hand. "About last night . . . you were wonderful, Kelly. The stuff of my dreams."

She blushed a bright red and looked at the kids, who seemed totally absorbed in the elephants and were far enough away that they couldn't hear. "You weren't too bad yourself," she admitted.

"Ah, grudging praise. I guess I'll just have to try harder next time."

His frankness embarrassed her even more, and her cheeks felt as hot as burning coals. She couldn't even speak. And it was no help at all when Seth just laughed.

Men, she thought, could be such barbarians.

Two days later, Kelly sat on the warm sand in a puddle of sunlight, watching Seth and his children play at the water's edge. They hadn't made love since that one night. In fact, she got the feeling Seth was avoiding the possibility as much as she was, and she couldn't blame him. What had happened between them was incendiary, and someone could get hurt.

But she was warming to him anyway, and not just because they'd made such spectacular love.

She was warming to him because he took such unstinting care of his children. Because he related to them so well, and so obviously loved them with his whole heart. She felt herself growing warm and gooey just watching them, found herself wishing she could be part of the magic circle that included the three of them.

As her girlfriends at home would have said, Seth was a prime catch. A domesticated male who loved his children. Not at all what she had expected.

As he sat helping them build a sand castle, he was patient, encouraging, and cheerful. The happy sparkle was in his eyes all the time now, whether his kids were climbing all over him like a jungle gym, or sleeping soundly in their beds.

And she had never in her life felt more like an outsider.

It wasn't that they didn't include her. The kids liked her and she liked them whole bunches, but she wasn't one of them. Seth included her in everything they did, but she knew why: because he was afraid to give Velvet an opening to come after him again. It wasn't because he wanted her to be part of that magic circle. He'd made it very clear that he was never going to marry again.

Which was just as well. She had her own life, and didn't really want to disrupt it for a man and his two kids. Besides, she didn't trust men. They were users, as Seth was proving right now, however good his intentions. He was *using* her.

Which was fine, as far as it went. She was agreeing to it. She was even enjoying it, despite the uneasy pressure at the back of her mind reminding her she had a customer deadline to meet and ought to be spending more time at the computer.

But enjoying it or not, she had never in her life felt as *alone* as she did right now.

A sigh escaped her, and she started drawing absently in the sand with her forefinger.

"Miss Kelly! Miss Kelly!" Johnny came running toward her, his short legs stirring up little geysers of sand. "Come see our castle!" He had to pause to hitch up his bathing trunks, then burst again into a run.

Smiling, Kelly rose and walked toward him. When they met, he reached up to take her hand and tug her toward the water's edge.

"It's a pretty good castle," Seth called to her. The sun was bringing out gold and red highlights in his dark hair, and his skin had turned a nutty brown. Kelly's own paleness was transforming into a golden glow that she rather liked.

"Wow, that's beautiful," she said sincerely when she reached the castle.

"Daddy showed me how to make the towers," Johnny said, and proceeded to explain in excruciating detail about the soda cans and the Sno-Kone cup.

"I made these," Jenny said, pointing to the crenellations and turrets.

"They're wonderful." She sat cross-legged beside the castle and looked at the three of them. "You did a fantastic job. I've never seen a better sand castle."

At the children's insistence, she added a tower of her own, and found a great deal of pleasure in playing in the sand like a child. For the first time, it struck her that in her pursuit of success, in her determination to prove to her family that she *wasn't* a failure, she had sacrificed an awful lot of life's pleasures.

Seth layered more sunscreen on the children, then they ate the lunch of sandwiches and orange juice they'd packed along for their beach picnic. Afterward, the children played a little longer, but their energy began to flag.

"Nap time," Seth announced, and they began the walk back to the house. Johnny tucked his hand in Kelly's, the way he was beginning to do more often. Each time he did it, her heart melted.

They arrived in the backyard just in time to see the veterinarian sedating the tigers with a dart shot out of a gun. Johnny and Jenny became immediately upset, sure that the tigers were being killed.

Seth scooped them both up in his powerful arms and hastened to reassure them. "They're just being put to sleep for a little while—like taking a nap. No one's going to hurt them."

The kids watched doubtfully as first Alex, then Nikki, collapsed to the ground. After a minute, Zelda opened the gate and walked in, bending to touch each of the cats.

"Out cold," she told Mike Halloran. "Seth, if you want to bring the children in, they can touch the tigers and see they're just sleeping."

Seth hesitated, and Kelly couldn't blame him. Even though she didn't fear the tigers as much as most people did, she never quite believed the tigers were as fully asleep as Zee seemed to think.

"Do you want to touch the tigers, kids?"

Hesitantly, both children nodded.

Seth carried them into the enclosure and squatted, letting them each stand on their own feet. Only Kelly noticed how he winced.

"They're sleeping," Zee said, squatting on the far side of Nikki from the two children. "See?" She reached out and ran her hand along Nikki's flank, then stuck her finger into his lolling mouth. "Having pleasant dreams."

Jenny was the first to step forward and tentatively touch Nikki. Johnny followed a moment later. "Why did you have to shoot him?" he asked.

"Well," Zee said, "tigers don't like to get shots any more than you do. But since their claws are so sharp, and they're so strong, we can't get close enough to give them a shot. Because they won't listen if we tell them to hold still and be good."

Johnny nodded. "Mommy says I have to be good, and I am."

"I'm sure you are. But you can't tell that to a tiger."

Johnny nodded, understanding. "Why do they have to have shots?"

"So I can make sure they're okay," said Mike, joining them. "I'm a tiger doctor, and I have to give them a checkup and make sure they have all their shots and things. I can't do that when they're awake." He squatted next to Zee and began his examination.

"See, I check their teeth, just like a dentist." Pulling back Nikki's lip, he revealed the astonishingly large, gleaming teeth. "Sometimes they need a cleaning. Not this time, though, not for Nikki."

"Good," said Jenny. "I *hate* tooth cleanings."

"So do Nikki and Alex," Zee remarked. "They're big babies."

That made the kids laugh, and took away the last of their fear. They watched the vet with great interest, and seemed almost hypnotized by the way it felt to pet the huge cats. Jenny even lay down beside Alex and put her ear to the tiger's chest, listening to the heartbeat.

Kelly slipped into her old role of helping Zee keep the tigers' heads elevated while they slept, and she rediscovered the ineffable awe of holding a huge cat's head in her lap while she stroked its fur.

Looking up, she caught Zee's eyes on her. "You really need to work with the cats again, Kelly," her aunt said. "You always had a way with them. And you love them."

"I've got other things I need to do, Aunt Zee."

"I'm not saying you should become a circus performer. Just that you ought to work with them a little."

She was saved from answering by the children's interest in the circus. Twenty minutes later, when the vet finished his examination, they all left the enclosure while he administered the antidote to the tigers. They started stirring almost immediately, and he followed the others out. Zee locked the gate behind him.

"You know," Kelly found herself musing, "it's such a shame that we can't get closer to them."

"*You* could," Zee said.

It was odd, she thought, how much she yearned for that contact. Odd, when she thought about it, how much yearning she'd been feeling since she came home—a place she had never wanted to be again.

"I'll think about it," she said to Zee.

"Good. You can help me give them their bottles later."

Nikki rolled over onto his stomach and lifted his head, looking groggily around. A moment later, Alex did the same thing. They shook their heads as if confused, and tried to rise, but their legs gave out. The kids giggled.

Nikki looked at them, as if offended by their laughter, then began licking his forepaws as if that would help wake them up.

"They are so beautiful," Seth murmured.

Kelly looked at him, and saw him utterly enthralled. Which was something, because he'd been here for months and must have seen the tigers nearly every day. But still he was enthralled, just as she was. She liked that in him.

Mike, who had been waiting to make sure the tigers awoke without problems, picked up his kit. "Just let me know when you need me to sedate them so the carpenters can get to work on the kennel," he said to Zee. "Otherwise, they're fine—as healthy as any fifteen-year-old cats I've ever seen. Better than most."

Just then the two elephants, who still had the run of the garden, came lumbering around the corner of the house. "Any luck placing them?" Mike asked.

"There's a place in Texas that's interested. I'm waiting to hear."

"I hope wherever they go they have plenty of room and plenty of other elephants."

Seth bent and scooped up Johnny in one arm and Jenny in the other. "Come on, kids, nap time. Thank Aunt Zee for letting you pet the tigers."

Both children thanked her obediantly, then, utterly oblivious to the wonder of elephants walking through the garden, put their heads down on their father's shoulders.

"Johnny wants to know if you're coming, Kelly," Seth called back to her.

She went, thrilled that Johnny wanted her.

They put the children down in their beds, and Kelly sat on the edge of Johnny's cot while Seth sat on the edge of Jenny's and read a brief story to them.

Johnny always wanted Kelly to sit beside him as he fell asleep for his nap. She assumed it was because he wanted the comfort of a woman's presence while his mom was gone.

But whyever he did it, it always made her heart swell the way he would cling to her hand and demand a hug and kiss. And sometimes he would curl right into her, as if he needed the reassurance of her closeness.

She stroked his hair gently as he listened to Seth read, and when he looked up at her and gave her a wide, sleepy smile, something inside her softened and cracked, letting though a warm, wistful burst of love.

After the children fell asleep, Seth and Kelly tiptoed out of the room and went to the kitchen, where Seth poured them tall glasses of iced tea.

On impulse, Kelly asked, "Are you ever going to let me see any of your sculpture?"

He hesitated, then shrugged one shoulder. "I don't know. Do you really want to be put in the position of having to lie and say they're great? Or worse, be in the position of being unable to speak at all?"

She looked at him curiously. "Do you really think they're that bad?"

"I don't think they're that good."

Before she could marshal a response, Bea walked into the room. "There you are," she said. "I just wanted to tell you that we've decided to take the children to Busch Gardens. Since it's more than an hour from here, we'll take them into Tampa with us tonight and stay at a hotel, so they're fresh in the morning. I'll pick them up around seven, if that's all right." Without waiting for Seth's response, she walked out of the house.

"What was that?" Seth said. "I feel like I just got sideswiped."

"I think they're scheming again."

"Ahh!" He suddenly grinned. "Well, what do we do? Seize the time alone together, or put a spoke in their plan?"

Kelly really, really wanted to seize the time alone together. They hadn't had any at all since that one night. But she hesitated, knowing how dangerous it might be to her heart to spend so much time with Seth.

Of course, it might be equally dangerous to try

to put a spoke in her family's plan. They might come up with something worse than taking the children to an amusement park.

But Seth was having other thoughts, thoughts that wandered far away from the family's scheming. "I don't want to be away from the children that long," he admitted. "And I'd really like to be there to share it with them when they see Busch Gardens for the first time."

"And to keep Zee from taking them on the big roller coasters," Kelly added wryly, even as her heart seemed to plummet. Well, she knew her place, she thought. Second to the kids—and that was as it should be.

But it hurt anyway.

Chapter 16 ✑

Bea professed to be delighted that Seth and Kelly were joining them. She also insisted on paying for their rooms and their tickets to Busch Gardens.

She picked the airport Marriot, she said, because the children would get to see the planes arriving and taking off. Both Johnny and Jenny professed to find this a splendid idea.

Kelly wasn't sure it was a splendid idea after they checked in and she discovered that she and Seth had been given adjoining rooms. Much as she would have relished a repeat of their lovemaking, she knew it wouldn't be wise. Then Seth alleviated her worries by insisting that the children would stay with him and not with Granny.

"But I thought I'd give you a little break." Bea protested, waving her cigarette holder so emphatically that the unlit cigarette tumbled out of it and the children giggled. "Besides, I adore Johnny and Jenny."

"I adore them, too," Seth told her. "And I've missed them for six months. I only have two short weeks with them."

Bea frowned. This was clearly not part of her plan. Kelly watched with amused interest as her grandmother sorted through possible roles that would accomplish her end. Clearly Faye as Joan Crawford and Liz as Virginia Woolf wouldn't make it. Finally Bea settled on Katharine Hepburn.

"Have it your way, dahling," she said with that perfect upperclass brittleness, and just a hint of dampness in her eyes.

"Trust me, I will."

The issue settled, they sorted out the rooms, but not before Seth said, "Bea, you really should have invited Lawrence to join us."

"Well, of course I invited him. Why wouldn't I? But he said he had quite enough tigers and elephants at home."

Seth looked at Kelly. "He may have a point."

Johnny tugged his father's hand. "But there aren't any zebras at home. I want to see zebras."

"And that's exactly what we're going to do tomorrow," Seth promised him. "And we'll see a lot more, besides."

The evening was spent dining out and taking the children to watch the planes. But then it was nine-thirty, and the little ones were soundly asleep. Kelly sat in her room watching something—she hardly knew what—on television, amused that Granny hadn't even suggested the adults have some kind of party after the children went to bed. She couldn't make it any more obvious that she wanted Seth and Kelly to have time alone together.

Well, she'd plotted for nothing, Kelly thought. Seth was staying firmly on his side of the adjoining door, as if he didn't want his children even to guess that it could be opened. Most likely a wise move.

And she was crazy. Absolutely, positively, totally crazy. Why was she beating herself up with disappointment over something she had known all along she could never have? Why was she sitting here wishing Seth would open that door, knowing that if he did, she was only going to get herself into worse emotional trouble?

She needed to have her head examined.

Seth was watching his children sleep by the light of one dim lamp and the television set. He had a lot of reasons to pay attention to whatever program was on, and a lot of reasons to forget that only an unlocked door lay between him and Kelly. He knew it was unlocked, because he'd heard her do it.

One by one, he went through his reasons for not taking advantage of that fact. Number One: Velvet. Number Two: Velvet. Number Three . . . Oh, hell!

He had vowed he was never going to trust a woman again, never going to give a woman a chance to eviscerate him the way Velvet had. The divorce had hurt, and one of the hardest things he'd had to deal with, apart from nearly losing his children, was the obvious, plain-as-the-nose-on-his-face fact that Velvet had never loved him the way he had loved her.

He had felt gutted when she told him to leave. He had watched all his dreams and plans turn to ashes that left him nothing but a bitter aftertaste. And for a long time, all he could think of when a woman expressed interest in him was Velvet.

She had never loved him. He'd bet on that now. She had seen an opportunity to live a life of ease and bask in the glow of his perceived importance and fame. The very instant he had decided to step out of the limelight, she had been finished with him.

What was more, it had come at the worst possible time for him. He'd just lost the career he loved, was facing the possibility he might never be able to walk without a cane again, and she had tossed him out on his ear as if he were no more than a used tissue. She'd done what no sportscaster or sportswriter or coach had ever been able to do to him: She'd crushed his self-esteem and had left him feeling worthless and useless.

Was he ever going to give anyone the power to do that to him again? Not likely.

Over the past year, since they'd split, he'd put himself reasonably back together again. He no longer felt he was slime on the heel of life. The custody case had been an emotional setback, but it hadn't wounded his self-esteem.

He told himself that he would never regret marrying Velvet—how could he when those two beautiful children had come out his marriage?— but he didn't have to be stupid enough to set himself up for another round.

The funny thing was, though, the more he reminded himself how untrustworthy Kelly was, because of the way she had avoided her family for so long, the more inclined he was to trust her. Her warts were in plain view for all to see, and he honestly didn't think she had a pretense in her entire body—unlike Velvet, who had had little else.

At least you knew what the package contained with Kelly. On the other hand, he didn't know if he was up to dealing with her family issues. He might understand them, might even believe they were natural to a child who had grown up surrounded by a family that was exceptionally gifted, but he wasn't sure he could deal with it. Or that he wanted to—simply because he had so many issues of his own.

But all this thinking wasn't doing a damn thing to quell the ache in his groin every time he thought of her. Her lovemaking with him had been tentative and unsure, but it had also been utterly without artifice. And once she had decided to give herself, she had given herself wholly. She didn't seem to have much experience with men, but she more than made up for it with enthusiasm.

She had struck him as fresh, and he liked that freshness in her. That sense that it was all still too wonderful to be believed. Her reaction had made it all fresh for him, too.

And he'd utterly failed at his original intent, which was to taste the apple so he wouldn't keep wondering what it was like. So he could walk away from it. That didn't make him very proud of himself, but it had seemed to make sense at the time.

But all tasting Kelly had done was to hook him more. He was beginning to have a strong suspicion that she might be more like an addictive drug than an apple. He had to keep clear. His body might ache for her, but his head was in charge.

Yeah, right. He was honest enough with himself to know that sometimes his needs overwhelmed his sense. And like almost anyone else, when passion was on him he was a damn good rationalizer.

Then he heard a tentative knock on the adjoining door.

Kelly was hungry. Nothing on the dinner menu had looked very good to her, so she had ordered a salad. By ten o'clock she was ravenous and ordered a burger and fries.

Her late supper arrived twenty minutes later, on a tablecloth-covered cart. She pulled the chair up to it and reached for the ketchup bottle. Naturally, the bottle, being full, didn't want to give up its contents. Wondering why anyone in the world would use a glass bottle for ketchup anymore, she pounded on the bottom of it until her palm felt sore.

Then the ketchup decided to cooperate. In one great big blast, it shot out of the bottle—all over her denim shorts. Annoyed, she wiped as much of it off as she could with a napkin, then went to the bathroom to pull off and wash the shorts.

Only the shorts wouldn't come off. The zipper was stuck on the denim. No matter how hard she pulled and tugged, she couldn't get it to let go.

So she tried washing the ketchup off the shorts while wearing them, thinking if she could get them clean enough, she could sleep in them and find a way to deal with it in the morning—or just wear them to Busch Gardens and cut them off when she got home the next night. The idea didn't exactly appeal to her, but she couldn't see any alternative.

After repeated scrubbings with a washcloth, she still looked like an accident victim. Once again she tried to work the zipper loose, rubbing it with soap, but it still wouldn't budge. And no amount of contorting could get the shorts to slip down over her hips.

She was doomed.

Then she remembered Seth. He was right next door, and he was awfully strong, besides. He could probably work the zipper free.

She hesitated for a long time, reluctant to turn to him for help over something this stupid, then knocked tentatively on the door, hoping he wasn't asleep.

Seth ignored the first knock, telling himself that he could pretend to be asleep. At the second knock, though, he decided something must be wrong. Concerned, he went and opened his side of the adjoining door. Kelly stood there, with an odd expression on her face, her shorts soaked with blood.

"My God, what happened?"

"Shh," she said, "you'll wake the kids."

Kids? Why was she worrying about kids at a time like this. "You're bleeding!"

"It's just ketchup, okay?"

Ketchup? Ketchup. It took a second for his consternation to clear enough to allow him to understand what she was saying. Then relief made him stupid all over again. "Ketchup?" he repeated.

"Shh." Grabbing his hand, she tugged him through the door and closed it behind him. "Don't wake the kids. This is embarrassing."

He wondered if she was becoming as crazy as the rest of her family. "Embarrassing? Everybody spills ketchup sometimes."

"It's worse than that."

The drama in her tone warned him. He hesitated. "What's worse?" he asked finally. "I'm sure the hotel won't charge for cleaning the rug. They have to do that all the time."

She shook her head. "Worse yet."

He smothered a sigh. "Are we playing twenty questions again? Because if we are, I'm kinda tired, Kelly." Tired because he'd been spending entirely too much time at night thinking about her instead of sleeping. And irritated because the last thing on earth he wanted was to be close to her in a hotel room. Or maybe because it was the thing he wanted most on earth.

"My zipper," she said enigmatically.

"Oh. What about it?"

"It's stuck."

"Ah." He scanned her quickly, then felt his heart sink as he realized there was only one possible place she could be hiding a zipper. "Uh . . . not your shorts?"

She nodded.

"Oh."

"I've tried everything," she said in a burst of frustrated embarrassment. "Soap. Tugging. Trying to pull my shorts off without unzipping them. I'm stuck."

"Mmm." His sense of humor was waking up, and he had to struggle against letting a grin show. "That's . . . difficult."

"No shit," she said caustically, then sighed. "Sorry. I've been struggling for the last twenty minutes, my hamburger is cold, I can't get the shorts off, and I sure can't wear them tomorrow looking like this. Besides, I don't want to wear them to bed, either. They're wet."

They certainly were, he thought, looking down at them. "What do you want me to do?" He was playing dense, although he knew exactly what she wanted, because he was entertaining the unworthy suspicion that her zipper wasn't all that stuck.

"You're stronger than I am. I thought maybe you could pull it open. Or even rip it out."

"Ah."

"Seth, please. I'm so frustrated I could spit. Could you just help me instead of standing there sounding like a Freudian psychiatrist? Ah. Mm. Oh. Sheesh!"

His grin peeked out then despite his best efforts. "Just promise you won't use the torn shorts against me at my rape trial."

"Oh, please! Don't be a beast."

"So, let me see the damage."

She lifted the hem of her T-shirt and showed him. The zipper was stuck right at the top.

And he was suddenly, painfully reluctant to touch her. "Show me," he said again. "What's it caught on?"

She pulled the pants out a little and rolled the fabric over so he could see the metal teeth biting firmly into a thick wad of denim. "It'll ruin the shorts if I rip it. Those teeth are going to leave a hole."

"They're already ruined."

Tentatively, he reached out and grabbed the waistband of her shorts with one hand, and the zipper tab with the other. He tugged. Nothing budged.

"You're going to have to pull harder than that," she told him. "I can pull that hard. And I did."

"What I'm afraid of is that if I pull too hard and jerk it loose suddenly, the zipper might bite you "

"Oh." Now it was her turn to sound Freudian.

"Umm ... stick your hand down inside your pants behind the zipper. That way it won't grab you where you're most tender." He glanced up at her eyes. "As a male, I fully appreciate that threat."

"I bet you do." There was a sudden spark of laughter in her gaze. She stuck her hand in her shorts. "Go ahead."

He reached for the waistband again, but it was too tight to grab with her hand behind it. "Suck in your tummy."

"Cripes," she muttered. "All this and insults, too. I'm not supposed to have a tummy."

"You have a very nice tummy. Perfect just as it is. But it's in the way."

She inhaled, and this time he got a better grip on the zipper. He yanked.

Nothing happened.

It was his turn to swear.

"You have to pull harder," she said again.

"I know, I know. I just don't want to hurt you."

"Well, I can't stand here all night with my hand

in my *own* pants, and I can't wear these dang things tomorrow."

"Wait. You gave me an idea."

She lifted her head from her study of the zipper. "What's that? You have scissors?"

"No such luck. Go lie down on the bed. It'll help to get as much of you out of the way as possible."

She did as he directed, laying back with her feet on the floor.

"Now," he said, standing over her, "I'm going to stick my hands in your pants so I can really grab the waistband, okay?"

She nodded. Hell, she didn't look even a tiny bit reluctant. But *he* was. Sticking his hand in this woman's pants was tantamount to lighting a powder keg. Except that he just had to control himself, no matter what. He was certainly a big enough man to do that. *Maybe.*

Moving cautiously, he inserted his hand into her pants until he could get a good grip and at the same time keep the zipper away from her satiny skin. Satiny skin was all he could feel against the back of his hand, and the sensation was sending hot little sparkles running along his nerve endings.

He forced himself to focus on the problem at hand, not on the beautiful, tempting woman reclining so invitingly on her bed, and grabbed the zipper tab firmly.

"Ready?" he asked.

"Ready."

He yanked as hard as he could, but the zipper still didn't budge. He tried several more times with the same result, and the knuckle of his index finger was beginning to feel raw from sliding off the tab.

"Hell." He looked around. "Did they send a sharp knife with that burger?"

"Just a butter knife."

"Shoot." He looked down at her again, and realized that he was feeling a very strong desire to bury himself inside her. An almost overwhelming desire. And she was locked up in a denim chastity belt. Hah.

"Well," he said finally, "I guess I'll have to rip them." He didn't tell her that the idea was appealing to him more every second.

"Be my guest. I've got to get these damn things off."

So he reached down, grabbed the waistband on either side of the zipper, and yanked with every ounce of strength in his arms.

There was a series of pops as stitches ruptured and the zipper pulled away from the fabric. Success!

He stood there, holding the separated fabric and looking down at an expanse of creamy, smooth skin just above her white bikini panties. He should have closed his eyes or looked away. He knew that. But they were glued to her tummy.

"Thanks," she said.

He still didn't move.

"Uh, Seth? I need to take them off."

He obliged her, pulling them off in one swift movement that left her looking stunned. He tossed them toward the wastebasket without even looking.

She looked uneasily toward the shorts, which were hanging half in and half out of the basket. "Seth?" she said again.

"Yes."

Their eyes met. The world stilled. Then she said just one word. "Yes."

For an instant he didn't move, letting her response resound through him, into the farthest corners of his being. His gaze drank her in, and he felt a sense of wonder he hadn't experienced in a long, long time. What she was offering him seemed infinitely precious, as fragile as the stuff of dreams. He could hardly believe his good fortune.

She looked beautiful—and vulnerable. How long had it been since he'd been aware of that kind of vulnerability? He couldn't even remember. Velvet had never been vulnerable.

But Kelly was different. He knew her insecurities, and it moved him that she was willing to trust him not to hurt her in these moments, either physically or emotionally. It was a big responsibility—maybe, if he let himself think about it, one of the biggest responsibilities he had ever faced. That moved him in ways he couldn't begin to express.

"Seth?" Her voice took on a note of uncertainty, and he realized he hadn't moved for a lot longer than the instant it had seemed to him. Summoning a smile, unable to refuse the gift she was offering him regardless of his sudden qualms about whether he would measure up, he bent and ran his fingertip over her smooth skin just above her panty line.

He felt her quiver, heard her sudden intake of breath—and suddenly felt more powerful than he'd ever felt, even in the middle of a perfect block. Gripping her panties, he eased them off her, taking his time, savoring every single moment of anticipation.

"You're beautiful," he said thickly. "Beautiful . . ." He liked the way the corners of her mouth curved up dreamily in response, liked knowing he could make her feel that good.

Down her legs he dragged the white cotton, feeling her flesh every inch of the way. Then he tossed the panties aside and knelt between her legs, holding her open to him. Her knees gripped his hips, almost as if she wanted to close them—or as if she didn't want to let go.

Her dark curls tempted him, and he brushed them gently, causing her to draw another sharp breath. In that instant he became aware of the exquisite sensitivity of his own body, a reflection of hers. The merest breath, the merest touch . . .

He took her gently by the shoulders and lifted her so he could pull her shirt and bra off. Then she was completely naked in his arms—and he was still fully clothed. It was the most erotic sensation he could remember.

She seemed to enjoy it, too, because her arms wrapped around him and she nestled into him, small, soft, and warm.

But then she apparently became impatient, because she pulled back and reached for the hem of his polo shirt.

He was only too ready to oblige. It went the way of her clothing, somewhere across the room, and after an impatient moment, so did his shorts and briefs and his shoes.

Then they were both naked, clinging as she sat on the edge of the bed and he knelt between her legs. And nothing, not ever, had felt as good to him, not even making an unexpected touchdown that won the game.

He was high on her. Higher than a kite. Higher than a satellite. In fact, he was sure he was looking down on the moon.

Then he flew even higher as she reached out and began to stroke him, at first almost as if she were petting a cat. He wondered if she knew she was faintly purring in the back of her throat as her hands learned him. The question was fleeting, though, as each of her touches carried him further from thought and further into the realm of feeling.

She was lighting a conflagration in him that was leaving room for nothing else.

Her hands seemed to be everywhere, rubbing his chest, stroking his back and bottom, finally even reaching out to close around his shaft.

The sensation electrified him, causing him to suck air through his teeth as explosions blew out the last dam of patience in him. Bending forward, he pushed her back down onto the bed and began to teach her what she had just taught him, using his mouth to paint her with aching yearning.

Her breasts, small and perfect, filled him with wonder and responded eagerly to his touches. But this time he hunted lower, dragging his lips and his tongue over the softest skin he'd ever known, until she was moaning softly.

And then he found her curls with his lips, and her delicate nub with his tongue. She cried out softly and almost twisted away as if the sensation were so sharp it was painful. He hesitated, then licked her again, and felt a surge of overwhelming triumph as she reached out to grab his head and hold him close.

Patiently, holding himself in check, he took her higher and higher until she was writhing against him, and lost in the maelstrom of her own passion. And only when she tumbled over the precipice with a long moan did he join himself to her to find his own surcease.

The explosion shook him to his soul.

Afterward, Seth kissed her and wrapped her in the blankets. "Be right back," he whispered. Grabbing his shorts, he pulled them on and went to check on the children.

She was past feeling abandoned. She was past feeling anything except a glow that made her feel more fulfilled than she'd ever felt in her life. Curled in the blankets, she closed her eyes and savored the feelings of happiness, satisfaction, and peace. She had crossed some kind of barrier inside herself tonight, and there was an incredible sense of freedom that she didn't want to look at too closely right now. There'd be time later. There was always time later.

"Still sleeping," Seth said as he returned. Turning off all the lights, he crawled into the bed with her and drew her into his arms. She came willingly, glad to share the closeness again in the aftermath.

After a while, he said, "I have to go back soon. Johnny still has nightmares sometimes."

She nodded, reluctant to let him go, because letting him go would mean that she had to face reality again. But she understood. And she couldn't be selfish enough to try to keep him from his children.

"I don't want to go," he said.

"I know." And amazingly enough, she did. For once in her life, she actually believed that someone wasn't just coming up with a polite excuse to move on.

"Do you?" He hugged her even closer, as if that pleased him. Then he said, "I think we've got a problem here."

Her heart nearly stopped. She didn't want to hear the answer, but she asked anyway. "How so?"

"We seem to be falling in with your family's plan."

"So?"

"Do you suppose they'll be unbearably smug if they find out?"

A small laugh escaped her as relief flooded her. "Probably."

"That's what I think. They'll probably even try to rub it in."

"Undoubtedly."

"I hate it when people rub my nose in things."

"Me, too."

"Especially when I seem to remember that just a few days ago, we were going to find a way to fix their wagons."

Feeling wonderfully amused, she kissed his shoulder and laughed quietly. "Yup. I think I vowed to do it more than once."

"Well, we have to keep our promises, don't we?"

"We should."

"So, the question becomes how." He squeezed her again. "How do we fix their wagons?"

"Beats me."

"Beats me, too." He chuckled warmly. "I'm feeling too damn good right now to care. But give me time. I'll think of something."

"I'll think about it, too. Except I have to warn you, Seth, I've never known them to take a setback without turning it to their advantage."

"Hmm. Maybe I should just dig us a foxhole instead."

"It would probably work better. Besides, they're not really being all that obnoxious about it, are they?"

"Well, the adjoining rooms, and Bea wanting to keep the kids tonight, was a little heavy-handed."

"But remember, they wanted to take the kids away for a whole day and leave us alone. We foiled that, and look what Bea managed to do anyway."

He sighed. "You're right. She's incredibly gifted at this, with X-ray vision, faster than a speeding bullet—well, whatever. She leaps resistance in a single bound. We're in trouble."

"At the moment, I think we're in trouble with or without Bea."

The thought sobered him, and he didn't speak for several minutes. Finally he said, "We're in only as much trouble as we let ourselves be."

Kelly wished she believed that. When he made love to her again a little while later, a sadness seemed to fill her, as if she were saying farewell to something she loved. It seemed to fill him, too, and their lovemaking was slow, lingering, more thoughtful, and less hurried, as if he, too, were saying farewell.

Later, when he went back to his children, she lay awake staring at the darkened ceiling, trying not to cry.

Chapter 17 ❧

They all had a wonderful time at Busch Gardens. The children loved every bit of it, and even Bea's need to take frequent breaks by riding the train, or the need they all shared occasionally to escape into air-conditioning by riding the monorail, didn't dampen the day at all.

What dampened them was the thunderstorm that moved in around three o'clock. It blew in fast, and they barely made it back to the van before they were caught in one of Florida's famous gullywashers. For a while the rain was too heavy to permit driving, and lightning and thunder frequently made them all jump. The children loved it.

When it finally started to let up, Seth drove them home. The rain seemed to follow them, and by the time they reached the bridge to the island, the gulf was churned up into a rough, gray sea. The children were getting cranky and tired, but for that matter so were Max and Jules, who began to squabble mildly about the artistic merits of a film they had seen recently. Kelly was just glad that Zee and Mavis had decided not to come—Zee because she couldn't leave her animals, and Mavis because she couldn't handle the sun and heat well.

It was still raining when they all tumbled out of the van as if glad to head their separate ways. Seth took the kids at a run toward the guest house, and the others made their way inside the villa.

Kelly took a quick shower, then went down onto the veranda. The tigers had disappeared into the protection of the woods, but the elephants were hunkered together in the rain, looking as if they were sleeping.

It would have been a good time to work, but she was feeling lazy and unwilling to apply herself. All she wanted to do was think about last night. Again and again and again, replaying every moment, every touch, over and over as if she needed to absorb it piece by piece in order not to feel overwhelmed.

She'd have been happy to stay there alone for the rest of the day, but solitude wasn't easy to come by in the Burke household.

Bea found her there and sat with a dispirited sigh.

"What's wrong, Granny?"

"Manuel quit. The elephants were the last straw. Evidently he told Zee that they had to go or he was going."

"I wouldn't worry about it too much. It seems to me that Manuel is unlikely to find another place to work where they'll let him wear dresses."

Bea's lips curved. "You're probably right. But the landscaper is furious, too, and I can't say I blame him. Of course, I can probably soothe *him* with money to do the repairs. And then there's Lawrence."

"What's wrong with Lawrence?"

"Nothing, really. He's still on the wagon and quite proud of the fact. But . . . I get the feeling that he's been drinking all along because there's something seriously missing in his life."

Kelly nodded slowly, not quite certain what she should say. Or how much she should say. Finally she decided on, "He's lonely, Granny."

"In this house? No one's ever alone."

"I'm not talking about being alone. I'm talking about loneliness. We're not Lawrence's family. Not really."

"What a silly notion." She waved her cigarette holder. "He's been a part of this family for forty years!"

"But maybe he doesn't feel that way. He's an employee."

Granny nodded slowly. "Maybe," she said after a few moments. "Maybe."

Kelly was feeling strangely helpless. But she didn't feel she had the right to tell her grandmother that she suspected Lawrence was pining for her. Besides, what if she was wrong?

"What's happening with the elephants?" she asked, wanting to change the subject.

"Oh, I don't know," said Bea airily. "We certainly can't turn the poor things out until we've found a good home for them."

Kelly was interested to note that her grandmother was now speaking in terms of "we" rather than "Zee." "A change of heart?"

"Me, you mean? Oh, my dear child, you know I've always been a sucker for animals. Why else would I have given up half the island to two tigers?"

That said, Bea excused herself and went back inside, a thoughtful look on her face.

Kelly sat on, watching the steady rain fall, unwilling to move or occupy herself in any way. It might have been that she'd had so little sleep last night and she was worn out from the trip to Busch Gardens, but she suspected there was something more going on.

In fact, she wondered if she wasn't heartsick.

She found herself remembering a Spanish parable she'd heard in her high school language class, about a shoemaker and his daughter. The two of them had been so happy that they sang and laughed all day long, increasingly annoying the rich man who lived across the street. He was a miserable, unhappy man, and finally he could take the obvious happiness of the shoemaker and his daughter no longer.

So he invited the two of them to come stay in his mansion for a day and enjoy all the pleasures of unfettered wealth. At the end of the day, the shoemaker and his daughter went home and never sang again, for the rich man had shown them all they didn't have.

She was beginning to think that that was what making love with Seth had done for her. Instead of feeling joy that she'd had such a wonderful experience, all she could seem to do was feel sad because it couldn't always be hers.

A long time ago, she'd realized that the secret of being happy was to want what you had, and not to keep wanting more. She'd tried to practice that philosophy and had believed she'd succeeded fairly well.

Until now. Now she knew what she was missing, and no amount of arguing with herself could ease the aching in her heart.

An hour later, Seth came running up, with Jenny and Bouncer hot on his heels. "Have you seen Johnny?" he demanded as he came running across the back yard.

Kelly felt her heart stop. "No. Why?"

"Because I dozed off while the kids were sleeping, and he apparently wandered out of the house."

Kelly leapt to her feet immediately and ran into the house shouting for Zee.

"Zee! Zee, I need you now. Everybody, Johnny's lost!"

The Burkes came tumbling out of various rooms in the house, as did Lawrence and Cook, all of them demanding to know what had happened.

"Johnny wandered off. Zee, you've got to lock up the tigers *now!*"

Zee didn't even bother to nod. She dashed out of the house.

"We have to search," Kelly said. "But somebody has to stay with Jenny."

"I will," said Bea from the top of the stairs. She started down, cigarette holder forgotten. "Where is she?"

"Out back with Seth."

Outside, heedless of the rain, they gathered. Bea took Jenny to the guest house in case Johnny came back. Cook was stationed to keep an eye out at the villa. The rest split up in groups of two as soon as Zee had the tigers in their travel cages. Neither Alex nor Nikki looked happy over this development, and they let out a few roars that disturbed the elephants, who promptly moved to a fresh patch of garden. No one cared.

Seth and Kelly set out together, heading down the path to the beach, since Johnny might have wanted to play in the sand.

And Kelly found herself thinking that nothing, *nothing* was as important as finding that child. She reached out and grabbed Seth's hand, holding it, trying to offer what little comfort she could.

"I shouldn't have fallen asleep," he said as they

hurried down the sodden path, great drops of water dripping on them from the foliage overhead. "And if I hadn't stayed up so late last night, I never would have."

"This could have happened in the middle of the night, Seth. Parents have to be able to sleep."

"But I knew he wouldn't sleep all that long. I was so sure I'd hear him when he woke up."

She couldn't think of a reassuring thing to say, and she had the feeling that right now he was going to beat himself up no matter what she said. So she just squeezed his hand.

"I *am* unfit," he said bitterly. "Velvet was right about that."

"No, she wasn't. Don't you dare tell yourself that. I've never seen a better father."

"What would you know?"

The words cut her to the quick. If she hadn't already been so upset about Johnny, she probably would have snapped his head off. Fatherhood wasn't a mere matter of genetics, and who knew better than she? She'd grown up with *three* fathers—Max, Jules, and Lawrence—and all of them were the best dads anyone could be.

"I should have called the police."

She looked at him. "I'll run back to the house right now and do that."

After a moment he shook his head. "We've got six people looking, and most of the island is fenced off for the tigers. If we don't find him at the beach . . ." He didn't complete the thought. He just quickened his pace.

Kelly noted that he was beginning to limp badly, but she knew that nothing short of breaking both legs was likely to slow him down now. He called for Johnny as they hurried along, and she called, too. But there was no answer.

The beach was deserted when they arrived, smoothed out and covered with freshly delivered seaweed from the storm-roiled waves.

Kelly spoke her biggest fear. "He wouldn't have gone in the water, would he?"

Seth shook his head. "I hope not. God! They've both been warned not to go swimming without an adult. But who knows? You try and try to warn kids without scaring them to death . . ." He trailed off, looking up and down the beach. "I guess we should split and circle the island. It'll save time."

So she took off to the right, and he and Bouncer took off to the left. After a little while, she could no longer hear him calling over the pounding surf.

She walked along the edge of the sand, keeping near the woods, scanning the dark depths of them as far as she could see, calling the boy. But it was almost like night in there, thanks to the overcast sky, and because of the surf she doubted she would even hear him unless he cried out loudly.

They were going to have to call the police to help. The island wasn't that big, but if they didn't find him in any of the obvious places, there was no way the six of them could adequately search the woods. And warm though it was, it was raining. Hypothermia would be a problem before long.

But as each catastrophic thought tried to worm its way into her brain, she rejected it. It couldn't be. She wouldn't *allow* it to be. She kept remembering the way it felt when Johnny tucked his hand in hers, or crawled up into her lap, or the way she felt when he threw his head back and laughed. It gave her some idea of the hell Seth must be going through, because she was going through a small hell of her own.

Twenty minutes later, she and Seth met at the far

side of the island. Their eyes locked, and they both shook their heads.

"I'm calling the cops," Seth said. He set out at a trot up the driveway, limping horribly, and she followed right on his heels.

They reached the villa, but Seth flew right past it, heading for the guest house. Of course he would, Kelly thought as she ran after him. If Johnny had come back, he'd go to the guest house first. Maybe.

She almost turned back to see if Cook had learned anything, then realized she'd find out just as fast at the guest house. If Johnny had turned up at the villa, Cook would have called over to Bea at the guest house.

They burst through the narrow band of wet woods that divided the guest house from the main gardens, and found Bea and Jenny sitting on the front porch—with Johnny.

"He was under his bed," Granny said as they came running up. "He had a nightmare and was hiding."

Seth didn't say a word. He mounted the steps, lifted his son into his arms, and hugged him as tightly as he could. Kelly, feeling a surge of relief that left her weak, collapsed onto the porch steps and watched as Seth closed his eyes, as a tear began to run down his cheek.

She looked away quickly, battling back tears of her own.

"Johnny was bad," Jenny said a short while later.

Kelly looked back at the group on the porch and found Seth lowering himself into one of the chairs, wincing as he did so, and taking his son on his lap. "Why didn't you come when I called, Johnny?"

"I was scared." The little boy's lower lip trembled, as if he had suddenly realized that he'd made a mistake and might be in serious trouble.

"Why were you scared?"

"The monsters."

Seth tilted his head to one side, studying his son gravely. "Johnny, are you afraid of *me*?"

For several heartbeats Johnny didn't answer. Then he stole an uncertain look up at his father. "Mommy says you're the Credible Hulk."

Jenny corrected him with scorn. "*In*credible Hulk."

"Jenny," Seth said gently, "be quiet, please, and let Johnny talk, okay?"

"'Kay."

Seth looked at Johnny again. "What do you know about the Incredible Hulk?"

"He turns green and ugly and hurts people."

"I see."

Jenny couldn't keep quiet. "It's just a stupid TV show, Johnny."

Seth silenced her with a look. "Johnny, I don't turn green, okay?"

The little boy nodded doubtfully.

"Really, I don't. I couldn't turn green even if I wanted to. But you know something about the Hulk?"

Johnny shook his head.

"Even if he does turn green and ugly, he only hurts *bad* people. Really bad people. He never hurts little boys. Not ever."

Johnny appeared to think this over. Then he relaxed, leaning into his father's chest and popping his thumb into his mouth. Seth held him, rocking gently.

"I'm not the Incredible Hulk, Johnny. Your mommy was just mad at me when she said that. You say mean things when you get mad, too, don't you?"

Jenny agreed. "He calls me a pig face."

"See? And Jenny isn't really a pig face, is she?"
Johnny shook his head.

"And I'm not really the Hulk. I promise."

Kelly reached out and touched her grandmother's hand, indicating it was time for the two
of them to go.

They left the Ralston family alone on the porch
and walked back to tell the others that everything
was okay.

"I won't even comment," Bea said.

"About what?"

"About parents who say bad things about each
other in front of the children. Velvet Ralston needs
a good slap."

"She probably never even realized how it might
affect Johnny."

"She wouldn't have *had* to realize if she'd just
followed the basic rule of not bashing a parent in
front of a child." Bea looked over at her. "When
you get around to having children of your own,
dear, keep that in mind. You can disagree in front
of the children—as long as you do it civilly."

"I'll remember that." Because she was never going to forget the last hour. Never.

Later that night, concerned about Seth and
Johnny, Kelly went over to the guest house. Seth
was sitting on the front porch, smoking a cigarette,
holding an ice pack on his knee.

"I didn't know you smoked," she said as she
climbed the steps.

"I don't. But either I do something suicidal this
evening, or I might be tempted to fly to Paris and
put my hands around Velvet's throat. Since that's
likely to upset the kids, I'll put a nail in my own
coffin."

But even as he said it, he tossed the butt out onto the rain-soaked grass.

Kelly sat beside him, looking out into the darkness. The rain had stopped, but moisture was still dripping from every leaf and branch, making the night sound alive. "How's Johnny?"

"He seems to be fine. I'm not sure he really believed what Velvet said, but I think it somehow got tangled up with his nightmares."

"Is he having a lot of them?"

"Yeah. I'm not sure yet whether he's having more than usual for a child his age. I'll need to keep an eye on it. Of course, with the divorce and the custody battle—and God knows how much he's heard about *that*—he's got enough reason to be having problems."

"I guess so." She wanted to reach out and take his hand, but sensed that he wasn't ready yet to be touched.

"Anyway," he said, "I'm feeling like a royal shit, and wondering if I shouldn't have taken that broadcasting job just to keep Velvet happy so the kids wouldn't have to be going through this. Maybe I should have given in for their sakes. It was just a damn job, after all."

"I don't know." And she didn't. She had no easy answers for this one, and she wasn't about to tell him that for her own selfish reasons she was glad he'd refused to take the job. God, what a petty, selfish thought.

"At the time . . . at the time I was pretty much in a state of shock. I mean, I couldn't believe that she'd throw me out over a job. I even think I was in denial until the divorce became final. I had myself convinced that she'd change her mind. God, what a jerk I was."

"I don't think so. I think your reaction was normal."

"Maybe. Maybe not. But what I *didn't* do in the midst of all that upheaval was give serious thought to what the divorce would do to the kids. Christ, everybody I knew was divorced. Most of this society is divorced. I just figured if they could do it, so could I. I'd just work it out and do a good job of it."

She nodded.

"Anyway, after that shock wore off, I started facing the fallout. I started lying awake at night thinking about the kids. About how they feel about it. About what it might do to them. And just about the time I was making a concerted plan of action to ensure I was very much a part of their lives, even if I wasn't living with them, she filed a custody suit."

"Why did she do that?"

"Because I had joint custody. Fifty-fifty. A little hard to do when they're in school, but basically I was going to keep them over all their school breaks and a couple of weekends a month. When she started to balk because a particular weekend wasn't convenient or whatever, I insisted, and I guess she got mad. So she filed suit for full custody. I'm not sure when she decided that she wanted to bar me from seeing them at all. Or why. She just did, and I didn't know about it until I got the papers."

"She's cruel."

"Apparently so. Or just too angry with me to see what she's doing. God knows. All I know is that the price of this hassle is too high for the kids. Maybe I ought to just bow out."

Kelly couldn't restrain herself any longer. Reaching out, she took his hand. "Don't do that, Seth. Don't ever, ever do that. They need you. Even if they can't see you much, they need to know that you love them. Trust me, I know about *this*. Do you know how many nights I lay awake wondering if my parents really loved me? Long after I stopped missing them with every cell in my body, I wondered if they loved me. Don't do that to your kids."

He was silent for a while, but finally said quietly, "No. I won't do that."

She squeezed his hand again and started to let go of it, but he clung. They sat on in silence for a while, listening as the breeze began to pick up, rustling the leaves and clattering the palm fronds. The air suddenly felt a little drier.

"Well," he said presently, "maybe the custody fight's pretty much over anyway."

"She said it was."

"She's said a lot of things, many of them untrue. I'll believe it when I get it in writing from her lawyer."

"I can understand that."

He squeezed her hand, then let go of it. "Be back in a sec. I want to check on the kids and put this ice pack back in the freezer."

She listened to him limp across the porch and into the house, heard the screen door creak closed behind him. She could hear his air conditioner turn on out back, and realized that he had it running but had kept the door open so he could hear the children. He was a good father. Period.

He returned a few minutes later, carrying a couple glasses of orange juice. He handed one to her, then eased himself down into his chair.

"How's your knee?" she asked.

"I'm icing it every twenty minutes in the hope that I'll be able to walk tomorrow."

"Not good, huh?"

"I shouldn't have been running on it. Especially

after all that walking we did at the amusement park. It'll probably swell and get stiff for a few days. No big deal."

Kelly thought it was a big deal, but she didn't say so. She was just glad when Seth reached out again to take her hand.

"Life," he remarked, "is one hell of a learning experience."

A soft laugh escaped her. "No kidding. And it's been intensive the last few days."

"Yeah. What have you learned?"

"That I was seeing my family through a fractured mirror of my own insecurities. Which is not to say I'm completely over it, but I keep getting banged on the head. It'll sink in eventually."

"I think it already is. You seem more comfortable and confident than you did when you arrived."

"You've helped with that," she said impulsively.

"Thanks. I appreciate that. But you're doing it yourself, Kelly."

No, she wasn't. He was making her see herself in a different light with his comments—and with his loving. He was helping her to discover an innate sense of self-worth that had nothing to do with her family or her business. He was making her feel that it was good enough to be Kelly Burke just because she was Kelly Burke. It was a delicate, fragile feeling, but she was nurturing it because it felt so good.

"What about you?" she asked finally.

"Well, I'm learning how good intentions aren't enough. How much devastation divorce can cause to children. I'm learning that I can't go the rest of my life without seeing them, no matter what."

She nodded, but inside she felt a furtive sense of disappointment that he hadn't mentioned her. She would have liked to think that she was helping in some small way, just as he was helping her.

But he was silent, and only the breeze filled the emptiness between them. Finally she drained her glass and set it on the little table, preparing to go back to the house and bury her wounded ego.

"You know," he said suddenly, "you've been a big—"

But before he could continue, a cry from within the house cut him off. Seth jumped up instantly, and disappeared inside. Johnny was having another nightmare.

Kelly waited a few minutes, then left, walking up to the house with a heavy heart. Other people affected her in huge ways, but apparently she didn't affect anyone else at all.

Insignificant. That was what she was.

Behind her, the phone rang in the guest house, but she didn't hear it.

Seth ignored the phone. He sat on the edge of Johnny's bed, hugging him awake. The night-light wasn't enough, he decided. He needed to find something brighter for the boy to sleep with.

But with his father's arms around him, Johnny seemed to have forgotten his fear.

"Wanna tell me about it?" Seth asked.

"I dreamed a volcano."

What the hell was Velvet letting these kids watch? he wondered. "Where did you learn about volcanoes?"

"On TV."

It figured. "So what was the volcano doing?"

"Making lava. It was chasing you, Daddy."

"Well, there aren't any volcanoes around here. None. So I don't think we need to worry about it."

Johnny looked up at him. "It was just a dream," he said seriously. "I know that."

"Good."

The phone, which had stopped ringing a couple minutes ago, started again.

"That's Mommy," Johnny announced.

Probably, Seth thought. Velvet hadn't called once since she'd left the kids with him, despite her promise. And of course when she remembered to do it, she'd call in the middle of the night. That was Velvet. "If it is, do you want to talk to her?"

Johnny nodded.

They went to the living room together and Seth answered the phone. It was indeed Velvet, and she wasn't in a very good mood.

"Where the hell were you? It's after ten there. The kids should be in bed."

"The kids *are* in bed. Johnny was having a nightmare. I might ask you what you're doing calling at four A.M. your time."

"I just got in."

"Really. Well, Johnny's awake and wants to talk to you, and I'll go wake Jenny up, unless you want to call back tomorrow at a more reasonable hour."

"Wake her up," Velvet said. "My day is crammed tomorrow."

He handed the receiver to Johnny and went to wake Jenny. In her usual fashion, she was instantly alert. She tumbled out of bed almost before her eyes were open and ran to the living room.

Watching her almost broke his heart, because he had a feeling these kids loved their mother more than she deserved. Maybe he was just being bitter. Either way, he needed to halt this train of thought.

After talking to their mother for about five minutes, both children took themselves back to bed. Which left Seth to talk to Velvet.

"Is he ever going to get over these nightmares?" she asked.

"I hope so. Speaking of which, what are you letting him watch on TV? He was dreaming about volcanoes tonight."

"Their nanny is supposed to limit them to the children's channels," she said dismissively. "She was probably sneaking on shows that she wants to watch."

"Well, straighten her out. Nightmares are normal, but feeding them isn't good."

"And speaking of nannies," she said as she continued on her own agenda, "mine has quit. I don't have time to find another one right now, and I won't be coming home in two weeks the way I thought."

"Why not?"

"Because I've decided to go on to Rome and Greece with my . . . friends. The kids can stay with you, can't they?"

He wanted to say that they could stay with him forever as far as he was concerned. But he resisted the impulse. "Tell you what, Velvet. You have your attorney tell my attorney in writing that you're dropping the custody suit, and you can extend your trip however long you want. But if you don't do that, you'd better come back at the originally scheduled time."

"Or what?" she demanded. "Are you threatening me?"

"Not exactly. But my lawyer might decide to make a case for abandonment, if you get my drift. He's a real shark, and I can't always rein him in."

She was silent for a moment before saying tightly, "Seth, you're a son of a bitch."

"I had a good teacher. Look, Velvet, it's wrong to tear up the kids' lives this way. It's bad enough we got divorced. It won't be good for them at all if they lose either one of us completely. Try to see reason."

"Reason. Hah! You wouldn't see reason about that job."

"This is different."

"*You* might think so." But she fell silent again, and the whisper of the satellite phone connection could be heard. At last she said, "All right. What the hell. I'm getting tired of the whole thing anyway. I want to move on."

Of course she wanted to move on . . . to her friends. Or her *friend*, he thought bitterly. But anything that worked was fine by him.

"Okay. Make sure my attorney has that paper before the two weeks are up."

After he hung up, he went to get ready for bed. Then he used blankets to make himself a pallet on the floor beside Johnny's bed.

Tired as he was, he couldn't sleep. Instead of thinking about Velvet, and the kids, and how the biggest fear of his life might be fading into the past, he found himself thinking about Kelly.

His obsession with her was beginning to bother him. For safety's sake, it might be a good time to cut her right out of his life. Which sounded good, but it didn't help him sleep at all.

Chapter 18

The next days passed quietly. For whatever reason, Florida was defying its own weather edicts and had remained socked in ever since the storm had started when they were at Busch Gardens. Torrential rain alternated with drizzle, and the cloud cover never broke.

The Burke family seemed content to ensconce themselves in their various portions of the house and poke their noses out only for meals. Seth and the children stayed mostly at the guest house.

Kelly attempted to work, but she couldn't concentrate very well when she felt that Seth was deliberately avoiding her.

Granny found her in the library, hunched over her laptop, wrestling with strings of code as she debugged a website she was nearly finished with. Bea looked over Kelly's shoulder.

"What's that, dear? It looks like alphabet soup."

"It's code."

"Code? Like a secret message?"

"Not exactly. They're directions that tell a computer what to put on the screen for people to see. It's how I make my web pages."

"Oh, my. That doesn't look like fun at all."

"Right now it's not." But she clicked a button and brought up the graphical view of the web page she was trying to fix. "That's what all that alphabet soup looks like on the screen."

"Kelly, you're a genius."

She doubted it, but smiled anyway. "Thanks, Granny."

Bea sat down at the reading table beside her. "I swear I'm going to go out of my mind."

"What's wrong?"

"This weather! Lawrence is moping around the house until I want to scream. You're depressed. Even Seth had disappeared into his bolt-hole. *Everyone's* blue, and it's enough to drive me nuts. We need to do something about it."

"We do?" Kelly didn't know if she liked the sound of this.

"Yes, we do," Bea said firmly.

"What are you thinking about—keeping in mind that I haven't agreed to anything."

Bea *tsk*ed. "You're beginning to sound like a lawyer. I just think we ought to have a party or something. It's too short notice to invite anyone outside the family, but certainly we could have the Ralstons over and all do something together this evening."

Ah, thought Kelly. Granny had evidently noticed that she and Seth weren't spending any time together and had decided to do something about it. The stubborn part of Kelly wanted to argue with her, but the rest of her wanted too desperately to see Seth again.

"What kind of party?" she asked, without committing herself to anything.

"Oh, I don't know. We've got trunkloads of old clothes in the attic. I suppose we could have a costume party."

The idea appealed to Kelly. "I remember when you used to let me dress up out of those trunks. Such fabulous things: paste jewels, feather boas, cloche hats."

Bea patted her arm. "We did have fun, didn't we?" Then her face saddened. "What did we do to drive you away, Kelly?"

Instantly Kelly's throat locked up and tears started to burn her eyes. It took her a moment to find her voice. "You didn't do anything, Granny. It was *me*."

"You always were such a serious child, and I always felt there was this deep hurt in you, but I could never soothe it."

"It's soothed now, Granny. Really." And she meant it. Her family hadn't been to blame for her feelings, and at long last she accepted it.

"So you won't stay away as long again?"

Kelly shook her head. "I promise."

"Good." Bea smiled. "But this party . . . maybe Zelda would even do an animal act for us, you know? And Mavis could sing, and Jules could play, and I could do a scene from *Steel Magnolias*—I'm certainly as good as Shirley—and maybe Max could show us a painting."

Kelly was warming to the idea. "That sounds like fun."

"Wonderful." She waved her cigarette holder and inadvertently smashed the unlit cigarette against the back of the next chair. She never noticed. "Go get Seth and the children and tell them to come pick out their costumes. I'll get the ball rolling on the rest."

Kelly shut down her computer and did as she was bade, admitting finally that she wasn't as opposed to her grandmother's scheming as she had originally been.

Seth welcomed her pleasantly enough, but with clear reserve, and that began to annoy her.

"I don't have cooties, you know," she said irritably as he invited her in.

He closed the door behind her. "I don't recall saying you did." But he had the grace to look embarrassed, so he clearly understood exactly what she was saying. "We're playing Monopoly. Care to join us? I'll spot you some properties."

He was trying to be gracious, but she wasn't fully prepared to let him off that easily. "Are you sure I'm not contagious?"

"Actually, no, but I'll chance it."

She wanted to bean him, and refrained only because she was so aware she'd asked for it. "Granny's throwing a party tonight for the family. She wanted me to come get you and the children so you can choose your costumes."

"Costumes?"

"She's got all these old clothes up in the attic. Great for dress-up."

"Sounds good to me. Let me get the kids."

She stood in the small foyer, fuming at the way she was being kept waiting by the door like an unwelcome visitor—which she probably was, a realization that did nothing to mellow her mood.

Thirty seconds later, Seth returned alone. "Why don't I meet you up at the house?" he said. "Johnny wants to go to the bathroom first, and he's hungry. I figure I'll make them a peanut butter sandwich first."

"Fine with me." Annoyed that he was sending her on her way, she turned sharply and opened the door.

He caught her arm. "What's wrong, Kelly?"

"Don't touch me. You might get cooties."

"I might get frostbite. Look, we agreed we didn't

want to get involved. I'm trying to keep that from happening."

She looked over her shoulder at him. "You don't have to try very hard. Getting involved with you is the last thing on earth I want to do."

He frowned. "Good. We're in agreement. We'll be along shortly."

It was very lowering to realize, on the way back to the house, that she'd behaved badly. They *had* agreed not to get involved, and Seth had probably sensed, the last time they were together, that they were in danger of doing exactly that. So he had pulled away, the only wise thing to do.

The realization did nothing to make her feel any less irritated.

As soon as Seth and the children came up to the villa, Granny appeared in the foyer, as if materialized by a magic wand. "I'll take the children up to choose their costumes," she said to Seth. "I'm sure they'd like to suprise you. You and Kelly can go on up when they're done."

Seth opened his mouth as if to argue with her, then snapped it shut. He waited until Bea and the children had disappeared up the stairs, then looked ruefully at Kelly. "Foiled again."

"This is another matchmaking scheme, you know."

"That just occurred to me. Apparently two of my brain cells were dozing earlier. Well, she's doomed to failure."

"She most certainly is."

He nodded. "After all, we're each so unbearably repulsed by the other that we can't stand to be in the same room."

"Oh, I'm not repulsed by you."

He looked at her, lifting his eyebrows. "No? Be still my heart."

"No, I'm not at all repulsed. There are times, however, when I'd like to feed you to a *Tyrannosaurus rex*."

"Really?" He appeared to consider this possibility. "Wouldn't an alligator be easier?"

"Nope. I've considered that. You're too big and too thick-skinned."

"Ah. Well, I don't know where you can find a *T rex*."

"That *is* a problem. Genetic engineering would take too long."

"No doubt. And you'd have to lock yourself up in your basement laboratory for years, until your hair turned white and your hands became claws. For the impact, you know."

She nodded, beginning to enjoy this ridiculous conversation in spite of herself. "What do you want to feed *me* to?"

He grinned. A huge, devilish expression. "Me," he said bluntly.

Before she could respond with anything more than a flaming blush, the front door opened and Manuel walked into the house wearing a lime green slacksuit and navy-blue pumps. A matching blue leather purse was slung over his shoulder.

"Alligator," he said.

"What?" Kelly asked.

"We have an alligator on the front porch." He headed in the direction of the servants' quarters.

"Uh, Manuel," Kelly called, stopping him. "Is it alive?"

"It opened its jaws at me and made that hissing sound, you know? I didn't feel like arguing."

"Are you coming back here for good?"

Manuel tapped his toe on the tile. "I suppose. *If* someone gets the alligator off the porch." He turned and disappeared down the hall.

Kelly looked at Seth. "There's an alligator on the porch."

"So I heard."

"I can't imagine what it's doing here. We've never had one before. I don't think they like salt water."

"Hmm. Should we look?"

"I don't know. What if it's right outside the door?"

"They don't bite people, do they?"

"Not usually. They tend to avoid us."

"But? I hear a but."

"But they do like little kids—for food, I mean—and if this one's really hungry . . ."

He nodded. "We've got a problem."

Lawrence emerged from the back of the house. "Manuel says there's an alligator on the porch."

"We know," Kelly and Seth said in unison.

Kelly suddenly had a thought. "Where's Bouncer?"

"He was sleeping in his bed at home when we left. He can't get out."

"Well, he's probably too big for the gator anyway."

"Quite," said Lawrence. "However, Master Johnny is about the right size. Where's Miss Zelda?"

"I don't know," Kelly answered. "Somewhere in the house, I think. Why?"

"She'll know what to do about it. She rescued an alligator once before. I'll go find her."

"Lawrence," Kelly suggested gently, "why don't you just use the intercom? It'll save time."

Lawrence never used the intercom. No one ever did in this house. It had been put in years ago when Bea had started fretting that if she took a fall and hurt herself, no one might notice for hours. So the intercom had been installed in all the rooms, at great expense, and hadn't been used since it was tested. Most of them didn't even remember it was there. Which was true of a lot of things in this house.

"Excellent idea, Miss." He walked into the living room and punched the button. Kelly and Seth could hear him say, "Paging Miss Zelda. There's an alligator on the porch."

He might as well have said there was a fire in the house. Doors flew open everywhere, and soon everyone except Granny and the children were gathered at the top of the stairs. Manuel even came out of his room into the foyer.

"An alligator!" Mavis exclaimed. "Haven't we got enough fauna with the tigers and the elephants? This place is beginning to smell like a zoo."

"I'll get my machete," Max said.

Zelda glared at him. "You'll do no such thing! There's no need to hurt the animal."

Jules said, "Well, it's obviously lost. It wouldn't be here otherwise. Poor thing."

Max, who was covered with paint splatters, said only, "How big is it?" Kelly suspected he was trying to decide what size knife or sword he was going to need.

Manuel answered, "Huge."

"Oh, my God," Mavis said. "I'm going to faint."

Zelda began to descend the stairs. "Hold off, Mavis. It isn't in the house yet. That's something you want to save for when it's eating you."

Mavis clearly enunciated an uncharacteristically unladylike word.

Just then, someone knocked on the front door. The entire group fell silent, and every eye fixed on it.

"No," said Jules. "They don't knock."

"It could have been his tail," Manuel suggested. "He has a big tail."

But the knock came again. Lawrence didn't move, as if he were uncertain what might be out there. Finally Seth went to answer it.

"Don't!" Mavis shrieked. "Don't let it in!"

Seth paused to look at her. "Mavis," he said patiently. "Only people knock on doors. Therefore, the alligator isn't right outside the door. Okay?"

Mavis looked doubtful, but remained silent.

Seth opened the door to discover Blaise Corrigan standing there.

"Hi," said Blaise. "Did you know you have an alligator on your porch?"

"I was just about to deal with it," Zelda said, reaching the bottom of the stairs. "What can we do for *you*?"

"I'm here about the elephants, but it can wait."

Seth spoke. "Maybe you'd like to come in, Chief. So I can close the door before Mavis faints from fright."

Corrigan obligingly stepped inside, then looked up at Mavis. "It won't bother you if you don't bother it."

"That's what everyone says about bees, too, but I've lost count of the times I've been stung." She remained safely at the head of the stairs.

"It won't take much to deal with it," Zelda said.

"You can't kill it," Corrigan reminded her. "It's illegal."

She shook her head. "I thought you knew me better than that. I might kill a person, but I'd never harm an animal."

Seth looked at Kelly. "I'm glad to know where her priorities are."

Zee ignored him. "Manuel, I need my pole snare and some duct tape."

Manuel stayed where he was. "I can't let you do that, Miss Zee. It might bite you."

"It's not going to bite anybody. Unless I decide to feed *you* to it. Get my things."

Manuel looked as if he were about to argue some more, but turned and headed toward the back.

Lawrence then decided to step forward. "Really, Miss Zee, you should let me take care of it. I couldn't abide it if you were hurt."

Zee paused in front of him. "Lawrence, I love you dearly, but you're seventy years old, and there's no way you're going to wrestle with an alligator. Seth will."

"Seth will?" Seth repeated. "Thanks so much for telling me."

But to Kelly's discerning eye, he didn't look all that reluctant. In fact, the macho fool looked as if he rather relished the prospect.

Blaise spoke. "You should just let me call a trapper. They'll get it out of here."

"They'll just kill it," Zee said.

"Well, I do think that's what they usually do when gators become troublesome."

"This one hasn't been troublesome at all. It just happens to be on the front porch."

"Yes," Seth said, "I agree. Except for one thing, Zee. What are you going to do with it when you catch it?"

She waved a hand. "I'll deal with it."

Kelly looked at Seth. "I love her insouciant approach to deadly animals." He grinned.

Manuel returned with a long pole on the end of which was a rope loop, along with a roll of duct tape and a coil of nylon rope. "You forgot to tell me to get rope," he said. "But you're going to need rope."

"Good thinking," Zee said. Then she turned to Seth. "Ready?"

"I guess. What am I supposed to do?"

"A little alligator wrestling."

"I suggest we go out the back door in case the gator's moved."

There was no way Kelly was going to wait inside for the outcome. Ransacking her brain for some way to convince Zee and Seth to forget this madness, she followed them out the back door, with Blaise Corrigan, Max, and Manuel on her heels.

As they passed the elephants, the baby reached out to touch her with the tip of its soft, leathery trunk. She paused, and found herself looking deep into the youngster's limpid eyes, eyes that were framed by the longest lashes she'd ever seen. Forgetting her worry about the alligator for a moment, she reached out and petted the baby's trunk.

"No time for that," Zee called back to her. "You can babysit later if you want."

Kelly raced to catch up.

Out in front of the house they gathered to look at the problem. It *was* a big alligator, but not too terribly huge. Maybe six or seven feet in length. It was just lying there on the veranda with its eyes closed.

"It's lethargic," Zee said. "All this cool, rainy weather. That's good."

Seth stood with his hands on his hips. "Okay, what's the drill?"

"I snag him around the snout with the snare," she said. "So he can't open his mouth. He'll fight it for a while, and we let him. I might need help holding the snare."

"Okay. And then?"

"Then you get on his back and hold him still while I wrap duct tape around his snout. Be sure to rub his throat. That calms them. Then we tie him up and move him."

The thought of Seth actually climbing onto the alligator's back was more than Kelly could bear. "You can't do this," she said to him and Zee. "Someone will get hurt. You need to call someone who knows what to do."

"I vote for that," Corrigan said. Manuel nodded.

"I've done this before," Zee said. "It's not that difficult."

Kelly had her doubts. Zee had a way of minimizing things. And she was soon proved right, because the instant Zee approached him with the snare, the gator became considerably more animated. He opened his huge jaws and fussed at her. And each time the loop got close, he shook his head and evaded it.

"Time to pull up the lawn chairs and get the popcorn," Seth remarked to Kelly. "Might as well enjoy the show."

She looked at him. "If you had an ounce of useful brain, you'd know how foolish this is. Both of you could get seriously hurt."

"Hey, Refrigerator Perry was a bigger threat."

"But *he* didn't have claws. And jaws like that."

"You know who Refrigerator Perry is? I think I'm in love."

She glared at him, a look that should have withered him to dust. Unfortunately, he just wiggled those damn eyebrows at her.

Then he climbed the steps and went to stand beside Zee. "Want me to do that?" he asked. "My reflexes are a little quicker."

He was enjoying this, Kelly realized. The pigheaded, macho fool.

Zee handed over the snare and after only two tries, Seth had it around the gator's snout and tightened. At which point, the creature realized he was in serious trouble.

"Look out," Zee shouted when seven feet of muscled lizard began to twist sharply, trying to free itself. A cast iron chair went flying as the gator's tail struck it. Seth's arm's bulged with the effort of holding on to the steel pole, and he grimaced.

"Max and Manuel," he called, "you come up here and hold this pole so I can tackle this guy."

Max and Manuel exchanged looks. After a moment, Manuel kicked off his pumps and handed Kelly his lime-green jacket, revealing a cream-colored silk blouse. "Hold this, please."

Then he mounted the steps, Max trailing reluctantly behind him. The two of them approached cautiously, then stood on either side of Seth and gripped the pole.

"Just hang on tight," Seth said. "Give me a chance to grab him."

When he let go, the gator jerked Manuel and Max to one side. They immediately braced their feet and leaned in opposite directions.

Kelly's heart lodged in her throat. She couldn't believe Seth was doing this. But he walked around until he was beside the gator, measuring the situation. Then, almost too quickly to be believed, he jumped on the gator, lying lengthwise on it, grabbing its front legs with his hands.

The gator froze. Then it made one concerted effort to throw Seth off by twisting its body, but he clung with all his might. As soon as the gator stilled, Seth reached out one hand to rub its throat.

"Zee," Seth said calmly, "get the damn tape up here."

Apparently the alligator knew it was bested, though, because it didn't make a move, except one small jerk of its head, as Zee wrapped duct tape around its snout several times.

"Okay," she said.

"Now the rope," Seth said. "Quickly."

Between them, he and Zee wrapped the rope around the animal, tying its legs close to its body.

Then Seth stood up, looking rumpled but otherwise no worse for the wear. "That was fun," he said.

Kelly, who was sure she hadn't breathed once in the last five minutes, glared at him. "You super-macho jerk!"

Seth looked at Zee. "What did I do?"

"You risked your neck," she told him.

"Not really. I wouldn't have done it if I hadn't seen how it could be done. It wasn't that difficult."

"Hah!" said Kelly. "Hah!"

Seth shrugged. "Once his mouth was bound, it was perfectly safe."

Manuel and Max exchanged looks. They were still holding the pole snare, but with the gator quiet now, they didn't have much to do. "Safe?" said Manuel.

"All a matter of perspective, I guess."

Seth spoke. "I'm sorry I frightened you, Kelly. I thought you *wanted* to feed me to an alligator."

She could only glare at him.

"The question," said Corrigan, "is what you're going to do with the gator *now.*"

Just then, the front door opened and Bea stepped out. She took one look at the gator, then frowned at Zee. "You didn't listen to me, did you? I *told* you I didn't want any alligators on this island, but you brought one here anyway."

Kelly looked at her aunt, aghast. "You didn't!"

Zee didn't answer.

Bea poked her cigarette holder, with its broken

cigarette dangling, in the direction of her daughter. "That animal *goes*. I don't know where you've been hiding it all this time, but it goes right now. I won't be responsible for it hurting one of the children."

"Mother, it's been in the fenced area for years."

"It's not in the fenced area now. It *goes*." Turning sharply, she disappeared back into the house.

Zee looked at Manuel. "Get the van."

"Okay, okay. But where are we taking it?"

"Back into the fenced area. I'll figure out where it managed to get out."

"Mrs. Bea said not to do that."

Zee sniffed. "When have you *ever* listened to her, Manuel?"

He shrugged and went to get the car, picking up his purse and jacket on the way.

"Uh, Zee," said Seth.

"What?"

"Bea made a good point about the children."

"I said I'd find where it got out, and I will. There's no place in this entire state where you can be totally sure you won't run into an alligator, Seth. As a general rule, they avoid us."

Seth turned to Kelly. "That's the best argument I've ever heard for living in New York."

"She's right, though," Kelly said, defending her aunt. "They avoid us like the plague."

"This one's avoidance instinct seems to be malfunctioning."

He had a point. Kelly looked at the now-docile gator and wondered if Zee wasn't making a big mistake.

"I think," said Corrigan, "that Animal Control should be called. Seth's right; this animal isn't avoiding people."

Kelly nodded reluctantly, ignoring Zee's frown.

"Zee, they're right. You rescued this gator, didn't you?"

"Well, yes. Some people were complaining that it was in the retention pond behind their houses. Someone even said it ate their dog."

"It's *that* gator? You see? It has a history of not avoiding people."

"But it's hard to avoid people when they're building houses everywhere," Zee said reasonably enough. "We move into *their* territory, then get all in a tizzy because they don't leave. Except where are they supposed to go?"

Kelly walked up onto the porch and touched Zee's arm. "I know. It's terrible. And it's really all our fault. But this gator has done a little more than hang out in a retention pond. Apparently, wherever you were keeping him wasn't meeting his needs. Because here he is, away from water, on our front porch."

Zee studied the porch planks for a few minutes. "All right," she said. "But let me make a few phone calls first. Maybe I can find a better alternative."

She started to go into the house, but paused, looking at Corrigan. "You said something about the elephants?"

He nodded. "Junior has decided to drop the charges. The vet's report made him see sense."

"Good. Well, that's one load off my mind." Then she disappeared inside.

Max put down the snare. "I guess he's not going anywhere."

"Not right now," Seth agreed. He looked at Kelly. "I'm sorry I frightened you."

"You didn't frighten me. You made me furious."

"For some people," he remarked all too wisely, "it's the same thing."

Chapter 19

An hour later, a friend of Zee's in the animal rights community showed up to take the alligator away to his own farm in south-central Florida.

The children, who'd come out to see the creature, were all excited.

"Can't you just imagine," Seth said to Kelly, "what they're going to tell their mother about their visit here? Tigers and elephants and an alligator on the porch. She'll be out to scalp me."

"She might be right. You know, if you won't consider your safety for your own sake, you ought to at least consider it for the sake of the children."

His eyes narrowed. "I wouldn't have done it if I hadn't figured out how to do it safely. And I'm not the only one around here who could do better at considering the feelings of others."

She flushed, mainly because she knew he was right. No matter how deluded she might be about some things, she couldn't lie to herself that easily. So she changed the subject. "We'd better go pick our costumes for tonight."

"Chicken."

She longed to give him a Bronx cheer, but refrained because the children were watching. "At least I'm not foolhardy."

"Oh, stop it, you two," Bea said. "Go on up to the attic. I'll watch the children."

They climbed the stairs to the attic shoulder-to-shoulder in stiff silence—like children being sent to their punishment, Kelly thought with unwilling amusement. The worst part of all this was that she couldn't seem to stay angry with Seth for long.

The attic ran most of the length of the house. Huge enough to be a ballroom, it was well kept and clean, and well-lit. Granny had saved a great deal of stuff over the years, but it was all organized, thanks to the efforts of Kelly and the staff.

"Where do we start to look?" Seth asked, glancing around. "There's enough crap here to furnish two houses."

Kelly pointed. "Over in that corner. There are a half dozen or so steamer trunks and armoires."

"Good. I'd hate to think I had to plow through everything."

She led the way, feeling the whispers of childhood around the edges of her mind. "I used to play up here sometimes. In the daylight. I never wanted to come up in the dark."

"Funny how we think ghosts are limited to basements and attics. As if they couldn't just go wherever they want."

"I'm not sure I ever feared ghosts, but there are so many dark nooks and crannies that it made me uneasy at night."

"I can see why. Almost anything could hide up here."

They reached the trunks and the armoires, all neatly arranged in their corner. A tall, dusty pier glass stood there, too, showing signs of having been recently wiped at just about the height a child would need.

Kelly opened the first armoire. The hinges

creaked protestingly, and a musty smell emerged. Inside were Bea's discarded evening gowns. "You know, Granny could make a fortune selling this stuff."

"Why doesn't she?"

"Memories. I asked her once."

He nodded, looking sober. "Men's clothes?"

"In the trunks, I think." She forgot about him—well, tried to—while she looked through the gowns. As a child when she'd played dress-up, these had been off limits. She had a feeling they weren't now that she was grown up, and she looked at everything from gold lamé to white satin covered with pearlescent beads. The one she really wanted to wear, though, was dark green watered satin that seemed to change color as she moved it. Wondering if it would fit her, she pulled it out and held it up.

Seth looked at her. "Did she mean for us to look silly or gorgeous? Because you'd look gorgeous in that."

"Thank you." The compliment warmed her all the way to her toes. Looking at herself in the pier glass, she decided there was no way she was going to wear anything else. Her life so far hadn't offered her many opportunities to look like a princess, and she wasn't going to pass up the only one she might have. The waist would be a little tight, but not unbearably so.

"I'm wearing this," she announced.

"Good. I like it. However, I have a small problem."

She turned to look at him. "What?"

"Well, actually it's a large problem. I don't think any of the men in your family have been my size."

She looked at the tux he was holding up and a

laugh escaped her. "You're right." In his hands, the suit looked like child's clothing.

He shook his head and set it aside. "Bea doesn't always think these things through. Hey, what's this?"

He held up a little girl's dress, white dotted Swiss with little embroidered strawberries on it.

Kelly felt her heart turn over. "I wore that to my first day of kindergarten. I loved that dress."

"I'll bet you were adorable in it."

She had no idea if she had been, but sitting down on one of the trunks, she took the dress from him and smoothed it over her lap. "I remember that day so well. Granny and all the others took me to school. I was so frightened, but I felt so good in this dress."

He sat facing her. "The first day is scary."

She nodded, and her heart ached as she remembered that day. Remembered that year. Her parents had died only a few weeks before, and she'd been feeling lost and lonely. The family had been there every minute for her, holding her, hugging her, kissing her, praising her. She could even remember her uncle Max saying, "If you weren't my niece, Kelly, I'd marry you in an instant. You're so pretty you break my heart."

So she had felt good about herself when she walked into school that first day. She'd felt like the prettiest, most special princess in the world. Why hadn't that feeling lasted?

She looked up at Seth. "They were so good to me," she heard herself say.

He nodded.

"It couldn't have been easy for them, having to take over when my parents died."

"Somehow I doubt they even thought about that."

"Probably not." She folded the dress carefully and put it back in the trunk. "I wonder why Granny didn't bring all the stuff from my room up here."

"What stuff?"

"The closet is full of my old dresses, and there's a trunk full of my toys and awards."

"Maybe," he said slowly, "she didn't want them put away where it would be difficult to get to them."

The thought pierced her heart like an arrow. Grabbing the green dress, she stood. "I've got to go downstairs. Will you be all right looking for stuff by yourself?"

"I'm not going to look any further. I'll either have to make up something myself or go into town. Don't worry about me. I'll find my way down."

She nodded and hurried off, suddenly overwhelmed by a need to talk to her grandmother.

She found Bea in the solarium reading a script while the children drew pictures at the nearby table.

"Oh, the green dress," Bea said when she saw what Kelly was carrying. "I wore that to the Academy Awards in—'52, I think."

"It's beautiful," Kelly agreed, sitting beside her grandmother. "But it'll be a little tight around the waist. Is it okay if I wear it?"

"By all means. And if it's tight, that's only because we used to wear girdles back then, dear. I wore a special strapless, full-length one under that. Unfortunately, I think I threw it out. It did such nice things for my figure, though."

"Granny?" Kelly wasn't interested in girdles. She had more important things on her mind.

"Yes, dear?"

"Why did you keep all my toys and awards in

the chest in my room? And my formals in the closet?"

"Well." Bea looked down at her book, then closed it gently. "You know I never throw anything away."

"I know. But you didn't put it up in the attic, either."

Bea nodded. "Well, child, we wanted your things where we could look at them from time to time. We all rather missed you. You'll never know how many evenings we spent taking your things out and remembering . . ." Her voice trailed off and she looked away.

This time Kelly didn't wonder if her grandmother was acting. Not even Bea could have mastered that particular break in her voice, the way it quivered as if she couldn't breathe right.

Kelly tossed the green gown aside and knelt in front of her grandmother, throwing her arms around Bea and hugging the woman's slender body tightly. "I'm sorry, Granny. I'm sorry I went away for so long."

Bea's hand came up to stroke her hair gently. "It's all right. It's something children need to do."

"But I didn't need to do it for so long."

Bea hugged her back. "Yes, you did. You did it exactly as long as you needed to. It's all right."

"No, it's not. But I won't go away like that again, I promise." Tears were burning her eyes and leaving hot trails down her cheeks. "I'm so sorry . . ."

"It's all right," Granny said again, as she had so often when Kelly was a child. She patted Kelly's back gently, trying to comfort her. "It's all right."

Kelly sniffled and lifted her tear-streaked face so she could look at her grandmother. "Just promise me one thing."

"Anything."

"No more matchmaking."

Bea raised both eyebrows, giving her best innocent look. "I'm sure I don't know what you're talking about."

"Yes, you do. And no more of it."

A little while later, Kelly hunted up her uncle Max, who was in his studio, smearing angry colors across a canvas. She opened her mouth to apologize, then saw what he was doing.

"What's wrong, Uncle Max?"

"The weather. I haven't had any decent painting light in days. What, I ask you, is the point of living in Florida if it's going to be as gloomy as the Pacific Northwest?"

"I'm sure I don't know. But you're painting . . ."

"I'm exercising. I have to keep my control, my flexibility, my command of the brush . . ."

To Kelly it didn't look as if he were controlling anything, but rather as if he were just painting angry streaks and blotches of color. With a sigh, he set his palette and brush aside. "What can I do for you, honey?"

"I just wanted to apologize."

"What for?"

"For staying away so long."

"You really don't need to do that."

"Yes, I do. For *me*."

He smiled and held out an arm. She came close and hugged him.

"You've always been a great dad, Uncle Max."

"I tried. I realize I shouldn't have given you those painting lessons, though."

She laughed quietly. "Well, I learned I can't paint."

"But you *can*. Maybe not with oil, but you paint in light on your web pages, don't you? I especially like the one you did for that woman's health center, with the silhouette of the woman outlined in rainbow colors. Very artistic."

His approval was a balm to her soul, and she looked up at him with misty eyes. "Thanks, Uncle Max."

"I'm just telling the truth. Ask Mavis. She'll tell you. The only reason we have that computer in the house was so we could follow your work. We're all very proud of you."

Next, Kelly went into the conservatory to find Jules or Mavis, one of whom was always in there practicing during the day. Stepping into it, she found that the smells carried her back to the hours she had spent here taking violin and piano lessons, and voice lessons from Mavis. Had it really been so bad?

No. It had not. And right now she was feeling a strong wave of nostalgia.

No one was in there. Propelled by memories, she wandered around, touching the keys of the piano, remembering their smooth, cool feel under her smaller hands.

There was some sheet music on the holder, hand written. Apparently Uncle Jules was composing again. He'd done some violin concerti in the past that had received wide acclaim, and looking at his carefully penned notations, she found that she had not forgotten nearly as much as she thought she had. Or perhaps she had learned more than she thought, because reading the notes filled her mind with the music. She could hear it as if Jules were playing it, and it was a lovely, lovely piece.

Wanting to experience more of it, she flipped back to the beginning . . . and felt her heart stop.

The piece was titled "Kelly's Song."

Almost without realizing it, her throat tight and her eyes burning, Kelly sat down at the piano and began to play the notes before her. She was not a gifted pianist and would never stand on a concert stage, but she could play quite adequately. As the notes filled the air around her, she felt peace beginning to fill her. Uncle Jules had always had a gift for haunting melodies, and she felt that this one would always be in her heart.

When the last notes faded away, she was reluctant to let go of them. She thought about playing the piece through again. But she was aware that it was unfinished, and no matter how many times she played it, it would never fully satisfy her until Jules completed it. An unfinished work—like her.

She heard a sound behind her and turned to see Jules standing there. "It's not finished," he said, looking embarrassed.

"Uncle Jules, it's beautiful."

"You played it beautifully. With exactly the kind of feeling I wanted. It's nice to hear someone else play it through. Thank you."

"No, thank *you*."

He came to sit beside her on the bench. "I've written other versions of it over the years, but was never able to finish them. It was odd, you know? I knew it was your song. Somehow it expressed you perfectly . . . at least to me. But it wasn't until you came home this time that I thought I could complete it. Here. Listen."

He put his hands on the keys and played the piece from the beginning while Kelly turned the pages. It sounded just the way she had played it, as if he were mimicking her interpretation, but when he reached the end of the handwritten music, he kept playing, taking the original melody and weaving it in and out, carrying it higher and higher until it was full and almost majestic, like a fulfilled dream.

When he stopped playing, she couldn't even speak. She closed her eyes and let the dying notes resound through her.

Finally he asked, "What do you think?"

She opened her eyes. "I think it's the best piece you've ever written."

He smiled at her. "I had the best inspiration."

She turned and hugged him. "I'm sorry I stayed away so long."

"That's okay. We understood you needed to."

A short while later, she had much the same conversation when she attempted to apologize to Mavis. And afterward, her heart felt lighter than it had in years.

Which only left Seth to trouble her, she realized. She had made her peace with her family, but there was no way to make peace with Seth. He was avoiding her, and she could have predicted he was going to avoid her, although not to this degree, when she had tumbled into bed with him. At least he, unlike other men of her acquaintance, hadn't promised undying love. He'd been utterly straightforward from the outset.

And she'd agreed anyway, so she had no one but herself to blame for the way she was hurting now. She hadn't wanted to get involved, either. But for the first time in her romantic life, she'd let her wants overrule her common sense, had even deluded herself into thinking that she wanted a fling without attachment.

Apparently her brain had slipped out of gear.

So she couldn't make peace with Seth, and making peace with herself promised to be difficult. She'd never been able to forgive herself for being a fool.

Deciding that she couldn't hang around here any longer, Kelly picked up the phone and made a reservation to fly home the next morning. She'd already dragged this visit out a lot longer than she had intended, long past the point when she'd realized that Seth was no threat to the family's fortune. There were no more excuses for hanging around.

Afterward, she told herself she felt better. But of course she didn't. She hurt worse than ever.

Bea insisted she would dress the children for the party to surprise their father, so Seth brought them over early. They were both so excited they could hardly contain themselves.

Seth, however, decided to beard the lion. "Bea, could I have a word with you?"

Bea nodded and motioned him to come to the far side of the sitting room while the children explored a set of hand-painted coasters she'd brought back years ago from Brazil. "What's wrong?"

"Nothing, really. I just want you to know we're on to you."

She lifted a brow and brought the tip of her cigarette holder to her lips, as if she were going to inhale. "How so?"

"Kelly and I both figured out your matchmaking scheme."

"I have no idea what you're talking about."

He nodded slowly. "You're a great actress, Bea, but whenever you lie, there's this little tic at the corner of your eye."

She made an outraged gasp.

"I don't know whose brilliant idea it was to make Kelly think I had designs on your fortune, but it didn't work. And trying to come up with activities that will throw Kelly and me together, or take the kids away and leave us alone together, is so transparent I'm ashamed of you. I thought you could do better."

"Well." Bea puffed on the end of her cigarette holder and pretended to blow a cloud of smoke toward the ceiling. "The whole thing about you handling the family finances was designed to get her home for a visit. That was *all*."

"Why don't I believe you?"

"Maybe because you're plagued with a suspicious mind. Really, Seth, I thought you knew me better than this."

"I do. Which is why I'm suspicious."

She shook her head. "Well, you're wrong. As you say, I'm a far better schemer than that. I merely wanted to take the children with me to Busch Gardens because it's so much fun, but so terribly boring to go without children. They give one such a *refreshing* view."

He began to wonder if he'd mistaken the whole thing. But then he remembered Cook. "Then why did you tell Cook to hide in one of the bedrooms so Kelly would have to cook?"

"Mavis did that," Bea reminded him. "And it was simply to teach Kelly a lesson. One doesn't offend the staff needlessly unless one is willing to do without them."

"Really. So then she comes over and asks me to help Kelly cook? Bea . . ."

She waved her hand airily. "Because we did want to eat. *That* was pure self-interest."

"Mm." He was beginning to seriously think he'd misjudged everything, and was feeling a little like a fool. "So this isn't some matchmaking scheme?"

"Good heavens, no! You two are ridiculously ill-suited."

Seth felt himself bridle at that, and although he didn't want to, he asked, "Why?"

"Because you're an ex-football player. Kelly needs someone who is more cerebral and less physical. I'm surprised you can't see it."

"Don't be ridiculous."

Bea arched a brow. "I'm not being ridiculous. She's sensitive, perhaps too much so, and you're blunt. Her sensitivity would drive you crazy, and your bluntness would wither her. Give me *some* credit for common sense." Then she turned and went back to the children, leaving Seth feeling annoyingly off balance.

Hanging around with Bea, he thought, could be dangerous to one's sense of reality.

He was just coming out of Bea's rooms when he encountered Kelly in the hall. She was wearing the green satin dress with black pumps, and had done something to give herself a remarkable cleavage. For an instant he could look at nothing else and felt all his resolutions to be wise, sensible, and intelligent blow away like dust before the overwhelming need to pounce on her.

"Um," he said, thunderstruck. "You, um, look *stunning*."

Her mouth twisted wryly. "The compliment would be more flattering if you didn't sound poleaxed."

"Huh?"

"You don't need to sound so shocked that I can look good."

"Oh." His brain cells were beginning to talk to one another again. "I didn't mean that. I just meant you . . . uh . . . look good enough to devour." Then he grinned, and wiggled his eyebrows at her.

"You have a problem," she said tartly.

"What's that?"

"Your brain has slipped."

"Slipped?"

"All the way down into your pants."

"Oh, that. That's my *other* brain."

Then he experienced the sheer delight of watching her dissolve into laughter.

"You're hopeless," she said.

"Probably. But so is your family. We need to talk."

Her smile faded and she searched his face. "Sure. About what?"

"Someplace where we can't be overheard."

Seeing Kelly all dressed up was doing things to him. Stupid things. He found himself offering his arm the way he hadn't done in years. For a moment she looked at it as if she weren't sure what to do with it, then, tentatively, she put her arm through his.

"I can hardly breathe," she confided. "Bea says she used to wear a girdle with this."

"Believe me, you don't need one." As soon as he spoke, he wished he could snatch the words back, because she'd probably take them wrong. Well, not really. He'd intended them just the way he'd said them. He just didn't want her to take offense—although he didn't know why. Having her angry at him would make the keeping away from her part a whole lot easier.

Instead all she did was smile almost shyly and said, "Thank you." Which threw him off balance again. He was beginning to realize that he could never predict exactly how she was going to react—and he rather liked that.

They decided to sit on the veranda out front. The rainy weather had passed, leaving the world feeling cleaner, cooler, and drier.

"So?" she said to him when they were seated.

"I told your grandmother to quit with the matchmaking."

"You didn't! Seth, now she'll really be on her mettle!"

"Wait, wait," he said, holding up a hand. "She denied it."

"Of course she did. Granny never confesses to her schemes."

"Well, that's where you're wrong."

Kelly lifted a brow. "What are you talking about?"

"She admitted to the scheme to get you to believe I was likely to embezzle the family fortune. She said they did that so you would come home for a visit."

Kelly flushed miserably and looked away, lowering her head. "It worked. I'm just so ashamed they had to scheme."

"Be that as it may," he said, focused on his own agenda, "she denied that they'd been scheming to throw us together. She said the thing with Cook was just to teach you a lesson about not offending the servants. And getting me to come help you cook was just to make sure that they actually had a meal to eat."

Kelly's head snapped up, and fire lit her eye. "Really. I'm glad to know they have so much confidence in me."

"I agree."

"But what about the trip to Busch Gardens?"

"Bea swears that was only because she wanted to go and it's so much more fun with children."

Kelly chewed her lower lip. "It's possible, I guess."

Seth shrugged. "Maybe. I know *I* enjoy some things more with the children."

"Well, of course."

"Anyway, Bea said they'd never be foolish enough to try to get us together."

"Why not?"

"Because we're not suited. That's what she said. Because I'm so blunt I'd wither you, and you're so sensitive I'd go crazy."

She gave him a doubtful look. "*Am* I too sensitive?"

He shook his head. "I don't think so. Am I too blunt for you?"

"Actually, I kind of like it. It's nice knowing where I stand."

"So they're wrong."

"Well, it wouldn't be the first time."

"I guess not."

They sat awhile in silence. Finally Kelly said tentatively, "But why did they hide the cookbooks so I couldn't cook?"

Seth looked at her. "Damned if I know."

"Unless Bea's lying about not plotting to matchmake."

Seth thought it over. "No," he said presently. "Her eye wasn't twitching when she said it. It's a dead giveaway when she's lying."

"Unless she's acting."

Seth sighed and leaned over so he could put his arm around her shoulder. "I'm surprised you didn't go nuts when you were a kid. Dealing with that woman must have left you feeling as if reality were shifting sand beneath your feet. Is she lying? Is she acting? Is this the real Bea?" He shook his head.

"I thought you liked her."

"I do. I adore her. She's a riot. But she didn't raise me."

"True."

Silence again fell, and Seth was pleased to note that Kelly didn't try to shrug off his arm. In fact, she even seemed to move a little closer.

"Well," he said after a while, "there's only one thing to do."

"What's that?"

"Pretend to be crazy about each other."

She looked up at him, bringing her mouth within kissing distance. The effort he exerted to refrain nearly tied him up in knots. "Why? What good will it do?"

"It will give them a fit—and I'm really in the mood to do it. I've been blowing it off since I figured out what was going on, but the more I think about it, the more I resent the fact that they impugned my honor by suggesting that I might be out to steal from them."

She nodded slowly. From his perspective, that would be extremely annoying. "Scandalous," she said. "Libelous."

"Well, I don't feel like suing. So I need another method of retaliation. If they're so sure we're a mismatch, then they'll be upset if we act like we're crazy about each other. They'll be seriously worried that you're making a major mistake."

The more Kelly thought about that, the wider her grin grew. "This could be fun. And maybe it'll teach them to quit meddling."

"Well, I don't know about that. Meddlers tend to remain meddlers. But it'll sure set them back on their heels." He glanced at his watch. "How long until the party? Forty minutes? I'll be back."

Then, before she could say another word, he dashed off in the direction of the guest house.

Chapter 20 ✎

Seth was late. They delayed dinner for him, until Cook threatened to throw the entire dinner in the trash.

"Well, I can't imagine where he's gone," Granny said, "but we may as well start without him."

The children were dressed up like characters out of a fairy tale. Jenny wore one of Bea's old cocktail dresses from the days of miniskirts, and on her it looked like a formal gown. She also wore clip-on earrings and a paste necklace, as well as a piece of feather boa that Granny had ruthlessly cut to size. Johnny had chosen to wear an old suit jacket that came to his ankles and a gray fedora that kept wanting to fall over his eyes.

Max had gone for the pirate look, with an old leather vest and a pair of baggy pants cut off at the knees. Around his waist he had tied one of Bea's old satin stoles. Jules was wearing an old football jersey and shoulder pads that kept trying to slip off. Mavis had strapped a golden breastplate from a long-ago opera over her plum-colored gown. Bea had decided to come as a bag lady, wearing a tattered cotton housedress and a man's sports jacket.

And Lawrence. Lawrence had been invited as a

guest tonight and sat proudly at Bea's right in his British army uniform. The smell of mothballs wafted down the table, and the uniform was loose on him, but he looked proud and impressive nonetheless in his scarlet coat.

And the way Bea was looking at him made Kelly's heart flutter hopefully.

Manuel served. Out of deference to the children, he had abandoned his maid's costume and tonight wore a simple black suit and bow tie.

"He's home," Manuel announced as he served the hot dogs and french fries—Granny's idea of a formal menu for children—on Wedgwood china.

"Who's home?" Bea asked.

"Mr. Ralston. His car passed the kitchen on the way to the guest house about fifteen minutes ago."

"Well, then he should be here at any moment. Thank you, Manuel."

Orange soda was served in crystal wine glasses, and Lawrence was tipping it down with all the panache of an inveterate tippler. The children's eyes were shining in great appreciation of the fancy dishes and the hot dogs. Kelly decided Bea knew exactly how to please kids. But she always had. She could remember other nights when the family had dined in their best finery on hot dogs or pizza selected just for Kelly.

But as the minutes continued to tick by, Kelly felt her spirits falling. Apparently Seth had decided to disappear again. Silly as it was, she felt as if the entire evening had been ruined.

But Seth was not trying to do a disappearing act. He'd planned to come to the party as a beach bum, wearing his own cutoffs and a tank top. Looking at Kelly all dressed up in the beautiful gown had changed his mind. Unfortunately, finding a tuxedo large enough to fit him had been a bit difficult. He'd finally found one that just barely fit and was struggling with the cummerbund when the phone rang.

It was Velvet.

"I'm in Tampa," she said.

He felt his heart sink. "What happened to Rome?"

"We had a fight."

"I'm sorry, Velvet."

"I'm not. The old goat. Anyway, I've met someone else . . . well, you don't need to know about that."

No, he really didn't. Much as he'd come to dislike Velvet over the past year, he still felt a wound to his masculine ego at the idea that she was seeing someone else, no matter how many times she did it.

"The point is," she continued when he didn't say anything, "I've decided to go to Japan."

The thought of Velvet in Japan made him feel sorry for the Japanese. The woman's notions of courtesy would probably try them sorely. "That's nice."

"We're leaving the day after tomorrow, and I'll be gone for three weeks."

"I'll be glad to keep the children—if I hear from your attorney."

"I already told him to write the letter, Seth. Your lawyer should have it by the end of the week."

"Good."

He tucked the phone between his ear and shoulder, and struggled to fasten the cummerbund, which was about an inch short for his waist. He glanced at the clock and almost groaned when he realized how late he was for dinner.

"Anyway," Velvet continued, "I want you to

come get me tonight. Or bring the children to see me. It'll be the only opportunity I have to see them for weeks."

His heart stilled and he forgot the cummerbund. For an instant, he felt nothing at all. Then he felt a fury of white heat. This woman had been messing up his life for the last year, and now she wanted to mess up this evening—his children's evening to have fun. Kelly's evening. Several moments passed before he could get a sufficient grip on his anger to speak calmly.

"Not tonight, Velvet."

"Why not? They're *my* children!"

"They're my children, too. And tonight Bea is throwing a costume party for them. At this very moment they're all dressed up and eating dinner, and looking forward to an evening of playing games and being entertained. I'm not going to ruin it for them."

"But I have plans for tomorrow!"

"Then cancel your damn plans for once and put the children first!" He slammed down the phone with a sense of immense satisfaction at having finally spoken his mind. Then he had a terrible, piercing sense of anxiety as he realized that he'd just pissed her off, and she might well resume the custody dispute.

But, God, he was sick of tiptoeing around her. Sick of never telling her what he thought of how she was caring for the children. Sick of having her dictate everything. Sick of having her decide when, if, and how he could see his children.

Tossing the cummerbund aside, he picked up the phone again and called his lawyer. It was late, the office was closed, but as always, Will was there.

"You need to get a new job," he told Will. "You work too late."

"Hey, the only time I can get any real work done is after the phone stops ringing and the court is closed for the day. What's up?"

Seth sketched the latest developments with Velvet, then waited as Will mulled them over.

"How nasty do you want to get?" Will said presently.

"I'm getting to the point where I'll do anything so that the kids aren't being shuffled around like baggage."

"She's left them with the nanny for several weeks at a time before, hasn't she?"

"This is the fourth time since we split."

"I can certainly make a case for abandonment, especially this time. I can't guarantee you'll win it, though. Listen, let me call her attorney and see what I can hammer out. Meantime, go enjoy your party."

As if he felt like enjoying anything right now. But he picked up the cummerbund, cinched it into place, and headed for the villa. He was *not* going to ruin the children's evening.

Or Kelly's. But what he didn't realize as he strode up to the house was that Kelly had become just as important in that equation as his kids.

Or maybe he wasn't ready to recognize it.

Seth arrived in the dining room in time to have a hot dog and ice-cream cake for dessert. Kelly watched him laugh and joke with his children, still feeling a strong yearning to be part of that circle. He also looked scrumptious in that tux, which surprised her, because she'd never particularly cared for men in tuxedos.

After dinner they moved into the conservatory, where a carnival atmosphere prevailed. Mavis sang an aria, accompanied by Jules on the piano, then

Jules played the violin for the children, weaving familiar children's tunes together. Max set up an easel and did portraits of Johnny and Jenny, first good ones in charcoal, then caricatures that had them screaming with laughter and demanding that he do one of their dad. Seth grinned as Max depicted him as a huge-bodied football player with an itty bitty head. The kids loved it.

Bea had dragged out the puppet theater that had once been Kelly's, and she and Lawrence did a little skit with hand puppets. Apparently they'd done quite a bit of rehearsing, and they had everyone laughing.

But eventually the children grew sleepy. Seth wanted to take them back to the guest house to put them to bed, but Bea insisted the evening was young, and the children were tucked in upstairs.

Then Jules put some music on the stereo. Lawrence rose and went to Bea, bowing grandly. "Dance, m'lady?" he asked.

She smiled and offered him her hand, and the two of them began to waltz around the room.

"They make a wonderful couple, don't they?" Seth asked Kelly. She nodded, her cheeks almost aching from the wideness of her smile.

"Maybe they've figured it out," he said.

"I sure hope so."

Max interrupted. "Will you dance with me, my dear?"

Kelly sailed off in her uncle's arms, remembering how he had danced like this with her when she'd been a mere girl, teaching her the intricacies of ballroom dancing. Seth partnered Mavis, who'd shed her breastplate, and soon three couples were whirling around the room.

Then Jules put on a tango. Max immediately

grabbed Mavis for the dance, leaving Seth and Kelly together.

"Now," said Seth, with a wicked glint in his eye, "let's leave them gasping."

"You know how to tango?"

"There's very little I can't do, sweetie. Just watch me."

Kelly, who had learned to tango under Max's tame tutelage, found herself in a dance that wasn't tame at all. It was downright X-rated. They soon had the floor to themselves as Seth bent her, bowed her, dragged her, tossed her—and did just about everything except make love to her on the dance floor. And what she was beginning to feel was definitely X-rated.

When the music fell silent, she was bent back over Seth's arm, panting for air, her cheeks flushed and her hair mussed. Their eyes were locked together, and the messages that were flying between them made her feel even more breathless.

Silence fell in the room, and it occurred to her that she had at long last succeeded in shocking her unshockable family. She rather liked the feeling, and started to smile.

"So *this* is how you have a party for the children?"

A woman's voice cut through the silence. Kelly felt her heart slam, and saw Seth's eyes narrow. An instant later she was upright and standing on her own two feet, no easy thing considering the rapid change of position had left her feeling light-headed.

She saw Velvet Ralston, wearing a neat, businesslike navy-blue dress, standing on the threshold. Beside her stood Manuel, his bow tie undone, looking as if he couldn't decide whether to kill her or just flee.

"I'm sorry," said Manuel. "I asked her to wait."

"I'm glad I didn't," Velvet said, storming across the room toward Seth. "A party for the children indeed."

Kelly could hardly believe her eyes when Bea stuck out her foot as Velvet barreled by her. Velvet took a sprawling fall.

"Oh, I'm so sorry," Bea said in a tone of sheer horror. "I'm so very sorry! I can't control that leg since my stroke, you know . . ."

Max made a sound like a swallowed laugh. Velvet picked herself up and glared at Bea. "Who are you? Some kind of servant?" Then she turned to Seth, jabbing her finger at him. "That was the most disgusting display I've ever seen. And why are you dancing with this trollop?"

Seth's response was low, dangerous-sounding. "Watch what you say, Velvet."

"I will *not*! I ask you to bring the children to Tampa to see me, and you tell me they're having a party. Well, what the hell kind of party is *this*?"

"The children have gone to bed," Seth said flatly. "And I don't think there's any law against dancing."

"Really? There ought to be a law against what you were doing. It was obscene."

"My," said Bea, rising from her chair. "How interesting. We were rehearsing a scene from my next commercial."

"*Your* commercial!" Velvet took a second look at Bea, and for the first time a hint of discomfort showed on her face.

"Bea," said Seth, "meet my ex-wife, Velvet. Velvet, this lady is my hostess, Bea Burke."

Velvet skimmed Bea with her eyes and her mouth curled. "Really."

"Really," said Bea, smiling too sweetly. "And

that trollop is my granddaughter. Would you like to start over again?"

Velvet looked nonplussed ... but not for very long. "What was I supposed to think, walking in on this? You look like a bag lady."

"That was the idea," Seth said. "We all dressed up and had a carnival for the children. I put them to bed just a while ago. Now I suppose you expect me to wake them up. Velvet, do you ever really take the children into consideration?"

She looked ready to spit nails, but reined in her temper. "Of course I do. Why else would I drive more than an hour out of my way to see them? But if this is the kind of environment you're exposing them to ..."

Seth cocked his head. "What are you going to do about it? Cancel your trip to Japan?"

Velvet backed down. "Of course not. But I think you ought to be more careful. You might think it's all right to live a wild bachelor lifestyle now—"

"Wild bachelor lifestyle?" Bea asked in amazement. Then she chortled.

Velvet rounded on her. "What's your problem?"

"The idea of Seth living a wild bachelor lifestyle. The man's practically a hermit, working on his dissertation. We have to all but lasso him to drag him out for some fun. Of course, he won't hear of hiring a nanny to look after the children so he can enjoy himself. He has some stupid idea that being a father actually obliges him to take care of the children."

Velvet's face darkened, and Seth hastened to intervene. "Bea, that's enough. This is between Velvet and me."

"You're damn right," said his ex.

"Well, excuse me for having an opinion," said Bea, looking offended. Turning, she went back to her chair and sat, her lips tightly compressed to make a point. Kelly felt a wild, totally irrational urge to laugh, but she stopped herself, not wanting to make things any worse for Seth.

Velvet was far from finished. "I can't believe you were dancing like that. What if the children saw?"

"Then I would have told them we were just being silly. It would probably be as easy for them to understand as when you have a man stay overnight."

Red spots of angry color began to burn high on Velvet's cheeks. "You have no right to say anything about how I choose to live."

"Exactly."

Silence filled the room again as Velvet digested his meaning. Finally she said, "I want to see the children. Now."

"Sure. Come with me."

Kelly watched the two of them leave the room, and her heart ached for Seth that he had to deal with this mess. It had to be just awful for him.

"You know," Bea said, getting Kelly's attention, "you don't want to get involved with him, child."

"I'm not involved, Granny."

"Maybe not yet. But keep in mind, if you get involved with him, you'll be getting involved with his ex-wife and the children. Are you sure you want to take that on?"

"We're not involved," Kelly said firmly.

"Good," said Max. "That relieves me of the need to kill that woman."

Kelly suddenly couldn't stand another minute in this room, listening to her family comment on what she should or shouldn't do. "I need some air," she announced. Picking up her skirts, she marched out of the room.

"I'm sorry," Manuel said again as she passed him. "I tried to keep her out front."

"It's okay, Manuel. You'd probably need to point a gun at that woman to keep her from doing whatever she wants to."

Outside, the night had cooled considerably. Kelly felt goose bumps rising on her bare arms—an indicator of how quickly she was readjusting to the heat here. Walking around the side of the house, she found the elephants. The baby came up to her and nudged her with his trunk, so she patted him and scratched his head.

Her shock at Velvet's behavior was starting to wear off, and tears began to sting her eyes.

She was already involved. It didn't really matter, because her feelings weren't reciprocated, but she was involved nonetheless. She wanted to strangle Velvet for the way she was hurting Seth. She wanted to strangle her for being such a neglectful mother. And she wanted to kick herself for being so stupid as to get tangled up with a man who had almost no interest in her, a man who came with enough problems attached that life with him would be one conflict after another about things over which she would have no control.

Deciding she was a fool, she sat on a stone bench with the baby elephant's trunk on her lap and tried not to cry. Here she had thought herself immune, had bellowed that she had taught her head to rule her heart. And now she discovered, too late, that her heart was ruling her head.

How dumb could she get?

Seth went upstairs with Velvet. He half expected her to tell him to get lost while she talked with the children. He wouldn't have blamed her if she had. But she didn't say a word when he stood inside the

door while she sat on the edge of their bed and
gently woke them.

His throat tightened when they climbed across
the bed and snuggled close to her, their sleepy
faces smiling when she hugged them. They loved
her and needed her, and no matter how angry he
was with her, he couldn't allow himself to forget
that. She was their *mother*.

They were clearly disappointed when she told
them she was going on another trip and couldn't
stay, but they brightened when she said they could
stay with him. They told her about the elephants
and the tigers, and about the party they'd just had,
and the trip to Busch Gardens. Afterward, they
snuggled back under the blankets and she kissed
them good night.

Outside in the hallway, Seth and Velvet looked
at one another.

"You'll have to enroll Jenny in school here," Velvet said after a moment. "I'm going to be gone too
much, and unless you want to move to New
York..."

He shook his head. "I never liked it there. You
know that."

"So put them in school here. I'll have my maid
pull all the necessary papers together for you."

"Thanks. I take it this is going to be longer than
three weeks?"

She sighed and looked away. "I don't know. I do
know it's going to take however long it takes to
sort out my own life. Listen..." She glanced at
him, then looked away.

"Yes?"

"You're not going to come back to me, are you?"

The question was like a punch in the solar
plexus. His lungs froze. Finally he managed,
"What?"

She shrugged. "I did a really stupid thing, Seth."

"What's that?"

"I divorced you. I thought I could make you take the network job. But you wouldn't buckle. So after the divorce was final, I panicked and filed the custody suit. I figured I'd get you back that way because you wouldn't want to lose the children, too."

"My God!" He was stunned.

She shook her head. "I was stupid. I know that."

"And manipulative," he said, still trying to absorb what she had said. This woman had ruined his life because she wanted him to take that job and thought she could force him to change his mind? That somehow seemed even worse than that she hadn't loved him at all.

"And manipulative," she agreed. "So, okay. I blew it. I misjudged you. And I guess, from the way you were looking at Kelly when you danced with her, that it's too damn late to apologize and try to win you back."

It was. The realization flooded him. All the pain and bitterness were gone now, but not because of what Velvet had just told him. They were gone because of Kelly. The realization left him almost thunderstruck.

"I thought so," Velvet said, and sighed again. "Oh, well. Live and learn. You keep the kids for now. I've got to replace what I threw away before I can really settle down again. We'll work out arrangements later."

She took a step away, then looked back to say, "I didn't love you enough. But you know what? You didn't love me enough, either."

He shook his head, checked on the children one more time and found them sound asleep. Then he went to look for Kelly.

Chapter 21

Kelly was still sitting on the stone bench when Seth found her. The baby elephant had decided to hug her, and had its trunk draped over her shoulder. Mama elephant didn't seem to mind; she just kept grazing on the remnants of the shrubbery.

Seth sat beside Kelly.

"How'd it go?" she asked.

"Velvet seems to be having a change of heart."

"Really?" Her heart lurched. Was he going back to his wife? But even as she felt swamped by dismay, she thought how unkind and selfish she was being. She had glimpsed Seth's pain over his wife's betrayal, and if he had the opportunity to make things right with her, she ought to be cheering for him. But she was in no mood to cheer.

"Yeah," he said. "She told me she divorced me because she thought it would make me change my mind about the broadcasting job."

"Major miscalculation." Which was the kindest thing she could bring herself to say. Right now, nothing she was feeling was kind. At another time, she might have been shocked by the violence of her own feelings.

"It sure was." He fell silent a minute, leaving her

to wonder what catastrophic news would come next. "Anyway," he said finally, "she told me the whole reason she filed the custody suit was to get me to change my mind and come back to her so I wouldn't lose the kids."

Kelly's anger flared to an uncontainable white heat. "What an awful thing to do to you! But worse, what a terrible, terrible thing to do to those children!"

"That thought *has* crossed my mind," he said. "I don't think she was thinking too clearly."

Now he was making excuses for Velvet. Kelly felt as if her heart were drying up, withering right in her chest.

He stood up suddenly. "Let's take a walk. The moon's bright enough."

It was indeed. It was high in the sky, a full moon, and it drenched the world in silver light. The baby elephant made a small sound when Kelly rose, but it backed away, then returned to its mother's side. The adult elephant reached around and gently touched her baby with her trunk, drawing him closer. Kelly felt her anger fade, and her throat tightened with disappointed yearnings.

Together she and Seth started down the path to the beach. The sea breeze was blowing, filling the woods with the sounds of leaves rustling and palms clattering. The night was alive with soft sound, and the breeze itself was a warm caress on Kelly's skin.

All her life she'd loved the nighttime sea breeze. It had always made her feel just a little wild, just a little excited, and very much alive. Even now, as she felt sure she was about to hear that Seth was returning to Velvet, she could feel the familiar touch of the night breeze, could cling to the memory of how good it had always made her feel.

The path was dark and shadowed by the trees, but worn smooth by many feet over the years. She and Seth were able to walk along it without any trouble.

At last they reached the beach, stepping out into an argent world where silver sparkled on the moonlit gulf and the beach glowed whitely. Kelly kicked off her pumps and stepped barefoot onto the cool sand. Her toes curled into it, as if seeking stability in the emotional whirlwind she was feeling.

Seth stood with his hands on his hips, looking up at the sky, as if he hoped to read a message in the stars. Kelly filled her eyes with the sight of him, suddenly realizing that this might be the very last time they stood here together like this. That it probably would be. She had already made up her mind to return to Colorado tomorrow before she got into any more trouble, and she wouldn't have been surprised if Seth packed his kids up in the morning and returned to New York. Not every man got a second chance with a wife who had divorced him, and from everything Seth had said, the split had hurt him badly. He'd be a fool not to take the chance Velvet had offered.

Eventually Seth dropped his hands from his hips and looked at her. "The question," he said, "is what do I owe my kids?"

She nodded, her throat growing so tight that she couldn't speak.

"Because," he said slowly, "I don't love Velvet anymore."

Kelly's heart took a furtive leap, then crashed again. As he'd said, the thing he had to consider was the children.

"The thing is, I don't think I could love her again after this, even if I tried."

She nodded, still unable to speak.

"She's hurt me too much. I couldn't ever trust her again. If she was willing to go to these lengths to make me take a job I didn't want, I hate to think what she might do over something *really* important."

Even though the words burned her throat, fairness prompted Kelly to say, "Maybe she's learned her lesson."

"Maybe." He reached out and took her hand. "Let's walk."

Why not? she thought. The waves were gentle tonight, but instead of their usual lullaby, they seemed to be singing a sad song, whispering of dreams wrecked on the shoals.

"The thing is," he continued, "if I went back to her, it would only be for the sake of the children. And I'm not sure it would do a damn bit of good in the long run."

"Why not?"

"Who's to say she wouldn't try something like this again? Or do something I absolutely couldn't live with? And we'd wind up in divorce court all over again, and the kids would have to go through all this trauma a second time. I just don't have a whole lot of faith in the notion that two people ought to stay together just for the kids. Especially two people like Velvet and me. She's willing to do nearly anything to get what she wants, and I'm not one to put up with a whole lot of crap in silence. We had some really vicious fights over that job— and over some other things through the years. I'm afraid it would only be worse now."

He squeezed her hand and she squeezed back but said nothing. It wasn't her place to speak. Besides, she was bitterly aware that she had no right to interfere in his decision.

"Anyway, I'm not sure that two miserable parents living together are all that much better than two parents living apart, at least for the kids. I know the theories go both ways, but in divorce it seems it matters more how the parents handle it. Velvet at least seems willing to handle it better now than she did before."

"Really?"

"Yup. She's leaving the kids with me indefinitely, until she sorts her life out, she says."

"That's a change of attitude."

"Isn't it? Words can't describe how I've been missing those kids."

"I can imagine." And indeed she could. When she boarded that plane tomorrow, she was going to be missing Johnny and Jenny nearly as much as ⁣as going to miss their father. In just a few ⁣they had curled up in her heart.

⁣e stopped walking and kicked off his shoes. ⁣en he shucked his jacket, bow tie, and cummerⁿand. "That's better. This damn suit is strangling me."

"Don't like formal dress, huh?"

"I don't mind it. But all I could find to rent was a size too small."

Kelly was feeling the same way in her dress, and on impulse, she turned her back to him. "Unzip me. I want to breathe."

He laughed and obliged, but the brush of his fingertips on her skin sent delightful shivers running through her, shifting her awareness from sorrow to something deeper and more atavistic. Apparently he felt the same spark, because his fingers paused, just barely brushing her back between her shoulder blades.

"You're beautiful," he murmured, his voice mixing with the susurration of the waves.

Helplessly in thrall to the needs pounding inside her, she turned and faced him. He was smiling, she noticed, a smile that warmed her to her toes.

Without a word, he reached out and tugged gently at her dress. Silently it slipped down until it was nothing but a dark puddle at her feet. She stood before him in her panties and strapless bra, reveling in the brush of the breeze over her bare skin.

One by one, he unfastened the buttons of his shirt, taking his time, his gaze never leaving her. He worked the cuff links loose and tossed them into his shoes. A moment later, his shirt followed. Thirty seconds later, he kicked his pants aside and stripped his socks. When he straightened, he stood before her tall, proud, and naked.

She had never seen a more beautiful sight than Seth bathed in moonlight. She could have stared at him for hours, but he reached out, drawing her against the warm shelter of his chest. She felt her bra clasp release and gave a sigh of pure contentment when he tugged the scrap of fabric away, allowing her breasts to meet his hard chest.

Her world spun, and she found herself lying on her back on his shirt, the sand beneath molding itself to her shape. He pulled her panties off and tossed them, then settled himself between her legs as if sure of his welcome.

For a long time, neither of them moved. The moon and stars wheeled slowly overhead as they clung together, finding warmth and comfort in their closeness. When Seth at last fitted himself inside of her, it seemed like a natural extension of their embrace, and part of the magic of the night around them.

He moved slowly, almost lazily, as if he were in no hurry, as if he didn't particularly care whether they reached the pinnacle. As if all that mattered was the feeling of closeness.

But eventually not even delay could withhold the inevitable. It came out of nowhere for Kelly, a sudden tidal wave of feeling that lifted her so high she felt as if she were flying among the stars. Moments later he joined her.

Afterward neither of them moved, reluctant to disturb the spell. But eventually, little by little, awareness returned. The sand felt hard beneath her, and cold. The tide was coming in, and from time to time she felt the chill of the spray fall on her feet.

At last Seth stirred and sat up. Then he pulled her to her feet and wrapped his white shirt around her, buttoning it with great care. For himself, he pulled on his pants.

Then he drew her close and hugged her.

He spoke. "Are you wedded to Colorado?"

"Most of my clients are there."

"Okay. No problem. What do you think of the kids?" he asked her.

Surprised, she looked at him. "What?"

"What do you think of Johnny and Jenny?"

"They're adorable. I love them to pieces already."

He nodded. "How would you feel about being their stepmother?"

Her heart stopped. "What?" she said again.

"I know it's a lot to take on. I wouldn't blame you if you said you didn't want all the disruption. A lot of people just wouldn't feel comfortable living with somebody else's kids. And then there's Velvet. As long as Johnny and Jenny are young, we're going to have to deal with her. That's a job and a half for anyone."

"Whoa," she said, feeling stunned. "Could you back up a minute?"

"Sure. Back up to what?"

"The part about being their stepmother."

"I thought that's what I was discussing."

"Seth . . ."

"Oh." He grinned sheepishly. "Good point. I should ask first, shouldn't I? Do you want me to kneel?"

Her heart was hammering so hard suddenly that her voice came out a squeak. "Forget the kneeling. Just tell me what you're talking about."

"Good. I'm not sure my knees can take much more tonight. Kelly, I love you. Will you marry me and my rugrats?"

"Oh, my God!" The words escaped her on a gasp.

"I knew it," he said. "It's too much to ask. But really, the kids won't be much trouble. I'll take care of them. I promise."

"Shut up."

"Shut up?"

"Shut up." She closed her eyes, fighting for emotional balance, trying to adjust to the change from the pits to the heights.

"Um . . ." Seth was beginning to sound very hesitant. "Could you let me down easy?"

Her eyes snapped open. "Why would I do that?"

"Well, if you kick me too hard, I might fall . . ."

"I'm not going to let you down."

"My knees—" He broke off. "You're not?"

She shook her head.

"So, uh, are you saying yes?"

She threw her arms around his neck. "I love you," she said in a heartfelt rush. "I thought I was going to die, having to leave tomorrow."

"Tomorrow! You're not leaving tomorrow. Not without me, anyway."

"No . . . no, I'll stay a little longer."

He let out a huge sigh. "So you'll marry me? Will you?"

"Yes. I will marry you."

He let out a whoop of joy, and lifted her right off her feet. "Let's go tell the kids now."

"Now?"

"Now."

"I have to dress . . ."

"They won't wake up enough to notice. Come on." He grabbed up their clothes and shoes and started hurrying her toward the house.

Twenty minutes later, after Seth yielded to Kelly's plea that she at least be allowed to go to her room and change into something suitable, they were sitting on opposite sides of the bed while Seth woke the children. Kelly knew an almost painful apprehension that the kids might not like this idea. That the glow in her heart, so newly born, might be doused by one cross word from either child.

Jenny woke first, sitting up to look quizzically at her father and Kelly. Johnny took a little longer; then, with a naturalness that made Kelly's heart melt, he climbed right into her lap and laid his head on her breast.

"I just wanted to ask you guys a question," Seth said. "What would you think if I married Kelly?"

Johnny popped his thumb in his mouth and didn't say anything. Jenny looked at her hands. Finally she asked, "Do we still get to see Mommy?" Kelly stopped breathing.

"Of course you do. She'll always be your mommy. But Kelly could be your stepmommy."

Jenny nodded. "Good. I like Kelly."

"Johnny?"

Johnny nodded. "I like Kelly, too."

"So we'll adopt her?"

Both children nodded approval.

After they went back to sleep, Kelly and Seth curled up together on the bed in her room.

Seth spoke. "Just a couple of weeks ago, I thought this would never happen to me again."

"What?"

"Love. Marriage." He snuggled her closer. "I love you."

"I love you, too."

"But there's one thing we have to have straight."

"What's that?"

"We're not going to live within a hundred miles of your family. They'll have to do their meddling long-distance."

"That's fine by me, but I thought you loved being around them."

"I love them all," Seth said, "but they'd drive me crazy in short order. I don't have to explain that to you. So we'll live in Colorado and come home to visit, okay?"

"It's perfect."

"Good." He sighed contentedly. "Well, they got what they wanted."

"No, they didn't."

"Hell, yes, they did. If you believe your grandmother's protestations, then you're mistaken. Our Bea got exactly what she wanted. The only thing that worries me is what she might want next."

"Grandkids?" Kelly suggested.

"Oh, well . . . in that case I'll just have to give in. Unless you don't want any more kids."

"Of course I do."

"Well, then." He sighed again, then a while later he laughed. "'All's well that ends well.'"

"Hmm?"

"I'm just thinking that it doesn't really matter who schemed what and why. All that matters is that I've caught you. And catching Kelly was a whole lot of fun."

She kind of agreed with him. Catching Seth had been a whole lot of fun, too.

And now that she had him, she was never going to let him go.

*Celebrate the Millennium
with another irresistible
romance from the pen of
Susan Elizabeth Phillips!*

The beautiful young widow of the President
of the United States is on the run, crossing
America on a journey to find herself. She
plans to travel alone, and she's chosen the
perfect disguise. Well, almost perfect...and
not exactly alone...

FIRST LADY
by Susan Elizabeth Phillips

Coming from Avon Books February 2000

Dear Reader,

If you loved the Avon book you've just read, rest assured next month are four terrific love stories that I know you'll keep an eye out for.

Historical lovers won't want to miss Karen Ranney's *My True Love*. Her heroes are men you'll never forget. Here, meet masterful Stephen Harrington, the Earl of Langlinais — he's battle weary and longing for peace. Instead he rescues a beautiful woman who stirs in him feelings that are anything but peaceful . . .

Here's a name you'll need to remember: Christie Ridgway. She's destined to become a star, and her first full-length contemporary romance Wish *You Were Here*, will show you why. Yeager Gates is a hot-shot flyboy, grounded by injury but still very much a full-blooded man. Zoe Cash is a life-planner extraordinaire, a woman who leaves nothing to chance — until she meets Yeager. This is a memorable love story written by an author you'll be seeing more of.

He's a rascal and a rogue, the favorite of all the ladies of the court. She's prim and proper, determined to live a quiet life in the country. But when the king forces Richard Blythe and Elissa to wed, the passion that flares between them surprises them both. *A Rogue's Embrace* by Margaret Moore is a delicious confection of a book.

When the townspeople of Burr, Wyoming see a big, broad bed being pushed down Main Street, they know that Jack Donovan's looking for a woman to share it with. But no one expected that woman to be Sarah Calhoun. Debra Mullins' *Donovan's Bed* is a battle of the sexes where everyone wins!

Until next month, happy reading,

Lucia Macro

Lucia Macro
Senior Editor

AEL 0100